I0662373

The Winter Wolf

The Seraphimé Saga, Volume Two

By

S.M. Carrière

ISBN: 0-9866976-8-0

ISBN-13: 978-0-9866976-8-5

Http://smcarriere.com

Other Books in This Series

The Summer Bird

Other Books by S.M. Carrière

The Dying God & Other Stories

Ethan Cadfael: The Battle Prince

Acknowledgements

I would like to thank everyone who helped me create this book and this series. To my parents who have been both stern and supportive.

To my beta readers, who helped make this story stronger and better and to Éric especially who kindly stepped in at the last minute.

To Laura, for the beautiful work she has done for me on this book cover and her unflinching good cheer and professionalism.

To all the people I have forgotten to put on this little list who have contributed to my writing, even in the smallest ways, you are so valued and I am so grateful!

To all my readers who have been so incredible to me since I started this journey.

The Winter Wolf

The Serephimé Saga, Volume Two

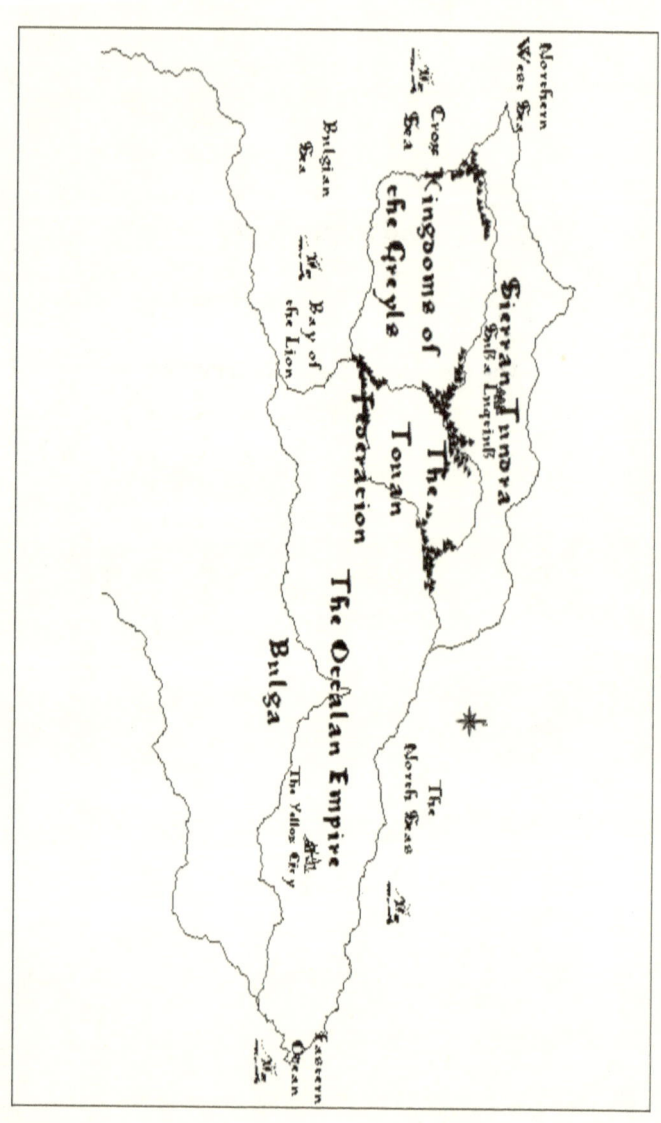

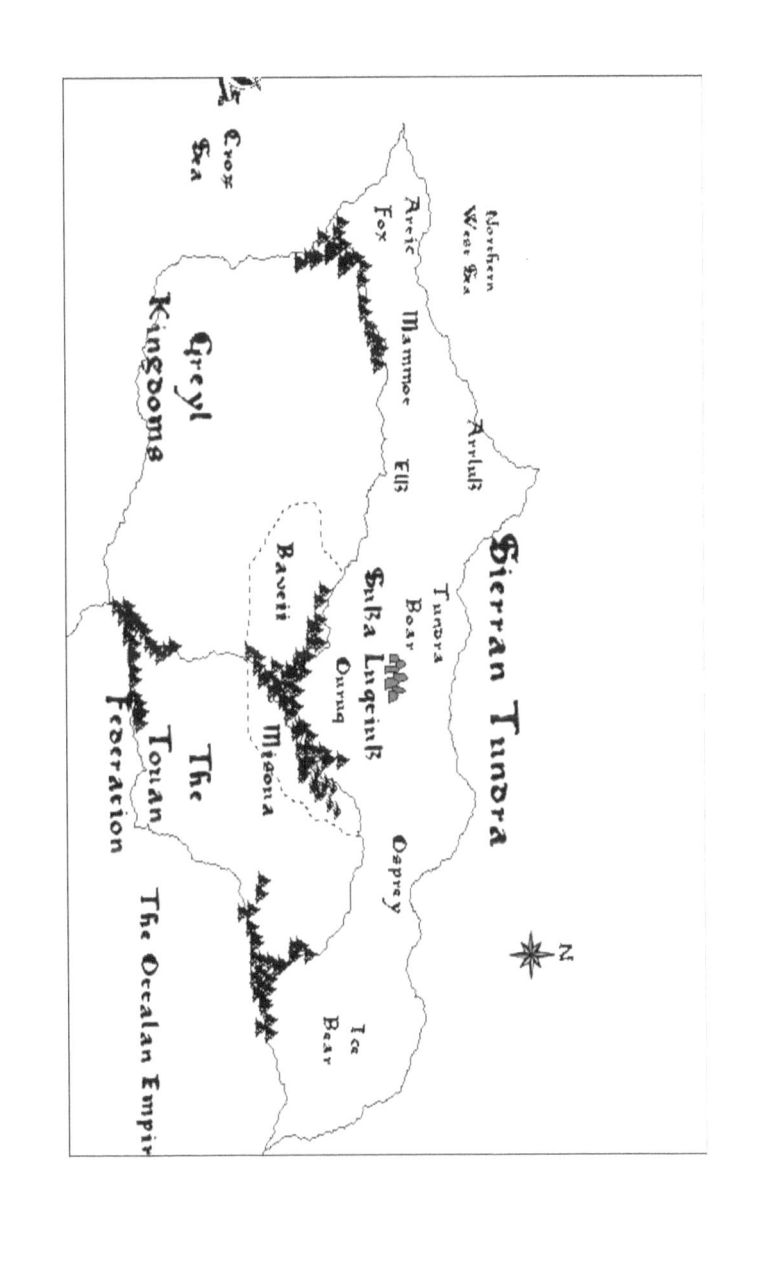

Prologue

The gods of the desert were cruel and hard, like the land itself. They required what life required – constant battle. Susa Ottal despised them. The battles they demanded, the blood they required, had taken away his family. His father was killed in battle, defending the well that was the village's only source of water. His mother was sacrificed upon the altar of the gods. A child of only ten-years-old, he became a slave, carrying his dying infant sister on the long march back to the invaders' homeland.

The slavers were also men of the desert. Men with brown skin and dark eyes like his. They could have been kin. Even their clothing was the same. All Susa could think about was their similarities during the long, arduous march across the desert. They were his people, and yet they insisted on battling their brothers and sisters, raping and enslaving them. All for what? Because the gods decreed that only the strongest could survive? Because the gods required blood on their altars?

Susa kept his eyes down during the hot, dusty march, staring at the orange sand to hide the hate in his eyes. When he buried his sister in a shallow grave on the eighth morning, he took up a sharp stone and cut his forearm.

"I promise you this, Denna," he whispered as the blood soaked into the sand at his feet. "I will make them pay, the gods and their followers alike. I will play their game, and I will win. I will choke the life from them. I will be a god-slayer. You will see."

For the first few years of his enslavement, Susa worked the dry sand for his master, trying to glean a harvest year after brutal year. If there was no yield, all the slaves were whipped. His master was fond of the lash; almost as fond of that cruel tool as he was of young boys. Susa, being handsome and strong, attracted his master's attention more often than not. He bore the raping in silence, letting it cement his hatred and his resolve.

When he turned fifteen, Susa snuck the sharpened head of a hoe into his master's bedroom beneath his robes. Distracted by his lust, the master was easy to kill. Susa beat in his head with the head of the hoe, relishing the warm spray of blood and brains. Before the light left the man's eyes, Susa looked down at him with a sneer.

"You are the first," he said. "The first in a long line of deaths that will rain upon this desert, to cleanse it of kin-killers and the gods who reward them. Do not worry. Your death, all those deaths that I shall bring, will serve a purpose. The desert will be united, as it would have been but for the bastard gods."

Susa Ottal did not run. He walked from his master's house, still covered in the gore of his first kill. He walked through the village, a vision of Bubbugu – the demon-bull god of death – and presented himself before the village enforcers.

"I killed my master," he declared to them.

Giving no resistance, Susa was arrested and sentenced to the fighting arena to serve as entertainment for however long he should survive. There, he fought other slaves for his evening meals. Susa had never held a weapon before. His family were goat-herders. Even so, he was swift and vicious like a sand snake. For five years he fought. During the time he spent in the dungeons of the arena, he forged an army with promises of freedom and a new age for the slaves and, the day before he turned twenty, he led the Great Slave Revolt.

No slave had ever challenged the authority of the Masters before. Perhaps that was the reason for their victory. Whatever the cause, Susa and his army of slaves were victorious. They not only won the arena, but attacked and won the village. All the slaves were freed and masters became slaves. The new slaves were made to build fortifications around the village, the very first of their kind.

Tall walls of fired yellow clay, thick enough to allow three men to walk abreast, surrounded the village. Many of the bricks came from the arena, which was frenetically torn down upon the slaves' victory. They built a fort in the centre of the village so strong no besieging army has ever managed to take it.

All the altars and sanctuaries of the gods were destroyed, their idols smashed into dust. Susa, leader of the Great Slave Revolt, forbade the worship of gods of any kind and deemed each man's fate the property of each man alone. Susa was proclaimed king by his followers.

Word spread, and it was not long until the name Susa was whispered in the ears of every slave, filling them with the fire of hope as they have never been filled before. Other revolts occurred. Some were successful, others not. Those slaves who revolted or escaped, fled to Susa's free city where they joined the cause. The ranks of King Susa's army swelled to proportions never seen before or since.

Susa's thousand-strong army swept through the desert like a sandstorm. They rode from village to village, freeing the slaves, enslaving the masters, and destroying the altars and idols of the gods.

"I am the King of the Desert!" Susa Ottal proclaimed.

"King of the Desert!" his followers cried in exultation.

In a campaign that lasted twenty long years, Susa led his armies against master, priest and god alike. When at last he had rode the entire length and breadth of the desert and subjugated all the people therein, he held for himself a festival, where he was crowned King of the Desert, true king at last. At the festival, he pronounced all the gods dead, and forbade their worship. A hundred slaves who had once been masters were beheaded before him, a sacrifice for the King.

Susa also declared that no man of the desert would ever again be a slave, and proclaimed a law that to take a man of the desert and make him a slave was punishable by death. The masters and their once high families, however, remained slaves for eternity thereafter. Justice, he proclaimed, for the crime of their families owning slaves for the eternity that stretch back before this.

Every year, on the anniversary of Susa's final victory over the desert, a festival in his honour was held, and every year, the men of the desert affirmed their devotion to Susa, the freer of slaves.

He forced many a master's wife to his bed until one at last gave him a son. The moment of the child's birth, he had the mother executed. The child was fed on the milk of goats and raised a warrior, filled with the hatred for the dead gods just as his father was.

The year following Susa's death, that son proclaimed Susa a god. For who else but a god could have battled the other gods and won? Susa, God of the Yellow City, bringer of law.

It was unfortunate that Susa's law against slavery did not extend to all peoples, for before Susa Ottal's proclamation against enslaving the men of the desert, none in the West had ever heard of the Ottals.

Come to death, strong men of the stone,
Come to death, for He rides tall and is unending.
Come to death, tall men of the woods,
Come to death, for He rides tall and is a-hunting.

- Baveii Equinox Song

I do not fear, my brothers,
I die in honour and glory,
For though I die, my brothers,
I take twenty souls with me.

- Pamisii War Chant

One

Walking the breadth of the desert was not easy. *I should have taken a horse*, Guild thought bitterly to himself. Guild wasn't his name, but his name was dangerous now; a thing that may bring death to him if others learned it. He reflected on his life. He had been a simple farmer, living in the shadow of the Holy Yellow City. His mother's family owned the well in the village, and used it to irrigate their crop – figs. He had been born wealthy, compared to most. He was also one of twelve children.

His family could have done without the extra mouth to feed and so, the moment he reached manhood, he eschewed marriage and became a member of the Fortu Guild – a hired sword, filled with the promise of adventure and plenty of coin. He rose through the ranks quickly. First he was Tigil. Then Braddard. Then, at length, Guild Master of the Fortu.

Now, he was Guild Master no longer, robbed of his title by a former friend, bent on vengeance; a man who would not hesitate to have any opponents killed. So he called himself Guild.

I should have taken a horse.

On horseback, it was no more than three days between villages, between water and beds and food. On foot, it was well over a week.

A week without water did strange things to a man. Shapes appeared in the shimmering desert heat. Women, translucent and enticing, who danced strange dances appeared frequently to Guild.

After months of walking, visiting village after village and almost dying of thirst each time, he almost believed in ghosts.

"Iris," he whispered, tears of regret staining his dusty cheeks as he stumbled across a dune. Iris. Her memory haunted him now more than ever. A slave, no more than a slave, and yet the only woman to have ever captured his heart. "I'm sorry. I'm so sorry. I should have done more."

Yet what more could he have done? He did not have the money to buy her, and even if he did, there could not have been any guarantee that she would not have died in a month regardless. Guild reached into his pocket and his hand closed around the clay wolf idol that remained there, hidden from the unfriendly eyes of the desert. The clay was ice cold to the touch, despite being alternatively pressed against his body and beaten by the sun.

Guild smiled grimly. It was winter in the tundra. He pulled the wolf out and pressed it to his chest. The cold hurt a little, but it was welcome relief from the unrelenting heat of the desert.

"Can you hear me, Winter Wolf?" he whispered, directing his thoughts to the idol at his chest. "I'm coming. I'm coming."

* * * *

Seraphimé, who most knew as Otsana, shifted uncomfortably in her sleep. She was sweating profusely, though it was the middle of winter.

"Otsana?" Bran whispered softly. He shook her gently. "Otsana? Are you all right?"

Seraphimé slept on, groaning a little as she shifted yet again. Bran chewed on his lower lip. He looked at the walls of the onion-shaped pavilion that had become his home. They were starting to lighten, the painted forms of the animals and symbols that decorated them slowly becoming shadows cast by the sun.

Bran had chosen to stay with his wife's people after the Great Gathering. The majority of his entourage were sent back home to the territory of the Baveii with instructions to relay the situation the people of the tundra faced to his father there. No doubt his father would relay it in court, and a debate would rage as to whether or not the Baveii should involve themselves.

The tribesmen of the Sierran Tundra were now kin. That fact alone should move the Baveii into action. So Bran hoped, at least. That had been the plan since the beginning, and the whole reason for his marriage to Seraphimé in the first place.

Bran placed his cool hand on Seraphimé's burning skin once more. "Wake, Otsana," he whispered. "The sun has come. It is day now."

This time, Seraphimé's eyes fluttered open and she looked around. Her green eyes met Bran's and she smiled.

"Hello, little crow," she said.

Bran smiled in return. His heart still skipped a beat when she looked at him. "Are you all right? You are burning to the touch."

"I had a dream."

"Oh?"

"I saw a small desert wolf. He was orange, like the sand, and the sun. He was coming, coming to me, in answer to my call."

"The desert is where the Ottals live. They are all snakes there."

"Perhaps one is a wolf."

Bran chuckled. "I think you place too great an import on dreams, Otsana."

Smiling in return, Seraphimé said, "When we are sleeping, we travel to the spirit world. There, we are shown things. I think you place too little import on dreams, my crow."

"In this, I think we can agree to disagree."

Seraphimé nodded. "When are your messengers expected to return?"

"Not until the council has decided."

"Will they decide in our favour, do you think?"

"I certainly hope so."

Seraphimé stretched, exposing part of her naked body to Bran. He leant forward and kissed Seraphimé on the now exposed crest of her hip. She laughed and turned to face him.

"We can be late to breakfast, can't we?" Bran asked, his blue eyes wide and hopeful.

Seraphimé laughed again and traced Bran's face with her fingers. "I don't think anyone will mind."

* * * *

"Your fault."

"Go away."

"Don't you growl at me. You might be a god, but I'm her kin. She'll listen to me before she listens to you."

"You're an annoying hag."

"Perhaps."

The Lord of the Hunt, Master of Animals and God of Death turned his gaze to the old woman on the cairn in his clearing. His expression was hostile, twisted by an unexpected jealousy. Hers was perfectly amiable, except the twinkle of mischief that sparkled in her vivid green eyes.

"Why are you here?"

"Because, when you so callously drove her away, she asked me to intervene on her behalf. And so I came here to tell you precisely what I was thinking. God or no, you are an idiot."

The Lord of the Hunt turned away again. The constant howling that had sounded in his private world since he had banished Seraphimé to marry had stopped some months ago. Some part of him yearned to hear it once again, to know that she had not forgotten him.

"You should be glad she's made peace with it. There is no more pain."

"I should be," he agreed. Here in the clearing, as it was in the land of the living, it was winter and the Lord of the Hunt wore his armour and helm of the skull of a great deer.

"But you are not."

The Lord of the Hunt rolled his broad shoulders in a bid to relieve the tension that had settled there.

"I knew it! You love her."

"Go. Away."

"No. I. Won't."

"Do not mock me, woman!"

The old woman sighed. "You are just going to have to compromise."

The Lord of the Hunt turned back and looked at the old woman with an expressionless gaze. She had been around him long enough to know that meant he was curious, but did not want to be.

"You've fashioned her into the Winter Wolf. She is on her way to ascendancy. If all goes according to plan, she shall become the tundra, yes? The goddess who chooses her kings, yes?"

The Lord of the Hunt cocked his head in acquiescence.

"Then you have no choice but to set her free to make that choice."

The Lord of the Hunt turned away again. "I want her."

"Yes, well a god cannot be a mortal king as well. She cannot lie with you anymore, not again, not yet."

"Not yet?"

"The kings of the tundra will need her blessings with the return of the sun and the herds. The spring and summer months belong to the mortal kings. But the winters, my Lord; the tundra bears no fruit then."

"So I must share her."

"If she will have you," the old woman said with a smile.

The thought was enough to drive the Lord of the Hunt wild. "I will not!"

"Fine. Then you must learn to live without her at all. She will not abandon her husband now."

The Lord of the Hunt growled.

"Besides," the ancient woman said as she closed her eyes and leant back. "I like him."

* * * *

Ur awoke first, carefully dressing and exiting the pavilion so as not to wake Inna, who was still fast asleep. Precious few others were awake. No one had started a cooking fire yet. Ur stretched and yawned, turning sightless eyes towards the birthing sun. He paused for a moment at a lone figure on the horizon. A man, dressed in the skins of a deer and wearing a helm made of a stag skull. He was not an Ayal.

Ur smiled a little and walked towards him, knowing where he was by some power other than sight. Once at his side, Ur turned back and looked at the village of the Osprey Clan. It was not as big as it ought to have been.

"You are sad," Ur said after a deep silence.

"Yes," the figure replied, his voice deep and silken.

Ur smiled a little. "About Otsana." It was not a question.

The figure did not speak for a long while. "Yes," he said at last.

Ur remained silent. "Two men who love the same woman," he said, shaking his head. This time the figure drew his attention away from the portable village and looked down at the boy at his side.

"You see much, for one who has no eyes."

Ur smiled. "I have been gifted," he said. "When my eyes were taken, I received sight in return."

"What else do you see?"

"I see Otsana as Chooser of Kings. I see her as the Wolf of War. I see her as High Queen. Not just now, but always."

"What is she queen of?"

"That depends on you, King of the Dead."

With those words, Ur smiled serenely and walked back to the village. The Lord of the Hunt watched him go with a frown.

"Clever boy that," the old crone said from behind the Lord of the Hunt.

He groaned.

* * * *

"I don't believe it," Algar said bluntly as he paced in front of his brother at dinner. He had been in a meeting all day with his father and a member of the Holy Wetouan Council, the arm of the Holy Yellow City within the Tuan Federation. "The yellow robes have declared Holy War on the tundra."

Alam almost dropped his cutlery. "*What?*"

Algar threw his hands in the air. "Convert or kill. They aren't pleased with the ascension of a heathen war-leader over all the tundra. They consider it an act of treason and have declared war."

"There wouldn't be a heathen war-leader if the damned yellow robes told the desert idiots to stay the hell away."

"It's a culture of slavers, and they aren't allowed to acquire goods from the desert. Where else were they to range?"

"Acquire goods. They're people, not cattle! And that is no justification! What has father said?"

"What can father say? What the council decrees we must ratify."

"We were going to trade with them. Now we must fight them?"

"So it seems."

"That's just stupid." Alam was infuriated beyond words. They had just last year dispatched a messenger to the Osprey Clan informing them of their desire to trade, and now they were to ride out to slaughter them. Alam's mind turned to Gabija, the Chieftain of the Osprey Clan. He had promised her friendship, and had hoped for more.

Algar grunted. "The word is, the tundra has enlisted the help of our Greyl neighbours."

"Which ones?"

"Our closest ones."

"The Baveii?"

"Yes."

"Oh dear."

"Hardly surprising though, is it? They share gods still. The Greyls are primitive and yet to convert. And then there was that Otsana girl who married one of the Baveii princes."

"How so very convenient."

"Political marriages happen all the time."

Alam grunted. "If the Baveii have joined the fight in the tundra, we'll have an enemy on our left flank. That's a terrifying thought. Drawing the Baveii into a Holy War will draw in the rest of the Greyl tribes, who have long taken offence at strangers telling them how to think and behave. Do you know the size of the potential Greyl fighting force?"

"Expansive, I'd imagine."

"That's putting it mildly."

"But they lack discipline, Alam."

"And more than make up for it in courage and zeal."

Algar grunted. "This is going to get messy."

"Very."

"Damn it."

* * * *

Once Tigil and now Guild Master, Mtsusa, head of the Fortu Guild had been busy indeed. He had been twice to the Yellow City to speak with the Ottalan High Council. The council members had, at first, been dismissive of the Guild Master, but were moved by the threat of members of the guild converting to the religion of the tundra.

It was not true, at least as far as the Guild Master knew. However, a perceived threat was the same as a true threat. Great Susa knows, the stories of ghosts and gods in the tundra had made the circuit more than once, and the Guild Master had noticed a growing reluctance on the part of the Guild members to venture to the land of frost again. It irked him. Hired swords were not supposed to be cowards, and he'd be damned if he let a handful of them tarnish the Guild's reputation. Not while he ruled.

The second visit to the Yellow City proved much more promising. The council, greedy for slaves and sensing an opportunity to expand their influence over a larger territory had decided to back the Guild Master at last.

The Guild Master knew enough about the Holy Council to know that it was new slaves they desired, though they had used the excuse of ghosts and gods, just as he had.

The Ottals were all alike; power-hungry and greedy. It was a good thing, for more righteous men were less easy to manipulate. Mtsusa smiled with smug satisfaction as he rode away from the Yellow City.

Those frozen tundra bastards would pay for all they had done.

The council need only send out word to all the converted peoples under its control, and they would have an army like no other. The tundra would be crushed, and their cursed gods and ghosts with them. The thrill of the thought made the Guild Master lustful. He had taken a Sierran girl as a personal slave and he allowed himself the luxury of anticipation wash over him as he rode back to the Guildhall. She told him she was from the Ice Bear Clan. No ice bear would ever match the ferocity of his ravishing, he promised himself that.

His self-satisfied smile became vicious.

Two

*B*ran was pleased with the progress that had been made at court. News sent from his father claiming that the Baveii King had fully half the families ready to fight for Seraphimé and her people had Bran dancing in his seat as he told his wife.

"The other half will likely capitulate soon."

"The delay is worrying," Seraphimé told him.

"It will be sorted shortly, if it hasn't been already."

Sighing, Seraphimé turned her attention back to the spread of maps that were strewn on the table before her. Bran watched her auburn braid fall over her shoulder, which she flicked back in irritation. She looked up at her husband, her bright green eyes capturing him unexpectedly.

"This is where they come from then?" she asked, pointing to a large yellow splodge that was roughly the shape of a heart.

"Yes."

"They have religious ties with the Touans, correct?"

"Yes. But that does not guarantee the Touans will fight for them."

"Unless they declare Holy War."

"They wouldn't be stupid enough for that. Holy War will rouse the rest of the Greyls, and that is something no one wants to see."

Seraphimé was not convinced. "What if they do?"

"If I catch wind that they're even thinking of pulling such a stunt, I'll immediately petition the rest of the tribes. At least when it comes to that, we Greyls will unite."

"Will you?"

"I hope."

Despite her concern, Seraphimé laughed. Bran flashed her a quick grin before turning his attention back to the maps.

Later that day, when the sun began to sink after only three hours in the sky, Gabija visited. She did not smile her bright smile at either of them when she entered their pavilion and her face was several shades paler than usual.

"Gab," Seraphimé greeted with a smile. Her smile faded when she noted Gabija's trembling. "What's going on?"

"Sera," Gabija replied. She stumbled on her words and turned to face Bran. "Husband of my sister," she greeted formally.

Bran raised his dark brows, his blue eyes growing round. "Yes?"

Gabija opened her mouth, but there were no words.

"Gab, what is it?" Seraphimé asked.

"Bran, there's a... there's someone outside who wishes to speak with you."

Bran looked briefly at his wife, who scowled. "Who is it?" he asked.

"I dare not speak his name," Gabija whispered.

Seraphimé immediately tensed. It took Bran several moments to understand. The colour drained from his face.

Seraphimé turned to him. "I'll go."

"No," Bran said, his voice steady and authoritative despite the fear that quickened his pulse. "He asked to speak with me."

"Bran...."

He silenced Seraphimé with a pointed look. She understood. Bran could not be seen to be cowardly when faced with the Lord of the Hunt. He was husband to the god's favoured warrior, who now ruled a substantial army as Marshal of the Tundra. That made him a high king, of sorts, and should anything happen to Seraphimé, command would fall to him. No one would follow a coward.

Seraphimé nodded. Bran stood, squared his shoulders, and walked to the pavilion entrance and drew the flap back. Beyond the edge of the village, he could see the figure of the god in the snow, waiting.

"Wait," Seraphimé called after him. Bran turned, the flap still pulled open. Seraphimé ran to him and kissed him boldly in full view of their guest. There was no act that Seraphimé could have performed that Bran anticipated least and could not be more pleased about. The unexpected kiss told the Lord of the Hunt in no uncertain terms Seraphimé's choice.

Bran stroked his wife's face fondly, kissed her briefly again and, fortified by his wife's wordless declaration, walked to the Lord of the Hunt with square shoulders and bold strides. When at last he stood before the god he did not bow and forced himself to look at the god in the eye, or as much in the eye as the stag skull helm permitted.

"Walk with me," the Lord of the Hunt said bluntly. Not waiting for an answer, the god turned and walked away from the camp. Bran looked back and raised a hand to reassure his wife, who remained standing by the pavilion. The camp was long out of sight before the Lord of the Hunt spoke again. He began the conversation with a sigh.

"She loves you," he said. His voice was deep, and Bran could detect the slightest hint of an accent.

"I believe she loves you also." Bran spoke the words between clenched teeth. He had never before had to fight for a woman's affections, and though Seraphimé had made her choice many months ago and things had been blissful between them, he never forgot the anguish of loving a woman who loved another as fiercely as Seraphimé loved her patron god.

The Lord of the Hunt turned to Bran and studied him a moment. Bran held the gaze fearlessly, though his heart was pounding frenetically against his ribs. The Lord of the Hunt grunted.

"I have been informed by the first king of the Baveii of your blood vow."

Bran grimaced. "I'm beginning to rue ever making it."

The Lord of the Hunt smiled slightly. "You will release her once this war is won?"

"Yes."

The Lord of the Hunt nodded and sighed again.

"It'll probably kill me," Bran muttered to himself. The sharp ears of the King of the Dead did not miss the words. Again he studied Bran.

The sensation of having a god look at him, *through* him was an uncomfortable one. Despite his desire to appear brave, Bran's brow betrayed his fear in glistening beads. He shifted his weight, but did not look away.

"I have a proposition to make," the Master of the Wilds said quietly. Bran scowled at his rival in silence.

"Otsana has a grand destiny. She will one day assume the mantle of the tundra in the flesh, and when she dies, her spirit shall become the land. She is the Chooser of Kings, none shall rule in the tundra unless she first permits it."

"I'm not sure I am following."

"Otsana will, one day, ascend."

"Ascend. As in become a goddess?"

"Yes. And no man shall rule over the tundra unless she chooses it."

"How does she choose it?"

"She lays with him."

"Oh."

The Lord of the Hunt laughed. "If I could, I would keep her to myself. I find myself... completely at her mercy."

Bran nodded in agreement. "Love is a little like that."

"As her mortal husband, Crow, you are the first to rule the tundra," the Lord of the Hunt noted with a grunt.

"Otsana rules the tundra."

"While she lives, yes."

"While she...? What exactly are you planning?"

The Lord of the Hunt sighed. "Otsana cannot truly ascend unless she leaves the mortal realm." He paused. "Unless she dies."

"Yes," Bran growled. "I understood the implication."

The Lord of the Hunt smiled a little. "If I could, at her death I would take her away to be my wife."

"Queen of the Dead."

"But it is not my choice. While she lives, and after she dies, it seems I must be prepared to share her or lose her altogether."

"I'm not sharing my wife with you," Bran said flatly.

"Not yet."

Feeling his hackles rise, Bran's fists closed into tight balls and his shoulders bunched together as his body prepared to fight in response to the sharp jealousy that now ripped through it. "Not ever."

"And when she's dead?"

Bran growled, but knew well that even were she alive, he'd have little recourse. When Seraphimé decided something, there was no contending with her. Her will was made of ice and iron.

"Crow," the Lord of the Hunt said quietly, as he removed one glove. "Take off your mitt and take my hand."

Bran stared blankly down at the god's golden-skinned hand. He looked up.

"Why?" he asked guardedly.

The Lord of the Hunt did not answer. He simply stood, holding out his hand. Bran scowled. He slowly removed his mitt and took the hand of the King of the Dead. The moment his flesh touched that of the stag-helmed god before him, a great storm of images and emotions roared through Bran with the strength of a gale. The entire history of the Lord of the Hunt was laid bare for Bran to see, and experience. The shock and grief of his first kill, mingled with the joy of watching his family eat after months of starvation. Most pronounced, however, was the perpetual ache and hopeless longing that plagued the Lord of the Hunt.

The wilds were his home, but the wilds had denied him what he longed for most – a wife, a woman of his own to love and who loved him in return; children, grandchildren and the joys of watching them grow and find great loves of their own.

Then Seraphimé's face came into view, and the desperate longing of a thousand ages fell away, replaced by awe and wonderment. Everything that Bran had felt when he first laid eyes on Seraphimé was matched by the Lord of the Hunt, with all the power that befitted a god.

He understood, at last, that the decision to send Seraphimé away to be another man's wife tore at the Lord of the Hunt more than the god would ever permit himself to show. He felt the desolating loss as it was felt by the Master of the Wilds when at last Seraphimé made peace with her life, and allowed herself to love another.

The contact broke abruptly and Bran staggered backwards. There were tears in his eyes that threatened to overflow even as his chest threatened to cave in on itself, collapsing into the hole left by a ravaged heart.

"Now you know," the Lord of the Hunt whispered. He did not meet Bran's eyes, choosing instead to stare down at the lavender-coloured tundra grass. Bran trembled as he replaced his mitt.

"What is your proposition?".

Three

*G*uild shivered pointlessly in the cold. He had never been this far north before, and no amount of trembling could warm his frigid body. Though he was still in Ottalan territory, it was unbearably cold in the northern climes of the desert. The sun shone often, but feebly, and sometimes during the nights it snowed, though the snow had all but disappeared by the time the sun rose.

"You are dressed like a southern man," the Well Guard noted as Guild approached. Guild nodded. The sun was moments from rising, casting its wan warmth over the flat-roofed huts of the small village he had stumbled into moments before. Guild could not feel his finger or toes. His nose stung as if bitten by a swarm of tiny blackflies and his ears, peculiarly, felt like they were on fire. Parts of them had turned black and could no longer be felt at all. A small blessing for Guild. They had hurt him terribly.

"Where you headed then?" the guard asked amiably.

Guild observed the man a moment. The man wore the archaic armour associated with the position, and it was meticulously kept. No scratch or dent could be seen. It also gave the man more bulk than his lean face would otherwise suggest, and Guild suspected that the armour was not made for him, bur rather passed down from one generation of guards to the next.

The Well Guards were an archaic tradition; the remnants of a time when Ottals sought slaves amongst themselves. They meant nothing in this day and age.

Lord Susa had kept them as a measure against thieves, to put out village fires and in case any outside force ever decided to invade the desert. None ever did, and so the Well Guards tended to be lackadaisical people capable of snuffing a flame or two and little else.

"My uncle's village," Guild lied easily. "In the north-west."

The Well Guard shrugged as he handed Guild a large ladle filled with water drawn from a bucket at the edge of the well. Guild gratefully accepted the drink. It was freezing cold and set Guild's teeth chattering but he was much too thirsty to stop. The guard shook his head.

"You travelling on foot?" he asked.

Guild nodded, unable to unclench his frozen jaw.

"Well, you shouldn't go west dressed like that. You'll freeze to death. The tundra lies that way, and there is always ice there. You'll be dead before you get to your father's village."

Guild shrugged and the guard laughed.

"I get off my shift when the sun rises," he said. "Come back to my house. My wife will get you full of hot soup and into a warm bed. We ought to be able to dress you properly as well. We'll send you on your way good and warm."

"I can't pay," Guild managed to stutter through chattering teeth.

"Pft!" the guard said, waving his hand about. "Don't you worry about it. We don't want nothing for it. We are good folk and we know that Lord Susa smiles kindly upon charity to our fellows. Here. Bundle up, or you'll drop dead where you stand. Sit, sit. You're bound to collapse soon anyway."

Guild smiled wanly, gratefully accepted the thick camel hide cloak the guard wore and did as he was told, sitting on the stone wall of the well and leaning against the post. He closed his eyes and allowed himself to drift into blissful slumber as the guard rambled on and on about life here in the northern province of the desert.

The dawn came, as did the guard's replacement. The night Well Guard woke Guild gently and the former Guild Master stumbled wearily after him as the man retired for the day. It was not long before the cloak became too much, and Guild had to take it off or die of heat exhaustion.

"It gets hot here fast," he murmured.

"It's the desert. Of course it does."

Guild smiled thinly. "It gets cold at night in the south, but nowhere near as cold as it was here last night. How do you live with such extremes?"

"Very carefully. We're home."

Guild looked up. They were standing before a very small mud brick home, built in the stocky cube that had become standard throughout the Ottalan Empire. Unlike the buildings to the South, however, these northern houses were not whitewashed. The guard opened the door.

"Wife!" he called. "I'm home!"

Two young girls scurried into the room, which, Guild now noticed, was the kitchen. They quietly took the cloak from Guild and helped the guard with his ceremonial uniform. Trailing behind, looking sleepy, an older woman wandered in.

"Morning husband," she said yawning. It was quite a while later before she noticed Guild standing behind her husband. "Who is this?"

"Wife, this is...uh...."

"Guild," Guild supplied.

"Guild. He's off to visit his father in one of the villages west of here. Came from the south, and almost died from exposure. Cook him up a soup and find him some clothes."

"Yes, husband."

The woman left the kitchen through a smaller side door and descended down the rickety-looking ladder into the cellar that lay directly beneath the house to keep the food cool.

"Sit," the guard said, waving his hand at the small table and chairs. Guild did as he was bid, feeling entirely drained. He did not much care for food now. He just wanted a good night's sleep. It was cool in the house and it sent Guild shivering again, though no one would have called it cold.

"You're getting sick," the guard noted. "No wonder, what with you roaming around at night in nothing but an open vest and sandals. You best sleep for a few days. My wife will make sure you're well again before you leave."

"I'm in a rush," Guild said.

"You'll die if you rush too much. Relax here a day or two, Guild."

All Guild managed to reply with was a grunt. The guard's wife returned carrying a basket of various vegetables and a few sand pigeons. The guard beamed happily.

"She's a good cook. Got her for next to nothing. Her father just wanted to be rid of her."

Guild grunted again. The guard's wife was a beautiful woman, though starting to get a little flabby with age. Her dark hair was thick and shone lustrously, and her dark eyes sparkled. Without a word, she set to work. A fire was lit, the vegetables were cut and soon birds and all were boiling merrily away.

The kitchen filled with an enticing aroma, and Guild suddenly felt very hungry.

"Guild looks ill," the guard's wife noted.

The guard grinned. "He does. I've just convinced him to stay until he's better."

"Good. T'won't do to have him wandering around in a fever. Where will he sleep?"

"Put him in with the girls. He'll like that when he's strong enough."

Guild barely understood the exchange. He felt himself drift in and out of consciousness, pulled into wakefulness by the smell of soup and the constant chatter of the guard and his wife. He felt cold and shivered, and yet the places where his clothes touched his skin were far too hot to bear. He swayed dangerously in his seat as the guard's two slaves started to feed him the soup.

Without quite understanding what was happening, Guild ate his soup, let himself be led to his newly made bed and tucked in by the two slave girls who served the guard. He was asleep long before his head touched the pillow. As the sun beat down relentlessly on the tops of the houses in the northern province of the desert, Guild dreamt strange dreams of the ice and wind, and wolves and crows, stags and eagles, all of them at war.

* * * *

"Bran!" Seraphimé breathed as soon as Bran stepped into the pavilion. No sooner had he walked in than his wife abandoned her conversation with her sister and rushed into him, crashing bodily into his chest and throwing her arms around him. Bran pulled her close, closing his eyes and enjoying the strength of her embrace, the scent of her lightly anointed skin and hair and the warmth of her body against his.

"I love you," he whispered to her. Seraphimé made to pull away, but Bran wouldn't let her. He pulled her in tighter, holding her close as if it was the last time he would ever hold her. Seraphimé relaxed in his embrace and allowed herself to enjoy her husband's affection.

Bran's mind reeled with all that the Lord of the Hunt had revealed to him. He now knew that her life was destined to be glorious and, when it ends, she would live forever on, perpetual High Queen and Marshal of the tundra. A goddess.

The Lord of the Hunt offered Bran a way to be with her when at last both their bodies lay in coffins of permafrost. All it required was a small sacrifice. He would have to relinquish Seraphimé to the Lord of the Hunt in the winter. But come the spring, when life returned to the land, Bran, as the spirit of kingship, would once again be joined with his love.

The entire proposal hinged on one variable – Seraphimé. All would be revealed to her when the Master of the Wilds came to collect her and take her to the land of the dead. She could then choose. She could take one or the other, or both. Or neither. This thought shook Bran to his core. Seraphimé was, above all else, unpredictable.

Until then, Bran vowed to himself that he would cherish every moment of every day that he had with his beloved wife. So now he held her close, enjoying the strength of her embrace, the warmth of her body, and her gentle scent.

"I love you," he whispered quietly again.

"Bran," Seraphimé whispered in return. "I was afraid that you wouldn't return."

Bran pulled away and took Seraphimé's face between his large hands. He looked deep in her eyes and found bright warmth therein. He smiled. "Nothing could keep me from you." He leant forward and took her lips gently in his own. He had intended the kiss to be gentle, but it passion overcame them both.

* * * *

Gabija smiled to herself before she made her quiet exit. Neither Seraphimé nor Bran noticed her leave. They were both so far removed from anything but each other that they would not really have cared. They stumbled together to their bed and fell upon it in a frenzy of lovemaking.

Once outside, Gabija breathed deep the crisp fragrance of the autumnal air and, not for the first time, wondered if she would ever find a man who would love her the way Bran loved her sister.

Four

"*Y*ou're going through with it, aren't you?" Algar asked his father. "You know it's unjustified!"

The rotund king shifted uncomfortably under his two eldest sons' direct gaze and sighed. "What else can I do? Not doing so would be tantamount to declaring war on our own faith."

"You could go to the Yellow City," Algar replied. "And try to make the High Council see sense, since clearly, the Wetouan Council does not."

King Roger sighed. "If only," he said wistfully.

"You do know that a declaration of Holy War will raise the entire Greyl nation against us, don't you?"

"Yes, Algar, I am aware." He slammed his fist hard on the table in a rare explosion of temper. He immediately regained his composure and turned his back on his sons, staring up at the bright sun through the arched window of his private study.

"Father, they're fanatics of war...."

"Then we must hope that we win the day."

Algar sighed. "We'll have to strike at the Baveii first."

"Yes."

Alam cleared his throat.

"If they're in the North defending the tundra," he ventured. "There won't be many warriors at home."

The King nodded. "I thought much the same. We can wait until they engage the Ottals in the north, then we can strike at the Baveii heartland. We'll be onto the next tribe before they've had time to muster an appropriate reaction."

Algar grunted. "And in the North?"

"We'll let the Ottals take care of that. The Greyls are, at present, not unified, disorganised and completely unaware of the declaration of war. We'll have a distinct advantage over them. We can have fully half the Greyl territories annexed before they muster themselves enough to adequately provide resistance."

"And by then, they won't have the numbers," Algar mused.

"Correct. We can sweep around from the South up to the Sierran Tundra."

"And should the Ottals prove successful, drive the surviving Sierrans right to us."

"Precisely."

Algar sighed and flopped onto a nearby armchair. "A sound plan."

"You sound unhappy."

"I'm happy that it just might work. I'm not happy about this war."

King Roger grunted. "No one is."

* * * *

The Wise One of the Baveii woke in a sweat, his breathing ragged and burning fiercely in his throat.

"Spirits save us!" he whispered fervently. He threw aside the blankets that covered his thinning frame and scrambled from his bed. He dressed hurriedly, not bothering to comb through his short, white curls, and bolted from his hut. He raced on bare feet over the pre-dawn frost to the tall Mead Hall. He kicked open the doors and raced along the cold paved floor and into the back, which held the war room, court room and the King's personal chambers.

The Wise One burst into the King's bedchamber, kicking the door open with a deafening crash.

"My King!" he shouted.

Gofron bolted upright in bed, a small dagger clenched tightly in his fist. He stared blankly at the Wise One for a moment, before the sleep drained from his face.

"What the blazes?" he demanded after a shocked silence.

"My Lord, you must send word to the other kings! The Eagle is coming! The Eagle is coming!"

"What the hell are you talking about?"

The Wise One, still shaken by the images in his dream, looked at his king with wild eyes. "*The Eagle is coming!*"

Gofron raised his brows and turned the corners of his mouth down, less than impressed. "Did you chew on a strange fungus before you went to bed last night?"

The Wise One scrambled onto the bed and grabbed Gofron roughly by the collar of his nightshirt. "The Eagle is coming!" he hissed. He shook the King roughly. "None will be spared!"

This time the King listened, startled as much by the vehemence with which the Wise One spoke as the wildness in his unfathomable eyes.

"Take a breath," Gofron commanded gently.

"Rouse the warriors," the Wise One said, scrambling back off the bed. "I must warn the elders." With that, the Wise One exited the room, leaving King Gofron staring after him like a stunned fish. Moving with painful slowness, the King reached over and pulled hard on the bell pull by his bed.

Within minutes, a sleepy-looking servant appeared. "Your Majesty?"

"Rouse the house. Gather the emissaries and have them all assemble in the War Room."

The servant blinked. "The War Room, your Majesty?"

"Yes, you dullard. The War Room. Now snap to it!"

"Yes, your Majesty."

Groaning, Gofron threw his blankets aside and started to dress himself.

* * * *

A blaze crackled cheerily in the fireplace of the War Room barely a week later. It had not seen a fire for almost two hundred years. Good harvests had ensured relative peace amongst the quarrelsome kingdoms of the Greyls. Now, the last of the Baveii chieftains had arrived and it was time to make preparations.

Gofron was not the last to arrive to the painfully early meeting, and he seemed far more awake than the rest. He looked around at the room, taking stock of the minds and bodies of those he saw before him. He was not heartened.

"What is the matter?" his first wife whispered to him when she arrived, dressed as a queen ought. There was not a hair out of place.

"I'm not entirely sure, but the Wise One was virtually frothing at the mouth when he woke me last week."

The Queen nodded. "He has been plagued by bad dreams of late."

"Well, this one was bad enough to have him risk his life to rouse me."

The Queen said nothing to that, and she stood beside her husband as the rest of the court filtered slowly in.

"This better be good," someone rumbled in a grumpy-sounding voice.

"Is everyone here?" the King asked. All eyes fell on him and silence fell over the room. Someone coughed. Gofron raised his brows and waited for an answer.

"It looks like it," someone muttered at length. The King grunted.

"Good. I apologise for taking you from your beds at this hour. Earlier this week I was woken by our Wise One, who had himself been woken by a dream. He will be here momentarily to explain it all more fully, but while we wait I wanted to discuss the possibilities. It seems, from what little he told me, that we are soon to expect an invasion."

There was a general murmur amongst the lords gathered. "What exactly did he say?" someone asked.

"The Eagle is coming."

The room fell silent.

"The Eagle is coming," the Chieftain of the Kildurrow family replied with a small hint of disbelief.

"Yes."

Lord Kildurrow snorted a small laugh.

"The Ottals bear the standard of an eagle," Amwyl, Bran's mother and Gofron's third wife, noted too quietly for anyone but her husband to hear. The King turned to her.

"You think this may have something to do with the troubles in the north?"

Amwyl shrugged, suddenly nervous with the entire room looking at her. "It could be. Perhaps they are not content with just the tundra."

"That's ludicrous," someone noted.

"Is it?" Amwyl shot back. "Do we not have to suffer endless missionaries from their stupid Yellow City who warn of the wrath of their god?"

"She has a point," the Queen said, smiling a little at Amwyl. "Perhaps they have declared this a Holy War."

"If that's the case," Gofron mused quietly. "Then the Touans will likely fight on their behalf."

Another murmur shot through the crowd, this time it was laced with fear.

"This is just an attempt at fear-mongering. A power-grab by the priestly class and no more," the head of the Kildurrow family snapped. "We've seen it a hundred times before."

"I assure you," the Wise One noted from the doorway. "The Circle of Elders do not yet know of the threat that looms over us."

He walked boldly into the room and bowed low before his king.

"They will soon though," he informed the King. "I have dispatched messengers with all that I know. I have no doubt that we will, as we have only once before, bare steel in defence of our freedom."

"Before the court," Gofron said. "I want you to tell us everything."

The Wise One bowed again. "I had a vision," he began. "In my slumber...."

"It's called a dream when you are sleeping," Lord Kildurrow scoffed.

The Wise One continued speaking, pausing only briefly to glare at his heckler. "In my vision, I saw eagles in the sky, so thick that they blotted out the sun. They cast a menacing shadow over our vast lands. In the North, they were attacking a tundra wolf as big as a pony. Though that dog fought valiantly, she was brought down and the eagles turned their baleful eyes upon our lands. They surrounded us on every side. They rose in the air like a great wave of the sea, and came crashing upon us with the din of battle. It was then I awoke, and I was afraid."

Whispers greeted the Wise One's story. Some mocked, others murmured in awe. Gofron found himself in a difficult position. For many thousands of years, the Wise Ones were fully trusted, their visions believed and unquestioned. So profound was their sway over the Greyls that a simple satire would be enough to shame a king to death. They were once feared and respected by all.

This was no longer the case.

A plague of corruption had eaten the priestly class from the inside, their internal power-plays, and a long series of false prophecies designed to move kings and warriors around like pawns on a chessboard had stripped many of the Greyls of their trust and belief in the powers of the priestly class.

Powerful families, like the Kildurrows, no longer paid heed to anything the priestly class said or did and had gone so far as to banish them from their homelands entirely. Other families, like Amwyl's, were a very superstitious people and paid as much respect to the priestly class now as their ancestors did thousands of years ago. Yet other families were undecided, caught between wounded scepticism and a desire to believe in the world of spirits and magic.

"Hogwash," Lord Kildurrow said. He turned to his king. "You don't believe this drivel, do you, your Majesty?"

Gofron looked between Lord Kildurrow and the Wise One. "I do not know," he replied with measured pace. "I have never before seen the Wise One in the state he was in earlier this week. I admit it put a chill through me."

"You superstitious old bat."

Long used to Lord Kildurrow's blunt nature, the King laughed. "Perhaps. Even if it were not so and the Wise One's vision was only a dream –"

"The eagles are coming," the Wise Man intoned. "Mark my words."

Gofron gave him a flat stare, annoyed at the interruption. "Even if it was simply a dream," he said again. "There can be no harm in preparing for the possibility."

"Other than the profound cost, the interruptions to the harvest, the increased taxes, the...."

"All right, Kildurrow," Gofron sighed. "You've made your point."

"I believe him," Amwyl said.

"Well, of course *you* do," Lord Kildurrow grumbled.

"Mind the manner in which you speak to my wife," the King snapped at him. Kildurrow leant back in his seat, silenced, and Gofron returned his attention to Amwyl. "Say your piece."

"Prophetic dreams have been true before."

"Only in stories, Highness," Lord Kildurrow noted.

Amwyl ignored him. "Bran's wife, your majesty. Her name is Otsana. In the language of her people, it means 'she-wolf.' She has just recently been made Marshal of the Tundra. In this respect should the men of the desert, who march beneath the standard of an eagle, attack the North, eagles will most certainly be fighting a wolf. That much of the dream was true. Why would the rest of it be false?"

"Your Majesty," Lord Kildurrow cut in before the King had a chance to reply. "What is common knowledge can enter dreams also. That is not proof of the prophetic nature of the dream."

"I didn't know Bran's wife was a she-wolf," another lord noted aloud.

A sudden and very loud debate erupted in the gathering. The King sighed and let it continue for a while, staring at the far wall in deep thought. When his mind returned to the room, his eyes met those of the Wise One.

The old man had been an amusing diversion for the court prior to this, something he took on with a gentle humour. Now his eyes were sharp as flint, and so filled with knowing that Gofron could not help but be moved by it.

"All right!" he called. "That's enough!" No one heard him at first, embroiled in their arguing as they were.

"Enough!" Gofron roared. The silence that followed was sudden and deafening. All eyes turned to him. "Lord Kildurrow," he said with a smile. "Your position is duly noted and greatly appreciated. However, I would not go down in the annals of history as the king who simply sat by and did nothing when he was warned of a threat. I will be prepared in case the Wise One was indeed correct."

Lord Kildurrow rolled his eyes and issued an audible groan.

"Lord Kildurrow," Gofron said as he turned to him.

"Yes, your Majesty?"

"Criticism is healthy, and you have spoken well this morning. I would have you at my side as an advisor, that I might have a more balanced view of our troubles."

Lord Kildurrow raised his brows in surprise. "An unexpected honour, your Majesty."

The King shrugged. "A necessary one, I think."

"To keep me in line?"

"To keep myself in line."

Lord Kildurrow laughed. "In that case, I accept."

"Good. Thank you."

"The matter is decided. The Baveii will prepare for war. I'll have emissaries sent to the other kingdoms immediately. Business is now concluded, you are dismissed to find sleep or break your fast, whichever you fancy most."

The room slowly began to empty.

"Lord Kildurrow," the King said, drawing the tall man aside. "It would please me greatly if you were to break fast with me this morning."

"Another honour, your Majesty. One I am not so hesitant to accept."

"Excellent. Seek me out in an hour. I should have the messengers dispatched and all other business taken care of by then."

"Certainly."

"I shall be in my private dining room. The servants will show you the way."

"Thank you, your Majesty." Lord Kildurrow made his exit and the King turned to his family.

"Let us all retire and find the sleep we have missed."

They all bowed and filed out. Gofron caught the Queen's hand as she passed and gave it a gentle squeeze. She smiled to herself at the private signal and retired, not to her room, but to his.

* * * *

The King of the Baveii had not quite finished with the messengers when Lord Kildurrow arrived.

"Your Majesty," a servant squeaked from the study entrance in the awkward voice of a boy becoming a man. "The Lord Kildurrow has arrived and awaits your pleasure in the dining room."

"Thank you," Gofron replied, not looking up from his hasty scribbling. "Tell him I shan't be long, and send for breakfast."

The servant bowed. "As your Majesty commands." He vanished from the doorway to do as he was bid.

Gofron rushed his signature and sealed the small scroll in such haste, he spilled hot wax all over his fingers. Swearing profusely, the King handed the letter to the last messenger and dismissed him. The messenger made a hurried exit, daring to laugh only once he was out of the King's personal chambers and well and truly out of earshot.

Gofron strode into the dining hall petulantly sucking at his burnt fingers. Lord Kildurrow stood and observed with a small smile.

"Something the matter, your Majesty?"

The King grunted and waved Lord Kildurrow back into his seat. "Burnt my fingers."

"In the fire?"

"Sealing wax."

Lord Kildurrow laughed. "I've done that a few times. A hazard of lordship, your Majesty."

"Among others."

Lord Kildurrow nodded and smiled. The conversation was interrupted by the arrival of breakfast. It was no small feast. Lord Kildurrow brightened immensely. "Smells wonderful!"

Gofron nodded. "I tend to get extravagant at breakfast," he admitted with a small smile.

"I'm not sorry for it."

"Nor I."

"Your wives seem to get along rather well," Lord Kildurrow noted.

The King shrugged. "They have at least one thing in common. No doubt they discuss my shortcomings at length."

Lord Kildurrow laughed brightly.

"None of your sons accompanied you?" Gofron asked.

"No. My eldest is currently Lord of the Keep."

The King grunted. "He's a good boy. A solid fighter."

"He is indeed, though a little too fond of women for my liking."

"That is a healthy thing for any young man."

"Perhaps, but I'd rather not have to deal with bastard grandchildren."

Gofron shrugged. "Die early."

"With this war I just might," Lord Kildurrow said with a laugh.

The words wiped the smile off Gofron's face.

"I did not mean offence, your Majesty."

"Think nothing of it, Kildurrow. I do not want war any more than the next man. But I will not be caught unprepared."

"There is wisdom in that," Kildurrow said. "Even if it is because of some fool's dream. I suppose this now means that the Sierran nomads are most definitely our allies?"

"It would seem that way."

"Deftly done, I must say. Even if there was no threat, it is marvellous politicking to create a larger one in order to achieve the first objective."

"Don't tell my family, but I hate politics."

"That is a good sign, for a king."

"Is it? I wish I was clever about it, like my father."

"You father was very clever," Lord Kildurrow said with a smile. "Couldn't lift a sword though. Thank goodness he had the sense to make your mother his first wife. You are more like her side of the family."

"Why have we not spoken like this before now?"

"A long history of contention between families, I suppose. The Kildurrow family has a claim to the throne, you know."

"Too far back to be serious."

Lord Kildurrow shrugged. "That doesn't stop people being bitter about it."

Gofron tilted his head and smiled. That was true enough. "Then I hope to heal that breach."

Grinning, Lord Kildurrow asked, "Your eldest, is he married?"

Five

For two weeks, Guild was remanded to his bed. He slept solidly for the first four days, waking only to be fed and bathed by the guard's slaves. He felt weak and ill and it made him a miserable guest. He managed to wake on his own accord on the fifth day. Even so, the guard would not let him out of bed and gave his wife and slaves strict orders to do the same.

So Guild laid in bed, which was little more than a large mattress on the floor. Festooned with pillows, cushions and blankets, it provided ample comfort. The two slave girls slept beside Guild on it. He, in the meantime, gazed blankly at the ceiling.

His clothes had been taken to be cleaned and one of the girls had found the clay wolf he had stashed in his pocket. She was a sweet girl and she had placed the wolf on the floor by Guild's head while he slept. He turned his head to look at it. It seemed to him those green stone eyes were boring into him, deep into his very soul.

"Well, wolf," he asked of it. "Do you like what you see there?"

The wolf cocked her head. Guild jerked in surprise and stared hard at the idol. It stood by his head, as it always had, in the exact same pose it had always been in, and did not move again.

"You're losing your mind," Guild grumbled to himself. He turned his head away and, with one last glance at the idol just to make sure, he closed his eyes and drifted into a deep sleep.

* * * *

"Hello there," an elderly woman greeted him. She stood on the line where the orange sands of the desert met the green-grey rocks of the tundra. Guild blinked stupidly in response, and stared.

The woman was dressed in hides and furs, with strange fetishes tied into the fur of her hood and on thin hide straps from her coat. She was old, her hair as white as the snows that flurried around her. Her face was round and wide, with a flat nose and pronounced cheeks. Yet for all this, there was a beauty and grace about her.

"You are one of the ones who want to invade our lands," she said. "Yet, I do not sense any hostility from you."

Guild had nothing to say, so he continued to stare slack-jawed at the woman as she leant on her stick and regarded him with angular green eyes.

"You are coming to the tundra, yes?"

"Yes," Guild replied.

"Why?"

Guild reached into his pocket and withdrew the small clay idol. He held it out for the woman to see. She investigated it for a while then looked up at Guild, her eyes questioning.

"The enemy of my enemy is my friend," Guild said.

The woman smiled and nodded. "I see. You seek the Winter Wolf."

"Yes."

"Be wary, wolves are unpredictable."

"Yes."

"You may be risking your life."

"Yes."

"Do you want to die?"

"No."

"Then why have you come?"

Guild hesitated. "I have nowhere else to go."

The woman regarded him once more and then sighed. "Well, you'll have to ask permission of the Master of the Wilds to cross through here. It is he who guards these lands."

"I will ask him."

"You'll have to do it properly, or he won't hear you."

Guild frowned. "How do I ask him?"

The woman smiled. "You must stand at the edge of the tundra, and wait."

"Wait?"

"Yes. Wait."

"For how long?"

The woman shrugged. "I do not know."

Guild scowled.

"If you see a stag, you may enter. If you see a black hound, turn back."

Guild felt suddenly panicked. "I cannot turn back! There is nowhere for me to go. I am disgraced. My father will not have me. If I return to the guild, the Guild Master will have me killed. Please! Please, speak to him for me. Tell the Master of the Wilds that I must pass!"

The woman smiled. "Do you know what you just did, godless one?"

Guild shook his head.

"You have just asked an ancestor to intercede with a god on your behalf."

Guild's eyes remained blank.

"Welcome to the faith," the old woman said with a cheeky smile. She disappeared before Guild's eyes, fading into mist and blowing snow that drifted lackadaisically away into the heart of the tundra on a faint breeze. Guild scowled. He looked around him. Behind him stretched the Ottalan Desert; great dunes of orange sand, devoid of any sign of life. Before him stretched the Sierran Tundra, cold and rocky and just as inhospitable as the desert.

"Now what?" he shouted at the empty tundra. Only the wind answered. Sighing, Guild sat down facing the tundra. "I guess I wait."

* * * *

Guild woke slowly. It took him a long time to realise that he was not at the edge of two worlds, but safely wrapped in blankets in the home of a Well Guard in the northern province of Ottalan territory. He breathed deep, and his lungs filled with the pleasant scent of burning sweet bush.

"His colour looks better," he heard the guard say. He sat up and turned towards the door of the slaves' sleeping chambers.

"I'm feeling better," he said gruffly. "Though a little hungry."

"Not to worry. Wife's in the kitchen now." The guard came in and sat down. He looked at Guild squarely. "You in trouble?"

Guild blinked. "Pardon?"

"Three Fortu came through here tonight. Said they were looking for a southern man on the run. They had swords sharp for you."

Guild froze. He looked at his host in shock. "That slimy son of a bitch," he hissed. The guard raised his brows.

"Did you tell them I was here?"

"No. I said I saw you, and spoke to you and that you went east, to the sea."

Guild relaxed a little. "Did they believe you?"

The guard shrugged.

Guild sighed and shook his head. "I had struck a deal," he said. "I gave up my position as Guild Master of the Fortu in exchange for my life."

"He sent killers anyway."

Guild nodded. "I am so sorry. I did not foresee this. I did not mean to bring trouble on your house."

The guard grunted. "I must apologise, but it is too dangerous now to house you."

"I shall leave immediately. Thank you for all your hospitality."

"You won't go without proper clothing, or you will die."

"With the Fortu on my tail, I shall die regardless."

The guard smiled and said, "Don't make it easy for them."

Guild grinned.

"Bring the clothes!" the guard called.

Immediately, the two slave girls entered the room with bundles of skins and furs. With their aid, Guild hurriedly dressed. He went to the kitchen and was fed by the guard's wife, who would not let him leave until he had eaten.

"It is dark now, and I'm starting my shift," the guard told Guild as he handed him two large water skins. "Due west is a town. It is four days walk, then there is nothing. That must be the town you are looking for."

"What is beyond that?"

"The tundra, another five day's walk. But do not go there, Guild. There are ghosts in that place."

Guild nodded and smiled as he accepted a large helping of dried camel meat.

"Good luck," the guard said as Guild vanished out the door.

* * * *

One of the slave girls watched the figure of Guild disappear into the desert night while the other sat on the bed and combed her long black hair.

"Oh look," the girl combing her hair noted. "He left behind his statue." She snatched it up and went to the window. The other girl took it from her and sighed.

"Poor man," she said. "It seemed important to him." She reached down and placed it on the low table that held her grooming items and turned away from the window. "Here, let me comb your hair." She took up the brush and began to comb her sister's hair.

It wasn't until she had finished and placed the
brush back on the table that she noticed the statue was
gone.

* * * *

Certain he would have to avoid the town the guard
thought he was seeking, Guild ran through his situation
in his mind. Nine days on dried camel meat and with
only two water skins was bound to be taxing. It helped
now that he was dressed properly. He would travel by
night, and rest in the day. Search parties made camps
and firelight was easily seen and had the advantage of
destroying night vision. It would be much easier to slip
past his pursuers at night.

He reached into his pocket in search of the familiar
and soothing presence of the clay wolf and found it
empty. Guild stopped abruptly, then let loose a string of
curses. He had left it behind. Growling under his breath,
he marched forward. He could not turn back to retrieve
it now.

The guard had not been wrong about the distance to
the town. On the dawn of the fourth day, Guild crested a
dune and saw the town spread before him. With a sigh
he slid back down the dune and turned south.

When he thought he had walked far enough, he
stopped, drank a little water and stripped off his hot
clothes until he wore nothing but trousers. He made a
small shelter out of the clothes and settled in
underneath.

He struck his pitiful camp as soon as the shadows
lengthened and hurriedly dressed. The temperature
plummeted quickly. He was walking again before dark
had fully taken hold. It did not matter.

Any campfires would have been lit by now and thus easily avoided. Besides, at the night-time temperatures here, the only people foolish enough to be out of doors at sundown were the Well Guards. Guild was relatively safe from unfriendly eyes.

For two days more, Guild saw nothing but sand. Then, at last, the sand began to thin and harden until he noticed he was walking on packed earth. The colours in the dirt at his feet began to shift, first becoming paler, then assuming a greyish white colour. The air was colder and the days not nearly so hot. At the end of the ninth night of walking, the scene before him changed abruptly. The desert stopped, and the rocky, snow-covered ground of the tundra began.

Guild blinked. The change in landscape was so sudden as to be surreal. He stood at the crest of packed earth and observed the glistening white of the snow in awe. The sound of thunder turned Guild's head. He saw horsemen, Fortu horsemen, headed right for him at a gallop. There were not three, but twelve. Guild froze on the spot in fear before his screaming mind regained control of his body. He turned and plunged towards the tundra at a sprint.

It was useless. A man could not outrun a horse. Even still, Guild pumped his legs in a desperate effort to reach the snowline only to remember, upon reaching it, that he had been instructed to wait. He skidded to a halt and stumbled backwards a few steps. Spitting curses, Guild turned and faced the twelve riders, who now surrounded him without stepping foot on the tundra themselves. Guild smiled at that.

His grim smile turned into a grimace as the twelve riders dismounted and drew their weapons.

"Let me be," Guild growled angrily. "We had an agreement, the Tigil and I."

"The unnamed do not get to speak to us," one of the hired swords snapped back.

To Guild's disappointment, he did not recognise any of the faces before him. Of course the Tigil would have been careful to select members Guild did not know personally. It is always easier to kill a man one does not know or admire. Guild prepared for a fight. He was woefully outmatched and had no weapon. It was a fight that probably would not last very long.

They attacked as one. *Cowards*, Guild thought bitterly as he dodged the first strike, and managed to simultaneously disarm and knock out his target. *Sloppy cowards,* he thought as he picked up the now ownerless sword and engaged his next target. No sooner did he parry the first blow, than another man cut deep into his thigh. His furs prevented the wound from being as severe as it could have been. Still, it was enough to bring the broad man to his knees. He slashed out wildly, striking a similar wound into the leg of the person to his immediate right.

Everything from that moment seemed impossibly slow. His knees struck the hard earth, sending a jarring pain through his legs and spine. All he could see was a forest of legs and beyond it, the snowy fields of the tundra. There, in full view, seen between pairs of legs, stood an enormous stag.

It took what to Guild seemed an age, but to all others almost no time at all, to realise that the Master of the Wilds had just granted him safe entry into the tundra. With one last desperate lunge, Guild pushed himself up and forward, knocking his foes out of his way. Keeping his eyes on the stag, he sprinted once more for the snow.

Guild was wholly unused to running on snow and the first deep drift trapped him. He fell face-forward and immediately heard his attackers descend upon him. He covered his head with his hands, for whatever use it was. A fraction of a second later, he heard a squelching thud followed by a heavier thud and the deep, resonating bellow of a hunting horn.

Guild lifted his head and looked to his left. His eyes met the blank, dead gaze of one of his attackers. Guild pulled his range of vision back and noted with surprise that the man had an arrow clean through his skull, piercing one temple and exiting the other.

There was another thud and another man dropped to the snow, clutching his stomach and screaming, an arrow sticking out of it at an odd angle. Guild looked to the horizon and noted in dull shock a man dressed in a dark hooded cloak. He wore the skull of a stag, replete with many-tined antlers, and sat calmly on a tall dark horse as he nonchalantly notched and released arrows. He was not, Guild realised from the screams that surrounded him, aiming to kill.

The figure lifted a hunting horn to his lips and blew again and from somewhere behind him, three massive black hounds loped across the snow, their ruby eyes bright and keen as they closed in on their quarry.

The screaming rose in volume and octave as the beastly mutts descended upon Guild's wounded attackers. Guild buried his face in the snow and covered his ears and head as the snarls and screams mingled in his fuzzy mind. The screams died and Guild was left with the sickly sound of contented gnawing before he felt a gloved hand touch his shoulder.

"Can you walk?" a deep, accented voiced asked him.

Guild groaned and struggled to his feet. The moment he stood, his head reeled from the loss of blood. He would have collapsed had the quick reflexes of the antlered man not caught his weight.

"You must have those wounds tended," the antlered man said. He shifted Guild's weight until Guild was at his back.

"Take a hold of my antlers," the man said. "And whatever you do, do not let go."

Guild grabbed each antler firmly and felt the man lift him easily onto his back.

"Don't let go," he said again. All Guild could do was groan in response.

"Here we go then."

They were off, running at a remarkable pace. For all the speed that Guild noted in the scenery that whipped by, Guild was not uncomfortable and the man's gait was smooth. A man on the back of another man running would expect to be tossed around a good deal more.

It was then that Guild realised that he was not on the back of a man, but riding on the shoulders of a great stag, his hands firmly gripping the animal's sturdy antlers and his head resting on its noble neck. Confusion and shock almost released his grip, and he slipped.

The stag did not slow, and the shock and blood loss proved too much for Guild. He fainted, his hands still instinctively clutching the antlers of the great stag as the splendid Master of the Wilds flew across the snow.

Six

*S*eraphimé and Bran were in the middle of a serious tickle-fight when they were interrupted. A great, black shaggy body thrust itself onto the bed and a cold, wet nose dove between the two writhing bodies.

Bran screamed both in shock at the sight of the giant black mutt and in response to the sudden sensation of toppling backwards as he fell off the bed. He heard the sounds of his wife's bright laughter and a few happy barks as he struggled to his feet. When he stood, he found his wife's arms around the neck of a dog that could have easily carried her on its back. It looked at Bran. Bran looked at it, then at Seraphimé. She was laughing so hard tears streamed down her face, which the joyful dog happily licked while its curled black tail whipped back and forth.

"Bran," Seraphimé said, wheezing his name between breaths and laughter. She could say no more and broke down into hysterics once more. Bran grinned, but stayed warily away from the enormous black dog, which could only belong to the Lord of the Hunt.

Ur sprinted into the pavilion a few moments later.

"Otsana!" he said, barely even glancing at Bran. "Come quick! They've found a man."

Seraphimé looked at Ur with raised brows. "What man?"

"Inna thinks he's from the desert!"

"Thank you. Tell Inna I shall be along presently."

Ur nodded and left, leaving Seraphimé, Bran and the huge black mutt alone once more. Seraphimé sighed. "Is this your master's doing?" she asked the dog. The dog cocked her beautiful head in response and Seraphimé sighed again. "Never mind," she muttered. She looked at Bran. "Get dressed. We've someone to greet."

Bran pulled a face. He had hoped that clothes would not be needed for the rest of the afternoon. He grumbled as he pulled clothes from the a hanging wardrobe made from woven grass. Seraphimé joined him.

"Later," she murmured. "I promise."

Bran looked over at her and smiled. He leant over and kissed her on the cheek before turning away again and dressing. Seraphimé was dressed first, long used to the clothing of the Sierran nomads. She helped Bran with his.

"You've been here long enough," she chided with a smile. "You ought to know how to do this by now."

Bran grunted. "I do," he replied tartly. "I just like it when you touch me."

Seraphimé poked him hard.

"Ow!" he protested, snatching her hand in his.

Seraphimé laughed and pulled away. Bran pulled her back in.

"Not now!" she said. "Later!"

Bran wrapped his arms around her waist and kissed her neck. He said nothing and simply held her. He smiled when Seraphimé stopped struggling and leant into the embrace.

"We have to go," she whispered after a while.

"You go," Bran replied. "I'll wait here."

"You're coming with me," she said.

Bran sighed. "Why? I'm an outsider, they don't respect me."

"They will because I do."

Bran pulled back and looked at Seraphimé with large, surprised eyes and a small smile. "Do you?"

"Yes. You are my husband, Southern Crow. I need you by my side."

Grinning, Bran let his hands drop. "Let's go." He was up and out of the pavilion before Seraphimé could react. Moments later he stuck his head back in. "What are you waiting for?"

Rolling her eyes, Seraphimé joined her husband.

A beautiful spring day greeted the lovers as they stepped out of the tent. The skies were clear of clouds and the sun was bright and warm. Even so, the snow came up to Bran's shins and it did not look as though it would melt any time soon. Seraphimé took Bran's hand as they walked, the black hound loping gracefully at her side.

"Did I ever introduce you two?" Seraphimé asked.

Bran shook his head.

"Well then, Bran, this is Cabal. Cabal, this is my husband, Bran."

The dog looked at Bran only briefly before turning her snout forward again.

"She doesn't seem that interested," Bran noted.

"Be thankful for that. It would not be pleasant to be the focus of a wild dog's interest."

"I suppose not."

The couple stopped at the entrance of Inna's pavilion. Inna was outside the entrance waiting patiently for them.

"Otsana," he greeted. He nodded at Bran, who nodded in return. "The man was found in the snow, just a few hundred metres from here. He is heavily wounded."

"Did you treat him?" Seraphimé asked.

Inna nodded in affirmation. "Otsana... there were great deer tracks everywhere, and it was the black hound who led me to him."

Seraphimé nodded. "I suspected as much. Is he awake?"

Inna shook his head.

"May I see him?"

Inna stood aside and Seraphimé entered, with Bran in tow. On Inna's bed lay the man, covered in blankets, with a warming stone brought close to his feet. He was tightly bandaged in several places. Seraphimé went to him and placed a hand on his shoulder.

The stranger was a handsome man for a desert dweller, with tanned skin and a long face. His hair was dark and short, turning grey near his temples.

"I wonder why you were brought here," Seraphimé murmured.

She sighed and turned as Inna stepped into the room. "Well, the cold would have prevented too much blood loss and I have faith in your skills as a healer Inna."

Inna's mouth quirked.

Turning back to the man, Seraphimé said, "I am sure he will survive. The wounds?"

"All made by blades, Otsana. The man was attacked by other men."

Seraphimé nodded. "We shall see what he has to say when he is awake. Please call me as soon as he does."

"You have my word, Otsana."

"Thank you, Inna."

Inna grunted and shrugged.

"Well," Seraphimé said. "There isn't much else to be done here."

Bran was relieved, perhaps they could return to their pavilion and their play. Bran's hopes were dashed when they did return. Seraphimé needed to talk strategy and politics. With a resigned sigh, Bran sat at the table over a steaming bowl of tea and made plans with his wife.

* * * *

"Did you hear?" Alam noted casually. "The Baveii have mobilised. They're preparing for war. The whole kingdom is in an uproar. Weapons production has tripled. They're making armour at an astounding rate and many a young man has been conscripted into a newly formed regular army."

"That was to be expected," Algar said with a grunt. He sighed. "Any news on the other Greyl kingdoms?"

Alam shrugged. "None. Though, apparently the Elders are in a frenzy."

Algar raised an eyebrow. "Uh-oh. That can't be good."

"Not too many of the Greyls listen to them anymore."

"Yet they resist conversion. We shouldn't underestimate those people. Perhaps they've gotten word of the Holy War."

"Perhaps."

Algar sighed. "Does father know?"

"Yes. I only know because I overheard the messenger."

"Sneak," Algar said with a smile.

Smirking, Alam said, "I can be. So, what now?"

"That's entirely up to father. There's a messenger from the Yellow City here, with the plans for attack. Apparently they heartily approved of splitting the 'enemies of the true god' in half and preventing any sort of alliance. The Greyls will be worried too much about their lands to be able to send help to the Sierrans. As for the nomads, they live in the past. They're archaic armour and weapons won't be a match for Ottalan advancements. There's no doubt they'll be defeated. Their Marshal apparently has weapons made of stone."

"I imagine it relates to some tradition or another. One of their gods has weapons of stone."

Algar grunted. "Still, stone against steel? It won't be a war, it'll be a slaughter."

Alam nodded. "I know."

"Poor bastards."

* * * *

"They can handle the Ottals and we'll take the Touans," King Gofron of the Baveii said as he stared down at his maps.

"The Ottals also fight with steel, Father," his eldest said. "And the Sierrans with stone. They'll be obliterated."

The King scratched at his immaculately trimmed beard. "The Ottals are light cavalry. They rely entirely on their horses to fight. In the desert where it is all sand their horses are brilliant. But they won't be fighting in the desert. They'll be fighting in the tundra. That is no place for their desert ponies. I imagine fully half their horses will break their legs in that terrain."

"Not if they attack in the winter. Snow and sand aren't much different."

"Only a small number of Ottals know anything about the cold. They'll die of exposure."

"You're not giving them enough credit," Lord Kildurrow noted. "I am certain that they are not fools."

"Perhaps. But what I do know is that we cannot allow the Touans to join forces with the Ottals in the north. The nomads won't have a hope if that happens. If we engage the Touans, we can draw them away from the fight in the north, then swing around the southern flank and come at the Ottal force from behind."

"Assuming we win."

Gofron shrugged. "If we don't, then it won't matter, I suppose."

Lord Kildurrow grinned. "Then we best make sure we do."

"My thoughts exactly."

The fort was in a frenzy of activity. The bright ringing of steel being beaten and the grating sound of wood being sawed echoed in from the city as tradesmen of all kinds were employed to make weapons, chariots and war machines. Inside the fort itself, messengers and soldiers and kinsmen scurried about delivering reports and carrying out orders. The King, his eldest son and Lord Kildurrow were in the War Room, their heads bowed over a map as they threw strategies back and forth. They were interrupted by a loud knock at the door.

"Enter," Gofron said, not looking up.

"A messenger from the Marshal of the Tundra, your Majesty," a servant announced. The King looked up. He smiled as the nomad strode into the room.

"I do not like your walls," the nomad growled.

"I apologise, but fortifications have saved our skins and so we've learned to love them."

The messenger grunted. "Otsana sends her greetings and husband of Otsana asked me to give you this." The man extended his hand in which he held a small scroll.

"What's this?"

"The location."

"The location of what?" the King asked as he took the scroll and unrolled it.

"Trading post."

Lord Kildurrow raised his eyebrows. "We're in the middle of a war, and you want to talk trade?"

"No," Gofron said with a smile. "It makes sense. Much of the weaponry and armour we're making is going north. We can't have the nomads face steel in nothing but skins. In exchange they are sending us horses, some broken and some for breeding. With the nomads always on the move, a single spot for the exchange is a brilliant idea. It will also help to preserve their exact location, and ensure it remains a secret should one of us be captured."

"Clever," Lord Kildurrow noted.

The Crown Prince grunted. "Bran's wife is no fool."

"No indeed," agreed Gofron. "A fine choice for Marshal of the Tundra, I must say."

"That, and she has the Master of the Wild's favour."

Lord Kildurrow laughed. "You are all superstitious old bats!"

Gofron flashed Lord Kildurrow a wide grin before he looked up at the messenger. "We have enough armour and weapons to equip the warriors of the Osprey Clan, but none of the others yet. Will that be sufficient for the first exchange?"

The messenger nodded. "We have a mare, a stallion and five fighting horses. We will wait at the post. All further information to be traded there also, it is shorter journey."

"Perfect. Are you going there now?"

"Yes."

"Excellent. I'll have you escorted with the goods."

"Good." The messenger left without bowing and the War Room belonged to the three lords once more.

"Hey, you!" the King called as a serving boy scurried passed the door. The boy stopped and looked back in surprise.

"Yes, you. Come here."

The boy walked cautiously forward and bowed awkwardly.

"I need you to do something for me. What's your name?"

"Buddy, sir."

"All right, Buddy... Buddy? Really? Well, congratulations, Buddy, you've just been promoted. You will act as my personal messenger. You will report to me and only me, do you understand?"

The boy nodded, his eyes as wide as dishes and shining brightly.

"Good. I need you to run and tell the merchant's man Marillos that the goods are ready to go and they are to leave immediately with the Sierran messenger. Once you've done that, you tell the cook that we're all on rations. This war might be a long one, and it won't do to run out of food. Once you've done that, you come straight back to me, understood?"

The boy nodded vigorously.

"Good. Now go."

Buddy dashed off and the King shut the door. "Right, let's get back to this."

"All right, so we split the enemy into two forces. If we do this right, we'll have enough men to take the southern front and squeeze the Ottals between a heathen sandwich, am I correct thus far?" Lord Kildurrow looked to his king for confirmation.

"That about sums it up, Kildurrow. Any complaints?"

"Just one," the Crown Prince said with a smile. He had never seen his father this animated in his life. The war preparations had given him a sense of purpose and with it, fresh life.

"Yes?"

"There is no way we can engage the entire Touan force without the support of the other kingdoms."

* * * *

The priest smiled serenely as he stood before the Council in the Yellow City.

"My brothers," he said. "I have come to quell your fears, for the mighty Lord Susa has shown me the future. The tundra wolf will be killed. This war is just and righteous and we shall be victorious."

Seven

"So my father is planning to split their forces down the middle," Bran reported to Seraphimé as she gazed down at the map. Bran placed thirteen stones along the line that divided the Baveii kingdom and Greyl territory from the land of the Touans. "The Touans have an advantage. They are a federation, bound by their mutual faith and this call to Holy War, which you were right about, by the way. They are idiots. In any case, once he has the other kingdoms on side, they will strike along this front here, drawing attention away from the Ottalan front here."

Bran indicated the massive brown stone that represented the Touans and the red stone that indicated the Ottals. "Now, if father is successful, he intends to wrap around the Ottals here like so, and attack them from behind. The problem is, however, if father loses, the Touans will be free to do the same on our southern flank."

"I would advise a fighting retreat, or at least the display of it," Seraphimé mused. "They should give ground until they reach our southern flank and dig in there. They will lose less men of their own, take out more Touans, and make the Touans over-confident."

Not looking up, she continued. "Not only that, if there are outposts of a few hundred here and there, they can attack the Touan supply lines and starve them before that army ever reaches the southern lip of the tundra."

Bran stared incredulously at his wife. "Where the hell did you learn battle strategy?"

Seraphimé shrugged. "It makes sense is all."

It took Bran a moment to recover from his surprised admiration. The time he had spent amongst the generous and gentle nomads of the Sierran Tundra had lulled him into believing in their innocence. Seraphimé's grasp of military tactics did much to correct the overly idyllic ideas Bran had about his wife's people. They were clever, and they were strong. He turned his attention back to the maps. "If you are not upset over it, we can build a fort there and withdraw all the supplies and livestock to those locations, leaving nothing but burnt earth for the Touans to trudge through."

"Is that necessary?"

"If we are to starve them out, then we cannot leave crops behind for them to eat. We can always resow our crops afterwards. Besides, it looks like an act of desperation. If we want them to get overconfident, acting desperate is the best way to do it."

Seraphimé smiled. "I like that a lot. Could you divide your forces in half and have one half sweep behind the Touans once they reach the forts?"

"I think we could. I'll send word to father."

"Please."

* * * *

"Congratulations, Lord Kildurrow. The number is now seven. Seven out of thirteen is not bad," the King of the Baveii said with a smile.

"I'd be happier with all thirteen," Lord Kildurrow grunted.

"That will happen. With the overwhelming majority in our favour."

"We have only half."

"But a very powerful half. The other kingdoms will follow, mark my words."

"They're marked. If they don't, you owe me half of the Gutmoor county."

"Done deal."

Buddy appeared at the door. "Your Majesty, I have just returned from the trading post. Your son was there and he requested I give you this." Buddy held out a scroll.

"What is it?"

Buddy shrugged.

"Give it here then."

The young man did so and Gofron unrolled the small scroll. "You are dismissed, Buddy. Get some sleep. You look awful."

The young messenger bowed and left the room. The King stared down at the small map with lines scrawled all over it with a frown. His frown smoothed into a smile as understanding slowly reached his mind.

"Well?" Lord Kildurrow asked.

Grinning, Gofron said, "Kildurrow, there has been a change of plans."

* * * *

"You are certain of this?"

"Yes my Lord, I heard my father speak of it to my brother. They intend to engage the Touans to keep them from the fight in the north."

"How many of the kingdoms have aligned themselves to the Baveii?"

"So far, only five. Father is hoping the rest will follow soon."

"Thank you, young Lord Kildurrrow. That will do."

"They are going to keep their promise, right?" the young boy asked. "I will have the Kildurrow lands intact when the war is over, won't I?"

"If you continue to perform admirably," the man replied. The boy nodded.

"For now, my Lord, take this coin as payment,' the man offered Lord Kildurrow's youngest son a black purse filled with silver.

The boy took it. "Thank you."

"No, thank you."

The man stood and left, eager to return home and report to the Misouan king. The information should please him greatly. He grinned as he left the tavern. The Lord Kildurrow's youngest son had been an easy acquisition. He was a wonderful mix of ambition, trust and fear. Just ripe for the plucking.

The youngest son of Lord Kildurrow was equally satisfied. He resented being the youngest of four boys. The best inheritance he would ever get was the title of prince and a place in one of his brothers' houses. He was smarter than his brothers. It wasn't fair that he was born last.

Lord Kildurrow was a fool, daring to stand against the might of the Touan Federation and the Ottals combined. The Touans were generally fairly easy to beat when taken unawares during raids, but their discipline in battle was legendary. Even if all thirteen kingdoms took up arms, there was no chance of victory. This way at least, the Kildurrow lands would be preserved, and one of Kildurrow blood would rule it after all the dust had settled.

Young Lord Kildurrow smiled to himself as he drained his tankard in the noisy inn. His smile widened further when the food arrived. Braised pheasant, his favourite.

Eight

"*W*hat is it, Gab?" Seraphimé asked as Gabija slowly unrolled the parchment that Seraphimé's lieutenant handed her.

"It's a note."

Seraphimé's mouth quirked. "I might have figured that."

"It's writing. This is ludicrous. I can't read!"

Seraphimé extended her hand and Gabija handed her the small roll of parchment. She looked it over briefly. "Whoever sent it mustn't know us very well," Seraphimé said with a smile. "Surely they must know that we have no written language?"

Gabija sighed and Seraphimé laughed. "I suppose we'll just have to wait until Bran gets here. Perhaps he can read it."

"You know, he has settled so well into Sierran life, I keep forgetting that he is not one of us."

"He is one of us," Seraphimé quipped just as Bran walked into the newly made pavilion that was now reserved for talks of war. Bran had explained that there was a special room in his home called the War Room which was designed for such meetings. Seraphimé had the pavilion built as a private area for her and her advisors to discuss sensitive issues.

Messengers had been coming and going all week in preparation for battle. The other clans had begun their duties with vigour and their warriors were ready for war. The second shipment of armour and weapons had arrived from the south and now the Osprey Clan warriors were not the only ones better equipped to take on the Ottalan Empire.

By King Gofron's careful politicking and fear-mongering, all of the Greyl kingdoms had, for the first time in their history as independent kingdoms, united in a common purpose. Each had provided their northern allies with armour and weapons to aid in the defence of their tundra. In return, the nomads of the Sierran Tundra sent south a breeding pair of the massive tundra horses, a trade that profited both peoples.

"Bran?" Seraphimé asked as Bran bent to kiss her cheek.

"Yes?"

"Are you able to read this?" Seraphimé handed him the small roll of parchment Gabija had given her. Bran took it and flopped down on the furs beside his wife. He sat up again, with a frown on his face as he bent over the parchment in intense concentration. Gabija and Seraphimé looked on in curious silence.

"Well?" Seraphimé asked as Bran looked up with a stunned expression.

"Son of a bitch!" Bran spat.

"What is it?" Seraphimé's voice took on a sharper tone which snapped Bran out of his private thoughts.

"There's a spy in my father's house."

Seraphimé and Gabija tensed. "Are you certain?"

Bran nodded. "This note is from Alam of Misoua."

Gabija and Seraphimé exchanged a surprised glance. "Alam?" Gabija asked.

"Can you be certain he speaks the truth?" Seraphimé asked her husband.

"I cannot fathom what ruse would require this kind of trickery," Bran said, not looking up from the note. "He writes in a bid to restore his promise of friendship and hopes that he will be believed. He says here that someone is feeding them information. Their spy refuses to divulge the source, but it must be someone who is privy to my father's war room."

"He must be warned."

"Yes, he must! Will someone fetch me some parchment?"

Seraphimé looked at her lieutenant, who silently excused himself to do as Bran asked.

"Are they aware of the new plan?" Seraphimé asked.

Bran shook his head. "Not at the time this Alam person wrote this note. Is this Prince Alam, the second son of the King of Misoua?"

Gabija nodded. "It could be no other."

"Interesting. In any case, according to him, the Misouans think that the Greyls plan to confront them on the eastern front to divert attention away from the northern battles. He writes that they know of five kingdoms that have joined with the Baveii, but are making contingencies in case the rest follow, which they have. Damn it! This is the last thing that we need!"

The Lieutenant returned with parchment and charcoal. Bran scratched his message quickly and dispatched the Lieutenant with instructions to deliver it as fast as possible, and to the King's hands alone. That done Bran sighed and looked at his wife.

"Well, there isn't much we can do from here. Let's hope Father has a way of thwarting this turncoat. Son of a bastard's swine!"

Seraphimé smiled slightly. "Can we turn our attention to the finer points of the plan, if you please?"

Bran nodded and withdrew a map. "All right, chances are the Touans will be lured away from us to deal with the Greyls. We've been carrying raids into their territories for years now. There's a fair amount of bad blood between us. The Touans will jump at the chance to shut us up once and for all. With them split as they are, the Ottals will have their work cut out for them. It will be too cold for them to attack in the winter, and not safe enough for them to attack in the summer. Their horses will break their legs by the score. If our numbers were evenly matched, it would quickly become a rout."

"As it is, they outnumber us almost thirty to one," Seraphimé noted with a sigh. "It will come to blood no matter what evil befalls them in the tundra."

Bran nodded. "We need to avoid an open confrontation at all costs. They catch us on a flat and we're all meat for the crows." Seraphimé looked at Bran with a small smile and Bran flushed a little. "So to speak," he added.

"So we must also engage in a fighting retreat?"

Frowning, Bran said, "That'll put us all in Father's forts and completely surrounded. A full siege is not ideal at all."

Seraphimé studied Bran's maps with keen green eyes. "We split our forces. I will take half and hide far north, up past the rivers of ice. You take half and engage in the fighting retreat. My army will come in from the north and take them by surprise from behind."

"Like the Winter Wolf," Gabija murmured. Gabija looked at her sister carefully. About her moved shadows and light that were not of this world and she was afraid. Seraphimé hid within her bosom a secret store of great power.

And it was beginning to awaken.

* * * *

"What is it?" Gofron grumbled. It was the third time he'd been interrupted since he had made specific instructions not to be disturbed.

"Forgive me, your Majesty," Buddy said from the door of the War Room. "There's a messenger from the nomads here. He says he cannot speak to anyone but you."

The King exchanged a look with Lord Kildurrow, who threw him a knowing grin. Gofron sighed. "Very well. Send him in."

The nomad marched in and unceremoniously handed the King his message. He remained in the room and, with typical Sierran disdain, refused to bow. Gofron eyed him over with an unimpressed expression, before he unrolled the parchment. The nomad gazed back, his expression at once indifferent and mildly amused. Gofron clamped his jaw and concentrated on the parchment in his hands. The change in King Gofron was immediate. His shoulders bunched and his expression turned sour. Lord Kildurrow rose from his seat.

"What is it, your Majesty?" he asked with a frown.

Gofron handed him the parchment.

Lord Kildurrow's reaction to the words written there matched precisely his king's. He looked sharply up at Gofron and then turned to examine the people in the room. His three eldest sons were present, his two youngest were at dinner and were not old enough to be privy to the plans of battle. There were three other advisors besides himself. Last was the Wise One, who remained quietly in the corner, lost in grave thoughts. He turned back to Gofron and pulled him aside.

"We have to find out who it is!" he hissed.

The King gave him a flat look. "Thank you, Kildurrow. You have now established the obvious."

Kildurrow folded his arms, unimpressed as Gofron thought furiously to himself. "I have it," he said after a protracted silence. "We deliberately feed misinformation to everyone who might be privy to our plans one at a time. Based on the Misouan counter-plans we'll be able to detect who was our mole."

Lord Kildurrow frowned. "That's assuming the counter-plans are predictable."

"It also can't hurt to lie to our enemy can it? They won't be prepared for what is actually going on."

Lord Kildurrow grunted and eyed over the room again. "We're going to have to get our stories straight and keep track of what we told whom. That means a paper trail. That means an increase chance of our intricacies being discovered."

"Do you have a better plan?" Gofron snapped. Lord Kildurrow sighed and shook his head. The King grunted. "I thought as much. Meet me in my private quarters immediately following dinner. We have to sort this out, and we've not got much time."

Lord Kildurrow nodded and both men turned back to the curious mass of advisors.

Gofron smiled graciously at the Sierran messenger. "Thank you, sir. That is very good news indeed. Please accept our hospitality for the night. You must be tired."

The nomad looked at the King with an odd expression, before nodding his acquiescence. He left the room and followed Buddy to the special quarters reserved for messengers of the Sierran Nomads. It had a very large window, ensuring that the riders of the north could see plenty of sky. In truth, it did little to assuage them of their ill-ease at being encased in stone, but they did not complain. Much.

Turning his attention back to the crowd, King Gofron smiled. "Let's resume shall we?"

"Nathan," Lord Kildurrow whispered in his eldest son's ear as the King continued his speech from where he left off. "I need to speak with you tonight. In private. It's very important. Come to my chambers at midnight. Tell no one."

Nathan turned to his father with a questioning gaze and nodded.

It was precisely midnight when Nathan appeared in Lord Kildurrow's chamber. Lord Kildurrow himself was sitting on a thickly padded chair, with a glass of wine in one hand and his feet on a stool by the fire.

"Father?" Nathan enquired.

"Were you followed?" Lord Kildurrow asked, not turning to face his son.

"No. I don't think so."

"Good. Sit."

Nathan did as he was told. Lord Kildurrow observed him for a while in silence, making Nathan uncomfortable.

"No doubt you are curious as to the message his majesty received this afternoon?"

Nathan nodded.

"What I tell you is in the strictest confidence, do you understand?"

Again, Nathan nodded.

"We have a traitor."

Nathan's eyes widened to the size of platters.

"Someone is feeding information to the Misouans. That someone knows information that only those in the War Room would know."

Nathan frowned. "Are you certain of this, Father?"

Lord Kildurrow nodded. "Why?"

"Perhaps it's not someone in the War Room itself, but close to those who do attend the meetings."

Lord Kildurrow raised his eyebrows. "I hadn't thought of that," he admitted gruffly. "In any case, we have to be very careful about what we say to whom. I'm telling you this because I trust you."

Nathan scowled. "There is no one in that room who would betray your trust, Father. Or that of our king. He is much loved."

"Ambition does strange things to people, my son."

"You're trying to find out who it is, aren't you?"

"Well of course we are... now...."

"I'll do whatever I can, Father. I swear!"

"Nathan, stop interrupting."

"Sorry, Father." Nathan blushed a little. "Just the thought makes my skin crawl and my blood boil."

Lord Kildurrow grunted. "Listen, there has been a change in our battle plans. I'm only telling the few people I trust."

Nathan's brows rose.

"The truth is, we're no longer taking the Touans head on. We can't afford to, now that they know of our plan. We're going to the far south and try to swing around them and take them by surprise from behind. You're not to breathe a word of this to anyone else, do you understand?"

"Yes, Father."

"I mean it."

"I swear, I will tell no one."

"Good, you are dismissed."

"Good-night, Father."

"Sleep well, Nathan."

Nathan rose and left the room, his brow furrowed in deep thought. So intense was his concentration that he walked right passed his youngest brother, who had hidden himself in the shadows and listened.

The youngest lord of Kildurrow's heart was racing. They knew they had a spy. The good thing was, they thought it was someone in the War Room. He was safe; safe, and still in a position to rule his father's lands when this stupid war finally settled. Grimacing, the youngest lord of Kildurrow retired to bed.

* * * *

"The birds have come," Seraphimé said quietly to the gathered crowd of war chiefs and clan marshals. "We must prepare for battle, for with the spring the Ottal raiders will come. The Southern Crow and I have discussed matters at length. It has been decided that we will divide our forces in two. I shall lead the one half north to the rivers of ice, and with me shall come all those who cannot fight. They will live there until the threat has passed and they can once more return to their tribal homes.

"The other half, under Bran's command, will move to the three sisters and there await the Ottalan army. They will lure them further into the tundra. My warriors and I shall sweep down from the north and cut off their escape."

Seraphimé's lieutenant looked at Seraphimé, then at Bran, then at Seraphimé again.

"Are you crazy?" he asked bluntly. "He's not even one of us."

"He is my husband. I trust him."

"You might, but the warriors will not."

Seraphimé's eyes narrowed. Scouts had reported in the morning that the Ottal force was seen to be moving north. The war would start soon and Seraphimé had no time to waste on petty squabbles over cultural differences. She stood and faced the gathered crowd of war chiefs and marshals.

"Are the Greyls not descendants of our ancestors also?"

"So are the Touans!" one war-chief growled.

"Perhaps, but the Greyls still hold to our gods, not the god of the Yellow City. They, like us, have refused to convert. They, like us, have refused to be subjugated. They, like us, will fight our enemies to the death to keep these freedoms we all share! The Crow is one of us, and any who say differently may cross blades with me."

Gabija smiled a little to hear the vehemence in her sister's voice, to hear the challenge that she issued against any who would speak ill of Bran. These were signs of love. Seraphimé had hated him not more than two years ago. The change was striking; and welcome. Bran was a good man, in Gabija's esteem. He deserved to be loved.

The war chiefs and marshals murmured amongst themselves, but none rose to take on Seraphimé, Marshal of the Tundra, and incarnation of the Winter Wolf.

"Good," Seraphimé said, smiling sweetly. "Now, we will split each clan in half. Exactly half will travel with me. We shall take with us the people of each clan. Those that cannot or do not fight, will stay in the north until the battle is won."

"And if it is not won?" someone asked.

Seraphimé looked at the war-chief. She shrugged. "We will not lose."

"Indeed," someone grumbled.

Seraphimé levelled them with a flat stare. Gabija noted in uneasy silence how increasingly lupine Seraphimé's expressions were becoming. The Marshal of the Elk Clan, silenced by Seraphimé's green gaze, slumped slightly in his seat and folded his arms in a sulk.

"The desert savages are moving," Seraphimé
continued. "Their armies are on the march north. From
there, they will cross directly into the tundra through Ice
Bear Clan territory. Bran will meet them with his army
where the lands of the Ice Bear and the lands of the
Osprey meet. They will be lured further and further into
the tundra and I shall be on their heels."

"To the south," Bran said, taking his cue from his
wife's silence. "My father will draw the Touans away
from you and to their fortresses which have been built in
the northernmost regions of our territories. The Ottalan
Empire will not have the help of the Touan Federation."

"Whoever is victorious first shall ride to the aid of the
other army," Seraphimé finished. "That is the plan. Now
it is time to move. Divide your armies. Half come with
me, the other half must go with the Crow. In this life or
the next, we shall meet in the middle."

The war chiefs and marshals nodded to each other
and rose to their feet. They silently saluted to
Seraphimé and Bran and filed out of what Bran had
affectionately but unimaginatively dubbed the War
Pavilion. Bran took Seraphimé's hand and kissed it.

"Thank you," he said.

"For?"

"For defending me like that. You know, normally, it's
the man that defends the woman."

Seraphimé laughed. "Come on then, wife," she said.
"It's time to get ready."

Grinning, Bran walked with Seraphimé to their
pavilion. Inside, they found Ur and Inna waiting
patiently.

"Otsana, Crow," Inna greeted formally.

Seraphimé smiled. Everyone had taken to calling Bran by that name since they overheard Seraphimé say it. "Inna, Ur," she greeted. "It is time to move. You must come with me."

Inna nodded. "We will. We have gifts for you Otsana and Crow."

"Oh?"

Ur took Seraphimé's hand and led her to the bed. "Here," he said.

Seraphimé froze. Sitting beside her armour and weapons was a folded cloak and hood made entirely from wolf pelts. A bronze helm made up the hood of the cloak covered with hard leather fashioned in the shape of an enormous wolf with polished yellow-green stones placed into the eyes. Like the cloak, the helmed hood was covered in wolf pelt, giving the impression that the cloak came from the single pelt of a tundra wolf.

Immediately to the left was Bran's armour and another cloak, made entirely of crow feathers in hide. The hood was similarly fashioned as Seraphimé's, though in the form of a crow.

"By the gods," Bran breathed.

"Inna!" Seraphimé gasped. "This must have taken forever!"

Inna shrugged. "Many of the clan Shaman and Shamanka wanted to help. It did not take long at all."

"I am honoured," Seraphimé murmured.

"Otsana," Ur whispered.

"Yes, little man?"

"You are the Winter Wolf."

Seraphimé shifted uncomfortably.

Everyone knew the story of the Winter Wolf, the woman that was the tundra awakened, and of the destruction of the false caves of the ancestors. Seraphimé, despite all that had happened to her, did not believe she was that woman. She squeezed Ur's hand and walked forward.

"Will you help me dress?" he asked Inna. Inna nodded and Seraphimé immediately set to putting on her war dress. Once her armour was donned and her weapons attached, Inna carefully placed the cloak around her shoulders, and set the hood-come-helm on her head. Bran grinned.

"You look very frightening," he noted.

"Your turn," she replied. Bran dressed quickly and knelt down so that Ur could place the crow's helm on Bran's head. Seraphimé was grinning at Bran when he stood.

"Very fierce," she said.

"I look like a giant turkey," Bran said.

Seraphimé laughed. "You look like a giant crow."

"The wolf and the crow," Ur said with a smile. "The two beasts of war. The Ottals shall not prevail."

"Let's go," Seraphimé said, taking her husband's hand.

"We will dismantle your pavilion. Ours is already down," Inna said.

"Your charge?" Seraphimé asked.

"Healing, but slowly. He is asleep on our wagon right now."

Seraphimé nodded. "Thank you."

Inna shrugged as she and Bran exited their pavilion, carrying with them their horses' tack. Work halted in the enormous camp of the Sierran Nomads and all eyes followed Seraphimé and Bran as they walked to the horses.

"I feel like a fool," Bran muttered to his wife.

"Do not. Walk tall and breathe deep. There is power in your image Bran. Harness it."

Bran straightened and took a deep breath. He was immediately calmed and his blood rushed with a strange sensation. He laughed at himself for being such a fool, yet still the feeling of being in possession of power did not leave him. He grinned to himself, the expression turning ghastly beneath his helm.

They dressed their hoses and mounted. Together the Winter Wolf and the Southern Crow watched as the field of pavilions disappeared and was replaced by thousands of mounted warriors and family groups. It was not long before Seraphimé's lieutenant was at her side.

"The war chiefs have divided their warriors, Winter Wolf," the Lieutenant said. "We are ready to move."

Seraphimé nodded. She turned to Bran with a sad smile. "And so we part," she said.

Bran offered her a brave grin. "It will not be for long." He reached out and stroked his wife's pale cheek. The skin was smooth and soft beneath his touch. Seraphimé removed her wolf's head helm and his crow's head helm. Leaning across in her saddle, she took Bran's lips with her own.

Bran did nothing to shorten the public display of affection. It took every ounce of his will to pull away from Seraphimé when the kiss did end. She replaced Bran's helm and her own.

"We ride out," Bran shouted. He urged his horse forward and two thousand riders followed. Seraphimé watched him go with a weight on her chest, before turning her horse and leading the remaining warriors and the entire population of nomadic families and their possessions north, towards the rivers of ice.

* * * *

"Again?" King Roger of Misoua asked his spy.

"So my source has noted."

The King frowned.

"They're changing their plans so often, it's making me dizzy," Algar growled angrily.

"Your source must be mistaken," Roger grumbled.

"My source is living in the Baveii royal household," the spy noted sourly. "The news he delivered is from his father's own lips, he swears by it."

"And his father is?"

"A very close friend and advisor of the King," the spy replied tightly, cursing himself silently. He had revealed too much. "I will say no more of the identity of my source."

"What's this new plan, then?" King Roger asked.

"They plan to head north and help the Sierrans, so it was said. The idea is that the Ottals will starve and die, and the Greyl retreat north and our chasing them will yield similar results for us."

"It makes a certain sense, I suppose," Alam noted languidly. "We'd have a great deal of difficulty in the tundra."

"So would they," Algar grumbled.

"Only they have the Sierrans to help them."

"Every plan they've come up with makes a certain sense!" the King snapped angrily. "This is insane!"

Algar frowned. "Perhaps they're trying to confuse us."

"Pardon?" Alam and Roger asked in unison.

"They may know that we have an informant and are now using him to confuse us."

The King rolled his eyes and slapped his forehead. "Damn it!" he spat. "Of course that's what they're doing! Damn it! How did they find out?"

Alam's heart beat a frantic rhythm in his chest. "They must have a spy here," he noted casually. "Assuming that is true."

"It has to be true," Algar snapped. "Damn it!" The three men in the room sank into contemplative silence.

"We can try and beat them at their own game," Algar said after a while. "We'll use the same misinformation to make them as dizzy!"

"Oh brilliant," Alam said sarcastically. "And how do you plan to do that?"

Algar shrugged. "We have to find out the snitch first, then turn him back the right way around."

Alam grinned. "Oh, that's easy then."

"Stop it Alam," the King barked. "You're not helping."

Alam shrugged and turned back to his book. He had to find some way to get word out to Gabija. Surely they'd have moved by now. Any message sent would likely not arrive in time. Alam's hand trembled as he turned the page.

* * * *

What does it say, Kildurrow?" Gofron asked languidly from inside his wine goblet.

"Which one? The one from our mysterious friend amongst the Touans or the one from the nomads?"

"I like our mysterious friend. Read his first."

Kildurrow shrugged and unrolled the tiny parchment. "'They know you know.'" Kildurrow grunted. "Short and sweet. Now what?"

"Well, we can abandon our search for the mole," the King said with a sigh. "They won't trust him now, and he'll be no further use to them or us."

"I still want to know who it is," Kildurrow growled. "So I can strike off his head myself."

Gofron grunted. "We'll still need the cloak of misinformation."

"We will. By the by, my eldest said something interesting."

"Did he?"

"About the possible mole."

"Oh?"

"It mightn't be someone in the War Room at all."

The King sat up at this. "Go on."

"It could be someone who isn't privy to all the goings on inside the room itself, but might overhear conversations held in other chambers privately."

"An intriguing possibility, but I don't discuss anything outside the War Room unless it's here, with you."

"Then he'd have to be lurking around your private quarters," Lord Kildurrow mused rather loudly. The King frowned.

* * * *

The youngest lord of Kildurrow gasped quietly to himself. He pulled away from the door and turned, stepping straight into his eldest brother's plated chest.

"Hello, little brother," Nathan growled. He kicked his brother in the stomach so hard it sent him through the doors behind him and into Gofron's chambers with an almighty crash. Gofron yelped in surprise and leapt to his feet, spilling half his wine as he did so. Lord Kildurrow Remained in his seat, his face simultaneously sad and hard.

"I found this rodent skulking outside the door," Nathan growled as he marched into the room.

"Dylan," Kildurrow said in a quiet voice. "I did not want to believe it."

"Believe what, Father?" the young boy wheezed, clutching his stomach.

"What the hell is going on here?" the King demanded.

"I apologise, your Majesty," Kildurrow said quietly. "I have been doing some investigating of my own. I am profoundly saddened and shamed to say, I know who our traitor is."

Dylan's eyes grew wide. "I am not... I do not... Father... please!"

"Quiet Dylan," Lord Kildurrow said in an even voice. "I am no longer your father. No son of mine is a traitor."

Dylan started to cry and Lord Kildurrow had to close his eyes and turn away. Gofron understood and turned to Nathan, who looked pale and drawn, but determined.

"My Lord," Gofron said quietly. "Please escort the youngest lord of Kildurrow to the dungeons until I can think of what to do with him."

Nathan nodded and hauled the trembling Dylan to his feet.

"No! Please... please..." Dylan wailed. "Father!"

"Traitors, by law, must be put to death," Lord Kildurrow said quietly, not opening his eyes.

"Father! No!" Dylan squeaked.

Gofron nodded to Nathan, who then hauled the wailing lord down to the dungeon. The King turned to Lord Kildurrow.

"Your son," he said. "Is safe if you wish it, Kildurrow."

Lord Kildurrow grunted a mirthless laugh and shook his head. "A good king cannot ignore the laws he laid down, your Majesty."

"Then call me a bad king. He will be safe if you don't want to see him killed."

"I don't want to see him killed," Lord Kildurrow whispered. "So if your Majesty will excuse me, I will not be present at the execution."

Gofron nodded sadly. "Of course."

"Thank you." With nothing left to say, Lord Kildurrow bowed and left the King in shock by the fire, while he himself retired to his bed where he wept until he slept.

Nine

"Well, that does it," Algar said with a growl. "Our source has been compromised, and we have no idea which of the twenty or so plans relayed to us is the actual plan."

"Do use your head, Highness," the spy master said with a sigh. Algar looked at him with daggers for eyes.

"The new plans did not surface until the Greyls became aware of their information leak. Therefore, it is safe to assume that the plans that immediately followed were designed only to throw my source and thereby us, off the scent. It is logical then to assume that they are intending to proceed according to the original plan."

Alam shrugged. "Makes sense to me."

"Shut up," Algar grumbled. Alam laughed to himself.

"He's right," King Roger said. "It is likely that the Greyls mean to confront us head-on. They're bloody-minded enough for that. Proud, irascible bastards that they are. We'll crush them on the field, then swing around from the south to come behind the Sierrans, assuming that they are still fighting. I expect the Ottals will deal with them swiftly."

"Don't count on it, Father," Alam said. "They're a
bloody hardy people when they dig their heals in.
Perhaps you forgot that thirty Sierran warriors
decimated an Ottalan raiding party of over sixty."

The King grunted and Algar sank into his seat. "This
is stupid," he grumbled when their spy left the meeting.
"It's going to be bloody slaughter up there and all
because some raiding party didn't get what they were
looking for."

"It is because they do not believe," the King replied
absently.

"You know that isn't true!" Algar snapped. "This is
nothing but cold retribution for something the Ottals
brought upon themselves. Honestly, what did they
expect? That the Sierrans would simply shrug and beg
to be enslaved? Of course they were going to fight!"

"And still are," Alam said.

"And still are," Algar muttered.

"Are you going to defect?" Roger asked his eldest
son with a small smile on his face.

Algar sighed. "No, Father. But I want you to know
that I am fighting this war under duress, and I don't want
every Sierran slain."

"Neither do the Ottals," the King said, still smiling.
"Where else are they to get their slaves from?"

Alam exchanged a look with his eldest brother and
they settled into silence as they awaited their brooding
father.

* * * *

Bran missed having his wife at his side. He barely slept the first three nights on the march. It was not right, lying in an empty bed. His melancholy was duly noted by the army he led, but none felt comfortable enough around Bran to approach him. All the same, they admired Bran for the love he was not afraid to show his wife and the manner in which he honoured their Winter Wolf.

The fact that Bran wore a cloak representing his namesake, a gift from the last remaining of the Ice Bear Clan and the Shaman and Shamanka of all the tribes also ensured that Bran's orders were obeyed. All the same, Bran felt that he still needed to constantly earn the respect of the warriors who surrounded him. He was completely unaware that he was earning it with every passing moment.

The Baveii prince proved a very competent war-leader indeed. It was recognised, if somewhat grudgingly, by the war chiefs and marshals who accompanied him on this march. At dusk on the fourth day, Bran stood on a hill watching the eastern horizon, his eyes and nose hidden by the long painted beak of his helm, thinking of his wife.

Every thought sent a pang of cold fear through him. What if the Lord of the Hunt chose her for ascension before the war concluded? What if these were the last few moments of her life as a mortal woman; as his wife? She would spend it away from him. Several times he had to deliberately turn his mind to other matters to stem the welling of tears that continually threatened to rob him of his vision.

"How much farther," the war chief of the Ouruq clan asked Bran from beside him.

Bran started and looked at the man. He truly was a representation of his tribe's totem animal – ouruq, the massive, shaggy, bison-like beasts of the ice fields. He was not especially tall for a Greyl man, being as tall as Bran. For the Sierran's however, he was a giant and he was twice as broad as the Baveii prince; made entirely of muscle and bone. Bran was a little envious of his mass, but could not begrudge the man. It was not his fault. The man's father had been equally as large.

Bran shrugged in response. "Otsana told me there are three standing stones that mark the border between Osprey territory and the land of the Ice Bear. We will camp there."

"Will the Ottals find us there?"

Bran shrugged. "Only if they march in a straight line. Let's not overestimate their abilities though."

The war chief laughed. "Well Southern Crow, what shall we do if they pass us?"

"Assume they are remarkably stupid. It's a very idiotic thing indeed to leave an enemy at your back."

"But they will be. The Winter Wolf and her pack are in the north."

"Yes, but they don't know that do they?"

"Let's hope they aren't very clever."

"They'd have made the first engagement by the time they realised they are fighting a murder of crows instead of a pack of wolves."

The enormous man turned to Bran. "A murder of crows," he mused as he observed his commander. "I like the implication."

"For battle, I suppose, it suits."

The man remained by Bran's side in silence for a long moment before he spoke again. "You miss her, don't you?"

Bran nodded. "I am not used to being apart from her. It is not a good feeling."

The war chief grunted. "You are lucky. Every man envies you."

Bran grinned.

"I am War Chief Hotuaekhaashtait," his companion introduced himself.

Bran looked at the man and laughed. "I will never be able to pronounce that!"

"Then call me Bull. My sister does."

"That I can do, Bull." Bran extended his hand and Bull took it. They shook hands and grinned.

"Dinner is ready," someone called and the two men turned together and retired to their evening meal as the sun set on the snow.

* * * *

"Otsana," Ur said quietly from outside the light of the communal fire. Seraphimé turned.

"The desert man. He is awake now."

Seraphimé put down her meal immediately and quietly excused herself. She walked quickly to Inna's pavilion and entered, forgetting that she was still wearing her wolf cloak.

Guild's mind was still foggy from a fever that had not yet vanished.

He had woken slowly to find that he was being tended to by a man of strange appearance, with a wide, round face and angular eyes. His skin was not brown, but strangely golden and he spoke in a language that Guild did not understand. Even so, Guild knew him to be one of the Sierran nomads, and he did not seem pleased to be caring for Guild.

Why should he? Guild thought bitterly to himself. *Would I be content to care for one of a people who attacked and enslaved my own?* Guild knew the answer well. He was much more likely to drive a sword through them. Slowly.

There was a rustle at the door and both men turned towards it. What Guild saw took him by surprise and he cried out in shock. A wolf, as tall as a man, walked into the pavilion and looked at him with glittering green eyes. Fear struck Guild to the core and he started to pray, mumbling incomprehensible words as he clutched at his chest tightly. He squeezed his eyes shut as the wolf approached, growling at him in low tones of warning.

* * * *

Seraphimé turned to Inna with a raised eyebrow.

"He is still feverish," Inna said.

"He sees the wolf," Ur said quietly.

Seraphimé looked down at the man and then, remembering her dress, removed her wolf-head helm. The man did not notice. His eyes were shut tightly and he was rocking himself back and forth, muttering something no one could understand. Ur walked forward and placed his palm on the man's forehead.

"You must open your eyes, little eagle. You must open your eyes and face your fear. The Winter Wolf will not harm you."

The man tried in earnest to open his eyes, but whatever monster he saw when Seraphimé walked in dressed in her battle cloak he saw still. He shut his eyes tightly again and whimpered.

Ur sighed. "Open your eyes, eagle."

The man shook his head, blubbering in fear, his eyes still tightly shut. Seraphimé was losing patience.

"Stand aside, little man," she said gently. Ur looked uncertain, then did as he was told. Seraphimé laid aside her cloak and sat on the furs that were the stranger's bed.

"Look at me," she commanded.

The man's eyes snapped open and he stared at Seraphimé in terror. He shrank back from her curling into himself, his eyes wide and frightened but fixed on her.

"That's not unnerving at all," Seraphimé murmured to herself, earning a grunting laugh from Inna. Seraphimé sighed and reached out to touch the man's feverish flesh. He tried to pull away and whimpered.

* * * *

The giant wolf reached out and placed one massive paw on Guild's cheek. The touch was electric, sending shock waves through his already trembling body. Yet it was painless. The wolf did not press its sharp claws into his skin, but simply held its paw at his cheek. The man's trembling died down and his stare turned from terrified to filled with awe and the wolf before him began to change.

The enormous white Winter Wolf faded from sight and was replaced by a beautiful young woman with startling eyes of green that peered into him with concern.

The warning growls were replaced with words, words he understood, words in Touan. His mind immediately flew to the figurine he had left behind in the desert; the clay model of a long-limbed wolf with green eyes. All fear fell away. He stared at the woman with a slack jaw and wide eyes.

* * * *

"Do you hear me?" Seraphimé asked the astounded man. The man nodded slowly, closing his mouth.

Seraphimé smiled. "I am Otsana," she said.

"Wolf," he croaked in broken Touan.

Seraphimé frowned, but Ur nodded and smiled. "Yes," he said.

"You were found in the snow, not far from the winter home of the Osprey Clan," Seraphimé supplied. The man looked at her, apparently struck dumb. Seraphimé raised her eyebrows at him. "How did you get to be so deep in Sierran territory?"

"Stag," the man answered. "Man. Dogs. Carried me."

"Stag man?" Inna asked.

"The Lord of the Hunt," Seraphimé answered.

Inna grunted. "I suppose that means we have to let him live."

"I'm not sure."

"Help. Come to help," the man said. "Ottals coming. Led by enemy. Hate him. Help you."

It was all the stranger had strength to say. He fell back in a fevered slumber, muttering to himself before sinking further into sleep and fading entirely from consciousness.

Seraphimé observed his face for a moment. He was, the new scars notwithstanding, quite handsome and though he was one of the enemy, Seraphimé sensed that he was not false.

Ur looked at Seraphimé with empty sockets and Seraphimé returned his sightless gaze. "What is your heart telling you, Ur, that you so clearly want to tell me?"

Ur smiled. "I like him."

"Great. I hate him," Inna said, folding his arms and pursing his lips.

Ur turned to his kinsman. "Do not. He has been wronged by one of his own, and the spirits brought him here, to us, for a reason. Indeed, the Master of the Wilds thought it wise to deliver him to you Seraphimé. Do not discount his wisdom."

"Oh yes," Seraphimé replied a little bitterly. "Very wise."

Ur smiled again and took Seraphimé's hand. "The Stag loves you Otsana, like the Crow loves you."

"Well, I cannot have them both," she said. "Can I?"

Ur's smile did not falter. "Why not?" Ur released Seraphimé's hand and exited the pavilion, humming happily to himself. Seraphimé looked at Inna in astonishment.

Inna shrugged. "Don't ask me. He is further removed from this world with every passing day. Soon he shall wander entirely in the Otherworld with the spirits, and forget that he is alive."

Seraphimé looked down at her lap. "Do not say so, Inna. He is dear to me."

"And me," Inna replied, sitting beside Seraphimé. "But it seems he is called away from us for some purpose we cannot know."

Seraphimé sighed. "I miss my husband," she said suddenly. "I cannot sleep without him beside me."

Inna laughed. "I would offer," he said with a grin. "But I do not think that would be appropriate."

Seraphimé grinned and stood. "No," she agreed. "It would not."

"In another life then."

"Perhaps."

Inna grunted and kissed Seraphimé gently on the hand before she left to return to dinner.

Ten

"*You* must understand, Lord Dylan of Kildurrow, I take no pleasure in this," the King of the Baveii said gravely. Court had been summoned for the trial of the traitor, Lord Dylan, youngest son of the Lord of Kildurrow.

Dylan Kildurrow stood in the centre of the room, the eyes of every courtier boring into him. He was no longer weepy or trembling, and he stood sullenly facing his king, his father and his eldest brother.

Lord Kildurrow looked pale and tired, heavy bags sat over the dark circles that had settled around his eyes. His normally bright eyes were dull and lifeless. Nathan fared little better, but there was an edge to his misery, as there was bound to be. All young men who believed as fully in their cause as did Lord Nathan Kildurrow would harden themselves against the horror of a brother's execution, so long as it served the cause.

"Tell us everything, my Lord, and I promise clemency."

Dylan scoffed and looked off to the side. He said nothing. Gofron sighed and rubbed his face. The gentle touch of his first wife as she briefly squeezed his shoulder steeled his resolve.

"Very well," the King said at length. "How do you plea?"

"It doesn't matter what I plea, does it?" Dylan spat angrily. "I know what's going on! My brother is trying to get rid of me."

Nathan's face looked as if it had just been slapped. "What?" he breathed.

"You were always jealous of me! I'm smarter than you and would make a better lord, and you hated it!"

Lord Kildurrow's expression hardened, but he remained silent and let his eldest son speak.

"That is ludicrous," Nathan managed to bluster. "You are my brother…."

"And you're jealous!"

"Dylan!" Nathan snapped. "I wanted you in my household! I was going to grant you a manor of your own!"

"Oh very good," Dylan sneered. "Such charity."

"You are not helping yourself," Gofron said bluntly. "Your brothers cannot help the order of birth any more than you can."

"But father could've noted. He could've changed his successor."

"I had no cause to," Lord Kildurrow said quietly. "And now, seeing this, I am glad I did not."

"You're an idiot!" Dylan hissed. "You all are. Fighting the Touan Federation and the Ottalan Empire! Do you honestly think you stand a chance? They're going to kill you all! You inbred pack of fools! We'll all be bowing before the god of the Yellow City in less than a year. At least I tried to secure a place for the Kildurrow bloodline, that a Kildurrow might rule over Kildurrow lands when the rest of you are in pieces all over the battlefield!"

Lord Kildurrow put his head in his hands and could not answer.

"At what cost?" Gofron asked quietly. "That you abandon your honour, and the name Kildurrow be hated by all Greyls everywhere?"

"It wouldn't matter! The Kildurrows would be lords still, while your families prostitute themselves for their new masters."

"Enough!" Lord Kildurrow roared, rising to his feet. His ire was frightening to behold. His eyes turned to blue ice as he stared balefully at his son. "I do not know what I have done to be cursed with a son who cares not for the honour of his name. But I shall soon be rid of it." He turned to Gofron. "I would ask the court that it withdraw its offer of clemency. Give him the justice that becomes his crime and never, *never* let it be said that there is a traitor with the name Kildurrow."

Having nothing more to say and on the verge of a breakdown, Lord Kildurrow bowed stiffly and stormed from the court, leaving behind him an audience sitting in shocked silence. Gofron turned his eyes to Dylan, who was shaking with irrational ire and delusional self-righteousness. He shook his head sadly.

"The offer of clemency is withdrawn. Since you have shown no remorse for your dishonourable actions, I have no choice but to hand down the death penalty. At dawn tomorrow, Lord Dylan of Kildurrow, your head shall be parted from your shoulders. There is nothing more to discuss. This court is now dismissed."

Dylan was collected by three heavily armed guards and taken back to the dungeon, but not before he threw a baleful glare at his eldest brother, who could only watch, bewildered.

The court filed out of the court room in stunned silence, no one daring to talk until they were out of earshot of the King. Once the room was empty of all save the royal family and Nathan, Gofron stood.

"You are dismissed," he murmured to his family before walking to where Nathan stood, staring into nothing, with tears streaming openly down his cheeks.

"My Lord," the King said gently, taking Nathan by the shoulder. Nathan turned to the King, his expression blank. Gofron's heart cracked. Nathan was a young man, not much older than Bran. Throwing aside decorum, the King wrapped his arms around the boy's shoulders and pulled him into a fierce embrace, one which Nathan accepted with unquestioning gratitude.

"I'm so sorry," Gofron said. Nathan broke down and wept. For almost half an hour, the King hugged Nathan close as he released his grief.

* * * *

"Well," King Roger of Misoua said mildly when the news reached him. "At least now we won't have to give away the Kildurrow lands."

* * * *

The Lord Kildurrow was not in the mood for company when he heard three quiet taps at his door. He opened it anyway. It was a surprise to him to find Gofron's third wife, Princess Amwyl, standing before him with a small platter of food and a large carafe of rich wine. He silently stood aside and let the Princess enter.

"Your Highness," he greeted in a dull voice. Amwyl smiled sadly in return and placed the platter on Lord Kildurrow's table.

"You probably don't feel much like eating," she said gently. "So I brought only soup and some bread and butter. I imagine the wine is more interesting right now."

Lord Kildurrow managed a smile. "Yes," he replied. "Much." Though he did not mean to, Lord Kildurrow gave Amwyl an appraising look. She couldn't be much past thirty, and looked younger still. He found her face beautiful and her eyes kind. It reminded Lord Kildurrow a little of his wife, passed some four years ago from a strange affliction no one could diagnose. For the first time in a long time, a small flame of desire stirred in the pit of his belly. He immediately quelled it in shame. How could he think such a thing on the eve of his son's execution? And worse still, about a woman who was his friend's wife?

"I shall leave you to it," Amwyl said gently. She would have glided passed him, had not Lord Kildurrow instinctually shot his arm out to block her way. His hand rested on her hip as he asked, "Will you not stay?"

The contact was electric, setting Amwyl's heart racing and her stomach fluttering. She froze on the spot and stared in surprise at Lord Kildurrow, who himself looked equal parts surprised and conflicted. She herself was ashamed that she did not pull immediately away.

"I cannot stay," she managed to say. Lord Kildurrow smiled a little and nodded. He dropped his hand.

"Forgive me," he murmured.

Amwyl smiled at him and touched his cheek. "There is nothing to forgive," she replied. "Please try and eat something. I'll have a servant come to fill your bath."

Lord Kildurrow nodded and stepped back, allowing Amwyl to pass. Amwyl smiled as she walked down the hall. She felt as if she was floating.

* * * *

"You're in a good mood," Catrin noted as she came into Amwyl's residence. Amwyl was embroidering a new belt and humming to herself. She smiled up at her sister.

"I am. So?"

Catrin smiled. "Nothing. Would you like some tea?"

"That would be wonderful."

Catrin stoked the fire and added more wood before placing the kettle on the hook to boil. "So," she said as she sat down by her sister. "What's his name?"

* * * *

"Did you hear, Crow?" Bull asked Bran as they settled in for another cold spring night near the three sisters.

"Hear what, Bull?"

"There was an execution. A Baveii lordling sentenced to death."

Bran's head snapped up. "What? Who? What happened? How did you hear?"

Bull grinned. "Messenger," he grunted, tilting his head towards a tired-looking rider who had arrived earlier that afternoon. "Figured it wasn't secret planning stuff, so he told me. Treason, he said. The boy was feeding information to Touans."

"Who was it?"

Bull shrugged. "Kildurrow. Dion or something like that."

Bran's eyes opened wide. "*Dylan?* Dylan Kildurrow was the traitor?"

"That's the one. You are surprised?"

"I knew him a little. He's only five years my junior. He seemed... well, he seemed nice enough."

Bull shrugged. "You think everyone is a lovely person. You're too trusting Crow."

"Poor Lord Kildurrow. It cannot be easy to stand by and have your son sentenced to death."

Bull shrugged. "I'd kill him myself if my son proved to be a traitor."

Bran looked long at Bull. "You would, would you?"

"I would. It is a point of family honour."

Bran grunted. "I don't know that I could kill my child."

"I didn't say it wouldn't hurt."

Bran laughed. He leant back on the rocks that surrounded the fire pit and breathed deeply. The fragrance of the wood smoke was sweet, a product of the sap of the shrubs used for kindling and the bones that burnt long and hot in the centre. He turned his gaze up and stared a moment at the stars the glittered across the sky before turning his eyes and thoughts north.

I miss you, he thought fiercely. *I love you.*

Though he did miss his wife most dearly, he found himself content. There was something liberating in the open skies and the broad fields of snow that ran uninterrupted for miles in every direction. There was a freedom in the tundra. It filled Bran's soul.

"What are you thinking?" Bull asked as he gnawed on a bone.

"That I couldn't imagine anywhere else I'd want to live," Bran replied. "There is something captivating about the tundra."

Bull grinned. "Your wife."

Laughing, Bran said, "Other than my wife. It feels... right, like this is how life is supposed to be led."

Bull grunted. "You don't mind the walking?"

"You get used to it," Bran said with a shrug.

"You don't mind the cold?"

"You get used to that too. And the way the sun sets the snow sparkling on a cold day is stunning."

"Romantic. No wonder she loves you."

Bran's head turned at this. Though she seemed to tolerate his affections with good humour, Bran was certain that her heart still belonged to the Lord of the Hunt. She had never once said the words 'I love you' to Bran. "No wonder," he murmured a little sadly.

Bull noted Bran's melancholy in silence and decided a change of subject was in order. "When will they come, do you think?"

"The Ottals? Soon I hope. I'm not thrilled at the thought of battle. But waiting for one is torture."

"We really going to run?"

Bran nodded. "They're likely to outnumber us and badly, especially with half our army in the north. The more we can lure them over the difficult terrain of the tundra, the more horses' legs will break, the more tired and hungry they become, the easier they will be to kill."

"Seems cowardly," Bull muttered.

Bran grinned. "But necessary. We will lose a full out battle. This is the best chance we have of defending the tundra."

Bull shrugged and said nothing. Bran stretched. "I think I'll turn in." He left the fire to Bull and a few other war chiefs and went to sleep.

* * * *

"Otsana," Ur said so quietly it was barely heard over the noise from the makeshift pavilion city that had sprouted on the middle of a glacier. Seraphimé had walked from the city to the edge of the glacier. It was a sheer drop of almost twenty feet now that a large portion had cracked off. She gazed intently south.

"Yes, little man?" she replied almost absently.

"The desert man is awake. He is asking for the Winter Wolf."

Seraphimé looked down at Ur and smiled a little. In her war cloak she must surely look like a wolf that walks upright. "I am not that wolf, Ur," she said. Ur simply smiled. Seraphimé sighed. There was nothing she could say to Ur that would ever make him believe otherwise. She did not know why she bothered trying.

"Come on then," she said, holding out her hand. "We'd best not keep our guest waiting."

Ur took her hand and together they walked back to the pavilion city. Seraphimé's pavilion stood at the southernmost edge of the city and Inna's stood beside it. The pair of pavilions had become the unofficial gateway to the rest of the camp. Ur led Seraphimé into Inna's pavilion.

Guild looked up as soon as he heard the pavilion entrance open. The boy with no eyes who still managed to see, led in the woman he had requested to see. Now virtually free of fever, he could see clearly that it was simply a woman dressed in the cloak of a wolf. Yet still, there was some power that surrounded her and the fevered visions he had the last time he woke haunted him.

There was a long silence as the woman's hidden eyes observed him carefully. Eager to lift the discomfort he felt, he pressed his hand to his chest.

"Guild," he said.

The standing wolf before him cocked her head in a lupine fashion, made even more so by the fact that she was yet to remove the wolf's head helm.

"Guild," she repeated. Her voice was rich and pleasant. Had she appeared to him in anything other than her war cloak, Guild would have been seduced by the sound of her voice alone.

Guild nodded and the woman smiled. She lifted off her helm and Guild issued a quiet gasp. Pale skin contrasted beautifully with her dark auburn curls that were kept back in a braid. Green eyes, a stunning colour to Guild who came from a world with very little green, sparkled with keen intelligence. The woman pressed her hand to her chest.

"Otsana," she said.

Guild smiled. "Otsana," he repeated. He pointed at Inna, who stood not far away, his arms folded across his chest and a highly unimpressed expression painted on his features. The image made Seraphimé smile and it was all she could do to not laugh.

"Inna," she said.

Guild observed Inna a moment. "Thank you, Inna," he said in his limited Touan. Inna grunted and looked away. Guild turned back and pointed at the boy.

"Ur," Ur said. This took Guild by surprise. There was no way the boy ought to be able to see that Guild had pointed to him.

"Ur is a gifted boy," Seraphimé said in perfect Touan.

Guild smiled and nodded. "I have noticed."

It had been a very long time since Guild had reason to speak Touan. It was not returning to him quickly enough for his liking. He could hear his own accent as he spoke it.

Seraphimé nodded. "Why are you here?"

"I've come to help."

"Why?"

"It's a long story."

"Your people have not attacked yet. We have some time."

Guild sighed and nodded. He waited for Seraphimé to sit and he smiled a little as Ur climbed into her lap. Guild, struggling to remember the appropriate words, haltingly told his story. He spoke of Iris, and the idol she had carried with her to the desert from the south. He told them of the Tigil's raid against a clan in the tundra, and how his men had been badly defeated. He told her of the Tigil's burning hatred, and the way in which he seized power. Lastly he told of the slave woman who had interrupted his wandering and had given him the clay wolf.

"I came here because I had nowhere else to go. I am the youngest bastard of a lord who has more sons than he needs. He threw me out once, going to him now as a failure would ensure a speedy death."

"You understand that your people have committed heinous crimes against the people of the tundra?"

"Yes, Otsana. I place myself completely at your mercy."

Seraphimé narrowed her eyes at Guild. "I remember the attack that your Tigil deemed such a failure."

Guild looked at her with unasked questions in his eyes.

"Before I became Otsana, Marshal of the Tundra, my name was Seraphimé and I was a princess of the Osprey Clan. We were headed south when the Ottals attacked. In the raid my stepmother was killed, taking her unborn child with her. My father was slain trying to avenge her death. I was one of the warriors that defended the tribe. I was pulled from my horse. I was raped. Had not Inna come to my rescue, I would have died."

Guild lowered his head. "I am sorry."

"Are you?"

Guild sighed. "The Fortu are not slavers. Not really. We... they are swords for hire. They perform a variety of tasks, and in truth are more used for guarding trade caravans than anything else. However, our actions are directed by the one who pays us."

"Are you trying to say that those men had no choice?"

Guild frowned a little.

"Because I tell you now that they had a choice. There is always a choice. They chose poorly, and paid dearly for it and now this, this Tigil, has started a war because of it. They brought it all down on their own heads."

"The Tigil is Guild Master now. He believes that his victory is assured."

"All the information of value you have supplied is nothing we did not know already."

"Then let me help another way."

"How?"

"I know how the Fortu fight. I know all their strategies. I trained most of them. Surely there must be some use for me?"

Ur scrambled off Seraphimé's lap and she stood. "I will think on it."

Guild looked panicked for a moment before he surrendered. He nodded. "Thank you."

Seraphimé did not respond. She replaced her cloak and left the pavilion. Guild slumped where he sat. Coming to the tundra may not have been the best idea after all.

"If I were her, you'd have been strung up for the bears a long time ago," Inna growled before leaving the tent. Guild swallowed.

"Otsana," Inna called as he jogged across the ice to her. "You cannot seriously be thinking of permitting him to continue to live amongst us?"

Seraphimé sighed as she turned to face him. Ur stood beside Seraphimé, his hand in hers and his attention somewhere unknowable.

"I am not sure. There must have been some reason the Lord of the Hunt brought him to us."

"You can ask him if you like," Ur said absently.

Seraphimé frowned and looked down at him. Ur was still gazing distantly at the horizon. Seraphimé followed the gaze and froze. Standing in plain sight was a massive great stag, his antlers no longer there, having been shed for the winter. Milling at his feet were three very large, coal black hounds.

Seraphimé sighed. She turned back to Inna. "I will probably be late for dinner."

Inna grunted, throwing her a sidelong look. Seraphimé smiled at him and, releasing Ur's hand, started to walk to the deer. Inna watched for a moment. It seemed to him that the stag glowed a faint green, and Seraphimé a faint blue. It must have been a trick of the light. Glare from ice did strange things.

"I bet they're going to fight," Ur said cheekily.

"All right, little man," Inna said, trying not to laugh. "This is none of our business. Come and help me build the icehouse." Ur grinned and trotted behind Inna as they made their way to the centre of the pavilion city where the food was stored.

* * * *

Seraphimé could not help but admire the art with which the Lord of the Hunt was able to fool the eye. She noted as she approached that the stag appeared less and less like a stag and more and more like a man in a cloak, yet the act of changing form was not perceptible at all.

The Marshal of the Tundra folded her arms across her chest when at last she stood before her patron god.

"Hello Otsana," he said in his deep, gentle voice.

"Why did you bring him to us?" Seraphimé asked bluntly.

The Lord of the Hunt's mouth quirked. "Are you still angry with me?"

"Answer my question, and I'll answer yours."

"Your irreverence is most refreshing."

Seraphimé pressed her lips together and put all her weight on one leg. She glared at him in silence.

The Lord of the Hunt's smile broadened. "You are most beguiling when angry."

"Stop it!" Seraphimé snapped, stamping her foot.

The Lord of the Hunt laughed and wrapped his muscular arms around Seraphimé's shoulders. Seraphimé resisted at first before acquiescing and leaning her weight against him.

"I have missed you, Otsana," he whispered.

"Your own fault."

"You sound like your grandmother."

Seraphimé smiled at this. She could imagine what her grandmother would say to him if she were alive.

"Why did you bring him to us?" Seraphimé asked again.

The Lord of the Hunt shrugged and ran his fingers through the lose strands of Seraphimé's hair. "I like him."

Seraphimé pulled away. "You like him."

The Lord of the Hunt shrugged again.

"That's the reason? You like him?"

Silence answered her question. "What sort of reason is that?"

Seraphimé threw her hands up in frustration.

"He could be useful to you, Seraphimé. He does not yet realise, but he already has you in his heart. He will prove a most devoted follower."

Seraphimé sighed. "Fine," she said. She began to turn away.

"The Crow misses you," The Lord of the Hunt said.

Seraphimé snapped back around. "You've *spoken* to him?"

"We have come to… a peace," he said.

Seraphimé's eyes narrowed. "What peace?"

The Lord of the Hunt shrugged and Seraphimé rolled her eyes. "You vex me."

"I try," the Lord of the Hunt replied with a quick grin. Seraphimé smiled.

"Am I forgiven?"

Seraphimé thought about it a moment. "I suppose."

"Good." The Lord of the Hunt's tone became serious. "You must ready your warriors soon, Otsana. The eagles are coming. They are many, and they are hungry."

Nodding, Seraphimè asked, "They have crossed?"

"Not yet. They are on the march. They will enter the tundra a week on the morrow."

"We'll be ready."

The Lord of the Hunt nodded. "Otsana?"

"Yes, my Lord?"

The Master of the Wilds regarded her in silence for a while.

Seraphimé frowned in confusion at him. "What is it?"

"You are so beautiful," he breathed. He reached out and stroked her pale cheek. Seraphimé smiled a little before turning and walking away.

"Well then," an Osprey said from the snowy ground a few feet away. "That went well."

"What are you doing here, harpy?"

"I'm here to make sure you behave yourself, my Lord. Bran may have agreed to the compromise, but my granddaughter is yet to."

The Lord of the Hunt growled. He turned on all fours and trotted away, his hunting dogs in tow, and the chatty osprey flying low overhead.

Eleven

"This is the last village before the tundra snows meet the desert sands. There is a wide swath of hard-packed clay that begins a day or two before the tundra snows begin. The ice leaks water there. It would be a good place to camp before we march into the tundra itself."

Guild Master Mtsusa grunted as Braddard Asul explained the best route. He knew it all already. His mind wandered as the Braddard spoke.

"We'll be crossing through a territory that has been stripped of its population. Any given clan, I understand, is not permitted to cross into another clan's territory unless expressly invited by the hosting clan. Unless, of course, it is the time of the Great Gathering. We can expect no attacks for a few weeks."

"I don't like it," another Braddard grumbled. "We don't know the terrain, and I dislike going into places I know nothing of."

"It can't be helped," Braddard Asul replied irritably. "The clans will not cross this territory and come to us. We can't just sit on the edge of the tundra and wait for them to come. It won't happen."

The other Braddard grunted and remained silent.

It was coming to a head.

Soon the Ottals would be involved in a full-scale war with the nomads of the Sierran Tundra. The Guild Master, now General of the Holy Armies, had over one hundred thousand soldiers at his back. The army dwarfed the entire population of the tundra by at least fifty thousand. It would not be war, it would be slaughter. The thought made the Guild Master smile smugly to himself.

"We'll camp on the desert edge of the hard ground for a few days," Mtsusa said. "It will give us time to rest and to test this theory that the clans don't cross territories."

"They don't," Braddard Asul muttered. He rolled up his map. "I know they don't."

"Braddard Asul here is a scholar of the Sierran nomads," a Tigil sneered.

The Braddard looked sharply at the man. "I am. So you'd best listen to me. No one here knows them better."

"Enough," the Guild Master snapped. "Let us eat and find our rest. We move west at dawn."

The tent quickly emptied of people, all except Braddard Asul.

"What is it?" the Guild Master said with a resigned sigh.

"Forgive me Guild Master, but I must caution you. You will find the ice-dwellers much more organised than before. They are expecting us, and they are led by a mated pair of war-leaders they have taken to calling the Winter Wolf and the Southern Crow."

"I had heard something to that effect."

"Guild Master...."

"Go to bed, Braddard. Their feral leaders are nothing more than superstitious fanatics, foaming at the mouth. They will prove to be ineffectual against our numbers."

The Braddard did not look convinced. "As you say, my Lord," he said with a bow. He left the tent and paused, looking up at the clear night sky. Two red stars glittered dimly in the night mother's cloak. "I don't like the look of that," he muttered. "I don't like the look of that, at all."

* * * *

"Marshal," Inna said as he blustered into her pavilion. "The Ottals have crossed into the tundra."

Seraphimé almost dropped her tea she stood so quickly. "It's time to move, then," she said with a grimace. Seraphimé pulled on her chainmaille shirt. "Will you help me dress?"

"It would be my honour, Otsana."

Seraphimé sighed as Inna stepped further into her pavilion and picked up her padded steel breastplate, overlaid with leather in swirling designs. It had been a gift of special magnificence, made by the personal smith of the King of the Baveii, who had also sent a note saying that she had quickly become his favourite daughter-in-law. It had made Seraphimé smile. Now it made her sad. Her husband would be taking on the Ottals in less than a month. It was likely that her father-in-law was already engaged with the Touans in the south. This could all go very badly, very quickly.

"Please don't be so formal with me, Inna," Seraphimé said as Inna placed the breastplate over her and began to lace the sides. "We are supposed to be friends."

"And we are, Otsana," Inna said with a smile. "I respect you greatly."

"And I you."

"Me?" Inna grunted. "A clanless man?"

"As long as you live, so shall the Clan of the Ice Bear."

"War has a habit of ending lives," Inna mused darkly.

Seraphimé smiled a little. "Then stay close, Inna, and I shall do all I can to protect yours."

"I shall," Inna said with a smile. "But only to do all I can to protect yours. The Winter Wolf is much more important than a man who is the last of his kin."

"I do not agree."

Inna grunted as he started to lace up Seraphimé's archers' braces. He laced on her greaves in silence

"Ur wants to come," Inna said as he left Seraphimé's side and fetched her war cloak.

Seraphimé almost choked. "He cannot! He is just a child!"

Inna nodded. "I said as much. He is insisting. He would ride beside you, Otsana."

"I will not allow it!" Seraphimé snapped. "A child in battle?"

Inna smiled. "He would argue that he had left childhood behind long ago, when the Ottals killed his mother and stole his eyes."

Seraphimé shifted her shoulders a little to allow her armour to settle. "I cannot argue that," she replied. "But I could not battle if I was afraid for him."

"You need not be afraid for him," a deep, silken voice said from the pavilion entrance. Inna and Seraphimé both spun around. Inna turned white and Seraphimé gasped aloud at the sight of the Lord of the Hunt standing at her pavilion entrance, Ur beside him, his tiny hand holding the hand of the King of the Dead. "He will not fight, and comes only to witness; witness and remember."

Inna could not find a voice with which to respond, made mindless and mute by the power that radiated from the god standing before him. A faint green light emanated from under the god's cloak.

"Do not fear, Inna," Ur said with a smile. "He is not here to collect souls. Not this time."

"Why are you here?" Seraphimé asked guardedly. The pull the Master of the Wilds still had on her made her irritable. She thought of Bran and forced herself to remain steady.

"I am come to ride with the Winter Wolf."

"To battle?"

"To battle."

"Why?"

"Do you not remember our conversations, Otsana?"

Seraphimé's suspicious stare prompted a small smile to appear on the Lord of the Hunt's face. "I have a vested interest in the survival of your kin."

"You will remain Master of the Wilds long after we are all dead."

"Yes," the Lord of the Hunt agreed. "So long as I am remembered, I shall be."

Seraphimé smiled a little. "The Ottals have no gods," she said. "They have forbidden the worship of gods."

The Lord of the Hunt nodded. "All but one."

"The god of the Yellow City. If we lose, you shall be forgot."

"I shall."

"And will suffer death."

"Yes."

Seraphimé folded her arms across her chest. "I am almost tempted to defect," she said tartly. Inna choked on his breath at the unexpected tone Seraphimé employed. The Lord of the Hunt did not anger. Instead he laughed.

Seraphimé grunted and smiled a little. "I would be honoured if you were to ride with us."

"I bring Ayals with me. They are a force of close to a thousand."

Seraphimé smiled. "We could certainly use that."

"Then they are yours to command."

"What of you?"

The Lord of the Hunt smiled sadly. "Touch me Otsana."

Seraphimé frowned and reached out. Where her hand expected to contact with the Lord of the Hunt's chest, there was nothing. Seraphimé's hand passed through him. She stumbled backwards and gasped.

"In the Otherworld, I am solid flesh and bone, filled with warmth as any of the living may be. In this world, I am... an apparition. It can be seen, and I can speak, and I can walk upon the ground." He cocked his head.

"In this world, I can make the herds strong and the hunter swift, I can grasp the hands of the souls of the dead and lead them to where they, too, will become solid once more. But in joining this fight, I must bring all of myself, and should a blade pierce me when I do, I can be killed."

"And the Ayals?"

"They are the flesh and blood extension of me. Should they be struck in this world, they will collapse into nothing and cease to exist. Do not fear, Otsana," the Lord of the Hunt said when Seraphimé gasped. "It is a price they are willing to pay. Many remember their living kin. Many choose to die for them."

Seraphimé sighed. "We shall have to make do then. Inna, my weapons please."

"Allow me," the Lord of the Hunt said when Inna found himself incapable of movement.

"Inna," Ur said gently, his young voice rousing the large man from his stupor. "Come, we must prepare also."

Inna nodded mutely and took Ur's offered hand. Giving the Lord of the Hunt a wide birth, Inna and Ur exited the pavilion.

"You can be killed by mortal blades, then?" Seraphimé asked.

"Yes. If struck walking whole in the mortal realm."

"I shall keep that in mind."

"Will you?"

"'ware the wounded woman, my Lord."

The Lord of the Hunt laughed softly. "I consider myself warned."

"Good." Seraphimé smiled and turned. "Time to go."

Seraphimé walked from the pavilion to find a large gathering of curious faces. Word had spread quickly that the King of the Dead had been sighted in the camp. The residents of the entire pavilion city had gathered to see him.

Seraphimé's mouth twitched a little. She looked about and noted that her army was almost ready. They were gathering several metres west of the camp. By the entrance of the camp, pink tongue lolling happily out of her mouth, sat the Black Hound, Cabal. Seraphimé smiled at the dog, who came bounding forward to settle happily by Seraphimé's side.

"We must ride now," she told the gathered crowd. "Take good care. We shall see each other again."

There was nothing else to say. Seraphimé heard the crowd murmur and knew that the Lord of the Hunt had appeared behind her. She started to walk to the gathering army and the crowd parted in waves. Some grieved. They reached out to touch Seraphimé as she passed. Others murmured prayers, prayers to Seraphimé herself that she deliver them. The latter made her uncomfortable.

"It has already started," the Lord of the Hunt muttered.

"What has?" Seraphimé asked.

"You have sharp ears, Otsana."

"Perhaps that is why they call me the wolf."

The Lord of the Hunt laughed. "Perhaps."

Seraphimé mounted her horse and waited patiently for the rest of the army to gather.

The wait itself revealed what the Touans would believe to be a decided lack of discipline. There were no ranks, no files. All the fighters were mounted. There was no infantry of any kind. It would make battle interesting, if nothing else.

The Ottals were also horsemen. Horse against horse was always a close battle, and the Ottalan horses were smaller and by extension faster and much more agile. Whether or not that would be an advantage on the tundra was yet to be seen. With luck, the majority of desert horses would have broken their legs on the tundra's difficult terrain.

Seraphimé watched as family members ran to their loved ones in the gathering army to give them talismans, extra food and sometimes wine. Warriors said goodbye to their wives and children, to their mothers and siblings and, on the occasion, to their husbands and children.

Inna joined Seraphimé a moment later, Ur riding a tundra horse of his own. On another horse sat the Ottal deserter, Guild. Seraphimé looked at him with surprise.

"I can help you," he said, almost pleading.

"He is here at my bidding," Ur said with authority that belonged to a much older man.

"I hope you know what you're doing, Ur," Inna growled. It was evident that he was not at all pleased with the arrival of the desert-dweller. Seraphimé studied Ur a moment. His face remained impassive and serene. Whatever it was Ur believed, he believed it strongly. His faith could not be shaken.

"Very well," Seraphimé said. "I trust you, Ur."

Ur inclined his head. "I am honoured."

"I am relieved," Guild added. "For a moment I was worried you might strike off my head."

Seraphimé looked at Guild. Unsmiling, she said, "I still might."

Inna's face brightened.

* * * *

"I don't like this," Braddard Asul muttered to himself as his horse slipped for the second time in three steps. The heat of the desert wind at midday thawed the snow only to have it promptly freeze when the north wind blew in the evening. They were walking on rocks covered in uneven ice. Their horses were not coping very well. Movement proved painfully slow. The Guild Master wanted to make damn sure no horse broke its legs during the march across the territory of the Ice Bear Clan.

There was no life here; nothing for miles but the glare and sparkle of ice and snow. The Braddard looked back at the vanishing line of orange that marked the desert and sighed. He was homesick already. He did not want this war, holy or otherwise.

If a people wanted to be free of their gods, let them damn well free themselves. We have no business in the tundra… And the tundra knows it.

There were some nights, some disturbingly silent nights, that the Braddard was sure he heard voices. Insidious whispering flowed over the ice with the wind, bringing with it the feeling of being watched, of being discussed, dissected, weaknesses found….

The Braddard shook his head. He was letting the paranoia get to him. Too much talk from the soldiers about ghosts and a man that was also a stag. Too much gossip about ancient arrows and ancient curses. The Braddard sighed and looked to his right.

It was a chance decision to do so, but one that made the Braddard stop dead. The regiment of Fortu he commanded stopped behind him. They all looked to their right when they noticed the colour drain from the Braddard's face as he gazed at the scene before him.

Some hundred metres or so from the marching path of the Ottal army stood a raised stone platform. Encircling the platform, mounted on shoulder-height crucifixes were sixty-five headless corpses each dressed in the armour of the Fortu.

"Guild Master!" the Braddard snapped, his voice much higher than he intended it to be. It was not long before the entire army had halted. They all faced north with pale faces and slack jaws.

From somewhere near the head of the long train of marching warriors and soldiers, the Guild Master walked his horse forward to investigate. The Braddard, curious and a scholar of the tundra, was eager to observe that which was completely unfamiliar to him. He had never heard of such sites constructed by the Sierran nomads and it intrigued him as much as it frightened him.

Taking the Braddard Asul's lead, other leaders in the army also walked their horses to the site.

"Well," Mtsusa said as the Braddard Asul arrived. "What the hell is this?"

"I am not sure, Guild Master," the Braddard admitted as he dismounted. "The Sierrans are not noted to be great builders. They do not have the tools required to shape stone in this fashion. Look here, see how the joints are made? Lock and key and each layer slots in with the one beneath it with these ridges here. Absolutely fascinating."

"Brilliant," the Guild Master noted without enthusiasm. "So what does it mean?"

"It couldn't have been built by the nomads. They do not possess the inclination or the technology for the platform."

"They obviously must."

"But they don't. And where did they get the wood from? Those crucifixes are definitely wooden. No trees grow in the tundra. Shrubs maybe, but these posts are tall and thick. Definitely trees."

"So?"

"So, this construction wasn't Sierran."

"Then who?"

"Well, the stone work is archaic. And the Touans were prone to head hunting before they converted. It's a practice that has been largely abandoned all around, but some of the wilder Greyl warriors still practice it."

"So this is Greyl?"

"No. Not unless the Greyl that built this was thousands of years old."

The Guild Master looked at the Braddard for a moment.

The Braddard started to get excited. "Just look at the design. It's a bit like the way they used to build cairns, but with a little more sophistication. And to build something so sturdy on a foundation of ice and snow indicates a great deal of specialisation. I can only surmise that someone who was raised in the tundra, with the technology and knowledge to build in stone must have made it. There hasn't been a culture like that in this part of the world in well over eight thousand years! This is a spectacular...."

The Braddard's excited ramble was cut short by the Guild Master's very firm grip on his arm. "Shut up you idiotic scroll maggot!" Mtsusa hissed angrily.

Braddard Asul's mouth fell open in surprise. "Wha…?"

"Do you want to scare the men out of their wits?"

The Braddard looked around at the grey faces that looked at him with astonishment and he realised what he had been saying. "I didn't mean to imply that there would be someone hanging around that was eight thousand years old," he spluttered in a terrible attempt at retracting his words. "Just that the technology is very old…."

The Guild Master shook the Braddard hard. "One more word out of you and I'll take your head from your shoulders!"

The Braddard immediately clamped his mouth shut. A cold north wind began to blow.

"Ghost!" someone from within the ranks shouted.

The Guild Master and the Braddard both turned. The wind had whipped up the small deposition of snow that had settled in a little pile on the platform. As the snow swirled, it seemed to complete the image of a man, replete with empty eye sockets that stared unblinking down at the Guild Master. The image was there for only a moment before the wind blew it apart. It was enough. The men in the army were spooked. This in turn terrified the horses.

Mtsusa released the Braddard, who fell heavily on the ice, and turned towards his army. It was in shambles. Horses were bolting in every direction, many could not find footing and several broke their legs, falling to the ground with ear-piercing screams.

"Silence those horses!" the Guild Master roared at the top of his lungs. "And get yourselves back in line!"

The Guild Master had proven himself to be a formidable man. In the first month of his appointment as General of the Holy Troops, he demonstrated a tendency towards the hard and cruel. If there was one thing the Ottals would fear more than tundra ghosts, it was the wrath of their General. The horses with broken legs had their throats slit, their life gushing from them in a steaming rush of red. It did not take long before the other horses were under control and the men back in line. The Guild Master remounted and walked his horse to the men, all of whom still faced the grisly monument to their immediate north.

"Do you know why I started this war?" Mtsusa rumbled. He let silence flow after his question. "I started this war because I came to the tundra, and it made a coward of me. Foolish beliefs in false gods and ghosts and the superstitions of the barbaric people that surround us made me into less than a man." The Guild Master raised his voice. "There are no gods, but for the one true god of the Yellow City! I come to clear the tundra of the false gods, and to free its people, who cower under their sway! There are no ghosts in the tundra! Only wind and snow. That is all."

The men that had spooked now looked thoroughly ashamed.

"Now the next coward to cry ghost will meet the edge of my blade! To prove to the tundra tricksters that we are not afraid of their gimmicks, we will camp here for the night. Now, butcher those horses."

In silence, the army split into its regiments to set up camp as their General commanded. The Braddard, sore from his fall, limped passed Guild Master Mtsusa to take control of his regiment.

"And if you say anything else about the impossible," the Guild Master hissed as the Braddard led his horse past. "I'll have you stripped, flayed and left for the bears."

"Yes, General," Braddard Asul murmured. He mustered his men and went to do as he was told. He wisely chose not to go to the command tent to eat with the other officers that night. He knew he would be unwelcome. Any man the Guild Master did not want to see was made plainly aware of the fact. Instead he sat around the fire with his men and chewed on half-cooked horsemeat and dates.

"Is that platform really eight thousand years old?" one soldier asked.

Braddard Asul shrugged. "In all likelihood, no. Anything older than a few hundred years would have been destroyed by the glaciers that snake their way south periodically. The construction itself looked relatively new. The technique is, however, extremely archaic."

"But those bodies.... When he was still Tigil, the General went mad. You remember it, don't you Braddard? He talked about ghosts and a man that turned into a stag and hell hounds the size of horses! And now, all of a sudden, he doesn't believe it? I'm not buying it."

The Braddard shrugged. "None of us believed him, did we? Why do we suddenly believe what he used to say now, when he's saying something else?"

"Because, there are sixty-five bodies up there, sixty-five guild members, and sixty-five was precisely the number that the General lost on his last expedition to the tundra."

"That can't be them."

"Why not?"

"Because it's been over three years. Those bodies would have decomposed or have been eaten by scavengers by now."

"Then how do you explain it?"

"They must have beheaded some of their own and dressed them in Fortu armour."

"That doesn't sound likely."

"More likely than bodies that don't rot."

The soldier grunted and the conversation ended, the Braddard and his men brooded over the fire and chewed their meal.

* * * *

Seraphimé watched the Ayal approach with a certain amount of wariness. It was always taxing to observe a man change into a Black Hound at will. He was sighted first by the Lord of the Hunt's own three hounds. Cabal, always cheery, stood and barked at the approaching Ayal, happily wagging her tail.

The Ayal loped over the spring snow at an easy run, before leaping into the air and changing into a woman mid-flight. The woman bowed before the Lord of the Hunt and offered her lord a swift, wolfish grin. The Lord of the Hunt beckoned the Ayal closer with his finger and the Ayal whispered her message into the god's ear. This time, it was the Lord of the Hunt who grinned. He whispered something back before dismissing the Ayal.

The Lord of the Hunt chuckled as he approached Seraphimé and sat down beside her.

"What was that all about?" she asked him.

"Oh, nothing," he said innocently. "Some denizens of the Otherworld had concocted a devious plan, that is all," he added when Seraphimé levelled him with a flat stare.

Twelve

"*H*old the line!" Lord Kildurrow roared. Overhead whizzed the javelins thrown by the charioteers who galloped back and forth in the space between the infantry and the cavalry. Several members of the light cavalry rode with the charioteers, letting loose arrow after arrow.

The thundering charge of the Touan heavy cavalry faltered as the javelins and arrows found their marks.

"Reform!" the distant cry of their commander echoed down the field.

"Hold!" Kildurrow roared again. The heavy infantry pulled closer together, locked their shields and raised their long spears.

"Brace!"

An instant later the Touan heavy cavalry crashed bodily into the waiting infantry. The Touan's first line was obliterated, but there were twelve more lines of horsemen. Lord Kildurrow kept the fighting as brief as possible, weighing the costs of battle carefully.

"Break!" he commanded. The heavy infantry broke lines and fled to the waiting chariots, where they were swiftly whisked away from the much slower Touan heavy cavalry.

No sooner had the chariots vanished from the field than did the warriors of the Greyl kingdoms let loose their rage. With a mighty roar, the Greyl army surged ahead, clashing against the lines of the expansive Touan force in one great wave.

Cavalry and footmen raced together to engage the Touans. Fully half the Touan heavy cavalry had fallen before the Touans gave the command to withdraw. The cavalry retreated and the Greyls were hit with a line of fresh foot soldiers.

The King of the Baveii, elected leader of battle by the makeshift council of Greyl kings, noted the splitting of the light cavalry as the Touans tried to encircle the charging Greyl horde.

"Clever bastard," he said grimly before giving three blasts on his horn.

The charging Greyls stopped suddenly and made a hasty retreat, splitting down the middle to scare the Touan cavalry wide before rejoining. The enclosing Touan cavalry suddenly found themselves flanked by javelin throwers, archers and slingers, and were cut down in astounding numbers in the crossfire.

"Fall back!" the Touan commander screamed. Slung bullets and arrows rained on the retreating Touan army until they were out of range. Only then did the Greyls retreat to camp.

King Gofron met with Lord Kildurrow as soon as the Touans were safely inside their camp.

"Deftly done," he congratulated Kildurrow.

Lord Kildurrow shrugged. "We've lost more than I'd hoped," he said.

"But not more than required."

"We've been at this two days."

"Yes, the auxiliary troops have been set. We can retreat any time now."

"The next camp is prepared?"

"Yes."

"And it is?"

"A tiny village so it looks like we've just found a place to hole up in while we try and recuperate."

"Nicely done."

"Wasn't my idea, to be honest."

"You're the King. It's always your idea."

Gofron laughed and clapped Lord Kildurrow's back. His messenger, Buddy, approached.

"Buddy," the King said. "Send the wounded out. They're to go immediately to Oisín's Keep where they'll be tended to and made ready to fight once the battle reaches them. Buddy nodded and left again to do as the King bid. Gofron turned to Lord Kildurrow. "A short engagement tomorrow, and then we burn it and run."

Lord Kildurrow nodded. The King clapped his friend on the back and they parted ways for the evening.

Sleep did not come easily to Lord Kildurrow. His mind was always on his sons, all of whom he sent to the newly fortified ancient stronghold on the north westernmost frontier of Greyl territory. None of them were permitted to join the battle on the field, much to their collective disappointment. Lord Kildurrow had already lost one son in his lifetime and he would sooner die than go through it again. This way at least there was a lesser chance of that happening.

Lord Kildurrow's mind also turned to the beautiful Princess Amwyl, whom he could not get out of his head since she brought him dinner on the eve of his son's execution. He was ashamed and angry. She was his friend's wife. He had no business dreaming about her. Even still, the thought of her plagued him constantly. Amwyl, like the rest of the royal household, save a few princes, had been sent to Oisín's Keep in the northwest. The thought of seeing her again gave him both shame and immeasurable courage.

With a sigh Lord Kildurrow closed his eyes and dreamt of a beautiful woman in his arms.

* * * *

"Undisciplined, huh?" Alam demanded of his elder brother as the pair removed their helms. "We were obliterated out there!"

"We still outnumber them, Alam."

"They took out nearly the whole damned cavalry!"

"Reinforcements are on their way, and the Greyls are giving ground. They will be beaten."

"Ow, ow, ow!" Alam complained as a squire helped him remove his breastplate. Alam looked down at his side. It gushed blood from a wound he had not even noticed he had sustained. "Great," he muttered grumpily before the loss of blood overwhelmed him and he collapsed, caught at the last second by his brother.

"Surgeon!" Algar screamed.

As a prince, Alam was one of the first to receive treatment. Things being as they were, however, the surgeons were swamped with wounded. The ground in and around the medical tent was muddied with blood and worse

Alam had to wait and Algar sat with him, his hands pressing a rag onto his brother's side to stem the blood loss. It seemed much too long before a tired-looking surgeon approached.

Algar yielded his brother to the surgeon. He sat by his brother's bed, shaking as he watched a surgeon treat his unconscious brother. When the wound had been stitched and bandaged, Algar turned his attention to the surgeon.

"He will live, won't he?"

The surgeon shrugged. "There's a good chance he won't, your highness," the surgeon said gently. "The wound is deep and is already leaking bile. I'm sorry."

"He can't die," Algar whispered. "He can't."

"I am sorry." The surgeon left to wash his hands and treat the next in line, leaving Algar bereft by his brother's bed.

* * * *

"Father," Algar said quietly as he stood before the rotund King of Misoua in his pavilion. "Alam is dead."

King Roger dropped his wine and stared at his eldest in mute horrified astonishment. Algar took a deep breath in order to steady his voice.

"He took a wound in battle this afternoon. It pierced an organ. He... he lost consciousness when his armour was removed. He died shortly after. I didn't have time to summon you."

Unable to bear his father's gaze, Algar bowed stiffly and left the pavilion. His mind failing, Algar's legs took him to his own tent where he sank down on his bed and, at last alone, wept until exhaustion took him over.

* * * *

"We killed a prince!" the Greyl infantry roared in celebration when the scouts returned with the news of a royal burial. The chants and cheers woke Lord Kildurrow from his sleep. He wandered outside to where the celebrations were taking place.

"What is going on?" he asked one reveller.

"One of the knights slain was the second son of the King of Misoua," the infantryman replied with a broad grin. "Takes the heart out of the enemy, something like that!"

Lord Kildurrow grunted and returned to his tent. He paced a while, unable to share the joy of the infantry that danced and sang in the centre of camp. He turned on his heel and gathered his parchment and pens. He scribbled a brief message then, deciding it was not enough, he tossed it into the small pile of burning embers in his hearth. He dressed himself and stole quietly from the camp.

* * * *

"Forgive me for intruding on your grief, your Majesties," a soldier said meekly from the entrance of the King's tent where the King of Misoua and Algar sat in melancholy silence.

King Roger blinked, clearing his hazy vision. "What is it?" he croaked.

"There is a messenger, Sire, from the kingdom of the Baveii."

Algar and Roger frowned at each other.

"Send him in," Roger managed after a short pause.

"Your Majesties," the messenger bowed and exited.

A moment later, a tall, broadly built man with greying temples and kindly blue eyes strode into the tent. He walked tall and boldly, but his face was etched with the marks of grief.

"Your Majesties," the man said softly with a deep bow. "I am...."

"I know who you are Lord Kildurrow," the King of Misoua shot back bitterly. "What are you doing here?"

Lord Kildurrow sighed and straightened. "Your Majesties, I come before not as your enemy, but as a father who has also lost. I am so sorry."

"Your men are celebrating!" the King of Misoua spat.

"But I am not. No father should live to see his sons die. I wanted you to know that you are not alone in your grief."

"You risk your life to *console* us?"

Lord Kildurrow smiled a little. "Yes. Though it is only a risk if you ignore the rules of combat."

Roger stared incredulously at the man before him. "One word from me, and you'd be captured. Arrested. Tortured and held to ransom."

"Yes."

"And you risked that all to...."

"Extend my sympathies, your Majesties. The Greyls may be your enemies at the moment, but we are still men and we bleed when cut, and grieve when we've lost."

"Go to hell. Your kind has been raiding my lands since time began."

"Yes, and your kind raided ours before that. How many sons must be killed, how many grieving fathers must be made, before we learn, I wonder?"

Lord Kildurrow's softly spoken question struck the Misouan King dumb.

"Alam didn't want this war," Algar said softly, distantly. "He fought only because he had to."

"As do we all," Lord Kildurrow replied. "I will intrude on your grief no longer. I am sorry."

Lord Kildurrow bowed and turned. Roger opened his mouth to call the guard, but Algar stopped him. "Let him go," Algar murmured gently.

Lord Kildurrow left and, in accordance with the laws of war, was escorted to neutral ground where, he was surprised to discover, the King of the Baveii and a small host awaited him.

"Your Majesty," Lord Kildurrow said with a bow.

"Kildurrow," the King replied. After a searching silence Gofron asked, "Why did you go there?"

"The King of Misoua lost his son today," Lord Kildurrow replied. It was all he need have said. Gofron understood precisely Lord Kildurrow's motivation, even if some in his host did not.

"His son was a traitor," one of the guard noted darkly. "It runs in the blood."

The hurt that crossed Lord Kildurrow's face made Gofron react immediately. He turned to the soldier and glared hard at him. "The Lord Kildurrow has my confidence. If you insult his honour, you damned well better have some proof, or it'll be your neck to face the axe."

"Yes, your Majesty," the soldier replied sullenly.

The King grunted. "Everyone is dismissed. Lord Kildurrow, will you walk with me a while?"

Lord Kildurrow nodded and fell in step beside his friend. They walked for a time in silence and, in truth, it was easier that way. They both enjoyed the comfort of each other's company without having to create the discomfort of talk.

"You look exhausted, Kildurrow," Gofron noted. "You haven't slept much have you?"

Lord Kildurrow shook his head and the King sighed. "How did it come to this?" he asked.

"A lost wolf wandered in and stole the heart of a crow," Lord Kildurrow replied, his mouth quirking a little. The King of the Baveii threw Lord Kildurrow a flat look.

"It was a rhetorical question."

"Was it?" the false innocence with which Lord Kildurrow framed the question brought a smile to Gofron's lips.

"Have you had dinner?"

"No."

"Good. Join me in my tent. Let's eat."

Lord Kildurrow did not feel much like eating, but he could not refuse his friend and king, so he smiled and nodded and together the King and his closest advisor wandered to Gofron's pavilion.

* * * *

It had been three weeks of marching. The Ottals faced nothing but silent snow and ice for mile upon mile. It made the army uneasy and they shuffled warily along, their eyes wide and their shoulders tense.

The three weeks of travel into the tundra had been difficult. The terrain was brutal. Several more horses had broken their legs, bringing the number to just under two hundred. Suddenly, the Ottalan army, famous for their cavalry, had an expansive infantry. Walking happened to be no less difficult than riding through the tundra and several men seriously injured themselves falling. Two had died of exposure, and several others were marked with wide black scars as the frost ate at their skin.

Braddard Asul kept his mouth tightly shut and obeyed orders without question, but his mind was constantly at work. Waiting for the Ottals to come to them was the perfect strategy for the Sierran nomads. The Ottals were wholly unable to survive the tundra. Much longer now and the army would be completely broken.

The Guild Master would not hear it. He kept the pace even and did not slow for those who could not keep up. The march of the Ottals left a trail of dead and dying behind it. The Braddard did not like it, but could do nothing to convince Guild Master Mtsusa to slow his pace.

Spring was here, the Guild Master had declared. He was not wrong. The days were getting warmer and longer, but the nights were still frigid. The snow that melted during the day froze over at night, sometimes up to three inches thick, covering everything.

Often fresh snow would greet the waking Ottals, hiding the ice and making it yet more treacherous. When at last the grass began to show through the snow, the men's spirits lifted.

That was before the Ottals realised that the retreating snow and ice revealed a terrain even more difficult.

Exposed rock with wide, sometimes sharp-edged fissures played havoc with the horses' slender legs and dainty hooves.

Worse still, the supply wagons would periodically get stuck in deep patches of newly made mud, and the whole army had to pause and lend what strength they had left to pull the wagons free of the rocks. Three wheels had shattered thus far. Wagons had to be abandoned and others overloaded, making them more prone to getting stuck and on it went.

Everyone was miserable. Some even talked of desertion. When news of that reached the Guild Master's ears, he used death threats and the Yellow Robes. The priests walked amongst the soldiers, issuing prayers and uttering blessings. They fed the soldiers word of Susa's joy at their persistence, at the rewards that awaited them at the end of their long and difficult journey. Every night the priests held sermons, whipping the soldiers into a blind frenzy.

Only Braddard Asul remained immune. The scholar-sword was not convinced by the sermons. He did not share the wild hatred of the tundra that had formed in the hearts of his fellows during this march.

With each passing day in the miserable, inhospitable land of frost, he grew to admire the Sierran nomads more and more. They must be a hardy people indeed, to survive in such a clime.

The Braddard's thoughts were interrupted when a scout returned, trying hard to generate a trot from his tired and cautious horse. The Braddard happened to be in earshot when the scout spoke to Guild Master Mtsusa.

"General," the scout said. "They're just south of here. No more than half a day. And they're camped. It looks as though they've been waiting for us. One of them... he saw me."

The Guild Master's expression turned sour.

"I apologise," the scout said. "The bastard... he smiled and waved."

Braddard Asul almost laughed. He managed to cover it by pretending to clear his throat. "The cheeky bugger," the Braddard mumbled when the Guild Master glowered at him.

Mtsusa turned back to the scout. "We camp here. I want everyone rested when we meet our heathen foes. Spread the word."

The scout bowed and did as he was told. Braddard Asul turned back and went to the aid of his regiment. He felt the Guild Master's dark eyes bore deep into the back of his neck.

"Well?" one soldier asked the Braddard.

"They're a day south. We camp here. We march on them in the morning."

"About time. I want some fighting after all the freezing we've done up here."

Braddard Asul shrugged. "It's the tundra, what did you expect? We chose to come here. We've no one to blame but ourselves."

"I didn't get much of a choice. I was told to march, so I marched."

The Braddard grunted as he helped unload some firewood and set up a hearth. "War is a little like that."

The soldier laughed. "I suppose. You know, I think the more I travel in this accursed place, the more I think that the nomads are either insane or devils. Only the former would choose to live in such a place and only the latter would survive it."

"They aren't devils," Braddard Asul said with a sigh as he unwrapped a pot and filled it with water. "Insane? Well, perhaps. It's not a place I would like to live. Then again, perhaps that is why they choose to live here."

"How do you figure that?"

"Until twelve years ago they were completely untouched by anyone outside the tundra. They were safe."

The soldier considered it. "I suppose that must be true."

Braddard Asul grunted. "I suppose. We don't have any fresh meat, do we?"

"We do, and we'd best eat it fast. It was fine a week ago when the weather was still cold enough to keep it frozen. Now that the days are warmer it'll go bad real quick."

The Braddard sighed. "We'll have to salt cure it then."

"No time. We only have this evening."

"I can smoke it," another soldier said. "My mother used to smoke cure all kinds of things. She taught me."

The first soldier laughed. "Was she hoping for a daughter?"

"She was hoping for someone useful," the second soldier shot back.

"Enough," the Braddard said with a sigh. "Smoke it then. We'll use as much as we can in the meal tonight though."

"I need rocks."

"What for?"

"To build the smokehouse."

Braddard Asul nodded. "Get rocks then."

The soldier, along with a few others left the setting up of camp in search of enough loose rocks of appropriate size with which to build the smokehouse.

* * * *

Bran chuckled as the sun set over his camp. Bull grinned from ear to ear and there were bouts of laughter as the story spread.

"It was very good. Very good," Bull said, finishing his amusing tale of childhood pranks. "The poor bastard screamed in his sleep for three days!"

"You're a cheeky bastard," Bran said.

"If he did a better job of hiding himself, perhaps I wouldn't have been," Bull replied.

Bran laughed. "Hey, do you think if we all started howling, they'd hear us from here?"

Bull stopped stirring the stew and looked up at Bran's face with an impish expression. "It'll be full moon tonight."

"So that's a yes?"

Bull nodded, his brown eyes twinkling like stars.

Bran grinned. "Excellent!"

* * * *

"Did you hear that?" one Ottalan soldier asked, turning his head from the fire and looking south.

"Hear what?" the Braddard Asul asked in a dull voice.

"I could've sworn I heard.... There! There it is again! Didn't you hear it?"

"I don't...."

"Shhh!"

A curious silence fell over Braddard Asul's regiment as each man listened closely. A distant howl floated to their fire on the breeze.

* * * *

"Now," Bran commanded as he let loose another howl. It was the fourth he had ventured alone. Bull immediately joined in. Years of living in a world still heavily populated by wolves made Bull's howl more convincing. Soon all two thousand warriors raised their voices in the chilling call of the tundra's most revered predator.

Bran's long howl was the last one to die away, but even he could hear the answering call; the melancholy, primal howl of a wolf somewhere in the north.

* * * *

Seraphimé lifted her head at the sound of wolves howling in the night. Standing as she was on the rock, in the moonlight and still wearing her war cloak, she looked every bit the Winter Wolf. She closed her eyes and let the sound of the wolves fill her before she tilted her head and howled in return.

War had come, and the tundra had risen.

* * * *

Braddard Asul turned pale as the howls from the south were answered by a single long howl from the north. He turned his head and in his mind's eye saw on the far horizon, standing on the crest of an ancient cairn long destroyed by ice and wind one lone wolf, as large as a pony, tilting its head back and answering the army in the south.

The sound put a chill through the Braddard. Even more so as another wolf, further north answered the melancholic cry of the wolf on the horizon. Packs of wolves elsewhere in the tundra lent their voices to the chorus and it seemed, suddenly, that the tundra was alive. It lived and it was gathering its might, calling its warriors to battle.

The tundra had issued her challenge.

"Lord Susa save us," the Braddard whispered.

Thirteen

The change in Seraphimé was not physically noticeable. To most, it was not obvious that she had changed at all. She looked the same. She spoke in the same manner, with the same wit. She walked with the same grace. Yet something was different. The power that had remained hidden beneath had surfaced. It surrounded her. It filled her.

It struck her army with a new kind of awe. It was noted that though Seraphimé looked like a woman still, her eyes belonged to a wolf. Ever more frequently she had taken to wolfish habits. She began to recognise people by scent, noting who was where in the camp simply by testing the wind.

For Seraphimé, nothing had changed. She had always been this way. She always had this kind of power, these abilities. This was just another side of her. She no longer cringed when people referred to her as the Winter Wolf. The tundra was part of her, was her, or rather, she was the tundra. It had always been thus. It was only natural.

Ur was pleased. He now dressed himself in grey and black robes, tied at the waist with a simple sinew belt, the end of which held tassels made of wolf pelt.

It was understood by all that Ur had become the servant of the Winter Wolf, the first Shaman of her cult. The deference this afforded him was great. People made way wherever Ur walked.

The Lord of the Hunt and his Ayals remained with Seraphimé. The tundra had awakened, and though the Lord of the Hunt had influence over the animals, he was as much a servant of the tundra as the rest of the army. Like the animals over which he exercised his extraordinary powers, he too was subject to the moods of the land in which they lived. It was a servitude he bore easily, for it had always been so. Only this time, his mistress had a face, a body, and a voice.

"Ur," Seraphimé greeted as the boy stepped from his pavilion one morning in the week following Seraphimé's answering howl.

"Otsana," Ur said with a smile. "You look well."

"I am. Where did you get your robes?"

The Lord of the Hunt shifted his weight. Seraphimé understood immediately. "You sew well," she noted to him with a quirk of her mouth. The Lord of the Hunt grinned swiftly and Seraphimé closed her eyes. "They are almost at the three sisters. We must hold here until they are lured past before we continue south."

"Can you tell what's happening with the Greyls?" Inna asked as he too approached Seraphimé's fire. Seraphimé opened her eyes and shook her head. "My sight does not extend past the line of trees. I cannot see into the south."

Ur sighed and climbed into Seraphimé's lap. Inna smiled slightly. It was easy to forget that Ur was still a child.

Now, however, in the arms of his matron goddess, he was as a babe; content and safe. Ur sighed happily and Seraphimé smiled, kissing him gently on the top of his head and stroking his hair.

Guild was the next to exit the pavilion. He spied Seraphimé and halted, his dark eyes staring at her. Seraphimé observed his slack-jawed expression mildly.

"Is something the matter?" she asked him.

"You seem... different."

"Do I?"

"Yes."

"Am I not dressed the same?"

"You are."

"Do I not have the same face?"

"Well... yes."

"Is it not my voice with which I am speaking to you?"

"It is."

"Then what is different?"

Guild shrugged. "I don't know," he said with a frown.

"Otsana is awake," Ur said sleepily.

"I can see that," Guild replied grumpily.

Inna laughed. "You are still unfamiliar with our favourite child," he said. "He speaks in riddles."

"It was spoken plain," the Lord of the Hunt murmured.

"You don't understand. Otsana has woken," Ur said.

Guild frowned. "Yes," he said with deliberate emphasis. "I can see that."

The Lord of the Hunt laughed quietly. "Otsana is 'she-wolf,' desert man."

"And my name means 'council of men.' What of it?"

Ur giggled. "Silly boy," he said. "I shall teach you."

Seraphimé sighed. "I'm hungry."

"You are the tundra, you feed us," Inna remarked with a smile as he began to fill a cauldron with snow.

"Perhaps, but this body is mortal and requires sustenance."

"Soup?" Inna asked.

Seraphimé smiled and nodded. "Yes please."

Ur straightened. "Mmmm! Soup!"

"You all eat soup every day," Guild complained. "How can you not get sick of it?"

"Because it is warm," Seraphimé said with a smile. "And Inna makes it hearty and flavourful."

Inna shrugged. "Old mother showed me the recipe." The broad man sighed. "I miss her."

"She is not gone," Seraphimé said with a smile.

Inna looked up at Seraphimé and nodded. "I know, but it isn't the same."

"She said you use too much salt," Ur said with a smile, before turning his head again towards the south.

Inna glared at him. "That was your complaint."

"Strange."

"Indeed."

Fourteen

"What the devil?" Roger, King of Misoua said when the sky flared orange. He and Algar ran outside.

"Those bastards," Algar said. "They've burnt their camp. They're on the run. Again."

"And in the middle of the night. Cowards. We can't chase them until morning."

"That was the idea, I think. You see the fires up ahead? They're burning the crops as they go."

"As they like. We have supply trains."

"They must be getting desperate, trying to starve us out like this. Surely they're aware that this will only bring famine upon them also?"

Roger shrugged. "Well, we should report this."

Algar gave his father a sidelong look. "The council members have eyes, Father. They're all seeing this too."

"Damnable Greyls."

Algar sighed. "We should get some sleep. There'll be a hard ride tomorrow."

"Unless we wait for the reinforcements. It won't be much good to completely exhaust our cavalry when they're already in such poor shape."

"It will be discussed at a meeting, I'm sure."

"Your Majesties," a messenger of the Wetouan Council said as he jogged up to them. "A council has been called."

"Of course it has," Roger grumbled. The messenger raised his eyebrows and the King sighed. "We'll be along soon."

The messenger bowed and then jogged away, carrying the message to the next council member. With a resigned sigh, the King returned to his tent to dress properly.

It was only fifteen minutes later when King Roger and Prince Algar arrived in the council tent. The head of the Wetouan Council, as well as an overseer from the Yellow City, presided over the meeting. It was always the same. People would argue semantics for hours before deciding on the first suggestion made. It aggravated Roger no end and Algar bore it with equally poor humour.

"This is what's going to happen," Roger said as the crowd gathered. His blunt impertinence put a smile on like-minded council members, and earned him barely audible threats from other members. Roger didn't particularly care either way. "We're going to rest up here until the reinforcements arrive. Then we set off after the cowards and fight another few battles. Then they'll run again. And we'll chase them some more, and on and on ad nauseum."

"You will bow before the Wetouan Council," one man dressed in yellow robes intoned dully. He was sick to death of continually having to remind the King of Misoua of his place.

"Of course," Roger said. He did not bow. The member of the Wetouan Council rolled his eyes, but pressed the issue no further.

"The fact of the matter is, they're fighting hard. That last assault decimated our heavy cavalry. We need to revise our strategy," said the King of Gumoua.

"We're gaining ground," the King of Hitoua countered.

"But at what cost? Eventually, there will be no reinforcements left to draw upon."

"When that happens, the Greyl army will be so small it will hardly matter."

On and on the arguing went until, at last, the representative from the High Council of the Yellow City cleared his throat.

"This war is a Holy War, and cannot be abandoned. Those heathens that do not convert must be cleansed and their souls delivered to the true god so that they might find justice with him. I advise that we wait for the reinforcements and continue to chase the heathens until the last is delivered to the gates of heaven."

"What a wonderful idea," King Roger noted with a smile. "Very original. I second that."

Algar had to bite his lip to keep from laughing at the expression of the High Council representative. Any response he might have offered was drowned by the weary agreements of all members of the council. The council was thus concluded and, with the sun breaking over the horizon, Algar and Roger trudged wearily to their beds.

* * * *

"Damn it!" Lord Kildurrow growled as he withdrew with the rest of his troops. The battle went poorly indeed. They had lost more men than they could afford. The day's fighting was done and the Touans were celebrating.

As anyone would, Lord Kildurrow thought bitterly. He looked across at the King of Baveii as he crossed the line into Greyl controlled territory. Gofron looked drawn and tired.

"We need to revise," Lord Kildurrow said abruptly as he stopped in front of the man.

"You're bleeding all over the place, Kildurrow. Get to the surgeons, immediately."

"It can wait."

"The hell it can! Go now! I'll speak to you when you have been treated."

Lord Kildurrow growled, but complied. He marched to the surgeons' growing pavilion and sat heavily in line, sulking.

"Stop sulking," a young woman said with a smile. "You'll trip over that bottom lip."

Lord Kildurrow raised his head and blinked. "*Amwyl*?" he asked incredulously.

Princess Amwyl smiled and pressed her finger to her lips. "Hush, my Lord," she said. "The King will never forgive me if he finds out I am walking amongst his army!"

Lord Kildurrow was at a complete loss as to what to say. No less beautiful in plain clothes, Princess Amwyl seemed a vision to the Lord Kildurrow at the moment.

"Now," she said, kneeling down and removing Lord Kildurrow's helm. "Let's have a look, shall we?"

"Where did you learn to be a surgeon?"

"My mother. I was her only daughter and boys get into awful scrapes sometimes."

"Did she not employ a surgeon of her own?"

"She preferred to treat her children herself. Her father was poisoned by his surgeon and she had developed a profound mistrust for them."

"I see."

"Do you?" Amwyl examined the wound on Lord Kildurrow's head. "Well, it could be worse. Your skull wasn't quite split. I imagine your ears must be ringing."

Lord Kildurrow grunted.

"One more knock and we'd be trying to put your brains back in your skull though. I can treat this, but you won't be allowed back on the field until it has healed properly."

"There's a war to fight."

"There are enough healthy warriors to fight it without you."

"You can't keep me from fighting."

"The hell I can't. I'll have the head surgeon speak to my husband. See if you can object to him."

"I'd fight my way back."

Amwyl laughed as she began to clean away the blood. "With your head spinning as I'm certain it is, you won't get very far."

Lord Kildurrow grunted again and closed his eyes as Princess Amwyl cleaned, stitched and bandaged his head. She hummed to herself all the while.

"That's a lovely song," Lord Kildurrow mumbled.

"The Mother's Lament," Princess Amwyl said. "I forget most of the words, but it is about a mother whose son was sent to battle. She sits by the window watching for his return, but he never comes home."

Lord Kildurrow opened his eyes and observed Princess Amwyl through swimming vision. "What happened to her?"

"She died in her chair, and her ghost sits there still, hoping to see her son once more."

"Bran will be all right," Lord Kildurrow said gently. "I know he will."

Amwyl's eyes filled with tears. She smiled at him. "I'm more worried for you," she lied. "You're going cross-eyed. I'm almost done with the bandages. I'll fetch you some tea that will relieve your headache and help you sleep."

Lord Kildurrow nodded. "But first I must speak to your..." he spied Gofron enter the pavilion. "King."

Princess Amwyl smiled and, not sparing a glance for her husband, rose to fetch the tea. Lord Kildurrow, meantime, watched the King approach warily.

"So?" Gofron asked as he sat down by Lord Kildurrow. Lord Kildurrow was luckier than most. He, being a lord, was given a bed, while the common fighting men were remanded to any dry spot on the increasingly bloody ground.

"I'm not allowed out to play anymore," Lord Kildurrow slurred with a lopsided smile.

"Really?" the King replied with heavy sarcasm. "I wouldn't have guessed."

"Bastard," Lord Kildurrow muttered.

Gofron grinned. "I think we need to change tactics."

"Really?" Lord Kildurrow imitated. "I wouldn't have guessed."

The King laughed, then let the smile slip from his face. "A full retreat; to Oisín's Keep in the northwest. We can hold there until the Sierrans come to our rescue."

"*If* they come to our rescue."

The King shrugged. "In any case, we no longer have the numbers for an open assault."

Lord Kildurrow nodded, and immediately regretted it. "That's true," he agreed with a wince. "A suggestion, your Majesty?"

"I'd welcome it."

"Leave behind light cavalry to harry the supply trains. Burning the crops will do nothing if they can still ferry supplies to their army."

Gofron nodded. "Yes, that's true. We'd need several groups, to be commanded independently."

"Yes, so choose those commanders very wisely."

"You have a knack for pointing out the bleeding obvious, Kildurrow."

"That is why you took me on board, your Majesty." Lord Kildurrow closed his eyes and leant back on the rough pillows.

The King sighed. "I'll let you get some rest. You'll be moved out with the rest of the wounded as soon as I finish the meeting."

"As you like."

"We have to create a diversion to buy us some time to escape."

"Burn their camp." Lord Kildurrow was almost asleep when he said it.

Gofron smiled. "Kildurrow, you are a genius."

"Now who's pointing out the obvious?"

"Here's the surgeon with your medicine. I'll take my leave now. Rest up, Kildurrow. I want you fighting fit for the siege."

Lord Kildurrow opened his eyes and he looked at Amwyl with poorly disguised astonishment as she set the tray of tea down on his bed.

"Take good care of him, surgeon," Gofron said, blissfully unaware that it was his third wife who now curtsied before him, her eyes determinedly cast down at the ground. He patted Lord Kildurrow's shoulder and left the pavilion. Lord Kildurrow shook his head at Amwyl, who threw him a cheeky smile as she poured his tea.

"Here you are," she said handing him the cup. He shook as he took it.

"Drink it all down."

"You're insane," Lord Kildurrow rumbled back before downing the cup in one gulp. "You could have been discovered."

Amwyl shrugged and helped Lord Kildurrow into a more comfortable position. "Sleep well, my Lord," she said gently.

Lord Kildurrow grunted and closed his eyes. Unable to resist, Amwyl leant forward and kissed him briefly on the cheek. Lord Kildurrow smiled as he drifted into a very pleasant sleep.

* * * *

The King of the Baveii was blunt as he explained the situation to the war council.

"We're losing. That last battle cost us more than we could afford. I've spoken with Lord Kildurrow and we've both agreed that facing the Touans in open battle now will be the death of us. We have to retreat. A full retreat to the northwestern stronghold is the only option available to us."

His words were greeted with a low-toned murmuring as the lords began to discuss it between them. Gofron allowed it for just a moment before he help up his hand to silence them.

"We need to protect our wounded and ensure that they make it to the stronghold. We have no choice now but to employ a full scorched earth policy. The issue is that the Touans will be fed from supply trains that come in from Touan territory."

"You want to set up pockets of raiders to ensure that the supply trains and the reinforcements do not get to the Touan army," the King of the Pamisii guessed shrewdly. Gofron nodded. "Each group will have to be commanded autonomously. Once we're inside that Stronghold, there is no way we can get word in or out."

The King of the Pamisii nodded. "I have a son, he is young, perhaps, for his own command, but he is clever and brave."

"I'd have to meet him."

In an instant kings and lords were volunteering their children for the task, each vying with one another in an effort to achieve greater prominence. Gofron sighed.

"Thank you all. I will meet your candidates myself and take it from there. Now we must discuss our retreat."

The King of the Pamisii was the first to speak. "The wounded have already begun to travel north?"

"Yes, some. They've started the burning also. The rest will follow as soon as this meeting is adjourned. What we need to do is buy them more time."

"And how do you think that is going to be achieved?"

"We harangue the enemy," the King of the Baveii replied. "Starting tonight, we attack their camp under cover of night. We use stealth and fire to keep them at bay. It may also help reduce their numbers enough so that if they happen to catch us in the open, it'll be a fairer fight."

"There is little honour in that," the King of the Pamisii noted.

"It's that or hand our lands over to the god of the Yellow City."

That set the room rumbling. There was not a soul there who would simply stand by and allow that to happen. In one plainly spoken sentence, Gofron had cemented Greyl resolve. It was not long before the pavilion was awash with suggestions. The discussion ranged well into the night, when it was decided that it would be easiest to split the army.

A small section would accompany the wounded as a guard and ensure they reached the fortress intact. The bulk of the army would divide into two and disappear, each attacking the Touan force as they marched, or when they camped. After each engagement, a small section of each half would peel away and ride behind the Touan army and remain there to harass the reinforcements and the supplies.

Should those troops prove successful, they would relieve the pressure of the unavoidable siege, and they might yet be numerous enough to cause serious problems at the Touan's back once their army was entrenched for the siege.

As soon as this was decided the candidates for command of the various units of warriors were brought before King Gofron outside the pavilion and each was interviewed carefully.

Not one of them had been tried as commanders before now and Gofron feared it likely that, despite his best choices, they would utterly fail at the task at hand.

Even worse, young men are prone to grandiose thoughts and there was a real risk that they would lead their men against the Greyls themselves in a bid for power. Gofron watched closely for any signs of deception in the young men.

If there were any weaknesses, they were nigh on impossible to see. The youths were genuinely keen to lead commands against the Touans. The young Pamisii prince was a good deal more reserved than many of the others. He, unlike his peers, did not utter any anti-Touan sentiment or boast about his skills in battle, real or imagined, but remained thoughtfully quiet. At length he spoke.

"I know the forests of Pamisii fairly well, and know how to be invisible in them. The Touans will have to pass through there if they hope to reach the stronghold. We can hit them with arrows on either side and take down a good number of them with very little risk to ourselves."

Gofron observed him a moment. "Go on."

"There isn't much else to say. Those woods go on for days. Even riding at their hardest, it would take them three days to pass through. After that it's fairly rocky terrain for another few days. Another ambush could await them there, while the forest troops turn back and lay in wait for the reinforcements and the supplies." The Prince grinned.

"They'll be so exhausted by the time they reach the stronghold, they won't have the energy to start the siege for a few days... that will buy the Sierran's some time, assuming their campaign goes well."

"That sounds decent," Gofron mused. "Very well, since this is your plan, I grant you the command of the forest troops. We'll divide the army by...."

"If it pleases your Majesty," the young prince of the Pamisii interrupted. "I have a small contingent of people I trust. I would rather have them with me."

"I understand that, your Highness," the King of the Baveii replied with a smile. "But..."

"You are concerned I might make a grab for power once this war is over." The prince shrugged when Gofron gave him a startled look. "I am not offended, your Majesty," he said with a small smile. "It is a fair concern. I would consider you a fool if you didn't at least consider the possibility. Very well. I shall speak to my comrades and see which ones are most willing to stay behind."

"That would be none of us," a large, older man growled from the shadows by the pavilion entrance. "T'ain't none of us leaving you out there without a guard."

The prince sighed and smiled simultaneously. "Forgive the intrusion, your Majesty. This is Grunt. He is a ranger, and taught me all I know about the forests."

Gofron extended his hand and Grunt shook it.

"Pleased to meet you," Gofron said with a smile. Grunt grunted. The King almost laughed.

"Now, please tell me what the objection is to this prince braving the woods without you?"

"The lad's special," Grunt said simply. "We ain't leaving him."

"Special how?"

"Not now, Grunt," the Prince said, his cheeks flushing.

"T'ain't none of yer business is it?" Grunt retorted. Gofron, King of the Baveii and War-Leader Elect, raised his brows at Grunt.

"Grunt!" the Prince admonished. "I do apologise," he said to the King. "Grunt is in a foul mood today."

Gofron remained silent, but made it clear that Grunt was excused.

"Grunt seems to think that I have been gifted with a special ability."

"Blue ghost," Grunt said bluntly.

Raising his eyebrows again, Gofron took a moment to collect himself. "*Blue ghost*?" he demanded incredulously.

The Prince sighed. "I'm not," he said.

King Gofron gave Grunt and his prince a sidelong look. The Blue Ghost was a popular myth; amongst rangers especially. It was the spirit of the trees, which wandered through the woods, killing those who trespassed for mischief and aiding those who came with respect into the forest. It was said to be particularly fond of blue glass, and rangers everywhere left pieces of blue glass in the forests as offerings to the spirit in order to keep it on their good side.

On occasion, so the myth went, Blue Ghost would take on a mortal form and live a mortal life. This occurrence was extremely rare, occurring only in times of great need, when the forest was most threatened.

"What threat to the forest is there?" Gofron asked Grunt with curiosity.

"Not the forest, the spirit. The new god from the east that looms over us would have us forget Blue Ghost. Then Blue Ghost would die."

"I see."

"The rangers stay with him."

"Appease my curiosity a moment. What happens if Blue Ghost dies?"

"No one to take care of the trees."

"What about the Lord of the Hunt?"

"Animals," Grunt grunted. "Master of Animals. Blue Ghost is older than he."

"I see."

"Do you?"

Gofron breathed deeply. "No. Not really." He turned to the young prince, who, now that it had been mentioned, did possess an otherworldly air. "I've been convinced. You may take your rangers. You will depart from the rest of the army when we've entered the Pamisiian woodlands."

"Thank you, your Majesty," the Prince said with a bow.

Gofron nodded. "By the by," he said. "Do the Touans believe in Blue Ghost?"

"They have converted, your Majesty," the Prince said with a frown.

"That wasn't the question," the King replied. "Nonetheless, make them believe."

The Prince's face immediately lit up with the thoughts of a thousand cruel pranks designed to unsettle and terrify. "I can manage that, Majesty."

"Good."

* * * *

"What the devil is going on?" the Guild Master roared at Braddard Asul. The entire army had awoken, only to find that their camp had been surrounded by seventy-seven blackened heads, twelve still recognisable, on spears. It was clear that the sixty-five heads had belonged to the raiding party that had been slaughtered when the Guild Master was still just a Tigil. The other twelve heads belonged to Fortu Guild Members, but none save the Guild Master had any inkling as to how they ended up in the tundra.

"I do not know, General," the Braddard snapped back. He'd had quite enough of his commander. He was reviled and belittled often, but when Mtsusa wanted to know something, it was he that was summoned.

"The Sierrans and the Greyls both are head hunters. So too were the Touans before we civilised them. It is likely the Sierrans snuck here in the night and planted those heads there."

"Without being seen?"

"How the hell am I supposed to know?" the Braddard growled. "I'm not a clairvoyant."

"You mind the way in which you speak to me!" the Guild Master growled.

"You first," the Braddard shot back.

"I'll have your head."

"Oh good. You can add it to the seventy-seven heads just outside your door. At least I wouldn't have to march through a land that doesn't want us here!"

"You sound like the heathens!"

The Braddard exploded. "What the hell is wrong with you? You are so determined to prove yourself a man, that you're ignoring everything around you that contradicts your opinion! The tundra doesn't want us here. She told us so last week with the voice of a hundred wolves. The Sierrans have a god that is a man and a stag both, and has with him three Black Hounds. You yourself found one of his arrows the day the Braddard Rema was killed. You said you saw him with your own eyes!"

"I was mistaken."

"I don't believe you."

The Guild Master's eyes narrowed. In the command tent all eyes darted back from the Braddard's face to Guild Master Mtsusa's in shocked silence. No one, not one, dared to speak to the Guild Master the way the Braddard Asul did, let alone spout heretical statements with such vehemence.

"Dare you call me a liar!" Mtsusa hissed.

"You're going to get us all killed if you keep ignoring the signs!"

"The god of the Yellow City will not allow us to be defeated."

"The god of the Yellow City holds no power in the tundra!"

The gathering took one collective gasp and the Guild Master straightened.

"Non-believer," he growled. "Arrest him!"

Braddard Asul struggled as two members of the Guild Master's personal guard grabbed him roughly and dragged him outside.

"You have to listen to me!" the Braddard screamed as his legs flailed uselessly. The Guild Master took up his sword and followed the guards outside.

A large crowd had gathered outside the pavilion the moment the shouting started. They watched on in mute astonishment

That is well, the Guild Master thought grimly. *Let everyone know how I deal with insolent insurrection.*

"You must listen!" the Braddard screamed. "The tundra has issued her challenge! You cannot ignore the signs we have seen! You are leading us to death!"

It was all Braddard Asul was permitted to say. The Guild Master ran the point of his sword through the Braddard's throat, leaving him alive long enough to gurgle thick blood, before the Guild Master twisted his sword, wrenching the Braddard's head from the rest of his body.

Braddard Asul's body shuddered, then fell to the ground.

* * * *

"He's a cruel bastard, isn't he?" Bull whispered to Bran. Bran grunted. They had stolen up to the camp at the first sign of dawn under the guise of a reconnaissance mission. In truth, they simply wished to appease their curiosity about their enemy. The Ottals had not moved to engage them in a week though they were less than a day's ride away. Together, they had witnessed the brutal execution of Braddard Asul.

"One thing's for certain," Bran muttered back. "The tundra has them spooked. If they're desperate enough to enforce obedience under pain of death, they're not having a fun time of it."

Bull grinned. "Lovely thought isn't it?"

"Time to turn back," Bran answered with a scoff. "They'll strike camp soon."

Bull nodded and they slithered down the snow together. The camp was so focused on the execution, not a single one of them knew they were being watched.

"Well?" the other war chiefs asked as Bran and Bull raced each other back to camp.

"I win!" Bran exclaimed, leaping into the air with boyish glee.

"Bulls are not made for speed," Bull acquiesced, puffing a little. Bran grinned, slapped his friend on the back and turned to the expectant war chiefs.

"They are many. They outnumber us in more ways than I care to count. However, they are spooked. I say we play with their minds a bit."

"How?"

"I'm not sure. Any ideas?"

As the warriors struck camp, the war chiefs huddled close and devised elaborate pranks together. It had been Bran's idea of a pleasant distraction while they awaited the battle that would surely come later in the day, and it worked. Some of the ideas offered had the war chiefs guffawing with sheer glee and it was infectious. Soon the entire camp was smiling. Indeed, they were looking forward to the impending engagement.

Fifteen

"That clever son of a...." Algar growled as he tried to douse the fire that had engulfed his tent. The entire Touan camp had been set ablaze. The Greyls, in a bid to escape, had managed to launch flaming missiles into the heart of the Touan encampment during an unexpected midnight raid. It did not take long for the blaze to take hold.

The smoke was thick and made toxic by the dyes in the cloth that now burned, and Algar coughed as he slapped at his tent with his cape until the cape caught fire. There was nothing for it. The smoke was too thick. Algar had no choice but to retreat past the billowing fumes. He was, he noted sourly, not the only one. Tired and grimy soldiers, knights, lords and vassals had scrambled from the camp and now gathered and watched as the camp slowly crumbled into ash.

Algar looked west. The Greyl army had already fled. They would get a good few days ahead of the Touans, who would have to sift through the wreckage of their camp to retrieve what they could. Then there would be all the waiting for the reinforcements, and more supplies, and to regroup, and to collect the horses, many of which, Algar noted, had been stolen or had bolted.

In utter frustration, Algar let loose a tirade of curses, pacing and stomping about like a toddler in a tantrum.

It could take as long as a week to recover from this, and Lord knows where the Greyls would have fled to.

"I hate this," Algar told the sky. The sky did not answer.

"Well, that was rather unexpected." King Roger said cheerily from beside his son.

"Why are you smiling?" Algar demanded.

The King shrugged. "You have to admit, if you're trying to run away and make sure you have some distance, this would be the way to go about it."

"How could we let this happen?" Algar demanded, recommencing his pacing.

"I think it was because we overestimated our enemy. We did not expect them to flee. We were expecting a single, decisive, brave, if poorly planned battle. Turns out we don't know our neighbours very well. At all."

"They are fighting for more than just themselves," a rasping feminine voice said from behind them. Algar and Roger spun around and found only the tree to which he and his father had retreated. Algar frowned and started to turn away.

"I'm up here," the voice said again.

Algar looked up and noticed nothing out of the ordinary. He searched the tree, passing over the bird of prey that sat on a low branch nearby. It was only after the fourth pass that Algar noted that the osprey was looking intently at him, its neck stretched out and chest puffed up so that it looked bigger than it was. It settled back after Algar noticed it.

"Took you long enough," the voice said as the osprey began to preen.

Algar's jaw fell open. "I'm going insane," he muttered to himself.

"No. You're just waking up, that is all."

"The raid and fire woke me up," Algar growled.

The voice chuckled as the osprey cocked her head to the side and observed Algar with disturbingly keen eyes. "That was a stroke of genius. The crow's father is a clever man."

"The crow's.... you mean Bran, don't you? Prince Bran, who married the Tundra Marshal, whom everyone is calling the Winter Wolf."

"Otsana, yes," the voice said. The osprey ruffled her feathers. "She's my granddaughter, did you know that? I'm so proud."

"That's ludicrous. A bird cannot be kin to a wolf."

"As ludicrous as talking to a bird," the osprey shot back. Algar pressed his lips together and turned away.

The bird behind him chuckled. "Do you know where you come from, Prince?" Without waiting for an answer, the bird spoke on. "No? I'll tell you then. A long time ago, two tundra clans journeyed south together as friends. They were the Crow Clan, and the Lion Clan. They took up lands beside one another and remained good friends for centuries. In the west, the Crow Clan fathered thirteen kingdoms. In the east, the Lion Clan fathered fifteen.

"Generations of Lion and Crow married, to keep the friendship strong. Yet still, time made friends forget one another and slowly friends became enemies, and the fighting started." The osprey paused.

"It was not long after that the Eagle rose from the east and the Lion forgot his friends and his gods. I speak to the chiefs of the Lion and Crow clans that travelled south together every so often. They are sad; sad that they are not remembered, and their friendship is not remembered. Do you want to know their names?"

"I really couldn't care less."

"Greyl was the chief of the Crow Clan, and his warrior name was Bran. Toua was the chief of the Lion Clan, and his warrior name was Algar. Bran Greyl and Algar Toua were friends and, through marriage, kin."

"Go away, you old harpy," Algar rumbled. He threw a look at his father who was staring out into the distance, pretending, very poorly, that he was not listening to this exchange.

"You are fighting kin, Algar Toua."

"Go. Away."

"As you like, kin of my kin."

"You and I are not kin."

"No? The crow has married an osprey, who became a wolf."

Algar turned slowly around to face the osprey perched on her branch. "I know that."

"You do, do you? Well, you're not as ignorant as some then. Seraphimé might even have liked you."

"*Seraphimé*?" Algar said the name a little louder than intended and he had to wait until the curious eyes left him before he dared continue his conversation. "Seraphimé, princess of the Osprey Clan, whom Alam met and respected. Seraphimé, who was killed in battle? That Seraphimé?"

The osprey cocked her head at Algar. "Seraphimé was not killed. She was saved by the Lord of the Hunt and taken to the Shamanka of the Ice Bear Clan. When she healed, the Lord of the Hunt sent her south, to the land of the crows. There she met the Baveii prince, Bran Greyl who became her husband. Algar Toua, Bran Greyl is your kin, and he has married my kin. That makes us kin."

Algar shook his head and turned away. "This is insane. Seraphimé is dead. Alam saw it with his own eyes. And I'm talking to a bird. The fumes must have gotten to me."

"All right, little lion," the osprey said. "I thought you were at least as intelligent as the crow. It seems, alas, that Bran has more sense after all. It's a good thing it was him who married my granddaughter."

With that, the osprey took flight, soaring high above the dying fires to the fleeing Greyl army.

"That was interesting," Roger said quietly when Algar rejoined him, fuming in silence.

"What was interesting?"

"Hmm?"

"What was interesting?" Algar made it clear with his tone of voice that he wanted to deny the entire conversation he had with a bird. Birds do not speak and people most certainly do not speak to birds.

"Oh, nothing."

"That's what I thought."

* * * *

Bran donned his war cloak and, with Bull's aid, his weapons and armour.

"You look fearsome indeed," Bull noted.

"I look like a giant black turkey."

"With a very sharp beak and eyes of cold stone."

"Not to mention talons of steel."

"There you go. Now walk tall."

"Thank you, Bull."

Bull shrugged. "I want a cloak like this, but made of bull hide, with great big ouroq horns.

Bran grinned. "You are welcome to wear one, if you can make it."

Bull smiled and shook his head. "Only Shaman can make these cloaks. They are special."

"Are they?" Bran certainly felt special, though it was not the pleasant kind of special.

"They are imbued with power, Bran. The Shaman cast spells as they make these cloaks."

"Of course they do."

"You do not believe in the power of the Shaman?"

"I don't believe in magic, Bull."

Bull grinned. "You will."

"I'm sure."

The camp had been struck and a small force of trustworthy vassals had taken the supplies west. They would meet again, certainly. Bran had to lure the Ottals deep into the tundra. That was his task. Seraphimé would then come at them from behind. Bran hoped.

A scout came galloping across to Bran. "They're here," he said.

Bran nodded. "Mount up!" he called.

Everyone obeyed. Bran had long ago proven himself to them. There was not one war chief or warrior who would not now consider Bran one of them.

"Bull?" Bran asked as Bull moved his horse next to his. "Where are your warriors? I do not see anyone except your standard bearer."

Bull grinned. "You remember the story I told you of the first Bull, long ago chief of the Ouroq Clan?"

"Vaguely." Bran's eyes widened. "They're buried in the snow?"

Bull grinned. "Want to spook a horse? Have ghosts jump up from the ground. They'll lose many more horses today."

"Bull, if you weren't a man, I'd kiss you."

Bull grinned. "You'd have to fight my wife for the privilege."

"I could take her," Bran said with a cheeky grin.

"You say that now, but wait until you meet her. I might be as big as a bull, but she is as strong as an ox. You wouldn't stand a chance."

"Should make an interesting fight."

Bull laughed, the sound ringing clear through the crisp spring air as the first of the Ottal army crested the small hill yards away from the Sierran troops.

A distantly shouted command was uttered and the enemy troops began to form up. It was spectacular to behold. Three standard-bearers, each carrying a tall flagpole crested with a golden statue of an eagle, marched forward and stood in an evenly spaced line across the entire length of the enemy army. The flags that fluttered overhead were dyed yellow, with an orange eagle on each.

The standard bearers thrust them into the ground, thus marking the line that they now considered Ottalan territory.

Behind that line, tightly packed rows of horsemen gathered, each in perfect rows and separated into regiments, each carrying their own standard. The colours remained the same, orange and yellow, but the size and shape of the flags, as well as the arrangement of the colours varied.

By comparison, the Sierran army was in shambles. Each Clan had a standard, though it was not dyed and woven fabric, but ochre-painted skins, sometimes a simple strip of their totem animal's pelt or its stuffed tail, as in the case of the White Fox Clan, served. The armour of the Sierrans did not glitter as did the armour of the Ottals, covered in leather and furs as it was.

Horsemen formed in Clan groups, but there were no rows and no columns, just circles of groups divided by wide channels. Archers and swordsmen were not divided. There was absolutely no order whatsoever.

"Well, now," the Guild Master said with a small smile as he observed the small army waiting before him. "This should be easy. Let's go treat with them, shall we?"

He wasn't speaking to anyone in particular and no one answered him. He nudged his horse and rode forward to the centre of what was soon to become the battlefield with a small group of his personal guard.

"I have an idea for our next engagement," Bran said to Bull. "Remind me to tell you after this one. But for now, start laughing, and get the others to as well."

"Laugh, Crow?"

"Yes, Bull. Start laughing."

Bull did. He turned his horse around to face the warriors and began to laugh, winking at them as he did so. They caught on immediately and, not knowing how it would help, they too began to laugh. What began as a fine display of acting soon turned into genuine laughter, aided by the maddening effect of adrenalin. Chuckling himself, Bran nudged his horse forward, accompanied only by Bull. The pair approached the Ottalan commander with wide grins on their faces while behind them the warriors laughed and laughed.

Bran spared a glance for the highly disciplined soldiers of the desert as they stood at the crest of the small hill. They shuffled uncomfortably, turning to look at their comrades no doubt wondering at the reason for the Sierran's glee, or even at their sanity.

"Greetings," the Ottalan commander said to Bran and Bull in passable Touan once they had stopped a few feet before him. The two Sierran warriors were on horses that loomed larger than Mtsusa thought possible, towering over his own desert horse like great mountains of muscle and bone. He did not like it.

The pair were grinning like lunatics and Bran could tell it was making the commander nervous.

"Hi," Bran said and Bull had to cough to hide his amusement. Bran would not treat seriously with the man.

The commander of the Ottals frowned. "Are you the commander of this... army?" he asked, making sure to add as much dripping derision as possible when he uttered the word 'army.'

"No," Bran said with a smile. He offered no more. The longer he drew out these talks, the colder the army he was facing would become. He was certain there was no room in their armour for furs or wools, and steel gets very cold very, very fast.

"Then it is the Winter Wolf. I will treat with her."

"You can't."

"Why not? Where is she? Why is she not with her army?"

"Oh, she's with her army. Look down at your mount's feet, desert man. There is the Winter Wolf. Look up at the sky, so clear and blue and cool, that is the Winter Wolf. Look around you at the snows that will not disappear until the summer, and the grasses beginning to break through the snow, at the rocks that show through and at the men at my back. That is the Winter Wolf, and she doesn't much like you. Thus, as her representative, it is my task to tell you to go home, since you haven't listened to her thus far."

Bull laughed and the Ottal commander grew angry.

"I will speak to the Marshal of the Tundra, or to no one!" he snapped.

Beneath his beaked hood, Bran grinned. It was truly a grim sight "You will speak to me or to no one. You will turn around. You will return home, and you will never come to the tundra again. In return, you shall receive safe passage all the way to the desert sands, with nary a snow storm or even encounter with a bear. These are the tundra's terms."

The Ottalan commander looked at Bran through slitted eyes. "You don't honestly think that your measly band of men can out match my entire army, do you? You are hopelessly outnumbered and clearly outmatched."

Bran's grin widened. "Try us, desert man," he growled. "You are in the tundra now and nothing is as it seems."

"So be it. Take a look around, insolent, overgrown sand pigeon. This will be your last day on this frozen wasteland."

"Be nice," Bran chided easily. "The tundra is sensitive."

The Ottalan commander shook his head and glared at Bran before turning his horse and trying to trot back to Ottal controlled territory. Bran observed mildly as his dainty horse slipped twice and stumbled once on the short journey up the slope before he turned his horse and trotted easily back to his men, who had stopped laughing.

"I need you to laugh really hard, like I just told you something about sand boy over there," Bran informed his warriors. They acquiesced, letting a small burst of raucous laughter loose into the chill air. Bran was certain the Ottalan army could hear them, for the commander whipped around and stared at Bran. Bran could only smile back as many in the ranks took a collective step backwards.

"All right," Bran said, unsheathing his powder blue sword. "A charging line of horses will have many weak points. Some horses are faster and so on. You will wait for my commands before you ride forward to meet them. Hold your ground until then. I have a feeling many a horse will break its legs on the run down the hill. Let's let them." Bran raised his sword and, tilting his head up to the sky, howled. His howling had improved.

The other warriors unsheathed their weapons and joined in the chorus of eerie howls.

* * * *

"They're all insane," one of the guards whispered to the Guild Master.

"They're just trying to scare us," he replied. "It's strategy and nothing more, mark my words."

The guardsman nodded, but did not look convinced.

"It's that or they know something we don't," another whispered to the first guardsman. The latter nodded, but kept his peace. No one wanted to become the next Braddard Asul.

"Send the wings in first. They're small, we'll encompass them easily," the Guild Master told his lieutenant. The Lieutenant nodded and shouted the command. In an instant, the Ottals came thundering down the slope, forming a deep crescent as they did.

* * * *

Bran watched them approach. "White Fox take the left. Elk, take the right. Cut the heads off those spears and come around. The rest scatter in the centre."

It seemed a miracle to Bran that the war chiefs understood his commands at all, he wasn't even sure if he understood them. However, his intent was clear. The White Fox Clan and the Elk Clan immediately split from the group, charging with ease at the foremost riders of each end of the crescent. They would engage there and, if all went well, slip outside the circle the Ottals were trying to form.

The other clans rode forward at a gallop, seeking places in the approaching line of desert horsemen that had faltered. There were plenty of such lines to choose from.

The ride down the slope proved perilous for the Ottals. Almost one thousand riders were down without ever engaging their enemy. They tripped other horses, or made them jump over the tumbling bodies, causing injuries to both horse and rider.

Before the slope levelled out, there were five thousand injured horses that would have to be slaughtered. The Guild Master cringed.

The little desert horses were outmatched by their massive cousins of the tundra. Though slower, these beasts were sturdy and as sure-footed as any goat. They navigated the traps of the thinning snow and the rocks beneath easily. The men of the tundra were also in better spirits. Long used to the cold and much better dressed for it, they had no problems handling their weapons. The Ottals, however, were stiff with frost and many weapons were fumbled and dropped from fingers that were unresponsive to the mind's commands.

It was a bloody mess. The White Fox and Elk Clans were a proficient team and kept the rear of the main Sierran force relatively clear. The ground became soaked with blood, making it slippery and dangerous for both breeds of horses.

"Pull back!" Bran roared as he wrenched his sword free of an Ottalan soldier's belly. Inch by inch, the Sierran nomads moved back, searching for a clear space for their horses to find better footing. The fighting at the wings grew more fierce as the Ottals recognised the retreat and tried to prevent it.

Out of the corner of his eye, Bran saw Bull raise a massive horn to his lips. With a deep breath he blew one short blast. In the middle of the Ottal ranks, the entirety of Bull's clan jumped up from the snow with a deafening roar. The desert horses went wild as the men jumped and ran about them, screaming and barking like a pack of rabid dogs. It was the single most effective tactic of the battle, dispersing the enemy and causing such agitation that the Ottalan army lost all cohesion.

Many fled, forced to trip and tumble over the snow and rocks to reach the haven behind the line of flagpoles that marked Ottalan territory. Many more were cut down, even as Bran's army took flight, rejoining the clans and pulling back. The Guild Master grimaced as the battlefield was revealed. Of the thousands of slain there, fully twenty-five thousand of them were Ottals, the majority of them killed by their own horses. There were a further ten thousand wounded some of whom, should they live, would never walk again.

Of the fur-clad warriors of the Sierran Tundra, only five hundred had perished or were wounded. In relative terms, the Ottals had the advantage. They had only lost one fifth of their fighting force, while the Sierran's had lost a full quarter. Even still, it was closely fought and too many more encounters like that would likely leave the Ottals so crippled they would not be able to aid the Touans.

"Damn it!" the Guild Master growled angrily. He stared at the man dressed in the guise of a crow as the self-styled representative of the tundra raised his bloodied sword high and howled. It was not long before the remaining fifteen hundred warriors in the Crow's army were also howling, raising their weapons high.

When at last they fell silent, a single low howl drifted in from the north, carried on a sudden frozen gust.

"Archers!" the Guild Master snapped.

"General," one of his guard said. "The bows are unusable. They'll snap from the cold."

"I said," Mtsusa snapped as he rounded like a wounded dog on his guard. "Archers!"

The guard nodded and gave the command. There was a dry hissing as bows were unwrapped and arrows notched. "On my mark," the guard called. "One, two, mark!"

The arrows were loosed. At precisely the same moment another, much stronger gust of wind blew in from the north, forcing the arrows off target in its chilling gale. It kicked up snow as it blew, forming the famous ghosts of the tundra, some of whom appeared to reach up and take arrows right out of the sky with impossibly long arms. Then the gale was gone, leaving none of the Sierrans harmed. Not a single arrow had found a home.

A murmur spread through the Ottal ranks, silenced only by the Guild Master's hard glare. The Guild Master turned back around to find the Crow grinning hideously at him. It might have been his imagination, but Mtsusa could have sworn he saw, ever so briefly, a flicker of golden light surround the man dressed as a crow.

* * * *

"We head south!" Bran roared, turning his horse and pushing it into a gentle canter. Whooping and howling, the fifteen hundred warriors of the tundra followed suit and the Ottals were forced to watch their enemy disappear over the tundra while they were left behind to tend to their dead and dying. They had nothing to look forward to but another long march over an unforgiving terrain, in a land crawling with wolves and ghosts.

Sixteen

"They have crossed the three sisters," Seraphimé said, looking into the horizon. It had been close to a fortnight since she reported that the Crow had engaged with the Eagle. Many had died. It was a closely fought battle, so Ur had claimed and Seraphimé had agreed.

"Do we move south now?" Inna asked.

Seraphimé nodded. "We will pick up their trail at the three sisters. They will have difficulty moving through the slush and over the rock. We should catch up with them relatively quickly."

Inna nodded. "Good."

Ur sighed. "War is such a waste."

"Yes," Seraphimé agreed. "It is."

Ur shrugged and left Seraphimé's side. "Come, Inna," he said. "I'll help pack."

"Thank you, little man," Inna said quietly. He watched the Lord of the Hunt approach Seraphimé before turning back towards the camp. Even he, ancient and powerful, showed a great deal of deference to Seraphimé.

It seemed odd to Inna that the woman who almost died in his arms four years ago was now the object of the adoration of a god. The gravity of it, and all its possible meanings, occupied his mind as he and Ur struck their pavilion and saddled their horses.

* * * *

"That howl from the north," Guild Master Mtsusa mused from the head of the table. "That was the second time we've heard it."

"So?" one Braddard asked.

"So," the Guild Master said with a sneer. "My guess it that this so-called Marshal of the Tundra is up there, and they're using the howls to communicate."

The theory was met with stony silence as the members of the war council deliberated.

"Could be," another Braddard rumbled. "If it is...."

"That means they're planning to come up behind us," the Guild Master finished.

"Clever."

"But not clever enough. They've been discovered. Braddard Mamni?"

"Yes, General?"

"I want you to take your regiment and head north. Hide in ambush, then take them by surprise. I want that bitch on her knees in front of me."

The last comment was greeted with snickers and sneers. Braddard Mamni nodded. "If you will permit me, General," he said. "I should like the newly formed troop of foot soldiers also."

The Guild Master thought on it a while, then nodded. "Very well. Do what you want to the others, but leave this 'Winter Wolf' alive. There's a thing or two about animals I can teach her."

The sneers and snickers grew louder, and several people chuckled. It was decided. Come morning, the Braddard Mamni would detach his new command from the main army and head north to ambush the enemy that was planning to ambush them.

Morning dawned bright and clear, and bitterly cold. It was as if spring had changed its mind, and decided to release the land to winter once more. It did nothing to dull the movements of the Ottals, however. Last night after the war council adjourned the Yellow Robes had given a particularly rousing speech. The Ottals resolve was strengthened once more.

Not to be outdone, the tundra sent strong winds whipping in from the north, bringing with it hard pellets of ice that seemed to fall from nowhere. Nevertheless, the prospect of foiling the Sierran nomads' plans had the Ottals in a relatively good mood. After a quick briefing the Braddard Mamni and his men departed, heading north as quickly as they could as the rest of the Ottal force began their march to chase down the Southern Crow's army.

* * * *

Bran was surprised to see a messenger riding to him. They were two days from the trading post where, prior to the commencement of the war, messages and trade items were delivered. The messenger must have been waiting for them there.

"Your Highness," the messenger said with relief. He was wearing the livery of the Baveii. "Thank goodness!"

"How long have you been waiting for me?" Bran asked.

"A fortnight, Highness. I have an important message from your father."

"All right."

"The battle in the south isn't going well. They've issued a full retreat and will await you at the stronghold."

"They intend to dig in for a siege?"

"Yes, Highness. Your father expressed a wish to see you inside the walls, rather than outside them."

There was a general grumble of disagreement amongst the war chiefs. Bran chewed on his lip.

"We are going to have to revise our strategy," Bran noted. "There's not much point dragging the Ottals to the stronghold only to be sandwiched between them and the Touans."

"Let me take what men will come, and we'll join with the Winter Wolf in the north. You take the rest and go to the false cave. Wait for us there. We'll come to lift the siege," Bull said.

Bran scowled. "I don't particularly want to go to the false cave. I want to be with my wife."

"But you know about sieges. I don't. I couldn't lead the men through a siege."

"Who said I'd leave the command to you?"

Bull smiled and shrugged and Bran sighed. "Of course I'd have left it to you," he grumbled. Bull laughed.

Bran rubbed his face with one mitted hand as he mulled it over. "All right, it's a sound plan. You'll need to dust your tracks well. I'll have to keep heading west and leaving enough tracks to have them continue to follow me."

Bull nodded. "It won't work if they don't follow you."

"Thank you Bull, I had surmised as much myself."

Bull laughed.

"So," Bran said. "Who wants to go with Bull and reinforce the Wolf's army?" There was not a single war chief who did not raise their hands. Bran groaned. "I don't particularly want to travel to the false cave all by myself."

The war chief of the Elk Clan shrugged. "I do not trust walls," he said. "And if the siege will be with both Touans and Ottals, the Winter Wolf will need many warriors outside the walls with her."

"I know," Bran grumbled. "Here's the next issue. How is one rider supposed to leave the tracks of a whole army?"

The war chiefs remained silent at that. They did not have an answer.

"We give you spare horses, and double up. Two riders, one horse," Bull said.

"How will that work in battle?"

"Horse guards," the war chief of the Elk Clan said, his eyes sparkling suddenly.

"Horse guards?" Bran asked.

"Long time ago, when horses were first tamed, each took two riders. One would dismount when battle started. He would walk beside horse and rider and protect them," Bull explained.

Bran grunted. "Good enough. It'll have to do."

"We leave now?" Bull asked.

"I suppose so," Bran said.

Grunting, Bull stood. "Good then." He extended his hand to Bran.

"Good luck," Bran said, a small, sad smile painted on his face. Bull grinned and pulled Bran into a crushing embrace.

"Be safe, Crow. We'll come. You'll see."

Bran nodded. He and the messenger watched as the army mounted two to a horse and galloped north, leaving Bran, the messenger and a herd of riderless tundra horses behind.

"Well then," Bran said cheerfully as he collected his horse's reigns. "We should get going."

"Are we just going to leave the horses here?"

Bran grinned. "I ride the stallion of the herd. They'll follow. Now let's go."

Shrugging, the messenger mounted and followed Bran as the latter nudged his horse into a steady trot. The messenger turned to look behind as the rumble of hundreds of horses trotting caught his ear. It was quite a sight to see. The messenger had never seen so many horses together at once.

"That's quite a herd," he noted to Bran.

"The wild herds are never this large, kept in check by predators and so on. Because the Sierrans tend to these herds, they've managed to grow quite large.

"That's an understatement." The jealousy the messenger felt towards Bran's enormous mount, compared to his smaller southern horse, was evident in the man's tone and expression.

Bran grinned. "One day I'll let you ride one. It's one of the single most frightening and exhilarating things to be up so high on such a powerful beast. Thank the gods they have a kind disposition normally."

"Normally?"

"Much like men who are normally gentle, war turns them into monsters."

"There's a frightening thought."

"Indeed. I'm just glad that they are on our side!"

The banter continued for the rest of the long day.

* * * *

"You know," Gofron noted gaily as he trotted alongside the wagon bearing the wounded. "I never realised just how expansive Greyl territory is."

Jostling around in the wagon, Lord Kildurrow grunted. He was tired and sore and he didn't particularly care. His king's chipper tone was starting to aggravate him.

"You'd think that because we're facing such bleak times, the weather would adjust accordingly. Yet the sun is shining. Birds are singing. It's lovely and warm…."

"Would you just shut-up!" Lord Kildurrow grated.

Gofron looked over at him and smirked. "Headache, Kildurrow?"

Lord Kildurrow grunted and let his head flop back, immediately regretting the sudden movement.

"Serves you right for being so reckless out there," the King sniffed.

"Bastard," Lord Kildurrow grunted. Gofron laughed.

"Why are you so cheery, anyway?" Lord Kildurrow asked. "We're losing a war. We're on the run, and you're up there on that demented looking black bastard of a horse, grinning like a fool."

The King shrugged. "What can I say? It's a lovely day."

Lord Kildurrow groaned and closed his eyes.

Gofron laughed again. "We've just passed the Pamisii forest. We'll be at the stronghold in another week or two and you'll stop being jostled about on that wagon and everything will be fine."

"Except that we'll be entrenched in a siege with a massive army at our gates, living off gathered supplies and hoping for help from the north that may never come."

"Always the optimist."

"I'm a realist, Majesty. I don't think there is anything to be happy about."

"Oh, I don't know. It seems we have some friends in some very deep places."

"Deep places?"

"Oh yes."

"Like?"

"Well, Blue Ghost for one."

Lord Kildurrow's eyes snapped open. "*Blue*...Damn you superstitious fool! There's no such thing as Blue Ghost!"

"We don't know that for sure, Lord Kildurrow." King Gofron looked smug. "In any case," he added as Lord Kildurrow's mouth opened to reply. "It doesn't matter whether it's true or not. We'll have the Touans believing it is by the time they've cleared the forest we've just left."

The bright red colour of indignation that Lord Kildurrow's face had turned slowly faded and was replaced by a smile. "You're playing with their heads," he said approvingly. "I like that. Very clever."

Gofron grinned. "I thought so."

"Don't get cocky."

"Go back to sleep you old badger. I'll see you at the stronghold."

Lord Kildurrow grunted and closed his eyes. He opened them briefly to see if the King still rode at his side. He did. Contented and comforted, Lord Kildurrow drifted into an aching sleep.

The stronghold was visible from several days away. The original keep had been difficult to discern against the mountain from which the ancient structure was carved. With the new additions, however, it now stood like a great pale grey imitation of the dark mountain towering over it.

Only the scaffolding supporting the new construction surrounding Oisín's Keep gave the position away. The masons had worked extremely hard and even now were not quite finished. It was never a good idea to have wet mortar when a siege started.

The King of the Baveii watched impassively as yet another Pamisii regiment peeled away from the main army and vanished amongst the rocks. This was Pamisii territory and the Pamisii knew best how to defend it.

Of all the kingdoms of the Greyls, the Pamisii were closest to their wild roots. They spent as much time out in the wilds as they did indoors. Every man and woman was conscripted to serve as a ranger for the term of three years. It mattered not if they were lords or commoners. All were called into the wilds.

Some fell so much in love with the wild places of their kingdom that they chose to remain there and were made permanent rangers. There were men amongst that ragged group of rangers that would have been kings had not the wild called them so strongly. They now paid service to a man that would not have been king had not his cousin taken the Ranger's Pledge. The right to rule amongst the Pamisii was decided more by ability and desire than by bloodlines.

Gofron admired the Pamisii for this sentiment. He knew what it was to feel the call of the wild and have no choice but to deny it. It made for a life of misery. The King had missed his calling. If he could change it, he would have ridden into the wilds and never returned before he was crowned King of the Baveii. He thought of his youngest son and envied him.

"Bran," he whispered to the deepening air. "I hope you're all right. I miss you, little crow."

The King started as a large crow suddenly squawked and took flight from a nearby tree. He had not noticed the bird sitting there. He watched it fly away, heading north over the rocks and envied it.

* * * *

"The stronghold is now complete," a tired-looking mason reported some five days after the Greyl army had entered Oisín's Keep and settled in. "We've food supplies to last us two and a half years, provided the cellars do not flood, and our wives have started growing orchards on the gentler slopes of the mountain."

"Really?" Gofron asked. "That was a wonderful idea."

The mason shrugged. "'T'was the architect that thought of it. He saw the smoke from the burning crops and gave the job to our wives right away."

"This architect is a brilliant man."

"Yes, Majesty. Only, the herds of goats was my idea."

"We have herds of goats?"

The mason shrugged. "Easier to feed and take up less room than cattle. Their milk takes some getting used to, but it's drinkable. And we can make cloth from their wool. Plus goats don't mind the cold so much, and it gets mighty cold here, Sire."

"That's wonderful, Mason… uh…."

"Frond, Sire."

"Frond. Truly? Your name is Frond?"

The King of the Pamisii cleared his throat. "It is common practice for children to be named for plants here, your Majesty."

"Is that so? Curious." Gofron smiled warmly at the mason. "Wonderful then, Mason Frond. I would very much like to throw a feast in the masons' honour, but I'm afraid we can't spare the supplies, so it shall have to wait until the war is won."

The mason's mouth quirked a little as he bowed. The King of the Baveii seemed to him a most amicable man and his informality was refreshing. Only the King of the Pamisii could be matched for speaking to a common man as an equal.

"So I suppose we have no choice now but to wait," Gofron said.

"We wait," the war council agreed.

"I hate waiting."

Seventeen

The attack came suddenly and without warning. Confident in her plans, Seraphimé had not thought to look for an ambush. Two thousand screaming Ottals crested the hill coming at Seraphimé's army like an angry wave of steel. Taken on their right, Seraphimé's army did not have time to wheel around and face their attackers. The fight was nothing more than a desperate struggle for survival.

The Ottals, fuelled by the sermons of their yellow-robed priests and a hatred of the tundra created by the savage terrain, bitter weather and a devastating defeat were in a frenzy that could be matched only by starving wolves.

Seraphimé recovered quickly from her surprise. "Red Deer, Mammot to me!" She called. Immediately, the warriors of those clans disengaged their opponents and retreated to Seraphimé's position. From there, they formed an arrowhead and galloped hard through the melee, splitting the battle down the middle. Once through, they split and rounded on the fight, taking the fully engaged Ottals from behind. The wave of warriors that pushed through grew as Ottals were cut down and their opponents joined in the rush.

The leader of the Ottals pulled his forces right and Seraphimé's line of horsemen could not turn in time to meet them. The wave dissolved once more into chaos. A high shriek caught Seraphimé's attention as she sliced her opponents belly open with a wide stroke of her black glass sword. She looked up and saw Ur dragged off his horse.

It happened in an instant, the bubbling of anger that transformed her. Seraphimé sheathed her sword and leapt off her horse, landing gracefully on the ground on all fours. With a blood-freezing snarl, the Winter Wolf bolted forward, her sharp fangs crushing armour and bone, tearing into Ottalan flesh with brutal ease.

Ur's attacker was savaged, limbs torn and bent at impossible angles. She did not kill him. He could not harm anyone anymore. Her job was done. Her yellow-green eyes turned to Ur. Ur nodded. He was unharmed, having sustained nothing more than a gash on his cheek.

"Ur," a tall great deer said as it bounded into the fight. The stag knelt on his front knees. "Get on."

Without hesitation, Ur scrambled on and, pausing only to press his soft snout against the Winter Wolf's forehead, the deer bounded away, dodging through the battle to take Ur to safety.

The Winter Wolf turned her blood-splattered snout to the sky and howled.

* * * *

"Did you hear that?" the war chief of the Elk Clan asked Bull.

Bull nodded, his face pale. "We ride! Now!" He did not wait for the others as he spurred his horse forward. His mount danced easily across the rocks at a gallop, faltering only once on hidden ice. With two and a half thousand warriors behind him, Bull crested a hill and paused in shock.

Seraphimé's army was embroiled in a closely fought battle with a regiment of Ottals and, dead in the centre of the fight, an enormous tundra wolf, white and grey fur streaked red and brown with blood darted through the battle. She had become the focus of the Ottalan attack and the Sierran warriors scrambled to protect her.

Bull unsheathed his sword as his horse-guard slid out of his saddle and unhooked his axe. Standing in his saddle, Bull howled in answer to the Winter Wolf's call. The army at his back raised their voices in an answering cry. Before the Ottals could respond, Bull's army galloped down the slope, whooping and howling. They descended on the Ottals with all the fury of a storm.

The Ottals did not stand a chance. All but one, the Braddard who had led them, were slaughtered. When the fog of battle cleared, Bull quickly took stock of the situation. Over five hundred Sierrans were slain, many more had injuries from which they would never recover. Missing limbs and broken spines greeted Bull everywhere he turned. His calculations were interrupted when Ur returned to the field, holding the hand of a figure that could only be the Lord of the Hunt.

"Otsana!" the boy cried as he let go of the god's hand and ran to the wolf, who was struggling hard to walk through the battlefield. She had been severely wounded. A savage-looking gash split her pelt on her hindquarters and a deep stab wound in her neck gushed blood down her muscled chest.

Ur ran into the wolf, wrapping his arms around her massive neck. "Otsana!" he wept. One of the warriors tried to approach to pry the boy off the potentially dangerous animal and was greeted by a low growl and the flashing of sharp teeth. He backed away slowly. Ur pulled away, tears streaming down his face.

"Help," he sobbed. "Someone help her."

The wolf whined plaintively, licking Ur's salt-stained cheeks, even as her back legs gave out. The Lord of the Hunt's three hounds approached cautiously, or, rather, two of them did. Cabal bounded towards the Winter Wolf and, despite the wolf's lowered ears, began to clean the wolf's chest. Growling occasionally, the Winter Wolf bore Cabal's care with a flat stare and bared teeth.

Bull almost choked on his breath as he noticed that even the pony-sized hounds of the Lord of the Hunt were dwarfed by the mass of the Winter Wolf.

"They lived a long time ago, these particular tundra wolves," an osprey said as it glided to land on his shoulder. Bull turned to the bird in surprise. The bird's eyes twinkled, laughing at him.

"They were here before; when all the land was ice, and great herds of mammot, ouroq and great deer roamed it. They were here even before the Old Ones. Some live still, far in the north, were the ice meets the water; but their numbers are few now, and each year are fewer and fewer. All wolves in the world come from them. All wolves in the world know them; remember them. All wolves in the world will obey them. Do not be afraid, Hotuaekhaashtait. You must not be afraid. The wolves have heard, and they are coming. The tundra's first children are coming."

"We will ride with the wolves," Bull said quietly. "As in the days of fog, when the false caves of the ancestors were torn down."

"Yes," the osprey said.

Bull nodded, then grinned viciously. "Good."

The osprey chuckled and Bull turned back to the scene before him and watched as the Lord of the Hunt approached the wolf timidly.

"Who are you, ancestor of the Osprey Clan?" Bull asked.

The osprey ruffled her feathers and puffed her chest proudly. "I am the wolf's grandmother." With nothing left to say, the bird flapped her speckled wings and was in the sky before Bull could respond. Bull watched her fly before turning to his remaining men, who were all transfixed by the scene before them.

"Tend to the wounded!" Bull barked. "We camp here until the Winter Wolf is well enough to walk, then we head west. Our southern brothers need rescuing."

Immediately the Sierran warriors sprang into action. Half went to set up the camp for the evening, far enough away to avoid irking the carrion beasts that were sure to come. The rest immediately began to pick through the battlefield, searching for survivors. They gave the wounded Winter Wolf a wide birth.

Ur was still weeping as Cabal stood aside and allowed her master in to take a look at the Winter Wolf's wounds. The Winter Wolf laid back her ears and bared her teeth in warning, but did not growl.

"Otsana," the Lord of the Hunt said gently. He did not speak the language of the Sierran nomads but his own language, long dead with the last of those who spoke it. "You are going to need sutures."

The wolf growled.

"I know," the Lord of the Hunt replied. "But they are necessary. Will you allow me to treat you?"

The wolf turned her head away.

"Please, Otsana." Ur placed his hand on the Winter Wolf's neck, reaching through the thick, warm ruff there to stroke her skin. She turned to Ur and immediately her green eyes softened. "I'll be beside you, Otsana," Ur said quietly. "I'll be there the whole time."

The wolf swung her massive head back to the Lord of the Hunt and snorted a short sigh. It was an unhappy, resigned sound, but it made the god smile nonetheless.

"Good. Thank you. I cannot treat you here. Can you walk?"

The wolf snarled irritably, but tried to stand all the same. It took several tries before she was able. A torrent of blood gushed from the gash on her side. She limped beside the Lord of the Hunt and Ur at a painfully slow pace. She made it only a few paces beyond the battlefield before collapsing again. The Lord of the Hunt grimaced and shook his head.

"This will have to do," he said, kneeling beside the Winter Wolf and stroking her head. The wolf's laboured breathing slowed and steadied. "Ur, I need fire and two cauldrons of water, a needle and thread, salt and dried sage."

"You will summon the Bride of Fire?"

The Lord of the Hunt nodded.

Ur felt his chest swell. "Is it truly that bad?"

"It is serious."

Ur nodded and stood, eliciting a whine from the Winter Wolf. Ur smiled slightly. "Inna! Inna!" he called. In a moment, Inna came running from the battlefield.

"Ur," he greeted.

"The Lord of the Hunt needs a fire, two cauldrons of water, a needle and thread, salt and sage."

Inna nodded and ran to find all that the Lord of the Hunt required without question. Ur turned back to the wolf and knelt at her head. He tentatively reached out and stroked it. "It will be all right, Otsana," he said gently. "The Bride of Fire will come and everything will be all right."

The Lord of the Hunt watched and smiled. Ur was part of the Winter Wolf's pack. There could be no denying it. The fates had chosen their Shaman well. The Master of the Wilds observed Ur in silence until Inna returned, carrying a large sack with everything the Lord of the Hunt had requested.

"May I watch?" he asked Ur.

Ur smiled and nodded. "But first, bring the desert man here."

"Guild?"

"Yes, Guild."

"He is with the wounded. He sustained a fairly serious injury today."

Ur nodded. "I know. He tried to rescue me before Otsana came. He is conscious now and this is something he must see."

Inna frowned. "How do you know that?"

Ur smiled. "I can see it. Please, Inna. Bring him here."

Inna nodded and ran to the small city of pavilions a second time. He entered the hide-covered, makeshift pavilion that had been erected to treat the wounded. The flat, circular hide that was the ceiling had been painted in a series of designs in yellow and red ochre to ward away evil spirits and draw in the healing powers of the moon. The hide walls were rolled up, allowing easier access into what was, essentially, a plaza. Wounded and Shaman healers alike poured in. Inna found Guild sitting placidly near the far edge of the plaza, watching the Shaman and Shamanka work.

"Guild," Inna said, drawing the desert man's attention upwards. Guild blinked as his thoughts returned to reality.

"Inna," he greeted. The hostility he had come to expect of the last remaining member of the Ice Bear Clan, made so after Ur took up his mantle as Priest of the Wolf Cult, was entirely absent.

"Ur has requested your presence. He says there is something you must see."

Guild frowned. "And what is that?"

"I do not know. He and the Lord of the Hunt are treating Otsana."

Guild frowned. "She is wounded? Is she all right?"

"Did you miss everything that happened?"

"Ur was pulled off his horse. I fought, and I lost. I was certain I was dead when I first woke and saw nothing but the painted ceiling of this pavilion."

Inna nodded. "Well, I'll fill you in on the way. Can you walk?"

"Just lost some fingers and took a bump to the head."

"Come then."

Guild stood shakily and walked, slowly, with Inna to where Ur, the Lord of the Hunt and the Winter Wolf waited. As they walked, Inna explained to Guild the transformation that Otsana had undergone. Guild believed none of it until they arrived.

A wolf of pale grey and white, larger than any wolf he had ever seen, lay on the ground oozing blood from various wounds. Her green eyes were distant and glassy as Ur stroked her massive head. Beside her, the Lord of the Hunt built a large fire, murmuring incantations as he did so. The Lord of the Hunt did not look up as Inna and Guild came to a stop before the group. Ur did.

"Hello Guild," he said gently. "Otsana, Guild is here," the boy said to the wolf. With barely a tilt of her head, the Winter Wolf swung her gaze to Guild. The glassy look in her eyes faded briefly before she turned back and her eyes glazed over once more.

Guild swallowed hard and felt his knees buckle. He fell to the ground and knelt before the Winter Wolf, his eyes wide and filled with tears, where he remained throughout the entire ceremony.

It began as soon as the fire burned high and bright enough. The Lord of the Hunt's quiet incantations became a louder, though still softly uttered, song. The words chanted were far older than anyone present could understand and the tone and rhythm changed as the Lord of the Hunt tossed in the bones. As the fire grew hotter and the bones caught, Guild observed the flames changing colour, and changing again.

At length, with all the bones ablaze, the Lord of the Hunt threw in a handful of dried sage and salt. He did this three times, uttering an incantation each time. On the third instance, the fire flared and sparks shot into the air. They formed, for the briefest moment, the figure of a young woman with smoke for hair. The image faded as if on a breeze.

"Impetuous imp," the Lord of the Hunt growled. He threw another handful of sage on the fire and uttered the incantation once again. Again the fire flared, sending up sparks in the form of a young woman. Again it faded into the sunset.

The Lord of the Hunt's eyes narrowed. He threw one more handful of sage into the fire. This time, instead of an incantation, he uttered a command. "Come here, Brigd! Now!"

This time the sparks formed something more substantial. The flare died away revealing a pale young woman standing in the centre of the blaze. A flickering gown of flames danced in ever-changing patterns across her smooth skin. Her hair billowed out from her head, made of tendrils of sage-scented smoke. Her eye sockets were hollow, the eyes themselves replaced by fire. The vision before the gathering was both beautiful and horrific.

"What do you want you disrespectful oaf?" the young woman standing in the blaze said, stomping her foot petulantly. Wood snapped as she did so.

The Lord of the Hunt bowed low. "Brigd," he said with a smile. "I am pleased and honoured to see you once more."

The Bride of Fire crossed her arms over her chest and glared at the Lord of the Hunt. "I am almost as old as you, Chernos," she snapped, using the name mortals feared to utter lest they summon the King of the Dead himself.

"Yet so fair and beautiful."

The Bride of Fire raised one eyebrow and looked decidedly unimpressed. "Your kind owe your survival to me."

"And you owe your existence to my kind, Brigd. Without the strength of our collective belief and constant honouring you would not exist."

The Bride of Fire stuck out her tongue, nothing more than a lick of flame, at the Lord of the Hunt and he laughed. "I need your help, Brigd."

"Naturally. You wouldn't speak to me otherwise." The flame-wrought figure sounded hurt.

The Lord of the Hunt sighed. "Please, Brigd. The Winter Wolf is injured. We need your healing powers."

"What do I care if she is hurt?"

"She will die if you do nothing."

"So? It does not affect me."

The Lord of the Hunt shook his stag-helmed head. "You are wrong, Brigd. She defends the tundra and her people."

"And?"

"If she dies, the Eastern Eagle shall win, and all gods shall be banished. Everything you are shall be absorbed by the younger god of the Yellow City and you, beautiful Bride of Fire, shall cease to exist."

The Bride of Fire tilted her head in a pretext of thought. At length she stepped from the fire. In an instant the dress of flames she wore was quenched and became sable. Her smoke hair was replaced by waves of burnished copper and her eyes of flames became human eyes once more, honeyed brown in hue. She smiled at the Lord of the Hunt beguilingly, her cheeks dimpling prettily.

"Very well," she said.

"I have needle and thread."

"Those are unnecessary. They are much too clumsy." The Bride of Fire raised her hands to the sky, purple now with the last threads of sunlight. The fire behind her flared sending streams of sparks high into the air. They descended at the Bride of Fire's command and enveloped the Winter Wolf. Otsana twitched and yelped as the streams of sparks touched her wounds. The blood ceased to flow and skin grew over the gashes until there was but a thin pale line to show for the horrific gashes. The sparks streamed back to the fire, but did not disappear. Instead, they exploded from the fire once more and snaked rapidly towards the plaza, which contained the wounded.

The streams of sparks twisted around the wounded as they closed wounds and fed life back into the dying, just as they had with the Winter Wolf. On their way, they touched the ceiling of the plaza, which promptly caught alight.

"Oops," the Bride of Fire noted in a tone that told the Lord of the Hunt that the new blaze was not a mistake at all. She smiled and, with her shrug, the sparks returned to the flames and vanished. The plaza, now heartily ablaze, was hastily torn down by Shaman and warriors alike, who reacted quickly and with much shouting.

The Lord of the Hunt glared at the Bride of Fire. She smiled sweetly in return.

"Will that be all, my love?" she asked in syrupy tones.

"Yes," the Lord of the Hunt replied in a voice as flat as his expression.

The Bride of Fire crossed her arms and arched her brows at the Lord of the Hunt. The god sighed. "Thank you."

The Bride of Fire flashed a stunning smile at the Lord of the Hunt. She skipped over to him and kissed him on the cheek. Sighing happily, she pranced back to the fire. She stepped in and the morbidly beautiful vision of a girl wreathed in flames returned.

"You are so handsome," she told the Lord of the Hunt. "I wish you'd call upon me more often." She blew him a kiss, upon which floated some sparks, before the fire flared up and claimed her. She vanished in the flames and the fire went out, leaving behind only white ash. There was not even an ember.

"Teenagers," the Lord of the Hunt growled.

"Inna?" Ur called softly.

"Yes, little man?"

"Would you take Guild back to the pavilion. He looks faint."

"Of course. What about you?"

"Otsana needs to rest. I promised her I'd stay with her, and so I shall."

Inna sighed. He looked down at Guild, who did indeed look pale. "Come on, desert man," Inna said not unkindly. "Let's get you into a bed." Inna helped Guild to his feet. The movement stirred Guild out of his stupor.

"What did I just see?" he murmured to Inna as the pair walked to their pavilion.

"The God of Hunting summoned the Goddess of Fire in order to heal the Goddess of the Tundra," Inna said. Guild stumbled as his head whirled.

"Easy now," Inna said as he pulled Guild upright again.

"There are no gods," Guild intoned dully. "But the one true god."

Inna laughed. "Then tonight must have been quite a shock."

"There are no gods."

"Tell me Guild, do you believe what you see and hear with your own eyes and ears, or do you believe what others have told you."

"My whole life... my whole life..."

Inna grunted. "They taught you to believe only in the god of the Yellow City. I understand. This must be difficult for you."

"My whole world has just been shattered," Guild said quietly. "Everything's wrong now. Everything."

"Not everything. You were brought here for a reason, Guild. Perhaps you were meant to be made to understand."

"Understand what?"

"That belief is a choice."

"I have no choice now."

"No? I am sure a keen mind like yours can rationalise anything. You took a hit to the head, did you not? Perhaps you were hallucinating."

"But you saw it too!"

"Entirely beside the point. I'm an ice savage, and easily fooled by any conjuror's tricks."

Guild almost laughed.

"Do you know what I think?" Inna continued.

"No."

"I think you have chosen to believe, and I think you made that choice a long time before this."

They had arrived at Inna's pavilion and Inna laid Guild gently onto the bedding. "Iris," Guild murmured before he promptly fell asleep.

"Goodnight, Guild," Inna murmured. "You fought well today."

Eighteen

*G*uild woke the following morning with a pounding headache. He groaned as he sat up. Inna's head popped in through the entrance.

"You shouldn't be getting up," Inna noted.

Guild grunted. "I'm hungry. You making soup?"

"Yes."

"May I have some?"

"I was planning on letting you starve," Inna replied tartly. "Of course you may have some."

Guild tried to ruffle his hair, and feeling like something was amiss, he pulled his hand down and stared blankly at it. The three last fingers of his left had had been cut off. The memory of the battle and of the events that followed flooded into Guild's mind. He sat for a moment trying to collect his whirling thoughts. When he felt composed enough, he stood and wandered outside.

Inna barely looked up as Guild sat heavily down on the rocks by the fire. The smell of soup filled the air.

"I've been thinking about what you said; about me choosing to believe."

"Oh?"

"You might be right. The man who chased me from... from everything I knew was able to do so because he found an idol in my room. Idols are outlawed and have been since the Ottalan Empire was founded."

Inna stirred his soup and appeared relatively uninterested, but Guild knew that he listened keenly.

"It was given to me by a slave girl. Her name was Iris and she was from the deep south, near the flood plains. She was so beautiful. I wanted to buy her, and keep her safe from all harm, but I was just a Tigil at the time. I could not afford to. She gave me an idol the last time I saw her alive. It was the only thing of hers she had left. I saw her later. She had been only two months with her master and she was dead."

Guild had to pause to keep his voice from breaking. He took a deep breath.

"I kept the idol and I made an altar to put it on. I did not pray to that idol, but I would sit before it and think of Iris and I would feel... peace. I believed she was somewhere safe, not in the torturous hell the yellow robes always preached about. I don't know why I believed it, perhaps just to comfort myself, I suppose."

"You believed it because she told you so," Inna said softly. Guild looked up with a frown.

"That peace you felt, Guild, that was her. She was telling you not to worry, she was safe and happy."

Tears tumbled unbidden down Guild's cheeks. It was the first time since Iris died that he wept. Inna's comforting hand on Guild's shoulder served only to permit the tears to flow more freely. Inna waited patiently for Guild to find his self-control. In that time, the Lord of the Hunt made his way to Inna's fire.

Inna nodded an informal hello to the god. He silently chastised himself for the act, which he found impertinent. The Lord of the Hunt, strangely, did not. He noted Inna's abashed expression and smiled.

"I do not ask for accolades, Inna Ice Bear. Only that respect is afforded to the wilds and her animals."

Inna grunted. "All the same...."

"I was a man once," the Lord of the Hunt interrupted. "And I value being treated as one once again."

Inna nodded. "As you like."

Guild looked at the Lord of the Hunt, his eyes red from weeping. "Was the Bride of Fire once a woman?"

The Lord of the Hunt nodded. "She was once a young woman, not yet of marriageable age."

"Did you know her?"

"Only in that she was kin, many generations on from myself."

"Is Otsana recovered yet?" Inna asked.

"No," the Lord of the Hunt replied.

"Good. Then we have time for a story."

The Lord of the Hunt laughed. "As you like."

Inna stirred the soup as the Lord of the Hunt began his tale. "When I was a young man, the land that is now tundra was covered in a thick forest. We had no fire then. When I turned twelve years of age, there was a violent storm that did not offer any rain. It was only wind and lightning and thunder. The clouds sent forth a strike of lightning that hit an old tree, one that had long ago died and dried out. It caught alight and the fire spread quickly. We hid as the fire razed a large portion of the forest before the rains came.

"My father was a clever man, and it was he who ran out into the storm to collect the smouldering embers. He placed them in a stone bowl and brought the bowl back to the cave. There, he tended the ember and kept it hot. That night, he started a fire with the ember, and from the embers of that fire, he selected a new ember and so on and on it went, for generations beyond count.

"For many generations, my father's name became synonymous with fire and he ascended to become the God of Fire.

"Then, one stormy evening, the ember was stolen by a man from the neighbouring tribe. Rouki was his name. He was foolish and in the pouring rain, he did not cover the ember. When at last our warriors tracked him down, the ember had died and we had no fire once more.

"Bridg had been born thirteen years before the ember was stolen. She had grown into a beautiful woman, and she was very clever. She had noticed the spark that sometimes occurred when the men made weapons and tools. She went by herself into the woods and gathered together leaves and branches and then tried to start a fire using the sparks from struck stone.

"One day, after almost a year of fruitless attempts, her bundle of leaves caught. Her cleverness proved disastrous, however. She had started a fire she could not control. She panicked and ran. The fire chased her as a man might chase his beloved. She became encircled in flame. Though many tried, they could not rescue her, and they were forced to witness her burning.

"It rained soon after, and everyone was so stricken with grief none thought to collect another ember. That night, Bridg's spirit returned to the tribe and, through a dream, taught them all how the spark of stone could be used to begin a fire. My father appeared with her in the dream, and the tribe thought them to be married. She became, in essence, his bride.

"As time passed, my father's name became forgotten. They did not remember his face, only that he was fire and Brigd's spirit ascended into the position of Goddess of Fire. She was no longer the bride of the God of Fire, but the bride of fire itself. It is fire that her followers honour. In fact, the fire that burns perpetually in the centre of the tundra, guarded by the grey virgins, is made with the embers of the fire created under the guidance of Bridg's spirit."

"Are you not upset?" Guild asked.

"I do not understand."

"Your father, he no longer lives."

The Lord of the Hunt smiled. "My father is fire, and fire will always be."

"But, he is no longer the man who was your father."

The Lord of the Hunt shrugged. "Perhaps, but the temperament of fire never suited him. Only the fire's warmth could match his kindness in life. The death and destruction that is at the heart of the nature of fire was never part of my father. He was a kind and gentle man. Besides, death is inevitable. Even for gods. One day, I too shall be forgotten and fade."

Inna grunted. "I do not see how that could be."

The Lord of the Hunt smiled. "No?"

"Men will always need to eat, therefore men will always need to hunt. How can they hunt without assistance?"

"There are peoples in the world who no longer hunt. Even now, the Greyls are starting to keep herds of animals they eat. My name is invoked less and less by them."

Inna grunted. "I cannot believe you will be forgotten."

The Lord of the Hunt shrugged. "I have already lived much longer than most gods of man."

Guild frowned. "Gods of man?"

"He means ascendants," Inna said with a smile. "Men and women who once lived and were made gods by the people who remembered them. They are the gods who deal with the ancestors directly. Of those gods, the Lord of the Hunt is the oldest."

Guild observed the tall figure of the King of the Dead. "You have more than one function, do you not?"

"Yes. I reign over the Otherworld and am King of the Dead. I assist hunters as Lord of the Hunt, and I keep the wild animals healthy as Master of Animals. Yet for all this, I am subject to powers greater than my own. The tundra is a more powerful force than I, as is weather and all movements of earth and sea. These powers, too, are gods, but they are not concerned with the world of men, only with the natural balance that must exist for life to continue."

"Then why does the tundra fight for you?" Guild asked.

"The tundra fights for the tundra. Once before men were foolish enough to tear into her flesh and build false caves that interrupted the movements of the herds and flocks. She acted then as she acts now. It is not for the sake of men."

Guild sighed and rested his chin on his knees. "If she cares so little, why are you fighting for her?"

"Because we depend on her," Inna answered. "We depend on the animals and the seasons to live. We must protect that."

"If you changed the way you lived...."

Inna scoffed, interrupting Guild. "And what? Start herding? This place, it cannot be tamed like the gentler lands in the south. The tundra tolerates us because we are respectful. The day we lose that respect will be the death of us."

Guild grunted. He thought to ask if the Sierrans would consider moving to where the land was more hospitable, but he knew it would be a fruitless question. The Sierran nomads loved the tundra, despite her harshness. It was like loving a woman who was powerful and free. For all of her faults, perhaps most especially for those faults, she was adored.

The desert man pondered this for a moment as he cast his gaze around. Spring had arrived. Bright green blades of grass were pushing their way through the thinning ice and snow. Birds were singing in the clear sky and the sun was shining brightly and warmly on Guild's back. There was a certain peace here, a peace wrought by the never-ending cycle of life that was never made more evident than in the tundra.

"Then you understand," Inna told Guild, a small smile touching his face.

The spell was broken and Guild frowned. "I'm not sure I do."

"Men," the Lord of the Hunt said quietly. "Were also made for the wilds."

Guild laughed a little at that. "Then tell me why we must build walls?"

"Because of other men," Ur said. No one had noticed him. Now all eyes were on him.

"Is the Winter Wolf awake, young pup?" the Lord of the Hunt asked. Ur shook his head. "She sleeps still. I have come in search of food, and to see if I cannot take some back to Otsana."

"Will she stay like that forever?" Guild asked.

Ur shrugged. "I do not know. Perhaps once the threat has passed, she will return as Seraphimé, princess of the Osprey Clan. Perhaps not. There is no way to tell."

"Poor bastard," Guild muttered. He grinned when all eyes turned to him. "Her husband. Knowing he is married to an actual wolf rather than a woman with that namesake is bound to be a shock to him."

Inna laughed. It was a bright, hearty sound that almost everyone had heard. Immediately, the mood of the morning lightened and soon the entire camp was buzzing about their breakfast, sharing laughter around their fires.

Ur ate quickly. Then, snatching the bag of meat that Inna had given him, he went immediately back to the Winter Wolf.

"Did he stay with her all night?" Guild asked the Lord of the Hunt.

The god nodded. "He slept against her breast, buried almost entirely in her ruff."

Inna smiled. "I wish I had seen that."

"Will she sleep much longer, do you think?" Guild asked.

The Lord of the Hunt shrugged and turned. "The Bull is coming."

"The what?"

Guild need not have asked. It was not long before the massive war chief arrived at their fire.

"Inna Ice Bear," Bull said with a warm smile. "Good morning!"

"Good morning, Bull," Inna said with an answering smile. Though they had met on several occasions at various Great Gatherings, they had never really spoken overlong and knew very little about each other. Bull's warmth, however, was infectious and Inna found he immediately liked the enormous man.

"I have come to enquire about the prisoner."

"The prisoner?"

"The Ottal commander."

Inna's gaze was blank.

"The one we did not kill yesterday," Bull prompted.

"I was not aware that we had taken a prisoner."

"Oh. Well, we did. What do you want done with him?"

"Bring him before the Winter Wolf, when she wakes," the Lord of the Hunt said. "Let him stand trial."

"And how are we to understand the judgment the wolf passes?" Inna asked. "I don't speak wolf."

The Lord of the Hunt laughed. "Ur will know."

Shaking his head, Inna said, "I miss the child he was. I miss the woman Otsana, for that matter."

"The woman Otsana is still there," the Lord of the Hunt said with a smile. "Tell me if you do not see her smiling at you when you face the wolf."

Inna grunted.

"That is good, then." Bull said. He pulled a face. "Will someone tell me when she wakes? I have the prisoner in my pavilion, and I'm sick of hearing him blubber like a baby."

"I imagine he's never seen a woman transform into a wolf before," Inna noted with a smile.

Bull grinned. "Is that soup?" he asked.

"It is. Sit down and have some. Escape that blubbering for a little while longer."

"Thank you, Ice Bear."

Inna shrugged. "It's nothing." He handed Bull a full bowl of soup and the man sat and ate with relish. "That was good soup," he said when he put the bowl down. Inna shrugged. "The recipe was our Shamanka's. She died on the way to the last Great Gathering."

"I'm sorry."

Inna shrugged again. "I have the feeling she is watching still."

"That's probably because she is."

Inna grunted and Bull changed the subject. Guild, Bull, Inna and the Lord of the Hunt remained at the fire until a chilling howl disturbed their conversation.

"She's awake," the Lord of the Hunt noted mildly.

* * * *

Ur sat on the ground smiling to himself beside the great paws of the Winter Wolf as she turned her head to the sky and howled a second time. There was something in that sound that called to him, pulled him close. His smile broadened as an answering howl was heard in the distance. The Winter Wolf's ears pricked and she turned to face the sound. It came again, a little closer this time, and the Winter Wolf answered.

* * * *

The Prince of the Pamisii, who was also called Blue Ghost, paused, the ranger Grunt close behind. In perfect silence, Grunt knocked an arrow. The barely heard footfalls of a small group of four legged beasts came closer. The Prince signalled for Grunt to hold.

Not long after, a small pack of wolves appeared from behind the thick trees. The alpha paused in his tracks and turned eerie silver eyes towards the Prince. Grunt raised his bow.

"No!" the Prince whispered, pushing the bow down. Grunt looked at his leader in surprise, then turned back to the wolves. The alpha remained in position as the wolves slipped past, ignoring the men and heading north. Once the rest of the pack was clear, the alpha raised his snout to the heavens and howled, answering some call that only wolves could hear. Deeper in the forest, other packs answered, all of them drifting north. With one last, knowing look at the rangers, the wolf turned and padded gently into the scrub.

"They are called north," the Prince said. "The Winter Wolf has called her children home."

* * * *

"What was that?" Guild asked, rising to his feet and turning around.

"More," the Lord of the Hunt answered.

"More?"

"More wolves. They are coming."

"We will run with them," Bull said with a smile. "As in the Days of Fog, when the false caves were torn down."

Guild looked blankly at the war chief, who only smiled in return.

Ur stood as the Winter Wolf left her seat and padded forward. She moved so gracefully that, for a moment, Ur was too caught in watching her to follow. Only when she stopped and looked behind her did Ur force his feet forward. Together they padded through the camp, past the herd of uneasy horses and up to the crest of a small hill. There, the Winter Wolf howled once more and was heartened by the answering cries.

Ur gasped as the packs approached. Four packs of tundra wolves, each one at least six members large, approached from the north, howling in answer to the cries of the Winter Wolf and of fellow packs.

They stopped a mile or so from the Winter Wolf and their leaders broke away, approaching the Winter Wolf cautiously, their bodies close to the ground, their tails stuck straight behind them, wagging slightly and their ears flat against their heads.

The three pack leaders stopped a few metres from Otsana and sank flatter against the ground as the larger Winter Wolf approached. After what looked to the eyes of the onlookers like a silent conference, the Winter Wolf turned and trotted back through the camp.

The three leaders turned around and rejoined their packs, leading them around the outskirts of the camp to the western side. There they sprawled, reclining in the sun as they awaited the next decision of Otsana.

Otsana and Ur did not return to the place they had slept, but instead headed to Inna's modest fire.

"Otsana will see the prisoner now," Ur told Bull.

Bull glanced at the enormous wolf behind Ur, who gazed back at him with twinkling eyes, and nodded. He immediately left to fetch the man.

"Tell the war chief to take the prisoner to the western edge of the camp. Otsana will receive him there."

Inna nodded and Ur and the Winter Wolf turned to leave. The wolf paused a moment then turned back to Inna. She cocked her head at him before turning away and trotting to the designated meeting spot. In that gaze, Inna perceived laughter directed at him.

"Very funny," he muttered darkly.

Beside him, the Lord of the Hunt chuckled.

* * * *

Braddard Mamni trembled as the massive Sierran war chief dragged him forward. His trembling worsened as he caught sight of the colossal wolf that waited for him. Beside the wolf stood a small boy in grey and white robes with empty eye sockets. On the other side of the massive animal stood a man dressed in a dear skin cloak with antlers sprouting from the hood. It was a hellish scene.

The Braddard grunted as he was thrown unceremoniously forward. His knees hit the hard, cold stone of the tundra with a painful crack.

"Desert Eagle," Ur said by way of greeting. "Welcome to the tundra." The comment earned a few laughs from the crowd of warriors who had gathered to witness the wolf chastise the desert man.

The Braddard glared up at the boy. "You will burn in the deepest pits of Lord Susa's Torment," he spat. The wolf cocked her head, and a moment later, the boy smiled.

"If it pleases you to think so," he said.

"It does."

The boy shrugged. "We are not here to discuss my fate, invader, but yours. I have something for you to think on. What punishment would you give the men who invaded your lands and slaughtered your people?"

The Braddard scowled, but said nothing.

"Come now," Ur said gently. "What punishment would you give them?"

Still the Braddard refused to speak.

"There, you see, desert man. You would not like strangers coming into your lands and killing your kin. You would fight them, would you not?"

"Yes," Mamni agreed sourly.

"What made you think we would behave any differently?"

"I didn't think you would," the Braddard growled. "And I do not care. We have come to cleanse this land of your evil ways."

The wolf growled low.

"The land says that you are not welcome here," Ur translated. "It is for her to decide what ways prevail. Not you."

"The one true god will prevail, as he did against the old false gods."

"In the desert, perhaps," Ur said with a smile. "Your god has no power here."

"You will learn otherwise."

"I very much doubt that."

The wolf grumbled and shifted a little.

Ur nodded. "I am certain that you would offer any invader a slow death in the desert. You are fortunate then that Otsana finds little value in torture. You are free to join the rest of your ill-fated army, desert man."

Braddard Mamni's brows rose.

"You will march west with us and when we reach your kin, you will be free to join their fate."

"We will prevail," the Braddard said, his voice low. "I shall be there to gloat when our victory comes at last."

"Look around you, desert man," Ur advised. "You are the only survivor of your army. Your people are in a land they do not know, a land that does not want them here. How long do you think they will survive in this terrain, in these temperatures?"

The Braddard pressed his lips together.

"Otsana has decided," Ur said. "The desert man will come with us, and be made to understand the power of the tundra. Who will guard him?"

"I will."

The Braddard recognised the voice and turned his head. Though he knew the voice, the fact that its owner was among the savages he fought took him by surprise. His eyes widened when he spied his former Guild Master. Guild smiled at him.

"Hello, Mamni."

The Braddard's expression turned hard. "You, nameless man, have no right to speak to me," the Braddard hissed at Guild in Ottalan.

"I have a name Braddard. It's Guild," Guild replied in touan so that those gathered here would understand.

"You are a traitor!"

Guild shrugged. "I am a man who has been made to understand," he replied easily.

Ur and Otsana both observed Guild with their heads cocked in identical positions. Guild tried to ignore it as he stared down his former guildsman.

Braddard Mamni suddenly laughed. "I would never have believed a man of the desert, raised in the love of the god of the Yellow City, to fall prey to the tundra's evil tricks."

Guild grinned. "It was not the god of the Yellow City that saved me from an attempted assassination, Braddard," he replied. "I have seen things that would shatter you. Now get on your feet. I have to get some food into you. I'll not let you drag me behind the rest of the pack."

The Lord of the Hunt grinned at Guild's implication and Ur smiled. "I believe you will do," he said. Ur turned back to the Braddard who was still glaring at Guild. "Thus it is, desert man," Ur said. "You are to remain with us until we reach your army. Then you may die with them."

That was all that needed to be said. Seemingly bored, the Winter Wolf turned abruptly and padded into the midst of the waiting wolf packs, Ur trailing dreamily behind.

Guild marched forward and hauled the Braddard to his feet. He turned and, pulling a stumbling Braddard along, marched passed Inna.

"I'm going to need some help with him," Guild muttered to Inna as he walked past. Inna grinned and followed.

Nineteen

"Bran!"

It was the only thing Amwyl was capable of saying as she rushed into her son's arms. Having no need to disguise herself now that she was where her husband always believed her to be, she wore a queenly gown of red and gold. The long skirt did nothing to hinder her flight into her son's strong embrace. She said his name over and over again like a prayer as Bran held her close.

"Hello, Mother," he said after the long embrace. It had been a long, hard ride across the tundra with an entire herd of horses at his heels and Bran was tired and glad to be with his loved ones.

"Oh Bran! I was so worried for you!"

Bran laughed. "I've been fine, Mother. Honest."

"Oh!" Amwyl sobbed, throwing herself into her son's embrace again.

"Let him go, Amwyl," Gofron said gently. "You're crushing him."

Amwyl gave her husband an ill-hidden eye roll but stepped aside nonetheless. Bran and his father embraced roughly.

"By the gods, boy," the King said with a smile. "Have you grown?"

Bran grinned at his father and shrugged.

"Where is Otsana?" Gofron asked.

Bran's smile slipped a bit. "We'd best talk inside," he replied. "There was a change of plans as soon as we heard you were making a full retreat."

"Indeed? Well, we've changed our plans considerably too. Let's go inside and get you something to eat. You look hungry. And tired."

"Exhausted actually," Bran replied with a grin. "It's been over a month of travel, and I've been riding without rest for two days. Those tundra horses are miracles."

Gofron laughed and clapped his son on the back. Bran reached around his mother's shoulders and together all three walked into the stronghold to breakfast, where most of the Greyl lords were already dining. Lord Kildurrow limped in moments after Bran's arrival to join them. Amwyl barely ate a thing, busy as she was fussing over her son.

"So," Gofron said amicably as Bran finished his plate. "How have you been?"

"Never mind that," Lord Kildurrow interrupted. "What the hell kind of buzzard was that made out of?" He pointed at the feathered hide cape that Bran had slung unceremoniously over the back of his seat.

Bran grinned. "It was made for me by the Shaman and Shamanka of the Sierran nomads. It's a cape of my namesake. They wear such things into battle, or, at least, their important leaders do."

"You're an important leader, Bran?" Gofron asked, his face splitting into a proud smile.

Bran shrugged. "I'm the husband of the Marshal of the Tundra, the Winter Wolf. They call me Southern Crow."

"That sounds... odd," Lord Kildurrow noted with a grunt. He took a long sip of his steaming tea and leant back.

"It is a bit, if you're not used to it. To be honest though, their way of life is liberating."

"Liberating?" Lord Kildurrow muttered. "Out in the open to battle elements and slavers both. Right."

"Yes," Bran insisted. "There are no walls to fence you in. There are very few rules, save for the things that make sense. There is no money. Aside from personal attire and weapons, there are no possessions. Everything belongs to everyone. It feels more natural, somehow. More organic, like that is the way we are supposed to live."

"So you like it up there," Gofron asked, a wistful note to his words. Bran smiled at his father, immediately guessing his thoughts.

"I do. And so would you."

The King grunted. "I'm past the age of adventure."

"No such thing!" Bran declared with a wide grin.

Amwyl smiled to herself. Bran had become a man at last. He had found a place where he belonged, the place he had been looking for his entire young life.

"You never were one for walls and gardens," she reminisced aloud. "You were always happiest outside, turning your skin dark and getting so filthy as to be unrecognisable."

Bran laughed. "I still am. Speaking of which, I'd love a bath."

"After," Gofron said, waving his hand in the air. "First, tell me what's going on up there."

"Well," Bran said, accepting more hot tea. "The Sierrans are remarkable fighters. Our first engagement against the Ottals proved very good indeed. We lost five hundred, but they lost close to ten thousand. Of course, their numbers still outweigh ours by a staggering amount, but the terrain and the cold are taking their toll on the Ottals."

"Good," Lord Kildurrow grunted.

"When word got to me of your full retreat, the war chiefs and I decided that we should split up. I would ride here, and Bull, war chief of the Ouruq Clan, would head north to join with Otsana and her warriors. They gave me fully half the horses in order to keep the tracks similar enough to ensure the Ottals would still follow me.

"Otsana will follow the Ottals here, attacking any reinforcements and supply caravans that try to cross the tundra. She'll come in behind the Ottals once they're dug in for a siege."

The King grunted.

"What's been going on here?"

"We fought a few battles against the Touans. The first two were fairly evenly matched, but the last one was a complete rout. We lost more men than we could afford. It was decided that we should retreat here, and leave behind small regiments to harry the Touan army and take the supplies and reinforcements in ambush. All the crops are burnt. It will take a while for the Greyls to recover from this fight."

"War is like that," Lord Kildurrow noted sourly.

Bran observed Lord Kildurrow a moment. He was a handsome man, tall and broadly built with brown hair that was greying. His eyes were a soft blue hue, and they were sad.

"I heard about Dylan, my Lord," Bran said gently. "I was shocked, and I'm sorry."

Lord Kildurrow's expression hardened. "He brought it upon himself."

Bran did not force the issue and turned instead to his mother. "You look well," he noted.

Amwyl smiled. "Of course I am well! My son is near me again."

Bran could not help but notice the long look Lord Kildurrow cast in his mother's direction. Bran's father seemed blissfully unaware, so Bran chose not to make an issue of it. Instead, he asked his mother about it after breakfast on his way to the chambers that had been made ready for him. King Gofron and Lord Kildurrow had retired to the War Room to continue making preparations for the approaching siege and Bran had a few moments.

"So," he drawled. "Is there anything you would like to talk about?"

Amwyl turned to her son with a sweet smile. "No," she replied, completely oblivious Bran's implication.

"Truly? Nothing? Nothing at all?"

Amwyl stopped walking. "What is it Bran?"

Bran smiled. "Well…" He paused. "I couldn't help but notice that the Lord Kildurrow was… well… he kept looking at you…."

The conversation became suddenly much more awkward than Bran had intended. Amwyl scowled.

"There is nothing going on between the Lord Kildurrow and myself," she replied tartly. She turned and marched down the hall, leaving Bran to jog to catch up.

"He seems to like you a lot," Bran pushed.

Amwyl scoffed. "Whatever gave you that impression?"

"It was in the way he looked at you," Bran said. "He cares for you."

Amwyl wanted to smile, but she kept her face stony. "It doesn't matter in any case. I'm a married woman."

"I know," Bran said. "It's just that... well... I want you to know that it's all right if you care for him too. I mean, it's all right by me. I'm not sure about father."

Amwyl stopped dead and turned to her son. Her face was lit with surprise, her eyes wide and her brows higher than Bran had ever seen them before. Her mouth closed slowly and her brows lowered until they were knitted in a fierce frown. "I don't know how to respond to that."

Bran offered a quick grin. "Then don't. This conversation never happened. If anyone asks, I know nothing about Lord Kildurrow's feelings for you, and I most certainly never advised you to follow your heart."

Whistling in an effort to seem casual, Bran walked away, leaving Amwyl behind to mull over his words. With a sigh, she turned and retired to her room to take up her much-neglected embroidery.

* * * *

The Guild Master scowled. Yesterday had been a lovely warm day, with a gentle southerly breeze.

This morning however was frigid, as if spring had changed her mind yet again and retreated back south, leaving the tundra to the bitter mewling of Old Man Winter. The Guild Master pulled his cloak around him tighter and threw the hood up high to protect his frozen ears as the army slowly struck their camp.

The men were too frozen to move quickly. Morale had plummeted once again. There were superstitious mumblings amongst the men about the mood and sentience of the land here. The Guild Master did not like it. He ordered the Yellow Robes to deliver another sermon after breakfast. Even that had less of an effect than it used to.

The men were cold and weary. What they needed was a decisive victory, one they were sure to get as soon as they caught up with the fleeing Sierran nomads.

"The cowards," the Guild Master spat angrily.

Several more groups of horses had lost their lives because of the fickle terrain that was sometimes rocky and sometimes icy. These horses were used to the desert, to soft sand and warmth. They were not coping well with the ice and rock of the tundra. Worse still, they were all spooked.

Every night since the Braddard Asul was executed, wolves had been calling to one another. Sometimes the chilling howls were close, so close it woke the sleeping men and threatened a stampede of terrified horses. Some of the howls were different. They were not quite the usual howls of the wolf. Once, one of the men swore he saw a large black wolf with glowing red eyes just outside the light of his fire. That man never sat picket again. Instead he cowered in his tent, shaking and praying night after restless night.

Guild Master Mtsusa turned back to the tracks he spied in the lingering snow. The Sierrans had departed this place at a gallop. How the blazes they managed a gallop in this terrain boggled the Guild Master's mind.

"I sense a presence," one of the Yellow Robes murmured to the Guild Master. "It is not friendly."

"I see nothing," the Guild Master growled back. *Superstitious bastards.* The Guild Master glared at the Yellow Robe for a moment.

"Is something on your mind?" the object of the Guild Master's irritation asked.

"If you keep talking like that," the Guild Master noted calmly. "You'll spook the men. They're already behaving like frightened sheep. I don't want to hear any more of it."

The Yellow Robe bowed his head. "As you wish," he replied mildly.

"All right!" Mtsusa yelled, turning back to his men, "Let's get a move on. The last man ready to move will be digging the latrines." That worked. The army, despite the cold, burst into a flurry of movement. It was not long before they were all marching once more.

* * * *

"They are heading southeast," Bull said with satisfaction. He rose from the ground and turned back to the enormous Winter Wolf that padded quietly beside Ur's mount. His horse was now used to the presence of the sizeable predator and did not shy from her. "They will reach the place where the Southern Crow and I parted ways soon. Whether or not they figure out the plan is yet to be seen. As for now, they are headed towards the stronghold."

"That is good," Ur said, speaking for the wolf, who simply gazed at Bull with fathomless green eyes.

"Shall we continue, Otsana?" Bull asked.

"No," Ur replied. "They are moving very slowly. If we go too quickly we shall meet them before they make it to the stronghold. We must wait here until tomorrow."

"That's a long time of doing nothing," Bull said with a grin.

"Then we shall be well rested when we finally engage the Desert Eagle."

Bull nodded. "All right then, we'll camp here."

The Winter Wolf suddenly turned south, her ears pricked up high.

"What is it, Otsana?" Ur murmured, turning his sightless eyes south also. A slow smile crossed his face. "The children are coming," he said quietly.

"The wha...?" Bull need not finish his question.

A large pack of wolves crested a cairn that lay in the south. With a joyous yelp, the pack scrambled down the grave and headed at a run towards the pony-sized Winter Wolf. They were as pups when at last they reached her, yelping and jumping and licking her as if they were friends long lost and now reunited.

After what seemed an age of whining and tail wagging, the wolves departed and, circling around the Sierran army, joined their larger kin.

Bull grinned wildly. "We will run with them," he said.

Ur smiled and nodded. "More come every day. They have heard the call of their ancestors and they have come."

"Well," Bull said. "We'd best get some food in our bellies."

Ur brightened, sitting up on his horse with a smile. "Mmmm! Soup!"

Inna laughed. Behind him, Guild rode with the Braddard Mamni tied securely to the horse's tack. The man had paled several shades as he observed the exchange between the enormous Winter wolf and the pack of regular-sized wolves. He did not understand the Sierran tongue and he could only guess what religious discussions were happening between the sightless boy and the war chief who now led the army.

"Do you believe yet?" Guild asked him.

"There is nothing to believe," the Braddard snarled. "It is in the nature of wolves to communicate with howls."

Guild grinned. "It is not in their nature to share their territories with rival packs," he noted. "I wonder how it is that the packs gathered here tolerate each other's presence. Remarkable, I'd say."

The Braddard growled and Guild turned to Inna. "You were right, Ice Bear," Guild noted. "A man can try and rationalise anything."

Inna shrugged. "I did not expect he would ever be made to believe."

"I had hoped."

Inna smiled and turned back to face Guild. "You're kinder than you'd have us believe."

"Not all eagles are soulless."

Inna laughed and, sparing a moment to cast the Braddard a flat stare, turned back. "Looks like we're staying," he noted. With a disappointed sigh, he dismounted. "Come on, let's go cook soup for the wolf and her pup."

Guild grunted and dismounted. Dragging the reluctant Braddard with him, the three men entered the presence of the Winter Wolf with great care. Whether by fear or reverence, Braddard Mamni could not tell. Guild went so far as to bow, earning a tongue-lolling smile from the wolf and a giggle from Ur.

"We do not bow in the tundra," Ur noted with a smile as he affectionately ruffed Otsana's ears. The Winter Wolf returned the favour with a flurry of licks that sent Ur sprawling on the ground in a giggling mass. Guild and Inna grinned.

"You are still in there," Inna noted. The wolf turned to him and nuzzled his hand. Inna laughed and stroked Otsana, who grumbled happily.

Inna started the fire and began cooking as Guild and Ur conversed.

"Where did the Lord of the Hunt go?" Guild asked. "His Ayal are all still here."

"Not all," Ur noted. "He took some fifty with him and headed east. He is going to waylay the supplies that have crossed into the tundra. We should have more food than we can handle within the week.

"Assuming he is successful."

Ur shrugged. "The Ottals believe that their enemy is in front of them. Not behind them. I doubt the supplies will be heavily guarded."

"You know, I am glad to be on your side," Guild noted with a grimace.

Ur grinned. "I am glad you are glad. That might change once the fighting starts."

Guild shrugged. "If we lose this fight, I'm a dead man. If I turn back to the desert now, I'm a dead man. Seems to me I'm doomed either way. At least with you I have some chance of making it."

"I think that very pragmatic."

"Such is the nature of survival, I suppose."

"You are all going to hell," the Braddard muttered in Ottalan. He did not understand their conversation, but he did not care. Their good cheer irritated him.

Guild shrugged. "Perhaps," he admitted in Touan. "But then I shall be spending all eternity in good company."

Ur laughed delightedly.

* * * *

"Hold still!" King Roger roared at his horse. The beast pranced and pulled at the reins as Roger tried to mount.

"All the horses are spooked," Algar noted sourly. He had successfully mounted his beast, but that didn't stop the brute from shifting and snorting. The Touan army had reached the Pamisii forest, a dense fortress of trees and bracken that loomed over them like a gnarled portend of doom.

They had managed to come through a barrage of ambushes along the way, sending the majority of attackers fleeing before them, but the damage sustained was irreparable. Their numbers had dwindled and the reinforcements sometimes never arrived. King Roger was certain that not all the ambushes had been taken care of. He disliked the idea of leaving the enemy at his back, even if they were in small groups.

"The scouts have reported seeing at least twelve separate packs of wolves, all of them heading north," King Roger grumbled as he tried to mount once more. "That's probably what's spooking the horses."

"Speaking of scouts," Algar noted mildly. "Here's one now."

Roger turned his head as he observed the scout riding at a gallop from the woods towards the council members.

"Well?" a representative of the Yellow City asked the rider.

Algar frowned. The man was pale, and his lips were blue as he wheezed through spasming lungs. "By the gods," the scout whispered. "There are demons in that forest!"

Roger and Algar exchanged glances. "Do tell," Roger said nonchalantly as he kneed his horse for jerking away, again.

"Blue Ghost," the scout whispered, his eyes glazing over. "Blue Ghost."

The scout slid numbly from his saddle. It was only then that the sturdy wooden shaft of an arrow that protruded from the scout's back was seen.

Algar gave a shout of surprise as the scout's eyes rolled and the man fell forward, dead. The representative of the Yellow City walked forward and plucked the arrow from the man's back. He frowned as he stared at it.

"I have never before seen this make," he noted.

Algar, still mounted, snatched it from his hand. He stared at the arrow, with its black, glass-like head in utter disbelief.

"This is an ancient design," he noted. "I have arrow heads like these on leather thongs to wear around the neck. Arrows have not been made like this for several thousand years."

"What does that mean?" the Yellow Robe asked irritably.

Algar turned his attention to the woods. "I know of only one thing who would still use such arrows."

"Who?"

"The Horned God," Algar said, sending a buzz through the gathered crowd. "Master of the Wilds and Lord of the Hunt."

"Blasphemy!" the Yellow Robe hissed. "There is no such creature."

"Of course there isn't," the King of Utoua jumped in, throwing daggers at Algar with his eyes.

"I never said there was," Algar noted calmly. "Only that the myth exists, and the only one who would use such arrows as these would be the Horned God."

"What is this 'Horned God?'" the Yellow Robe demanded.

"They say he is half stag, half man and is most often seen in the guise of a man wearing a cloak of deer hide with a hood that hides a helm of a stag's skull replete with antlers."

"You mean like that man over there?" Roger asked his son. Roger had spent the entirety of Algar's explanation gazing at the line of trees.

Algar followed his father's gaze and froze as he observed a dark figure beneath a broad oak dressed exactly as he had described. In his hand he held a bow of unknown design. At his side sat one enormous black mutt, whose eyes seemed to glow red in the fading light. Both man and mutt were staring, as near as one could tell, at the gathered army. Algar felt a chill spill down his spine. He looked at his father, who had a strange expression on his face.

"They are simply trying to scare us," the Yellow Robe snarled. "That is nothing more than a costumed man. Send your archers forward! I want this man dead!"

In an instant several archers stepped forward and let loose their arrows. The dog turned and disappeared into the forest before the arrows landed, but the figure of the Lord of the Hunt did not. The arrows that should have struck him past straight through him. With a small smile, the Lord of the Hunt turned and faded from sight, not simply disappearing into the forest as his hound had done, but actually fading into nothingness. In the gnarled oak that stood behind him, three arrows quivered from their recent impact. Algar's jaw dropped as a stunned hush fell over the gathering.

"I'm not the only one who saw that, right?" Algar asked slowly.

"It was nothing more than a trick of the light," the Yellow Robe growled. "We must march on."

"I am not going in there at night," Roger snapped, finally roused from his bulge-eyed stupor.

"Why not?" the Yellow Robe demanded.

"Look, they have the Horned God on their side, and the scout mentioned Blue Ghost. I'll happily take them on during the day, but there is no way I am fighting ghosts and gods at night."

"Blasphemy!" the Yellow Robe shrieked. "There is only one god."

"Yes," Roger replied sweetly. "I know. But, the horses are spooked, the men are spooked, and I am spooked. I say we camp here and wait until the light of day before we head into that." Roger pointed at the forest. "That way, it'll be harder for these heathen bastards to play tricks with the light."

Algar grunted. "I'm with father on this one."

The rest of the war council agreed immediately and no amount of shrieking could avail the Yellow Robe this night. Outnumbered and angry, the Yellow Robe stormed off to his tent whereupon he began devising a sermon to damn those who do not trust in the power of the god of the Yellow City and who were terrified of ancient superstitions. It was a fine sermon and would serve to shame the kings of the Touan Federation.

Roger and Algar could not care less. They retired immediately to their tents to rest and await dinner. Algar could not help but notice how the servants trembled as they laid out the meal before the King and his eldest son.

"Don't worry," Algar said kindly to one boy. "It's just the Greyls playing with our heads."

The boy managed a small, yet unconvinced smile and Algar sighed. "You don't still believe in that nonsense do you?"

The boy shrugged. "My pa used to hunt. He said his grandpa was killed by the Lord of the Hunt for killing a pregnant doe when he shouldn't have. He said now he leaves the Lord offerings when he's out hunting, and prays the night before. It's best not to anger the gods, he reckons. I used to think he was crazy, believing in that stuff even when he went to sermon, but now I'm not so sure. That man at the woods today, he looked exactly like pa described. He even glowed green."

Algar grunted. "It's all just head games, boy," he said. "Don't you mind it."

"As my prince commands."

Algar sighed. That was hardly satisfactory, though forgivable. The page was young and one cannot simply stop believing because they are commanded to. He looked across the table at his father. "What do you think?"

"Hogwash," Roger grunted. "All of it."

"So you think it was a trick?"

"It could have been."

"That's hardly definitive."

"Look, we Touans converted centuries ago. Never was one single sighting of the supposed old gods ever recorded, so it was easy to convert. What was one deity over another, really? Not one of them ever had any impact on how we lived, and converting was easier than war which surely would have come if we had refused."

"Just like now."

"Exactly. Just like now. The only difference is, the Greyls believe in their gods with all their heart and soul. They have many reported sightings of their spirits and deities every single week." Roger sighed.

"Of the recorded sightings, The Lord of the Hunt is second only to the spirit of the forests that the Greyl Rangers call 'Blue Ghost.' Less frequently, they report seeing a lady wreathed in light over some body of water, or the impetuous Bride of Fire in a hearth. Still, such sightings have been reported, and with every report, their beliefs are affirmed. They believe in it so much, they are facing war and obliteration to defend it."

"So...."

"So nothing. I envy that kind of unshakable belief. That is all."

"You haven't answered my question."

"Hmph. What was your question?"

"Do you believe that we all just saw the Horned God or not?"

"I believe that it doesn't matter what I believe. We're too entrenched in this war to do anything but march onward."

Algar sighed. "You're particularly unhelpful."

"Belief is something that is personal, Algar. You have to work it out yourself."

"What if it's true?"

Roger shrugged. "Then it's true. Though, bear in mind, gods can be defeated. Lord Susa of the Yellow City managed it. Now they worship only him, and their old gods are entirely forgotten."

Algar grunted. "I somehow doubt that these gods will be going down without a fight."

"And the gods of the desert did, did they?"

Algar shrugged. "I wouldn't know. I wasn't around then."

"Don't be smart."

"I can't help it. It's a symptom of possessing a brain."

"Yet you can't decide matters of faith by yourself."

"Ouch. That was low."

"And entirely necessary."

"As you like."

"That's right."

Algar burst out laughing. "I am humbled."

"I somehow doubt it. Now finish your meal. I want to go to bed."

"Yes, Father."

"Hmph."

Twenty

"What do you think, Blue Ghost?"

The youngest prince of the Pamisii sighed. "I do wish you'd stop calling me that, Grunt."

Grunt grinned. He wasn't going to change his mode of address, and the prince knew it. Grunt so firmly believed that Blue Ghost had come to the mortal realm to join in the struggle against the desert eagle, that nothing the prince could ever say would ever change the ranger's mind.

Sighing again, the Prince said, "We could paint ourselves blue and go for a haunting. They are already spooked from the appearance of the Master of the Wild earlier this evening."

Grunt's grin widened. "That sounds like fun. Do you want bullroarers?"

"Let's do that. That ought to spook them well indeed."

"You can be cruel when you put your mind to it."

"Serves them right for coming into my forest with mischief on their minds."

"It does indeed, Blue Ghost. It does indeed."

The Prince cringed, but said nothing, and he followed Grunt's silent retreat from the hiding spot where they spied on the Touan camp for the better part of the day. The pair arrived back at their fire-less camp not an hour later.

"Well?" a ranger by the name of Bluebell asked. She was a pretty girl, with dimples when she smiled and a dainty build. For all of that, there was not a single ranger with the Prince of the Pamisii who was more dangerous. She was a deadly accurate shot, and fast and vicious with any pair of short blades.

"Blue Ghost is suggesting a haunting. Got any woad and chalk? We'll paint him blue and scare the desert god all the way back to his home!"

Bluebell smiled as she observed her prince. "I like this idea."

The Prince shrugged. "The war leader elect asked me to make believers of them, and so I shall."

"I like this man. King of the Baveii, is he not?"

"He is."

"Point him out to me when we meet him. I'd like to take him to bed."

"He's married Bluebell."

"So?"

"Nothing."

"All right then. Now, let's get you painted up. I can't wait to hear those idiots shrieking like little girls."

"You're a little girl, Bluebell," Grunt reminded her. Bluebell glared at him, and the argument was dropped. The Prince chuckled and clapped Grunt on the back.

"Let's go. They're just heading off to sleep, and I want to shake a few tents!"

Laughing quietly, Bluebell accepted the offered bowl of woad and chalk paste and immediately began to paint the Pamisii prince a charming pale blue.

"You know," Bluebell mused cheekily. "Blue Ghost strides the woods naked."

"Blue Ghost is also a ghost and thus impervious to arrows. I'll keep my armour, thank you."

"They'll be able to tell it's a prank."

The Prince glared at Bluebell and Grunt grinned like a mad man.

"It's true you know," Grunt said.

"You just want to see me without clothes," the Prince accused Bluebell.

Bluebell arched her brows at him. "And?"

Grunt barked a laugh and the Prince levelled him with another flat stare. "It's all part of life, Blue Ghost," Grunt noted.

"Stop calling me that!" the Prince snapped. He turned to Bluebell and started to unbuckle his armour.

"You owe me, Bluebell," he growled.

"Don't worry, Blue Ghost," Bluebell said sweetly. "I'll make it all worth your while."

Grunt watched and grinned until he caught the Prince's angry eyes. "Come on rangers," Grunt said. "Let's set ourselves up around the camp and ensure our Blue Ghost is adequately protected."

"If any of you make a big deal of this," the Prince growled as the rangers disappeared into the dark forest. "I'll have your heads!"

Now naked, and painfully aware of the beauty of
the girl before him, the Prince focused hard on the floor
of the forest as Bluebell painted his body pale blue.

"You know," she murmured as she traced her
delicate fingers across his torso. "You look a lot
scrawnier with all that armour on. It doesn't do you
justice."

"Just put on the paint and shut up," the Prince
growled.

Bluebell deliberately slowed down, moving her body
close to his as her paint-covered fingers reached his
upper thigh.

"Everything has to be painted, you know," Bluebell
said with a coy smile.

"Gods, you are a demon from hell," the Prince
breathed.

Bluebell shrugged. "Sent to tempt brave men into
folly," she agreed.

"You think I'm brave?" the Prince asked,
momentarily distracted from the sensation of Bluebell's
fingers stroking his leg. Bluebell laughed. She stepped
back and put down her bowl.

"How long has it been, Blue Ghost?" she asked as
she unclipped the shoulder clasps that held her armour
together. "Since you last knew the love of a woman?"

"I've had my share, Bluebell," the Prince replied. He
could not help but stare as Bluebell's leather breastplate
fell away from her body. Her pale muslin shirt clung
enticingly to her torso and fell loose around her waist
and hips. The Prince took an unwilling step forward.

"I have a job to do," he managed to rasp as Bluebell took his hand and placed it over her perfectly formed breast. He allowed himself the luxury of exploring it through the shirt.

"You will do it," Bluebell said with a smile. "I'm sure you could spare half an hour?"

"Bluebell…."

"I'll compromise."

"Compromise?"

"That's right. I'll send you off on your task as placated as a man could be. When you return, you'll please me."

The Prince frowned. "To what end?"

Bluebell smiled and took the Prince's hand once more. She kissed his palm before she removed her shirt and placed his hand over her breast again.

"Women have needs too, my Lord," she murmured.

The Prince had time enough to grunt before Bluebell's lips touched his. After the kiss was over, the Prince smiled. "We have a compromise."

Bluebell laughed. She pushed the Prince backwards until he was pressed firmly against a tree and sank slowly to her knees.

* * * *

"What's taking him so long, do you think?" one ranger asked Grunt. Grunt gave him a look that silently told the man that he was an idiot and he needed to be quiet. The ranger sighed and played with the feathers on his arrow.

"Lucky bastard."

"If you ask nicely, she might for you too," Grunt mumbled. He turned back just as the moon broke free of the clouds that hid it and spied a pale blue figure walking silently through the trees. Grinning, Grunt stood on the specially constructed platform in the tree and loosened his bullroarer. Making sure he was clear of branches, he begun to swing it around. The resulting roar seemed deafening in the otherwise silent night. The haunting had begun.

* * * *

"What the hell is that?" Algar demanded, sitting upright on his bed and staring at the tent entrance.

King Roger was also awake, staring at the entrance in a confused state. "S'Juss wolves," he slurred.

"No wolf I know sounds like that."

Algar slid from beneath his blanket. It had become a habit of his to sleep in his chainmaille since the first of the Greyl night-raids on the Touan camp. With his father following, Algar walked out of the tent. He found, thankfully, that he was not the only one who had heard. All the members of the Touan army had exited their tents and were staring wide-eyed and frightened at the forest from where the sound emanated.

"I don't like this," Algar muttered. The sound faded and, for a moment, all was silent again. Algar almost turned to go back to bed as some of the soldiers had done already, before the sound echoed from the woods again, this time from a different place behind the line of trees, too far away from the first for any mischief-maker to have travelled on foot. Algar marched forward to the front of the camp, noting that the Yellow Robe was also out of bed and staring intently into the foreboding forest before them.

"There!" a soldier cried out.

Algar turned in time to see something pale blue and glowing in the moonlight flit behind a tree and disappear. The sound died down again and all was silent and still for a while. Algar frantically scanned the trees.

The deep whirr sounded again, this time from the most southerly side of the camp. Algar turned towards it, in time to spy the pale blue figure in his peripheral vision. He turned to it, only to find it had once more disappeared, while the droning sound continued to drift in from the south. It was answered instantly this time from somewhere deeper in the woods immediately in the west.

"Archers!" the Yellow Robe squeaked. Algar almost laughed. The man looked as terrified as he sounded.

It took a moment, but soon archers lined the western front of the camp.

"If it is Blue Ghost," one of the archers near Algar whispered. "He will not harm us unless we try to harm him."

"Just shut up and aim," another archer grated. Algar noted that the speaker trembled violently.

"So," he mused to himself. "Centuries of conversion really haven't made people forget."

"Not yet," Roger grumbled from beside his son.

"Come to enjoy the spectacle?" Algar noted wryly.

"More mind games, Algar. It's all mind games."

"If you say so." Algar was not convinced. He had spoken to more than one ranger in his time and while he found their devout belief in the spirit of the trees profoundly amusing at the time, the seriousness with which they delivered their beliefs haunted him now.

Roger looked at his son with a sidelong glance. "Do you believe, Algar?" he asked.

"I don't know," Algar said.

The blue figure strode out into the moonlight, appearing in the north, while a whirring roar sounded almost at the very front of the woods to the immediate west. In an instant, the line of archers loosed their arrows only to find that the figure had vanished once more. Moments later, the whirring roar of the woods went silent and from the north a rain of arrows, their own arrows, were fired back at the Touans. Some found their mark and the line broke as several archers fell to the ground. One or two of the nobles present screamed.

* * * *

Grunt had to stifle a laugh as the screams echoed through the trees. It was just as Bluebell had predicted, high and girlish.

"Don't laugh," Bluebell hissed from under the tree. She had appeared there as silent as a cat.

"Hello," Grunt said amicably as he scrambled down to follow their Blue Ghost as did the other rangers. They were all there to collect the Touan arrows and fire them back when they had struck the first time, and they intended to do it all night. "Was it everything you dreamed of?"

Bluebell glowered at Grunt. "I'll tell you when it happens. Incidentally, I want everyone gone for several hours after we return to camp."

"Several hours? A bit ambitious, aren't you?"

"Our Blue Ghost is young and in fine form," Bluebell replied in a terse whisper. "Trust me, we'll need several hours."

Grunt grinned as they scrambled together through the scrub.

* * * *

After the third volley of Touan arrows were fired back into the Touan ranks, the Yellow Robe stopped demanding the Touans attack the eerie blue figure that drifted silently between the trees. Instead, they all remained still and watched warily, not willing to turn their backs in case Blue Ghost decided to attack.

Algar's breath caught as the figure stepped boldly between the two closest trees that marked the beginning of the forest. It was standing on the road, shaded from the moonlight by the tangle of leafless branches of the canopy above. Even still, the figure glowed a pale blue. Green eyes scanned the Touan ranks. It was a bright green, the colour of new leaves. It was not a shade of green seen in the eyes of any man.

The figure caught Algar's gaze.

You are not welcome here.

The words hit Algar with a physical force, though the phantom before them made no movement.

These are our woods. You are not welcome here.

Algar shuddered as the apparition drifted away, melting silently into the shadows like a cat and becoming invisible to the watching army. All the while the trees whirred and roared.

It was one hour from dawn when the last of the unnatural sounds faded and the woods fell silent once more. Algar was exhausted, but he, like the others, dared not turn his back on the woods until the sun broke free of the horizon and shone with gentle warmth over the camp.

"You," the Yellow Robe said, pointing an accusing finger at Algar. "Will come with me."

Algar raised one eyebrow but did not argue. He followed the Yellow Robe into the command tent and sat wearily down at the table. His father joined Algar soon after, though he had to threaten the Yellow Robe's guards in order to do so.

"You seem to be an expert on all matters heathen," the Yellow Robe drawled.

Algar clamped his lips together into a flat line and glared at the holy man. "Is that an accusation?" he demanded.

"Not yet," the Yellow Robe replied. "I need to know everything about this supposed 'Blue Ghost' the archers were so terrified of last night."

"Of course it was *just* the archers," Algar muttered under his breath. He sighed. "Where to begin?"

"The beginning will do."

Algar glared.

"Whenever you're ready."

Grating his teeth, Algar spoke. "Blue Ghost is a very old spirit," he said. "Older even than most of the gods that the Greyls and Sierrans worship. Blue Ghost was around before men walked the earth, when the seas were ruled by great monsters. In any case, Pamisii rangers especially believe that Blue Ghost is the spirit of the tree collective."

"The tree collective?"

"The forest. They believe that one tree alone is simply a tree, but many trees together form a singular consciousness, an entity of sorts. They believe that Blue Ghost is the spiritual manifestation of that singular consciousness that is the forest.

"This spirit guards the forest from harm, destroying any who wander the woods and wreak mischief. On the other side of the coin, Blue Ghost is said to protect and love those who protect and love the forest. He is, therefore, the guardian spirit of the rangers."

"Why does he appear in the form of a boy?"

"The rangers believe that he appears in the form of a young man because it is mimicking those the forest is trying to communicate with. Men can relate better to other men than to trees."

"I see. Then, might I ask, why is this 'Blue Ghost' concerned about us? We are not here to destroy the forest."

Algar shrugged. "I don't know."

"Because," Roger said grumpily. "You are here to debase the system of belief which honours and respects the forest and replace it with a god who comes from a land where there are no forests. Fighting this invasion is simply self-preservation for Blue Ghost. Assuming that was Blue Ghost."

"Do you believe it was this spirit?" the Yellow Robe asked.

Algar half expected the man to sneer as he asked, but this question seemed spawned from a genuine confusion.

Roger shrugged. "It doesn't matter what I believe. Though I have never seen a man glow blue before."

"It was the moon," the Yellow Robe dismissed.

"He was standing in the shadows."

The Yellow Robe scowled. "There is only one god."

"In the desert perhaps," Roger agreed. "But you are not in the desert any longer, Ottal. You are in Greyl territory, and this land has many gods and many more spirits. They have not been defeated. Not yet."

"Then we must defeat them."

Roger inclined his head. "Or try."

The Yellow Robe scowled again. "Very well. We will pack and march now."

Roger shrugged. "As you like."

"Dismissed, then."

Roger and Algar promptly left the tent. Algar eyed his father for a moment.

"What is it, Algar?"

"You just made the Yellow Robe admit to the existence of other gods."

"So?"

"According the their doctrine, there are no other gods."

"So?"

Algar laughed. "You bastard! You are messing with his head as much as the Greyls are messing with ours."

Roger grinned. "What's war if one can't have a little fun?"

"Just aim that fun at the enemy, would you?"

"I am."

Algar stopped dead and stared after his father in stunned silence as Roger entered his tent. After a moment, Algar retired to his tent, distractedly mulling over his father's words.

Twenty-One

"*Y*ou're shivering a little, Blue Ghost," Bluebell noted when the young prince of the Pamisii entered the campsite. Dawn had just broken through the line of trees and the forest was painted grey and gold as the birds began to sing.

"It's cold," the Prince grated. "I need a blanket."

"You need a bath. Let me heat some water for you and we'll wash off that paint."

"Where are the others?"

Bluebell smiled as she wrapped a thick woollen blanket around the Prince's shoulders and set a large kettle onto embers she had somehow set smouldering without a fire.

"That'll give us away," the Prince noted.

Bluebell shrugged. "They're all idiots if they aren't expecting more ambushes. They've been hit every step of the way."

The Prince nodded in silence. She was right, and he was far from protesting the warmth.

"Now, come here," Bluebell commanded. She slid herself into the Prince's arms, her weight barely registering as she sat on his cold-numbed lap. Without thinking, the Prince pulled her close. She was wonderfully warm.

Bluebell smiled. "See now, not so difficult after all."

"Shut up."

Laughing, Bluebell slipped from his grasp. "The water's almost boiling. I'll have you cleaned up in no time. Then I intend to hold you to your word."

"I'm exhausted Bluebell."

"Don't worry. I'm sure the bath will wake you up."

It did.

* * * *

Algar could not help but cast his gaze in every direction as the Touan army walked through the Pamisii woods at a fast clip. It was deadly quiet. Not a single bird so much as muttered a tune. The sun barely found its way to the forest floor through the thick tangle of branches, though they were yet to be clothed in the first leaves of spring. Somewhere in the distance, a crow called.

"Three cries," Roger muttered darkly. "A bad omen."

"That does it," Algar snapped. "Since when were you such a superstitious bastard?"

Roger grunted. "Since a very long time, my boy. There's just been nothing in Misoua to bring it to the fore."

"Well bury it again," Algar grumbled. "You're making me nervous."

Roger grinned. "Good!"

"Bastard."

Roger laughed and Algar observed him with a sidelong glance. "Did our family really convert?"

"My father's did," Roger admitted. "Many, many generations ago."

"But not Grandmother?"

"Nominally, I suppose. She did all the things converts were supposed to. She went to sermon, and her family even took a pilgrimage or two. Yet when it came to the fundamental necessities of life, they still turned to the old way. Your Grandmother was particularly fond of the Lady of Light."

"The goddess of water?"

"Yes, a healer, like the Bride of Fire, but less prone to temper tantrums and mind-changes. She called upon the Lady of Light every time anyone in the household fell ill. I suppose some of it has rubbed off."

"So you believe?"

"Sort of."

"Sort of?"

"I didn't believe that any gods truly existed. They were just figments of our imaginations that we conjured to help us deal with life. Certainly I attended the sermons, and even occasionally prayed, but my heart just wasn't in it."

Algar grunted. "And now?"

"And now I've seen an apparition that looked precisely as the Lord of the Hunt is described, and a young man wandering the woods glowing blue."

"You said they were all mind games."

"And perhaps they are. Perhaps not. Tell me why not a single arrow struck the figure of the Horned God, but quivered in the bark of the tree behind at precisely the height of his heart. Tell me how the moonlight can make a boy glow if he is standing in the shade."

"You know what I think?"

"No. I'm not a clairvoyant."

Algar ignored the sarcasm. "I think your faithlessness is your weakness. I think you want so badly to believe in something that you're falling prey to tricks and illusions."

"That may be."

"You don't sound convinced."

"I'm not."

Algar sighed. "Just don't go around spouting it aloud, all right? You'll be burnt alive for being a heretic."

Roger shrugged.

"It's not something to be taken lightly."

"Perhaps not."

Algar observed his father. He knew the man all too well. "You're plotting something."

"Perhaps."

"Tell me."

"I'm not sure I should."

"Why?"

"Because it involves breaking the Treaty of Wetoua."

Algar choked. "*What?*"

"I'm tired of being ordered about by a council that is so far removed from everyday life, let alone my kingdom, that they have no idea how idiotic their decisions are. I resent going to war for a cause that is not my own."

"Father...."

"A war that cost me a son."

Algar fell silent.

"And may yet cost me more. I want to be free of the dictates of a god who has no idea about the shape of my lands or the history of my people. Misoua would be better off free from the oppressive presence of the Yellow Robes."

"A break from the Federation will cause war!"

"I am certain that this war will have adequately drained all our resources enough that a war on Misoua will simply be untenable."

Algar chewed his lip. "It's risky father."

Roger shrugged. "It might never happen. But Misoua will never be an independent kingdom if someone doesn't act."

Algar remained silent. He was torn between the duty he felt towards the other members of the Touan Federation and the instinctive desire for independence; the love for his father and the anger he felt over Alam's death.

The Independent Kingdom of Misoua. Algar turned the title over and over in his mind and found that the more he did so, the more he liked the way it sounded. He sighed.

We're about to become traitors.

* * * *

"Where the hell are they?" a ranger named Yew grumbled as he stood up from his seat.

"Let them sleep a day. Blue Ghost was out all night and I'm sure Bluebell hasn't given him much rest. Besides, the Touans will be really on edge waiting for something that doesn't come."

"You're having more fun than you ought to be, Grunt."

Grunt grinned at Yew. "You have no idea."

Yew rumbled a laugh.

"Shh!" Fern, the youngest ranger, hissed. "They're coming!"

In an instant, the rangers vanished from sight, disappearing in order to spy on the army that was now jogging through the trees.

* * * *

The day proved entirely uneventful. The Yellow Robe sat smugly with the leaders of the Touan Federation and flaunted the fact, throwing in several references to the protection of the god of the Yellow City. The more the Yellow Robe ranted, the more irritated Algar became, even more now that the possibility of an alternative had been planted in his mind.

As the Yellow Robe ranted, Algar's attention began to drift. He turned his pale eyes to the forest. In the golden light of the dying day, the tiny buds that would soon become leaves were plainly visible on the ends of the gnarled branches. He was blissfully unaware that the entire council was surrounded by a group of rangers, silently observing them and snickering to themselves.

".... And so much for Blue Ghost," the Yellow Robe crowed. "There has not been a peep from him."

"Wait until the sun goes down," Roger muttered.

"Don't crow too loudly," Algar cautioned the priest. "We're only one day in and we've a week's more forest to ride through. Guaranteed there are rangers in these woods, just waiting for the right moment to attack."

"I do not fear them," the Yellow Robe snapped. "We have come through other attacks."

"But most certainly not unscathed. We've lost a good number of men each time, and the reinforcements and supplies have been sporadic at best."

"Dare you doubt the will of the god of the Yellow City!" the Yellow Robe bellowed at Algar.

Algar shrugged easily and turned away again in silence. He and his father exchanged a look. They were both firmly in agreement now. Misoua would become an independent kingdom.

* * * *

"What have the scouts reported?" the Guild Master demanded of his guard.

"There are no more tracks left. The snow has melted away and now there is only ice or rock. We do not know where they are."

"They could have swung around behind us, for all we know," a Braddard rumbled grumpily. "We could be marching into a trap."

The Braddards grumbled amongst themselves as Mtsusa leant back on his cushions to consider.

"What do the Yellow Robes think?" he asked. The Yellow Robe who had been selected to accompany the Ottalan army smiled placidly.

"All is well," he replied.

The Guild Master narrowed his eyes at him, certain that the man was mocking him, but he did not force the issue. There was not enough time.

"Then you think we should continue?"

"It would seem our only recourse, since that was the direction they were fleeing before we lost their tracks."

The Guild Master grunted. "There is nothing else to report?"

"Nothing, my Lord," the guard said stiffly.

"Dismissed."

The guard turned and marched away and the Guild Master turned to the council. "It seems our worthy representative of the Holy Yellow City is correct. We can only chase them as we have been. We will camp for now and resume our march in the morning."

With nothing else available to them, the council members agreed and retired to their regiments as the sun dwindled in the evening sky.

Twenty-Two

The morning dawned crisp and grey over the Ottalan army.

"Uh-oh," one soldier muttered as he looked up at the broiling sky. Trying his best to ignore it, he went about his chores diligently.

They had not been marching for an hour when the sky opened up and a flurry of rain and sleet crashed over the army. If travelling over the tundra had not been difficult enough, it was now downright disastrous. The rocks were cold enough to freeze the rain on contact, creating a thin coating of ice that sent horse and man alike sprawling. Horses were not the only ones breaking their limbs now.

Worse than the terrain was the bitter cold. Soaked to the core, the soldiers shivered and shook as they marched. They tried to cover themselves with shields, packs, even spare armour as they walked, all to no avail.

After a miserable half hour of marching, the Guild Master finally called a halt, and the soldiers scrambled to make a shelter. Those who were unable to walk were tended to, but it was well known that they would be left behind. The army was moving too slowly as it was. They could not afford yet more delays.

Several men wept on their cots at their terrible fate, left alive for the beasts of the tundra to tear them apart while their comrades marched forward to an unknown destiny. Many of them uttered prayers to their god, asking for a swift death, or salvation from death, whichever need was strongest. Others cursed their god, renouncing the mighty Lord Susa and swearing that should they survive they would avenge his cruelty.

Though he remained hard on his men, the Guild Master was not as cruel as he could have been. When the spring storm subsided enough to make another start, he left the wounded a single shelter, some food, and some of their weapons and armour. They would have to fend for themselves, but they at least had some tools with which to do it. Even still, the wounded watched despondently as the Ottalan host marched steadily away from them. Not one soldier looked back.

* * * *

"Bull War-Chief," an Elk Clan scout said as he ran swiftly over the fresh ice towards the commander.

"Yes?"

"There is a tent over the rise. I smell sand on them."

"Ottalans."

"Wounded."

"Wounded?" Bull turned to the Winter Wolf who had taken to loping at his side. The storm had hampered the Sierran army and Bull was not pleased. The tundra wolves were unaffected. Their coats were thick and their skin remained dry. One or two of their smaller kin looked about as miserable as Bull felt. Even still, he was certain the Sierrans, with their oiled hide cloaks, had fared a great deal better than the Ottalan invaders. The thought set him grinning.

"You must offer them a chance," Ur said quietly after a moment's conference with the Winter Wolf. "Those that will not fight for us will be killed. Those that do will live."

"We cannot afford to carry wounded with us. It will cause many difficulties."

Ur shrugged. "The tundra wolves can carry them."

Bull grinned. "Now that would be something to see. How many wounded?" he asked the scout.

"It does not matter," Ur interjected. "Not many will be willing to fight for us. There will be few enough to carry."

"Very well. We attack?"

"Not on this ice. Let us go to them and speak with them. We will camp until the ice fades."

"Very well. Let's go."

Detaching themselves from the rest of the host, who began to set up camp, Bull, Inna, Guild with the Braddard in tow, Ur and the Winter Wolf walked carefully over the small rise. They stopped at the crest and looked down at the lowly orange-trimmed tent that sat like a frozen blossom on the tundra's endless plain.

"Looks lonely," Bull mused.

Sudden activity in the tent as well as shouts and the hiss of drawn weapons drifted up to the small group on the hillock.

"Well," Inna said cheerily. "They've seen us."

* * * *

Millen hobbled into the forming semicircle in order to face the small group of savages that stood upon the hill. His eyes immediately fell to the massive grey and white wolf that, when sitting upright, was taller than any desert horse. It was more than frozen fingers that caused his sword to fall uselessly to the ground.

He was never a fanatical believer, but Millen had believed. He observed the holy days, went to sermon and even paid a little more than the minimum tithe. Yet now, facing the giant Winter Wolf, Millen found his faith had fled him. Truly the might of the god of the Yellow City did not extend into the tundra. His god had sent him into the land of frost and abandoned him there.

"You needn't be afraid," one of the savages bellowed in Touan. "Lay down your weapons and the Winter Wolf will show mercy. Fight us and you will die. Fight *for* us, and you will live."

"Millen," another soldier hissed at Millen. "Pick up your weapon!"

Millen stared dumbly at the man, then down at the sword at his feet, then up at the crest of the hill once more. His blood ran cold. The monstrous wolf had been joined by yet more enormous wolves and several packs of their smaller, more normal kin. Millen took an unwilling step backwards.

"Millen!"

The Winter Wolf turned her beautiful head towards the sky and howled.

* * * *

"Well," Bull said as the wolves whizzed past him down the slope in a snarling horde. "I suppose we needn't fight."

"The wolves are hungry," Ur whispered sadly. "They haven't a chance."

"They were given a chance," Inna growled.

The Braddard turned abruptly to Guild. "These are your people!" he shouted. "How can you just stand by and watch them be slaughtered?" He struggled uselessly against the ropes with which Guild had him tied. Guild watched him impassively for a moment from his saddle.

"Twelve of 'my people' attacked me in the desert. I would have died had the Lord of the Hunt and his hounds not saved me in the tundra. If it was the desert that had been invaded, I would have fought to the death to protect my home. But you came here to slaughter the nomads. You brought this upon yourselves and I spare no pity for you, or them." Guild indicated the now screaming crowd of wounded that were trying desperately to fight the wolves.

"You bastard!" the Braddard screamed before erupting into a series of Ottalan expletives.

"You can be very cold," Inna noted, not without admiration.

Guild shrugged. "So can the tundra," he replied as the screaming subsided.

Inna turned back. The tent had been toppled, and the area around it was covered in blood and gore. Inna was surprised at his detachment as a tundra wolf faced down the last remaining member of the Ottalan wounded.

* * * *

Millen could not control his trembling as the massive predator padded closer to him, teeth bared in an ugly snarl. His eyes watered at the sight of the demonic dog before him. He could not help but squeeze them shut and curl into himself as the wolf leapt at him.

The blow never landed. Millen heard a yelp and then growls and snarls. He opened one eye to see two of the massive wolves embroiled in a vicious battle. The other wolves had stopped feeding to watch with keen interest.

The fight seemed to last a long time before the victor finally threw the other to the ground. Instead of crushing the opponent's throat, the wolf growled down at the loser, who whimpered in return. Apparently satisfied, the victor turned to face Millen and sat down, staring at the Ottalan invader with knowing, green eyes.

* * * *

"Stay here," Ur murmured.

"Yes, master," Inna grumbled back as the sightless boy guided his enormous black tundra horse down the slope. Ur ignored him.

It was not long before Ur pulled his horse up beside the Winter Wolf. He spent a moment observing the Ottalan with sightless eye sockets.

"He is just a boy," Ur murmured to the Winter Wolf. The wolf looked momentarily at Ur before turning back to the soldier.

"What is your name?" Ur asked him kindly.

"M-m-m-millen, my Lord."

"Millen," Ur repeated. The terrified soldier nodded.

"Millen, I am called Ur. I was once a member of the Ice Bear Clan. That clan exists now only in one man. It was destroyed by Ottal invasions. I am now Shaman of the Winter Wolf. This is the Winter Wolf."

Millen's eyes fell to the enormous wolf, which remained motionless, staring at him.

"Do not be afraid. She saved you today from the jaws of her children. Do you know why?"

Millen shook his head.

"Because you did not fight against us. You understand, Millen, that the desert-dwellers would not be our enemy if they had simply left us alone. Now they've started a war and we have no choice but to fight, or else perish. But you, Millen, you have a choice. How will you choose? Will you fight for them? Or will you fight for us?"

"I just want to go home," Millen said, suddenly breaking down. The sobs that wracked his body forced him to the ground where he curled into a ball, weeping. Ur sighed. The Winter Wolf whined and moved forward.

Taking pity on the child curled on the ground, she licked him tenderly. It sent the boy into hysterics until her tender intent became clear. Millen's sobs slowly subsided and he uncurled. At last in control, he looked up at the Winter Wolf and found that her eyes were not the eerie cold eyes of a predator, but the warm, sparking eyes of a person. Millen tentatively reached up to stroke the muzzle of the wolf before him. Evidently pleased, the Winter Wolf's tongue lolled happily out of her mouth as it split into a smile. Millen smiled.

"You are young," Ur sighed.

The Winter Wolf turned back to look at Ur. Ur laughed suddenly.

"All right," he agreed. "We can keep him." He turned to Millen. "Otsana likes you," he noted. "And she has agreed to take you to the edge of the desert once this war is over. She even said you don't have to fight at all."

"I never wanted to fight," Millen replied. "They told me I had to, or I would go to hell."

Ur shook his head, but did not comment on it. "Can you walk, Millen?"

Millen shook his head. "I hurt my knee during the attack. I think it's broken."

The Winter Wolf whined and lay down, presenting her back to Millen. Millen frowned and looked to Ur for explanation.

"Get on her back," Ur said. "She will carry you to our camp."

Uncertain, Millen threw one leg over the Winter Wolf's side and buried his hand in her ruff, grabbing a firm hold of it. The Winter Wolf scrambled to her feet. Millen's shattered knee dragged on the ground a moment and he cried out.

"Sorry," Ur muttered. Together they walked carefully back to the crest of the hill, where the rest waited, Ur on his tundra horse, and Millen on the back of the Winter Wolf.

Inna scowled when he caught sight of the young soldier on the Winter Wolf's back. The wolf looked at him innocently and even went so far as to deliver a firm lick to Inna's face as she passed. Inna burst out laughing.

"Cheeky wretch," he muttered. Guild laughed as the group followed the Winter Wolf back down the slope to the camp while at their backs the hungry wolves fed.

Later that night, Millen found himself curled up against the Winter Wolf's belly, while Ur curled happily at her throat. Though Millen was several years older than Ur, he was still a child and the comfort the Winter Wolf provided ensured that the traumatised boy slept with a smile on his face.

Guild could not help but smile himself as he noted the two children curled against the enormous wolf. Before he dragged his captive into the pavilion he shared with Inna, he turned to the Braddard. "You see," he said. "She loves her children."

"Bastard," the Braddard spat back.

Guild laughed and, gagging the Braddard, turned in to sleep.

Inna rumbled sleepy laughter as well. "Don't worry, desert man," he mumbled. "She doesn't love you."

Guild laughed again, then promptly fell asleep, Inna following shortly thereafter. In the darkness, the Braddard struggled and plotted.

* * * *

"You awake?" the cheeky female voice asked for the third time.

Algar groaned and rolled over. His eyes fluttered open only to find the bright orange gaze of an osprey who sat on his pillow, its face inches away from his own. He woke with a start and jumped from the bed. He had tried to scream, but his voice refused to work. The osprey chuckled at him and turned to preen her wings a moment.

"*You*!" Algar hissed.

"It's about time you woke," the osprey said to him, though her beak did not move. The bright eyes of the bird of prey were fixed on him and they sparkled with impish mirth.

"Do you delight in scaring the ghost out of men?"

The osprey shrugged. "You should have seen your face!" she said with a chuckle. "I'd do it all over again just to see that!"

"What do you want, bird?"

"Well, I happened to be flying overhead last week, when I accidentally caught some of the conversation you were having with your father."

Algar's eyes narrowed. "You just happened to be flying overhead."

"Well, I was curious as to how your army was coping with the sudden appearance of the Lord of the Hunt and Blue Ghost. Realising such beings do exist can be quite shattering, or so I'm told."

"Do they exist?"

The osprey snorted. "If not, then I've had a lot of conversations with a nothing."

"A nothing?"

"The Lord of the Hunt is also King of the Dead and Master of the Wilds. I'm, in effect, dead. I've spoken to him often."

"I see."

"Do you, I wonder?"

"Not really. Why are you here?"

"I told you, I overheard your conversation with your father."

"And?"

"And I'd like to help."

"Oh? How?"

"You're going to need allies."

"Are we? I just figured we would return to Misoua after this war is over and announce our revocation of the treaty."

"And incite another war."

"There won't be enough of anyone's armies left to start another war."

"If you like."

Algar scowled. "I don't like that tone."

"Which tone is that?"

"The one you're using."

"The tone that implies I know something that you don't? That tone?"

"Yes," Algar grated. "That tone."

The osprey said nothing at that and began to preen again. There was a long, uncomfortable silence before Algar sighed.

"Why are you still here?" he asked.

"I was just waiting for you to think your plan through and notice its idiocy."

"Mind your manners, bird, or I'll stick you with my knife."

The osprey shrugged. "What do I care? I'm already dead."

"Clearly you're not."

"How is that clear?"

"You're sitting before me and talking to me."

"And?"

"And the dead don't talk."

"Obviously."

"Damn you, bird! Say your piece and be gone! I want to sleep."

The osprey glared at him for a moment before blinking and shifting her weight. "The moment you announce your break from the Touan Federation, the preparations for battle will begin anew. You will be a tiny kingdom, squashed between the Greyls on one side and the entire might of the Touan Federation on the other."

"Yes."

The Osprey narrowed her eyes at him. "I can't believe you are this thick," she muttered. With a sigh, she tried another tack. "The Greyl Kingdoms are all independent states. They are not bound to one another by any obligatory contract. They are free to trade with one another and to kingdoms outside of Greyl territory. No one central ruling power hold sway over all the Greyl Kingdoms."

"All right."

"Do you actually possess a functioning brain?"

"It's three hours until dawn. I'm supposed to be asleep right now. Don't make too many demands on my brain."

The osprey glowered at Algar.

"Make friends with the Greyls and the Sierrans," she snapped, turning each word into its own sentence for emphasis. "Then the Touan Federation will think twice before marching on your borders."

"And how do you propose we do that?" Algar snapped back. "We're in the middle of a war with them."

"Yes, fighting for the very people you intend to reject."

Algar sighed. "So? We'll deal with one thing at a time."

"As you like. Though, think on this Algar Touan, if the Touan Federation is broken in this war, how likely is it that they will attack your independent kingdom of Misoua? Them losing this war will benefit your cause as well as ours."

Algar grunted. It was true.

"Well then, you blundering oaf, I have to go," the osprey said, stretching her wings. "Try and use the mind I know is buried in that skull somewhere."

Algar glared balefully at the bird as she flapped her wings and was airborne, darting from his tent like an arrow. Algar grumbled angrily, then shuffled back into his bed.

* * * *

"Well?" the Lord of the Hunt asked as the osprey landed gently on his broad shoulder.

"He's thicker than a boulder," the osprey replied. "But I might have gotten through to him."

Twenty-Three

$\mathcal{U}$r was extremely pleased to watch the Ayals return with a large prize of horses, weapons and supplies, all stolen from the Ottalan supply trains. He was not concerned when he noted that the Lord of the Hunt had not returned, though the Winter Wolf growled low when she noticed.

"Don't worry, Otsana," Ur murmured gently to her as an Ayal approached.

"My Lady Otsana," the Ayal said with a smile. "We bring gifts for the soldiers."

"Otsana wishes to know where your lord is," Ur said as the wolf twitched her tail in impatience.

"He has gone south to aid Blue Ghost against the approaching Touan army," the Ayal replied. "He has commanded the Ayals to remain here with you."

The wolf grumbled a little, but was apparently satisfied. She turned her attention to the activity that the arrival of the stolen goods had spurred. The warriors were laughing as they unloaded everything.

"The horses are not good for this terrain," the Ayal said. "But would serve well to feed the wolves."

Ur nodded. "Indeed." Ur turned around to find the Winter Wolf thoroughly distracted by Millen, who was scratching her ears. "Otsana," Ur sighed. "Do concentrate."

The wolf replied with a muffled grumble and Ur laughed.

"I was telling Otsana," Millen said. "That the army is moving very slowly. We'd been on our own only two days when you arrived."

"That won't do," Ur said with a scowl. He looked at Otsana a moment, who gazed at him in return. Those present, including Guild and Inna, could only guess their private conversation.

At length, Ur nodded. "Very well." He turned back to the waiting Ayal. "Otsana will send the wolves to them and hurry them up. Their haste may yet leave more broken horses behind them. They will not reach the stronghold in good condition. She asks that the Ayals join."

The Ayal grinned. "We will represent the Black Hounds in this hunt," he said.

Ur nodded. "That is well."

The Ayal nodded respectfully to Ur and to the Winter Wolf and left to inform the rest of the Ayals. The Winter Wolf stood and howled, calling the wolves to her. She turned and loped west, the various packs of wolves and hounds in tow. The hunt had begun.

* * * *

"Did you hear that?" an Ottalan soldier asked his comrade. The Guild Master overheard and turned to reprimand him. Instead, he caught sight of the wolves and hounds as they loped across the rocky plain.

"Archers!" Guild Master Mtsusa screamed. The army halted and turned, the archers readying their weapons. It was too late. The wolves were too close and coming too quickly for the army to prepare. The horses went wild, screaming and fighting their riders. Many broke free and bolted. Some had become used to the terrain and found good footing. Others did not and broke their legs in the panic. Riders everywhere were thrown from their saddles.

It was absolute mayhem when the wolves struck. The Guild Master need not have issued the order to retreat. The army was fleeing regardless, shooting arrows behind them as they did so. The Guild Master turned his panicking horse and bolted forward. It was a mistake. Not two strides into the run, the Guild Master's horse slipped and toppled, screaming as its knee shattered.

Mtsusa toppled violently from his saddle. He tumbled across the tundra before skidding to a halt at the heels of his fleeing army. When he looked up, his dark eyes met the knowing green eyes of a wolf the size of a pony. The wolf did not attack - indeed the attack was over - and wolves and hounds of all sizes happily fed on the dead that lay sprawled around them.

The Guild Master stood slowly, his eyes never leaving the massive Winter Wolf before him. The wolf's ears flattened and she bared her teeth at him, issuing a vicious snarl. Terrified, the Guild Master turned and ran, stumbling and falling several times in an effort to catch up with the rest of his army.

The army, once he found it, was in utter disarray. It had shrunken considerably, and the exhausted men and exhausted horses milled around in dazed confusion. It took them a while to notice their commander, bleeding and bruised from his fall standing at their edge. The army fell silent as all eyes turned to him.

The Guild Master did not like what he saw in the eyes of his men. They were empty. The men were cold and tired. They had no hope of victory in them. They were broken. The thought roused the Guild Master from his shock. He straightened.

"We are not defeated!" he bellowed. "We still stand! Let the tundra summon her army of hell-hounds and we will teach her the might of the desert!"

Perhaps it was the adrenaline that coursed through the blood of the men that made it so easy for their commander to rouse them. They raised their weapons and shouted in response.

"We will not be caught by surprise again!" Mtsusa bellowed.

The army roared.

"So let her come! Let her face slaughter!"

The roar was deafening. Men were laughing hysterically, even as tears streamed down their faces. They smiled and danced and praised their god. They grinned at their commander as he walked forward to take his place once more at the head of the army. There were several spare horses now. He chose one to ride. Singing and dancing, the Ottalan army resumed its march west, with a new, mad resolve.

* * * *

"That was unexpected," the osprey said from her perch on the King of the Dead's shoulder. The god sat astride an ancient breed of tundra horse, watching the Ottalan army from a safe distance.

"I don't think we gave the desert-dwellers enough credit."

The god shrugged, earning an irritated squawk from the osprey as she flapped frantically in an effort to keep her perch. "It was a clever move," he said. "The army is now almost half its original size. The Touans will not be getting the relief they hoped for at the siege of the stronghold, and they will have a sizeable and well-rested army at their backs."

"Well, let's hope their fanaticism does not lend them too much strength."

"Let us hope."

* * * *

"Bastards! Villains! Vile, pustule-sucking vultures!"

"Oooh, that was a good one," Bull told Inna as their captured Ottalan Braddard spouted curse after increasingly imaginative curse. Inna burst out laughing.

They passed the field where the wolves had attacked and slaughtered a large number of Ottalan soldiers earlier that morning. The Braddard dissolved into his cussing as soon as he saw the blood soaked ground and torn pieces of Ottalan armour, picked clean by a large murder of squawking crows. He had not let up since.

The Winter Wolf stalked forward with her head level with her shoulders and her ears laid flat. She growled low in irritation and Ur was worried she might turn around and silence the Braddard permanently with a snap of her powerful jaws. As if reading Ur's mind, the Winter Wolf turned her massive head and gave Ur a flat stare. Ur sighed and turned back to Guild.

"Guild, can you not muzzle that yapping?" Ur asked wearily.

Guild shrugged. "He should lose his voice before long, Shaman."

"If he does not he might lose his life. Otsana is growing weary of his foul tongue."

Guild sighed and warned the Braddard in Ottalan.

"Good!" the Braddard screeched. "Then kill me! KILL ME!"

Without warning and with lightning speed, the Winter Wolf spun around and closed her jaws around the man's torso, squeezing just hard enough to hurt. He screamed and lost control of his bladder. The Winter Wolf released him and, with a disgusted snort, turned back to lope ahead of the army.

"You big baby," Guild muttered as the Braddard broke down and started blubbering.

"I think he's gone insane," Inna remarked mildly from Guild's right.

Bull turned back and observed the Braddard. "You might be right, Ice Bear," he noted before facing forward again. His lips split into a wide grin.

"Enjoying yourself, war chief of the Ouruq Clan?" Ur asked.

"I am indeed. How much farther to the false cave, do you think?"

"Well, if we were going at a better pace, it would be roughly a week. Trailing the Ottals as we must, perhaps three."

Bull sighed. "I just want to get this over with."

"We all do, Bull," Inna grunted.

"Gods let us get there soon."

"Stop complaining," Ur said.

"Yes, Master," Guild, Inna and Bull intoned together, before breaking out into laughter.

Ur sighed. "And you call me the child!"

* * * *

Algar observed his father's face as he relayed the conversation he had with the osprey a week ago. It was the first opportunity that Algar had to speak to Roger in private since then.

"You're certain you weren't dreaming?"

"Damn it, Father!" Algar snapped, rising from his field chair with considerable force. The chair toppled to the ground as if in protest. "You were there that time the damnable bird spoke to me after the camp caught fire! You know full well I wasn't dreaming."

Roger sighed. "I don't know anything anymore," he muttered darkly.

"In any case, she's right, isn't she?" Algar said with a grunt.

"Seems likely. It's true that a small kingdom like ours cannot stand alone against the entire Touan Federation, war-weary or otherwise."

"So, we have to seek out some way to contact the Greyls."

"As one who is both a prince of a very powerful kingdom and married to a Sierran woman, it is Bran we should be seeking out."

"Just how do you propose to do that? We have to somehow get past the entire Touan army, then find the man and then what? What would we say? 'Hi, we've just spent the last few months trying to kill you, but now we want to be friends.'"

"Mind your tone."

Algar picked up his chair and sat back down. His head hung despondently and his eyes closed in thought.

"Have you thought about it Algar Touan?" a familiar voice said. Algar's head snapped up in surprise. He swore profusely.

The owner of the voice was not an osprey, but an elderly woman, with a wide, round face and nut brown skin. Her eyes were angular and sparkling green. Bestial fetishes tied to the rim of the hood of the feathered cloak she wore. Her grey hair was loose around her face and the corners of her full lips turned upwards in an impish smile. Algar could see that she must have been a stunning woman in her youth. He stared at her with wide eyes in incredulous silence.

"Don't worry," she said as she settled herself on the rug-strewn floor of the royal tent of Misoua. "Blue Ghost has sent a fog so thick none can see past their own noses. No one saw me enter, though they wouldn't pay much mind to a stray bird in any case."

"You're not a bird," Algar said.

The woman raised one brow and pursed her lips in distaste. "Well, not now you dolt."

She employed a tone usually used when speaking to a very young child. Algar took offence. He crossed his arms in front of his chest and glowered at the woman who smiled placidly in return.

"I can see that," Algar grated.

"I was when I came in."

Algar scowled. "Not possible."

"My dear, I died many winters ago, yet here I am. Nothing is 'not possible'."

Algar remained frostily silent and his father gaped at the old woman in mute astonishment. She looked back and forth between the two for a moment.

"Well, King of Misoua, are your nobles behind you in your break for independence?"

Roger's mouth slowly shut. "Most," he managed to utter. She raised an eyebrow.

"And those that aren't?"

"They don't know anything. There are one or two that believe in the Touan Federation with everything they have."

"They will need to be replaced."

"Thank you," Roger replied with heavy sarcasm. "I was aware of that."

The woman flashed him a quick grin. "I just wanted to make sure. You are, after all, that dolt's father and intelligence, or lack thereof, flows in the blood."

Algar snorted. "Hag."

The woman shrugged.

"We have sons of aligned nobles who are eager for land of their own."

"Of course you do."

"You disapprove?" Algar asked. The old woman shrugged again.

"To think that land could belong to anyone, let alone one family, is not right. But I won't complain. In this case, the desire to own it works well in our favour. Now, as far as communication goes, I'd like to offer my services."

"Your services?"

"Yes. I know who and where everyone is at the moment. If there is a message you need sent to someone at all, I can do it."

Algar smiled a little. "Well, that solves that problem."

Roger grunted. He eyed the woman over. She arched her brow at him.

"How do you propose to do that?" Roger demanded at last.

"Fly," the woman said with a smile.

Roger scoffed. She remained unfazed.

"Do you know where Prince Bran of the Baveii is at present?"

"Yes."

"Where?"

"Not your concern is it?"

"Look we're allies in this –"

"Neither tested nor proved."

"Fine. Look, could you just tell him he has friends in the Touan army and we need to know what to do to be helpful."

"In exchange for protection against the Federation, yes?"

"Yes."

"Good then. I'll leave you gentlemen to sleep. Sweet dreams." The woman vanished and in her place on the ground stood a speckled osprey.

Algar and Roger stared. The bird winked cheekily at them, then took to the air, darting out of the tent in an instant. Algar and Roger exchanged a long look.

"Well," Roger said at last. "I'm going to bed."

"Me too."

* * * *

"Have the rangers anything to report?" the King of the Baveii and war-leader elect asked. The man before him shrugged.

"There isn't much out there but ice and the start of grass," the man replied. He was wearing a pale green and grey cloak, speckled to look like a rock covered in lichen. One of the Pamisii rangers, he was once a nobleman but bore none of the refinements that came with the blood. The man looked as ragged and rough as the lands he traversed.

"Wolves are drifting north. Not in itself a cause for concern but for the numbers."

"Oh?"

"Wolves normally follow the herds. This time of year the herds are all heading north to the tundra grasses and the wolves go with them. However, several packs, larger in size than any normal wolf pack, are now several days ahead of the herds. And they're noisy."

"And?"

"Wolves rarely howl, despite what people will tell you. Now they're howling every half day and they're being answered by other wolf packs."

"Which means?"

"I don't know, but it's not natural."

Bran smiled softly to himself, but remained silent.

"Anything else?" Gofron asked.

The scout shrugged. That was taken to mean 'no' and the scout was dismissed. The King cast his youngest son a sidelong looks.

"Wolves, huh?"

"The Sierrans believe that Otsana is the Winter Wolf incarnate. She has called her children and they are answering."

"So you believe she is?"

Bran shrugged. Gofron shook his head, then stretched. His first wife smiled a little and shook her head in kindly reproach. Stretching on a throne during a meeting was less than kingly behaviour.

"Is there anything else to report?"

The war room was silent and the King grunted. "Engineer's report?"

An engineer stood and, after an awkward bow, began his report. "The walls all almost dry and the ballasts, trebuchets and catapults are all in place. As of now we're just making ammunition and weapons and trying to find the weakest spots to strengthen.

"Good. Is there nothing else? No more reports? Anything?"

The war room fell into silence once again.

"I never thought I'd say this, but I'd give my right arm for another report. All this waiting with nothing to do is starting to wear on me."

A few of the members of the war council chuckled their agreement.

"I have something."

The voice was an unknown, feminine voice with a thick accent and a touch of mischief colouring the tone. All eyes turned to the back of the war room where, quite unnoticed before then, stood an old Sierran woman in a feathered cloak.

"Who are you and how the blazes did you get in here?" Gofron blustered.

"Never you mind that. I have something to tell Bran."

Bran's eyebrows rose. "Oh?"

"Well? Do you want to hear it or don't you?"

"I do."

"Oh good." The woman looked Bran over a moment. He waited in silence, his face revealing nothing but slight amusement. She smiled suddenly, a flash of dazzling white that matched her impishly twinkling eyes. "As it happens, you have friends in the approaching Touan army."

"We do?"

"Oh yes, but there's a price."

"Of course there is."

The woman smiled again. "They request the help of the Greyls after this war is won in their endeavour to break free from the Touan Federation."

Bran's eyebrows shot up and there was a collective intake of breath from the gathered war council.

"That Federation is a thousand years old!" Bran exclaimed.

"Yes. The current king of Misoua is tired of being ordered about by the Wetouan Council and, by extension, the Holy Council of the Yellow City. He wants to gain independence for his kingdom. Of course, any sort of break with the Federation is likely to incite another war. King Roger of Misoua would like your assurances that should such a conflict arise, you will come to his aid."

"I cannot speak on behalf of all the Greyl Kingdoms," Bran said. "Not even my own. That decision rests with its king."

The woman turned to look at the Baveii king, her green eyes keen and sparkling. The man stared at her in disbelief.

"Well?" she demanded after a moment of silence.

"How does he intend to aid us?" Gofron demanded.

"He has a sizeable army of his own, as one might expect of a kingdom that borders a land of raiders."

Gofron grunted dismissively.

The woman smiled. "That army marches now with the Touan host. They will be right in their midst when the battle starts. A fine place to turn, is it not?"

Bran looked at his father. The King was deep in thought.

"How do I know this is not some kind of trick?" Gofron asked.

The woman looked genuinely insulted. "It's not a trick!"

"Perhaps not on your part. What if the king of Misoua is tricking you?"

"Hah!" the woman crowed. "That would never happen. I can smell a lie a thousand yards off. Besides, he's not bright enough for that."

"I'm sure."

"Mind your tone." The woman's voice was crisp and sharp and the King of the Baveii allowed a small laugh at himself; it made him feel like a chastised child.

"It's a valid concern," Bran agreed. The woman glared at him a moment before her gaze softened and she sighed. "Oh well," she murmured. "At least I know I'm not dealing with imbeciles." She turned her attention back to the King. "I swear that this is not trickery, as I believe it."

"Why wouldn't it be?" Gofron asked. "The Touans are capable of any breech of honour."

"King Roger lost a son to this war," Lord Kildurrow noted. He had remained largely quiet through the whole meeting, his mind on other matters.

The King could tell that he was troubled, but did not press the issue. Lord Kildurrow was a profoundly reserved man, and the loss of his own child still weighted heavily upon him. When he wanted to talk, Gofron would listen. Until then there was nothing that he could do for Lord Kildurrow.

"The night I spoke to him, his eldest mentioned Prince Alam's reluctance to fight this war. I have learned since that they had extended an offer of trade to the Osprey Clan of the tundra. Then the war broke out and it was retracted."

Gofron grunted. "Then why would he risk more sons in an attempt to break free from the Touan Federation?"

"Because," the woman said patiently, cutting Lord Kildurrow off before he could answer. "Then his sons can choose the causes they fight and die for, rather than die for a cause not their own. That is Roger Touan's motivation."

Gofron eyed the woman over again. "I don't know if I trust him. Or you, for that matter. Who are you?"

The woman smiled. "When I was alive, they called me Asi. You may call me Asi also, if you like."

"When you were alive."

The woman smiled. "That's right."

"So, what are you now?"

"Not alive."

The King scowled. Asi ignored him. Instead, she turned her gaze to Bran and addressed him.

"My granddaughter is not far from this false cave. She is chasing what remains of the army of the desert here. They themselves believe they are chasing what remains of the Sierran warriors here, as planned."

Bran's jaw dropped. "Your granddaughter?"

"Yes."

"Otsana? You're Otsana's *grandmother*?"

"Yes."

"That's impossible! She died years ago."

"Did I just not say that.... Oh, never mind! You're almost as dense as that Algar Touan. Now, will you aid the kingdom of Misoua if they aid you?"

Bran turned to his father, who had now turned quite pale. The King stared at the feathered woman with an expression that was caught between disbelief and bewilderment.

"Father?" Bran prompted.

Gofron shook himself, bringing his mind back to the current proposal. "I do not speak for all of the Greyl Kingdoms," he said gravely. "Even as war leader elect. That said, the Baveii pledge to assist the Misouans should they aid the Greyls in the forthcoming siege."

Bran smiled and turned back to the woman, who now stared at the King of the Pamisii with a raised eyebrow.

"Grandmother of the Winter Wolf," the King greeted formally.

The woman chuckled. "No need to be so formal, King of the Pamisii. I am just an old woman, not worth much to anyone."

The King smiled. "I believe all ancestors are venerated by the Sierran nomads, are they not?"

"The ones that are remembered are."

"Then I must treat you with great reverence, for only an ancestor remembered may return to the world of the living."

The woman smiled. "You know a great deal about Sierran beliefs, King of the Pamisii."

"Our kingdom borders the tundra. Perhaps that is why we were slowest to forget the bonds of kinship and the traditions of our forefathers."

"Blue Ghost has taught you well, I see."

"He has been the most visible spirit to the Pamisii," the King agreed.

"Then may the King of Misoua count on your aid in the forthcoming split from the Touan Federation?"

"You personally vouch for them?"

"I do."

"Then, yes. I pledge on behalf of the Pamisii that we will aid the kingdom of Misoua when they decide to extricate themselves from the Touan Federation."

Bran snorted. "You talk too much," he noted mildly when the King shot him a disgruntled look. The King of the Pamisii scowled and the woman laughed brightly.

"You have spent far too much time in the tundra, Southern Crow," she said with a broad smile.

Bran shrugged and the woman turned her attention to the rest of the rulers of the Greyl kingdoms. One by one with nary a question between them, they agreed that they would aid the Misouan kingdom against the Touan Federation.

When all the pledges were made, Asi nodded curtly.

"This is good," she said. "I shall inform them at once."

"They are still a fortnight or so away."

"Only three days as the osprey flies," Asi quipped.

No one had a chance to ask how that was relevant. In an instant the woman shrank and changed until in her place stood a speckled osprey. The bird chirped at the astonished onlookers in a manner that was suspiciously like laughter before taking to the air and darting out of the window.

"So," the King of the Pamisii noted, seemingly not disturbed at all. "That's how she got in."

Gofron turned to him and stared incredulously.

Twenty-Four

The entire Touan army had been on the run for two days without rest. At dusk two days ago, there had been an attack on their camp. It came from nowhere. The air had turned suddenly cold and all sounds ceased. There was no birdsong, no creak of wood or rustle of leaves. There was nothing.

One of the sentries spotted Blue Ghost, drifting in perfect silence between the thick trunks of the trees. Then the wind blew fiercely, sending to the nostrils of the Touans all the scents of the forest – the smell of thawing soil and rotting leaves, the fresh clean scent of new growth, the warm, comforting perfume of rich black earth and the crisp scent of ice that had not yet melted. It was a potent mix of aromas which created varied responses in the men who sensed it.

Many men, who were raised behind walls surrounded by finely kept gardens, were terrified of the wilds and the very smell of it sent them into a panic. They gripped their weapons in wide-eyed terror as the wind strengthened and then died away,

Blue Ghost, glowing faintly in the dying light, stopped in full view of the entire encampment.

Algar was not afraid of the wilds, but the sight of Blue Ghost terrified him. Blue Ghost appeared as a young man in fine form and completely naked.

Yet with every movement, beneath the skin of the young man, Algar would catch sight of an old man, bearded in white and withered with age, whose sunken green eyes spoke of a knowledge well beyond any mortal's reach. Those baleful green eyes of the old man pierced all, and when they landed upon Algar, the Prince's heart skipped several beats, his pulse pounding in his ears.

"Gods," he whispered.

Blue Ghost turned away and stared into the soul of the Yellow Robe who stood bravely, though somewhat diminished before the spirit of the woods.

"You," Blue Ghost said. The words were not so much uttered as understood and the sounds that reached the ears of the Touans were akin to the dry rasping hiss of leaves in the wind. "You should not be here. Turn aside. Go home."

"Our purpose is righteous," the Yellow Robe squeaked in reply. "The god of the Yellow City has sent us here to purge this land of false gods."

Blue Ghost had cocked his head and almost smiled at that. "Your god holds no power here," the spirit rasped. "We are the power in this land."

"We?"

"The trees. The wilds," Algar answered in a whisper. A slow turn in Algar's direction told him that Blue Ghost had heard him. The look Algar received was something like kindly interest.

"How did he hear?" Roger whispered tersely.

"The trees," Algar whispered in return.

Blue Ghost turned back to the Yellow Robe. "Turn aside and we will spare you."

"We are righteous!" the Yellow Robe bellowed in a moment of inspired courage.

"As you like," Blue Ghost rasped.

"Archers!" the Yellow Robe screamed. In an instant, arrows were loosed on the figure glowing faintly blue before the army. Not a single arrow found its mark. Blue Ghost simply stepped between them as if he were dancing.

"So be it," Blue Ghost whispered before he faded from sight. There was a moment of silent calm before the attack started. A single horn blasted through the woods and Algar turned to see the Lord of the Hunt, sitting on his massive black tundra horse, surrounded by an army of giant Black Hounds. When the blast from his horn ended, the dogs lurched forward in one great sea of rippling muscle and snapping jaws.

Bullroarers sounded from the trees and arrows rained down on the army from every conceivable angle, yet no attacker could be seen. Panicked, the army fled, the snarling dogs at their heels as they mounted their horses and rode west.

The Lord of the Hunt called off his hounds after a few hours and Algar turned back to see them milling about the Lord of the Hunt's ankles at the crest of a hill. The running had not stopped, however, and the army fled still.

At dusk on the second day, the army slowed and stopped. Now they sat in sullen silence around hearths that contained no fire, eating hard bread and dried meat for they had left their supplies behind them.

Algar sat by his father in the open meeting area that should have been the war tent, had they brought it with them. The war council was in an uproar.

Kings and their vassals were shouting at each other, some desiring nothing more than to return home to a safe bed and a warm meal. Others, so desperately afraid that they clung tightly onto their faith, began ranting like lunatics about blasphemy and the will of the god of the Yellow City.

Algar and Roger Remained silent, as did the Yellow Robe. All three observed the war of words that erupted. Only when physical violence threaten did the Yellow Robe act. He rose to his feet in silence. His movement was enough to hush the fighting of the war council.

"My friends," the Yellow Robe said calmly. "I understand the sentiments of all members of the war council. Indeed, I admit that I was deeply disturbed by the appearance of the so-called Blue Ghost in the woods two days past. However, upon reflection, I now see that it was simply a trick."

"Tell me what trick makes a man glow blue!" one lord demanded angrily. The Yellow Robe put up his hand to silence him.

"The trick of the mind," he answered benignly. "Terror can play games with our minds, and our minds in turn play games with our senses."

There was a great deal of agreement and disagreement from the gathered crowd.

"The Greyls know this well," the Yellow Robe continued. "They have used it to their advantage."

"By making a man glow blue?" another lord asked in a hard tone.

The Yellow Robe smiled. "All who know the properties of light will know that he was not glowing blue."

"Sure as hell looked like it to me!"

"Ah, but what colour is the last to fade at sunset?" the Yellow Robe asked. "When we cast our gaze far across the horizon and see the white caps of the mountains that border our two lands, does it not seem like they are glowing? When we spy exposed chalk or quartz upon the ground at last light, does it not appear as if they are giving light of their own?"

The crowd fell silent as many a lord sank into thought.

"You see?" the Yellow Robe continued. "That boy was no more than a Pamisii ranger, painted pale blue so as to fool us into believing he was the spirit they call Blue Ghost. So pale was his paint that it too, like the snowy caps of the snowy ranges, and the chalk and quartz, held onto the sun's last breath and only appeared to glow. They used our terror against us."

The silence was now deafening.

"Our great shame, my Lords, is that we lost faith in the god of the Yellow City, and we allowed their gimmicks to frighten us." The Yellow Robe looked over the faces of the gathered war council. Many were indeed wearing expressions of shame. Others, like the King of Misoua and his son, remained stony and unreadable.

"It will not happen again," the Yellow Robe whispered. "We will march to our enemies with our heads held high and when at last we meet them on the field, we shall be victorious, for we engage them with all the force of our faith and all the might of our righteousness."

King Roger looked about him as his fellows began to sit straighter and resolve tightened their features. Some of his own lords, those whom he knew he could not trust, were among them.

"Sleep now, my children," the Yellow Robe said with a smile. "We shall rest safe in the warm glow of our god and when we wake, we shall find ourselves lighter in our purpose."

With nothing else to say, the Yellow Robe retired from the circle and the war council disbanded for the evening.

"Well, he is a master orator," Algar muttered darkly to his father as they walked slowly back to their quarter.

"That he is. I'm almost prepared to die for the cause," Roger replied with a small smile.

"It worked," Algar grumbled. "We're still marching west until we come to the Greyl host."

"Aye, and be thankful for that. We won't have Greyl support unless we help them. We can't help them if it turns out that there will be no battle. Misoua will be stuck in the Federation forever, chained to its every whim."

Algar grunted. He turned away from his father's conversation only to spy the Lord of the Hunt sitting quietly on his horse and surrounded by three Black Hounds.

So still was this deity of the Greyls and Sierrans that, had Algar not possessed keen sight, he'd have overlooked them entirely. The Lord of the Hunt seemed to be looking intently at Algar, though Algar could not see his eyes for the stag skull helm.

"Well," Roger said, happily oblivious. "I'm going to bed. Good night."

"Good night."

Roger was far too tired to note the distance in Algar's tone. He crawled beneath his horse blanket, the only blanket he had left after the army abandoned their camp in haste, and promptly fell asleep.

Algar did not go to sleep. He walked towards the Lord of the Hunt. The god gave Algar a curt nod and turned his horse. Horse and rider vanished into the woods. Certain that the Lord of the Hunt meant for him to follow, Algar walked on, well aware that doing so may cost him his life. He had been walking for some time before he found himself at the edge of a clearing ringed by ancient stones as tall as his waist. Standing in the centre was the old woman who could transform into an osprey and the Lord of the Hunt, still dressed in his cloak and stag skull helm.

Algar stopped at the edge of the ring. He had heard tales of such rings of stone. These rings belonged to the people of the Otherworld – Aqyn, the realm of the stag-helmed god. They were not to be entered at any cost. Both the Sierran ancestor and the Lord of the Hunt watched him expectantly.

"There is no way I'm going in," Algar told them, surprised at his own boldness.

The Lord of the Hunt smiled, but remained silent.

"Then don't," the elder woman said with a shrug. "And wonder for the rest of your life what might have happened if you did."

Algar cursed at her under his breath. They knew the weaknesses of mortals well. Curiosity was a compelling weakness indeed. Algar took a deep breath and stepped into the circle. The world outside the circle changed immediately. The forest vanished, replaced by rotting stumps as far as they eye could see. The sky was covered with smoke that rolled and undulated in sinister clouds.

To Algar's left, a sickly deer struggled past, its step faltering until it fell. It did not possess the strength to stand and simply lay until it sighed one last, ragged breath. To Algar's right, a small band of people he could immediately identify as Greyl walked the wasted land weeping. They were as emaciated as the deer. One woman carried an infant with a swollen belly and wide, uncomprehending eyes. Algar watched as the child was buried.

He glanced over at the Lord of the Hunt, who remained perfectly still.

"This is what we fear," a voice said from behind Algar. It was both young and old and which spoke with the creak of wood and rustle of. Algar jumped and spun only to see the spirit called Blue Ghost standing behind him. It was as it had been in the woods. He was a young man, yet shimmering beneath the young man's visage was an old man with white hair and unnerving eyes.

"It won't be like that," Algar replied.

"Perhaps, perhaps not. Those that lead this invasion hail from the desert, where there are no woods. They do not understand the forest, and how important we are."

"But the Greyls do," Algar said. "They will be asked to convert, but that is all."

"Is it?"

"That's how it was for the Touans. They did not destroy our lands."

"Your lands were less saturated by spirits, Lion Spear," Blue Ghost replied. "It was easy for you to forget and convert. The desert eagles are filled with rage and hate against us, and we fear they shall seek to destroy all that is sacred in these lands."

"Such are the consequences of fighting."

"Is that why you did not, when the Yellow Robes came seeking the souls of the Touan people?"

Algar shrugged. "It happened over a thousand years ago. Well before my time."

Blue Ghost observed him a moment. "Asi tells me your father wishes to break from the Federation formed from the Touan conversion."

Algar nodded. "Yes."

"The Greyl Kingdoms have agreed to aid you, Lion Spear," Asi said.

Algar turned to face her. "Provided we help them, no doubt."

"Yes."

Algar sighed and rubbed his temples. "This is my father's plan, why do you not discuss these things with him?"

"He cannot see," The Lord of the Hunt said quietly.

"He can. He saw you, on both your appearances." Algar turned to Asi and pointed his finger at her. "He saw you change into an osprey and he even saw Blue Ghost."

"Your father's ideals are admirable," the Lord of the Hunt replied. "But his mind is like that of the Yellow Robe. He does not see the Lord of the Hunt, he sees a savage dressed in the skins of a stag. He does not see Blue Ghost, he sees a young ranger painted blue. He does not see a Sierran ancestor, he sees an old woman in a feathered cloak."

"Who just happens to be able to transform into a bird."

"Ask him what he saw that night, Lion Spear," Asi said. "And he shall tell you about fog and shadows, and how war plays with the minds of the bravest men."

Algar scowled.

"How many men are with you, Lion Spear?" Blue Ghost asked.

"Almost all the lords but three, and so we're without their men also. The number comes to four thousand that will fight for us."

"They know of your plans?"

"The lords do, and they agree. I can only assume that their soldiers do also."

"Here," Blue Ghost said. He held out a clenched fist. In it was a large bundle of necklaces. They were nothing more than a simple thin leather thong on the end of which hung a single blue glass bead.

"What are they?"

"Talismans, Lion Spear. The men that fight for you should be given one to wear. All who face them shall know them as allies and they shall be safe from harm from us."

Algar reached out and took them. "Thank you."

"No, thank you Lion Spear. Though you fight for yourselves, we are nonetheless grateful for your aid."

"Tell me something Blue Ghost," Algar asked. "Why do you call me 'Lion Spear'?"

"There is one who could better answer your question," Asi said gently.

Algar turned to her only to see an enormous lion approach the stone circle across the barren wasteland that was the deepest fear of the gathered entities. Algar's throat constricted, blocking the shout of alarm that grew there. Lions were common in Bulga and there were even a few in the far eastern reaches of the Ottalan Desert, where the sands gave way to long brown grasslands before reaching the sea, but he had never once seen one.

The great maned cat padded easily into the circle and came to a halt, his yellow eyes fixed on Algar. The lion changed form and standing before Algar was a man, dressed in the skins of a lion, with a lion skull helm. He wore only trousers and boots. Blue tattoos covered his pale, freckled skin. Around his arms he wore leather bands decorated with beads and feathers and three black claws, and in his right hand, he held a tall, stone-tipped spear.

Algar stared as the man removed the helm, exposing a head of long blonde hair of almost the same colour as Algar's own.

"Hello son," the man that once was a lion said with an impish smile.

"You're not my father," Algar manage to utter.

The man laughed. "My name is Algar Touan, Chief of the Lion Clan."

"My… ancestor?"

"Yes."

"Impossible."

"If you believe so."

"You are my namesake."

The man in lion skins smiled. "No, Algar Touan of the kingdom of Misoua, you are my namesake."

Algar stared at the man before him incredulously. "I don't believe it."

"As you like. I was once a man of the tundra, but in foolishness I tried to tame her. She proved to be much too wild, much too wilful. I journeyed south with my brother in arms, Bran Greyl of the Crow Clan, when the Winter Wolf came and destroyed our homes."

"The Winter Wolf. The same Winter Wolf that has everyone in the tundra worked up at present?"

"The same. She wakes to defend the tundra once more, as it was in my day."

"Do you not hate her?"

The ancestor laughed brightly. "No indeed. It was my own foolishness that led to my exile. Indeed, in exile, I found lands much more supple and yielding. These lands allowed us to build, but I had learnt my lesson from the tundra well. Never did we build unnecessarily or wantonly.

"I brought with me knowledge of the gods, and of all the ancestors that came before me. I loved them in life as I do in death. It grieves me to know that their teachings have been cast aside in favour of a younger, more foolish god."

Algar suddenly felt ashamed. "It was convert or die."

The Chief of the Lion Clan grunted. "And now that you do not believe in the Federation? Who shall you follow then?"

Algar thought a moment. "That is for each man to decide for himself," he said at length.

The ancestor in lion skins grinned. "Then I have a gift for you, namesake."

"Oh?"

The Chief of the Lion Clan held out his stone spear. "I killed a lion with nothing but my wits and this spear. That is how I became chief of my clan. I now give this spear to you, as a symbol of our blood bond and as a symbol of kingship. You are now Chief of the Lion Clan, Algar Touan. The blood of the lion is fused with this spear. It will lend aid to he who wields it righteously."

Algar's eyes widened. "I do not know how to fight with a spear," he said. "But I accept this gift and am honoured and humbled."

"If you ask me nicely," the ancestor said with a cheeky smile. "I will teach you how." He handed Algar the spear. It was impossibly heavy for so slender a weapon.

"That is the weight of leadership," the ancestor of the Lion Clan said as Algar almost dropped it. "Honour it well, and you will find the burden less."

Algar nodded. "Thank you, Father."

"I am called away. Good luck Algar, Lion Spear. Know that the spirit of the lion walks beside you now. Trust in its strength."

Algar nodded and watched as his ancestor became a lion once more, loping away into the burning wilderness.

"Did you know that was going to happen?" Algar heard Asi ask the Lord of the Hunt.

"No," the Lord of the Hunt replied, not taking his eyes off Algar. "But I am heartened it did. There must be something in this one his father sees that we have all missed."

"We must depart," Blue Ghost said suddenly. "Dawn comes. Fare thee well, Lion Spear. Asi will come to you with news as soon as it is had."

Algar nodded. "And to you, Blue Ghost."

The glowing blue figure vanished, dissipating into fog. Asi turned once more into an osprey and flew from the clearing. Algar watched her go, wistful for a moment. It must be a remarkable thing, to fly. He turned his attention back and found that a great deer now stood in place of the Lord of the Hunt.

"Much is riding on you now, Lion Spear," the stag said without so much as moving his lips. "Fare thee well, and honour your gift." With that, the deer bounded away.

With a start Algar woke.

"Bloody strange dream," he grumbled to himself. "Father," he asked a little louder. "Could we start a fire? I'm freezing!"

There was no answer but the predawn mutterings of sleepy birds. Algar sat up abruptly, finding himself far away from camp. He looked about him in muddled confusion. He noted that he was in a clearing, surrounded by standing stones as tall as his hip. He scowled and struggled to his feet. It took him a while to realise that he had used a long, sturdy stick to help himself stand. He looked and there in his right hand was a strong, stone-tipped spear. In his left hand he clutched a bundle of four thousand necklaces, each with a single blue glass bead.

Algar's head spun and his knees buckled unexpectedly. Leaning heavily on the spear to support his boneless legs, Algar fought with himself. It was not a dream after all.

Honour your gift.

Algar looked again at the spear as bits and pieces of the night floated into his memory.

The spirit of the Lion walks beside you now. Trust in its strength.

Algar nodded. "I will not forget," he whispered.

A wind blew and rustled the leaves of the surrounding trees as if they were answering. Filled with a calm strength, Algar turned and made his quiet way back to camp in the grey of first light.

* * * *

"Do you feel that?" Ur asked Inna as Otsana paused mid-stride. Her keen eyes turned south.

"Feel what, little man?" Inna asked.

"The Lion walks again."

* * * *

"Blue Ghost?" Bluebell asked as the young ranger groggily rose to his feet. The ranger answered with a deep groan. Grunt looked over and grinned at Bluebell.

"What did you do to him this time?" he asked.

"Nothing, you oaf!" Bluebell snapped. "He couldn't be woken," she added in a dark mutter.

"Gods, my head!" the Prince of the Pamisii groaned. He staggered a few paces before Bluebell caught him and pulled him back down to the ground.

"You're not going anywhere!" she growled.

"What happened?"

"What do you mean 'what happened?' You went to bed last night, and you got up this morning. Though, you look quite ill."

The Prince glared at Bluebell before pressing hard on his temples. "Gods, my head!" he repeated.

"You didn't even drink!" Bluebell said, exasperated.

Grunt snorted. "Stay here, Blue Ghost. I'll find some lichen. We'll have that headache cured in no time."

The Prince made a face and continued to massage his head. Bluebell sighed and took over massaging the Prince's head.

"I had the strangest dream," the Prince mumbled as Bluebell's skilled fingers began to relax him.

"Do tell," Bluebell replied.

"The Master of the Wilds was there, and so was an elder osprey woman. I was there, and we were talking to someone. And then there was another man who came, but he was actually a lion, or he was a lion that was actually a man. I don't really remember. In any case, he gave the other man we were all talking to a spear. That's all I really remember. Ow!"

"Well hold still!"

"Don't press so hard!"

"I wasn't."

"You were, or it wouldn't have hurt."

"Don't be such a child."

"I can hear you two bickering all the way down to the brook!" Grunt grumbled as he trundled back to the ranger's camp. "You sound like a married couple."

Bluebell grunted. "Well, we're not. Did you get the baby's medicine?"

The Prince turned and stuck his tongue out at Bluebell.

"Promises, promises," Bluebell replied tartly.

Grunt laughed as he began to scrape a mixture of bark and lichen into a bowl.

"Light a fire would you, Bluebell?" he asked. "This is better had when warm."

The Prince pulled another face. "That stuff is revolting."

"Well, you either drink it and cure that headache, or you don't and suffer with it the rest of the day."

The Prince groaned and flopped back down on the ground.

"You and I are going for a walk when that headache's gone," Bluebell told her Prince matter-of-factly. The Prince opened one eye and observed her a moment.

"As you like," he replied, before closing his eye again.

Grunt laughed.

Twenty-Five

Algar did not ask his father what he thought of the woman who turned into an osprey right before their very eyes. He told himself that he did not need his father's opinion to be certain of what he knew, but he knew that the real reason was that he didn't want his father's reasoned explanations to destroy the magic of the memories. That magic had come to mean a great deal to him.

Roger and Algar sat at a small fire shared with their loyal lords and fellow conspirators, eating breakfast. Algar's spear leant against his shoulder. He had no intention of ever putting it down. When asked where he had acquired it, Algar disclosed only that an old friend had given it to him.

"We're relying too heavily on the Greyls," one lord was saying quietly. "We don't know their plans. How are we supposed to respond to them if we know nothing of their plans?"

"We have a contact," Algar said quietly. "She'll tell us what we need to know. Until then, we have no choice but to sit tight."

"But...."

"Leave it Basil," another lord said. He looked at Algar carefully as he spoke. "The Prince is right. There is nothing we can do until we know more."

"How can we be sure this contact is on the level?" Basil whispered.

"That reminds me," Algar said. He put down his breakfast and turned to his saddlebag. Everyone watched on with interest as he extricated a fistful of necklaces. "She gave us these. These necklaces will mark us as allies. Anyone who fights the Federation will leave us be if we're wearing these."

Basil looked at Algar cynically. "Will they?"

"Yes."

"I would expect something more... obvious."

"Anything more obvious and the Yellow Robe will suspect something. Trust me. Wear these. There is enough for one for each of you and your men. Take what you need."

Basil, though uncertain, was moved by Algar's conviction. He was the first to count out the hundreds he needed for himself and his army. Roger leant over and whispered in his son's ear, "When did she give you those?"

"Last night," Algar replied.

"And she gave you the spear?"

"No."

Algar refused to speak any more and Roger turned back to his meal with a sigh.

"I'm not plotting anything against you, Father," Algar said with a smile.

"Then why all the secrets?"

"Because I'm worried that you won't believe me."

Roger turned to his son with a frown.

"Do you remember when you told me that matters of faith were for each man to decide for themselves?"

"Yes."

"Well, I've decided."

Roger looked at his son a moment. "So, it isn't the god of the Yellow City."

Algar shook his head and Roger nodded.

"I didn't really intend on changing the faith of our kingdom."

"Then don't," Algar said with a shrug. "But allow each man to choose for himself, just as you told me to do."

Roger smiled at his son. "For all your youth, Algar, you have moments of wisdom."

Algar grinned and said, "But only moments."

* * * *

"They still follow us, General," the scout reported.

The Guild Master nodded. He did not expect the wolves to give up their trail.

"So be it," he said. "We shall leave them plenty of Sierran bodies to feast upon when this war is over. If any more horses break their legs, leave them for the wolves. That ought to keep them sated enough to avoid a second attack.

The scout bowed and exited the pavilion which Guild Master Mtsusa had converted into a meeting hall. He brushed the shoulder of another who arrived in great haste. The scout bowed. "General," he reported. "There is a large fort nestled in the mountains due west of here. It's occupied, General. It is likely that the Sierrans fled there."

The Guild Master was genuinely surprised. "I did not think the Sierrans would much abide being enclosed in stone."

"Desperate times call for desperate measures," a representative of the Holy Yellow City noted dispassionately. "We knew they were allied with the Greyls. Perhaps this is where both have chosen to make their final stand."

"We are not equipped for a siege."

"No, but we can be. You have engineers in this army, General. I suggest you use them."

"There is a forest a fortnight from the walls of the fortress," the scout said. "We'd have wood enough to build siege engines."

"And what of stone?"

"There is enough rock in this damnable tundra to sate even the hungriest of trebuchets," the representative of the Yellow City noted.

The Guild Master grunted. "And supplies?"

"More will be coming in from the desert. In the meantime, I'm certain that the Touans will happily share what they have." The representative of the Yellow City looked positively bored. "We will be victorious."

The Guild Master nodded. "Good then. Spread the word, scout. We are to prepare for a siege."

The scout nodded and bowed, exiting the makeshift tent in a hurry to do as he was bid.

It was springtime in the tundra. They were farther south than they had ever been, and the grasses had started to grow tall and thick. Birds of all kinds flocked to the land in the hope of a feast. Animals started to drift back in.

With skilled hunters, the Ottals ought to be able to hold a long siege. The Guild Master just hoped that the siege would be over before winter struck again. If the spring had killed so many of his men, he dreaded what the winter would do.

"Send for a messenger. We ought to get word to the Touans about this fortress."

Before long, a messenger arrived and bowed before the Guild Master. With strict instructions on whom to speak, the youth went south with all haste to seek out the Touan army.

"Well," the Guild Master noted. "If we're to dig in for a siege, we'd best get there as soon as possible. I want to be well and truly set up for when the reinforcements arrive."

The break was over. With a collective groan, the Ottalan raiders rose to their feet and resumed marching.

* * * *

"There it is!" someone shouted from the head of the column of marching Touan infantry. News of the sighting spread through the ranks like wildfire. The end of the forest had been sighted. Suddenly the oppressive ranks of trees with their bright green buds did not seem nearly as sinister. There was a way out.

Eager to get away from the forest and the ghost that resided there, the Touan army picked up its pace. They had reached a jog by the time the first few broke through the line of trees and spilled gratefully into the sunshine that pounded the pale rocks of the slopes leading to the few areas the Pamisii had for pasture.

The pastureland was entirely devoid of cattle, but rising on the butt of the mountains that loomed over the pastureland towered a new feature – a tall and imposing fortress.

"Well now," Roger said when he and Algar breeched the line of trees. "That's new."

Algar held down a laugh. "How did they manage to keep that monstrosity a secret?"

"Hardly surprising, is it?" Roger asked. "They fed us so many different plans that we had no idea which was which and what was what."

Algar grunted. "Look," he said, nudging his father and nodding at the barely visible road that wound around the rocks. "A messenger."

"Oh goodie. That means another meeting."

Algar rolled his eyes.

A meeting was indeed called. Roger and Algar both looked surly as they wandered to the space that had been cleared for it. After some indecision, Algar decided it was best not to carry his spear to the meeting. The Yellow Robe might ask questions.

They all took their seats and the representative from the Holy Yellow City stood.

"Well, all those with eyes have not missed the fortress that appears as a dull grey smudge against the blackened back of the mountains."

"That was very poetic," Algar grunted to his father, who flashed a grin in response.

"What the Ottalan messenger tells us is that the fortress appears to be occupied. They have been chasing the Sierran nomads west since the beginning of the war. We have been doing the same with the Greyls. I think that it is safe to surmise that both Sierran and Greyl forces are locked tight behind those walls, which means only one thing. We must dig in for a siege."

"It's a good thing I thought to bring engineers with me then, isn't it?" the King of Hitoua noted.

"Calm down," Roger replied. "We all have engineers, Majesty."

The King of Hitoua threw Roger a foul look, but did not respond.

"That is well indeed," the Yellow Robe said amicably. "We have a forest behind us and rocks before us. There is more than enough material to prepare for a siege. I ask now that we push our troops forward to meet with the Ottals who will be settled into their camp in less than a week. Until then, we shall rest here...."

The Yellow Robe was interrupted by the King of Stetoua clearing his throat. "If it pleases the council," he said, "I would propose that we use the daylight we have left to move as far from the forest as humanly possible."

Algar did laugh that time, managing to control it enough to turn it into a hiccupping snort.

"Excuse me," he mumbled as all eyes turned to him. "I ate breakfast too quickly. In any case, I agree with his Majesty of Stetoua. We should move away from the forest as much as possible, if only to give our soldiers peace of mind and therefore a good rest."

"Good cover," Roger whispered to his son as the matter was turned over to the rest of the council for deliberation.

"Thanks," Algar whispered back.

"Very well," the Yellow Robe noted once a consensus had been reached. "We shall march the rest of the day and camp in a suitable location further from the forest."

With nothing left to say, the War Council disbanded and the Touan army marched once again. Algar chanced a glance behind him as he mounted his horse and noted nothing amiss. It appeared to be simply an old forest. He regretted the axes that would soon tear down the trees in order to make war machines from them. With a sigh, Algar faced forward and rode tall on his horse, his spear in hand.

* * * *

"Here they come," Bran noted from the lookout tower, the tallest structure of the fortress. By some miracle of design, the back wall had been carved directly from the mountain, creating a pillar of stability that the rest of the fortress relied on. Only if the Ottalans and Touans came at the mountains themselves could this fortress be brought completely down.

"Both of them?" Gofron asked, taking Bran's place at the window.

"The Ottals are closest in the north. The Touans have just breeched the forest."

"How can you see all that?"

"I can't really see it in detail. There's a blob moving just beyond the forest line. Since the Touans were the ones that came through that way, I can only assume it's them. As for the north, well, the Ottals chased me here, so it can be no one but them."

"I don't see anything moving."

Bran shrugged. "Yes, but you're getting old."

"You brat!" Gofron laughed. Bran grinned and dodged his father's playful punch quite easily.

"You'll never catch me, old man!" he exclaimed in glee as he fled laughing from the tower, his father in pursuit.

"Just you watch me, little crow!" King Gofron hollered after him. "I may be an old man, but trust me when I say experience counts for something."

The pair bolted down the stairs and through the kitchens laughing, startling the cooks, who responded with nervous giggles.

"Hah!" Bran laughed as he narrowly missed his father's lunge and took off into the dining hall.

Lord Kildurrow and the members of King Gofron's royal family were having lunch there when Bran burst through the kitchen doors.

"Thank you, Mother," Bran said as he raced past and snatched the bread roll Amwyl was buttering.

"Bran!" she exclaimed in exacerbation. She picked up another roll, only to have that one snatched by her husband as he ran passed. She did not even have time to break it open.

"Thanks, dear," the King called as he chased his youngest son out of the dining hall. Amwyl stared open-mouthed at the backs of her husband and son as they tore through the fortress in a game of chase.

After a moment of stunned silence, Lord Kildurrow bellowed a laugh.

* * * *

"They are in sight of the fortress," Ur said quietly as the enormous Winter Wolf curled herself up by the fire. Millen was resting happily against her, stroking her soft white fur and daydreaming.

"How do you know?" Inna asked.

"A crow told me," Ur answered.

Inna drew his attention away from the fire and looked around. There were several birds nearby, but no crows. Inna looked up and one lone crow flew overhead, turning north as soon as it was spotted.

"You talk to crows now?"

"Why not?" Bull asked. "He talks to wolves."

The Winter Wolf grumbled and gave Bull a stare that was at once irritated and playful.

"Otsana is still Otsana," Ur said with a smile. "No matter what skin she wears."

Bull shrugged as he continued to spit the rock hens. It had been a good hunt and the entire Sierran host were feasting happily on fowl of all kinds.

"So we will engage them soon?" Bull asked hopefully.

"Otsana wants to wait until they are settled in. Something important is happening in the Touan Federation. She wants to ensure it does happen and we don't destroy its chances by striking too early."

"What's happening in the Touan Federation?"

Ur shrugged. "I don't know. She won't tell me." He sounded irritated.

"Women need their secrets, little man," Inna said with a smile. Ur grunted and the Winter Wolf growled a chuckle.

"I think she's just putting you in your place, Ur," Bull said with a grin. "My wife does it to me all the time."

"Traitor! Villain! *Nameless!*" the captive Braddard shrieked as Guild walked passed him, a fat goose slung over his shoulder. Guild ignored him.

"He's starting to get on my nerves," Bull grumbled.

The Braddard was tied to a thick stake sunk so heavily into the ground even Bull could not shift it. It had become habit to simply tie him to such stakes when the Sierrans stopped marching for the day. Guild was sick of hauling him around everywhere.

"I can gag him for you," Guild offered brightly.

Laughing, Bull said, "If he keeps yowling like a queen, please do."

Guild grinned and began to pluck his catch.

"Did you get that by yourself?" Inna asked.

"I did," Guild said, proudly tapping the sling he had hanging from his belt. Ur laughed and Inna smiled at Guild.

"Good! We'll turn you into a man yet."

Guild shrugged and turned back to his task. "You know," he said after a moment of reflection. "For all the walking and despite the fact that we are at war, I rather like it here."

Inna grinned. "It is home to us," he said with a smile. "And we love it."

"What happens when this is all over?" Guild asked suddenly.

Everyone except Millen turned to look at Guild.

"I mean, when the war is over, and if we've won, everyone will go back to their lands and live their lives as they did before this war. But I don't have a clan, and I have nowhere to go."

At this, the Winter Wolf rose to her feet and padded around the small fire to Guild's side, leaving Millen looking disappointed. She lay down again and rested her head on Guild's lap. Guild smiled and stroked it.

"Otsana wants you to stay with us," Ur said.

Guild didn't seem to hear, he was so taken with petting the wolf at his side. Ur smiled softly and Inna and Bull grinned.

With a sigh, Millen rose to his feet and rejoined the Winter Wolf. Ur rolled his eyes. "You are spoilt, Otsana," he said, waving his spoon at her.

The Winter Wolf simply blinked at Ur in response. Bull rumbled a quiet laugh and settled in to turning his rock hens on their spit.

* * * *

"Hold!" The King of Stetoua roared as his quarter of the circle wavered under the onslaught. No sooner had the soldiers put down their packs than they were attacked by a large group of rangers and other Greyl warriors who had been hiding amongst the rocks and boulders that stood between the pasturelands and the Pamisii forest.

"Gods be damned," Roger grunted as he defended against his second opponent. His counter fell a little short and he only managed to slash a small gash through the ranger's chainmaille. No sooner was that achieved than the low droning sound of a horn echoed around the rocks and the attacking Greyls withdrew and immediately vanished from sight.

The speed at which they disappeared from view unnerved the already high-strung Touan army. They held position for a while longer, scanning the rocks for any signs of movement. There were none. After what seemed an age to the tightly wound soldiers, they slowly lowered their weapons and began to unpack.

A horn sounded again and immediately, the soldiers were back into formation.

Yet there was no attack. They stood or sat on their horses, their weapons drawn, preparing for a battle that did not come. No sooner had the first makeshift tent been pitched than the horn sounded again, and again the Touans took up arms and prepared for a fight that never arrived.

Thus it went throughout the night. Every so often a blast of a horn would sound and the Touans would form up. As dawn approached, the Touans were exhausted and worn beyond compare.

"Cruel bastards," Roger groaned as the light breeched his eyelids.

"Clever though," Algar admitted. "Without drawing anymore blood, they've left us without our strength."

"Yes, well, when you've stopped admiring them, you might want to know that there is a Holy messenger here. There's going to be another meeting."

Algar groaned. "Gods I hate those."

"I feel for you, princess," Roger said, rolling to his feet. "Time to go. Get up."

Algar groaned. His limbs ached and his head pounded. He had been visited by the other Algar Touan in what little sleep he had. In that time, he had been training to fight with a spear. Using that weapon was unlike anything he had ever experienced, and it fascinated Algar. He had trained hard in his sleep and it left his limbs feeling like lead.

Algar paid no attention to the opening formalities of the war council. His ears only heard when the King of Jatoua spoke.

"If we march straight through, we'll be leaving the enemy behind us," he roared.

"They are a small number," his brother, King of Doua, countered. "Hardly significant enough to lift a siege!"

"But significant enough to cut us off from our supplies and reinforcements," the Jatouan king countered. "We already left a gang back in the forest, and now we're proposing to add to their number at our backs by ignoring this mob?"

"His Majesty of Jatoua is correct," the representative of the Yellow City said. "Even if we do not exterminate the vagrants in the forest, we should not be so lax as to add to their numbers."

"So what do you propose?" Roger asked.

"Wing 'em," the King of Fanoua said. All eyes turned to the slender, quiet-spoken man. "They're likely to attack from behind for as long as we march. I say, let them, and when they've passed our back ranks, have those ranks peel off and come 'round them. They are not many, not more than twenty or so. They will not last long sandwiched between Touan soldiers outnumbering them as we do."

The Touan war council fell silent as each member searched for a flaw large enough to abandon the plan.

"He's right, you know," the King of Doua said at length.

"Then it is decided," the Yellow Robe intoned gravely. "His Majesty of Fanoua shall lead the next engagement."

Robert sighed, and the war council was disbanded for the day. The attack did not come for another two days of marching, though the constant taunting continued each night. They were almost at the edge of the rocky tumble when the attack did arrive.

There was no warning. The Greyl warriors seemed to simply appear out of nowhere, sometimes out of the very rocks themselves. The exhaustion of the Touan army was evident. It took them more time than it should have to muster themselves into the appropriate formation.

The King of Fanoua did not seem overly fazed. He sat on his horse at the centre of the army and watched with steel nerves until the moment was right. The only signal he gave was a clenched fist thrust high above his head, but his warriors understood it well. In an instant they peeled away from the main force and scurried over the rocks to surround the attacking Greyls. The Greyls saw the ploy too late and the attack ground to a halt; the rangers completely surrounded by Touan soldiers.

"Lay down your arms and you shall be given a merciful death," the King of Fanoua bellowed. "Convert and you shall be given new life."

Algar cringed. He could see the temptation of surrender in the eyes of the Greyls until the offer of conversion was put forth. In that instant the Greyls hardened. One held his weapon high in the air.

"I go to my ancestors!" the man bellowed, before charging at the Touans where their line was the thickest. Following him, the small Greyl force roared with the might of a thousand voices and charged forward.

The ensuing battle was brutal and short. All twenty Greyl warriors lay dead on the ground. Not a single Touan was hurt. The Touans began to laugh.

"Leave them," the Yellow Robe said, cutting the laughter short. "We march on to meet with the mighty Ottal host."

"You can't just leave them!" Algar protested.

The Yellow Robe turned to him with cold eyes. "They are abominations in the eyes of the only true god and do not deserve to be buried."

"They are still men, men who fought bravely for their cause. Give them at least some respect in their deaths!"

"Algar," Roger whispered. "Leave it!"

"I will not!" Algar snapped back. "These men will be buried."

The Yellow Robe looked quite taken aback. "These savages are not worthy of a burial. The matter is decided."

"The hell it is. They will be buried, even if I have to do it myself."

"Then do it yourself you will," the Yellow Robe sneered. He turned his horse and began to trot away. "Onward!" he commanded the army. Slowly, the men began to follow the Yellow Robe, leaving Algar and his father behind.

"You'd better go," Algar told his father. "The men need their commander."

Roger simply looked at his son.

"What?"

"I don't think I've ever told you how proud of you I am. It takes a great deal of courage to defy the voice of the power behind the Federation."

"Misoua is no longer part of the Federation," Algar growled. "Now go. I'll catch up in a day or two."

Roger nodded. With a nervous glance back at the forest, he mounted and rode to catch up to the rest of the army. Algar sighed and turned his mind to the burial of twenty bodies in a land that was made entirely of stone.

King Roger caught up to the Touan army without much difficulty. He found himself walking beside the Yellow Robe.

"You will need to discipline your son, King of Misoua," the Yellow Robe told him loudly enough for others to hear.

"I will not beat his good conscious out of him," Roger retorted. "That is your task." He turned his horse aside, and rode to join his men, all of whom had overheard him. They walked straighter behind King Roger and his loyal lords.

Later that evening as the Touan army settled to camp, King Roger was approached by a small, ragged-looking band of his men.

"Beggin' your pardon, your Majesty," one man said with an awkward bow. Roger acknowledged him with a nod. "I have nine volunteers with me. We want your permission to return to Prince Algar and aid in the burial of the Greyl warriors."

"In the dark?" Roger asked.

The man nodded. "'Twould be easier to slip away unnoticed, Majesty. That way you won't be getting into trouble with that Yellow Robe."

Roger smiled. "Very well, you have my permission." It did not escape his notice that all the men who stood respectfully before their king wore a necklace with a single blue glass bead.

"Thank you, Majesty," the man said with another awkward bow. He shuffled backwards away from the fire and, with a curt nod to his companions, slipped away into the night, his men with him.

* * * *

Algar had managed to line up the bodies and position them ready for burial before night fell. What he was supposed to do after was something of a problem. There was precious little soil beneath which to bury even one body, let alone twenty. Deciding that it was far too dark to do anything until morning anyway, Algar built himself a small fire and settled beside it.

As a child, Prince Algar had always been terrified of dead bodies. They were so sinister things – appearing alive, but with all the qualities of cold stone. He didn't much care for statues either. However, now in the chill spring night of the rocky slopes before the Greyl fortress, he could feel only peace.

These men died with no regrets. They had fought for what they loved, and willingly gave their lives to defend it. Algar envied them. Not so much for himself, but for his brother, Alam, who had given his life for a cause he had despised.

Algar felt his own resolve harden. It would never happen again. When the kingdom of Misoua fought, it would be for a cause the kingdom of Misoua believed in. Algar played with the bead around his neck.

"Can you hear me, little brother?" Algar asked the empty night air. "I was too late for you, but I can help others. I will help others."

A gentle breeze wafted over the rocks and ruffled Algar's hair. Algar closed his tear-rimmed eyes and thought of his brother. He was asleep in an instant.

Twenty-Six

"Let me try," Alam insisted. At ten years old, Alam was a bold child, and unafraid of taking risks. Algar admired that about him.

"You're too young," the weapons master said with a smile. Alam pouted.

"I'll show you later," Algar promised.

Alam immediately brightened and he threw his arms around his older brother.

Algar knew then that he was dreaming, and his chest tightened in grief. He did something in this dream of a memory that he should have done when the memory was made. He wrapped his arms around his brother and held him close.

"I love you," he murmured.

When Algar looked up, he found that he was holding a pillar of dust and not his brother. He leapt backwards with a startled oath.

"You're so easy to scare," Alam said from behind him, prompting another jump and curse. Alam laughed brightly.

"Alam," Algar breathed.

"In the flesh. Well, sort of."

Algar was not sure whether to laugh or cry. He stared at his brother, mute.

"Nice spear," Alam noted with a quick grin.

Algar nodded in silence and Alam laughed again. "You know," he said easily, "I rather like that you've taken on both the Ottalan faith and the Touan Federation all in one go."

"Oh."

"But Algar, make sure that what you do is for yourself, and for those that might still benefit from it. Doing anything for me is utterly useless. I'm already dead."

The last sentence hit Algar like a kick to the chest. His eyes watered suddenly. He bit his lip in an effort to curb the tears. "I am doing it for them," he managed to choke. "No one will ever have to die for a cause not of their own again."

Alam laughed. "Unless the cause is for Misoua."

Algar managed a small smile. "Well, that, I suppose."

"Well, I'm taking you from your training. I will see you later."

"Will you?"

"Don't worry Algar. As long as you remember me, I will never leave you."

Algar watched hopelessly as his younger brother wandered away across the formless land that was Algar's dream.

"Are you ready, son?" the Chief of the Lion Clan asked gently from behind him. Algar drew a deep breath and nodded.

"I am."

* * * *

Prince Algar woke moments before dawn. He had several new bruises from his dream-training and did not feel like moving. He had bodies to bury, however, so he groaned and rolled onto his side and came face to face with a boot. He followed the boot up to the leg, and up further still until he came to the face of a soldier wearing the livery of the kingdom of Misoua. Algar frowned.

"Morning, your Highness," the soldier said. "We reckoned you might need a hand with all this mess, so we back-tracked. It'll take many hands to build a cairn large enough to cover twenty men."

Algar struggled to his feet, picking up his spear as he did so. "Thank you," he said uncertainly.

The soldier shrugged. "I've sent Gout and Rat off to find the rocks. The rest of us will help clear some space for you."

"Thanks," Algar said again, taking stock of his surrounds and noting seven grubby-looking soldiers standing in a small pack behind the man who spoke. "And your name is?"

"I'm Bob."

"Gout, Rat, Bob," Algar repeated, not quite sure if he had heard the names correctly.

"Yep," the soldier replied.

"Right. Well, Bob, we need to find a place flat enough to bury these poor fellows."

"We have a place," someone said from behind Algar.

All eyes turned to the voice's owner. He was a tall, broadly built man dressed in a simple smock and trousers of dark brown and green. He was unmistakeably a Greyl ranger. Algar felt his shoulders tense.

"My name is Grunt," the man said.

Algar could have laughed. He ran through the absurd names he had heard in his head. *Bob, Gout, Rat, Grunt.*

"I am Algar," he managed to say, once the urge to laugh had passed. "I'm from–"

"We know who you are, Algar, Prince of Misoua. We recognise your face from amongst the Touan army."

Algar clutched his spear a little tighter. Grunt's eyes narrowed as he spied both the spear and the blue glass bead about Algar's neck.

"Look," Algar said, misreading Grunt's expression. "We don't want any trouble. I'm just here to bury the dead."

"I know," Grunt said. His tone was distant and thoughtful. "We were just coming to help. We overheard your argument with the Ottal and we were going to let you return to your army without incident once the work was done; a token of our appreciation."

"You were, as in past tense 'were,' as in you're not anymore?"

Grunt grunted. "Bluebell!" he snapped.

Appearing from a crevice as if she sprang from the very rock, a young female ranger came into view.

"You called?" she asked mildly.

"I want to speak with Blue Ghost."

"Is that so? Well, you know where he is."

Grunt turned and faced Bluebell with a frightful scowl. "Bring him here," he growled.

Bluebell raised her brows, looked uncertainly at Algar and then vanished once more.

"How do you people do that?" Algar asked.

Grunt grunted once more. "It takes years of training. Bluebell is special. A natural."

"Oh. So, are you going to try to kill us?" Algar was not sure why he asked, and he truly did not mean to employ such a casually arrogant tone either. He wondered where the calm courage came from. Grunt simply looked at Algar.

"I'm here," a young man said. He had arrived so quietly that none had noticed him standing a few paces away, despite the fact that he was still painted pale blue. In the light of day he looked nothing more than a young ranger painted blue, though every so often, Algar would spy the old man beneath who would shimmer into view when there was movement.

"Blue Ghost, this is Algar," Grunt said.

The young ranger that Grunt called 'Blue Ghost' jumped easily across the rocks to stand before Algar. He extended a hand, which Algar shook.

"Hello Algar," he said with a smile.

"Hello."

It was then that the ranger noted the glass bead around Algar's neck. He stared at it a while, before pulling his vision back and noticing the spear also. His eyes went wide for a moment before he looked Algar in the eye again.

"Lion Spear!" he breathed.

Algar twitched. How could this boy know that?

Grunt nodded. "I thought as much."

The young ranger's astonishment turned into a grin. He took Algar's hand once more and shook it more vigorously. "I'm very happy to meet you," he said brightly.

Algar blinked and tried to smile in return. He did not understand.

"Now do you believe, Blue Ghost?" Grunt asked quietly.

"Stop calling me that!" the ranger snapped in return.

"You aren't actually Blue Ghost?" Algar asked.

"No."

"Yes," Grunt said. The younger ranger gave him a stern look and then sighed. "You are here to bury the men you killed," he noted.

"Yes. I could not, in good conscience, leave them unburied. It is a disrespect of the most severe kind."

"That it is. Are you familiar with Greyl burial custom?"

"Only in that a man is buried where he died."

"For that is the place where the land claimed him," the ranger said. "Good. There is a flat rock just behind that large boulder on your right. We can lay them there and build a cairn over the entire thing quite easily."

"Two men have already gone in search of rocks for a cairn."

"We know. In the meantime, let's take the bodies to the flat rock."

It took very little time for the bodies to be moved. The rangers of the Pamisii woods were strong and efficient. Algar was surprised to learn that there were only ten. Such was the havoc they wreaked upon the Touan host, that he expected a larger force to inhabit the forest. Algar had to laugh at it. They were crafty.

The building of the cairn took much longer. It was not easy to find rocks of the appropriate size for the base of the cairn and the manner in which the Greyls built theirs was remarkably different from the manner in which the Touans did.

It was less a cairn than a tomb. No hollow was filled with soil and debris. Rather, each rock was placed in such a fashion as to create an open cave around the bodies, with the capstone placed at the height of a man's shoulder. The task took the twenty men the entire day to complete.

Exhausted, they retired to Algar's small hearth. "Tomorrow we will apply the clay," Grunt said as Algar started the fire. Algar looked up.

"Your cairns are very different from ours," he noted.

Grunt smiled. "Not so different."

"We fill ours," Algar said.

"Do you?" asked the young ranger Grunt insisted on calling Blue Ghost. Algar nodded.

"Interesting."

Grunt prepared the food that evening and all twenty men shared it in peace. Algar breathed deeply.

"Why can't we always cooperate," he mused to himself.

Bluebell snorted. "Because you are men."

"I have stories to tell you about how women behave, Bluebell. Do not tell me that a woman's cooperative skills are greater than a man's," Algar said with a laugh.

Bluebell glared at him.

"Careful," Grunt mumbled to Algar. "I know that look. You'll find yourself married afore long if you aren't cautious."

"I will never marry!" Bluebell declared vehemently.

Algar smiled. "Why not?"

"Because I refuse to be put into sanctioned slavery."

Algar laughed. "No married woman I know is a slave."

"Then you do not know any very well."

"Perhaps, but most men I've spoken with note with much regret how much they are controlled by their wives."

"There's another reason to not marry."

"Oh?"

"I prefer men with some spine. I'd lose interest the moment we got married and he lost his."

Algar laughed uproariously. "One day Bluebell, you shall meet a man you find you cannot live without."

"I doubt it," she rumbled. She accepted a bowl of steaming hot water and eyed Algar thoughtfully.

Grunt observed the exchange with a silent grin.

The evening proved eventful for Algar. His sleep was interrupted by Bluebell tapping hard on his forehead. Algar sat up and rubbed the spot where her strong finger repeatedly struck.

"Oh good," she noted with heavy sarcasm. "You're awake. You've only wasted half the night."

Algar raised his eyebrows. "Sleep is never wasted unless it isn't had," he whispered back.

"Very wise. Now follow me." Bluebell stood.

"What? Why?"

Bluebell did not answer. She simply turned and walked away. Confused and curious, Algar did as he was told, taking with him his spear and a dagger. He followed Bluebell's slight form until he could not longer see the small camp.

"What's going on?" he whispered harshly to Bluebell.

Bluebell ignored him. Annoyed, Algar lunged forward and grabbed Bluebell by the elbow. With all the speed of a viper, she turned and suddenly Algar found himself on the flat of his back. Bluebell sat on his chest, her hand pressing firmly on his shoulders.

"Very sloppy," she noted. With a swift twist, Algar turned and threw Bluebell on her back, with his entire weight pressed against her.

"Because you're so sharp," he noted with sarcasm. Bluebell fought back, and it was not long before the fighting on the ground turned into something else, just as Bluebell had intended.

When morning dawned at last Algar, who had crawled back to bed only moments before, was exhausted. Bluebell seemed completely unfazed and hummed happily to herself as she stoked the fire back to life and put the remnants of last night's meal on to heat. The rest of the men woke slowly, each coming gratefully to the warmth of the fire and sitting in contented silence. At length, Algar rose to join them.

"Good morning!" Grunt greeted cheerily.

Algar simply grunted and sat heavily down.

"You look tired this morning," Grunt noted.

"Exhausted," Algar mumbled.

"Here," Grunt said, handing Algar a bowl of reheated dinner with a knowing smile. "This'll help."

Algar grunted his thanks and accepted the bowl. It took a while before he roused himself enough to begin eating.

"You may return to your army today," Blue Ghost said to Algar. "There is little left to do on the cairn, but to put the clay on and seed the grass."

Algar nodded. "Thank you, but if it's all the same to you, I'd like to see it through."

Blue Ghost shrugged. "As you like."

"Then I'm going to go back to bed and sleep until tomorrow."

Grunt laughed loudly and clapped Algar hard on the back with his meaty hand. Algar managed a smile as he caught Bluebell laughing quietly to herself.

"Highness," Bob said suddenly. "Can we siphon off about a hundred troops to the woods without anyone noticin' do you think?"

"Why?" Algar asked. Grunt and his prince listened in closely.

"Well, it seems to me that all the problems we've had coming here was due to more than just one group of rangers, right?"

"It is conceivable."

"Right, which means there's probably a fairly sizeable force behind our army right now waiting for the order to attack, right?"

"All right.

"Well, they aren't likely to be that sizeable, right? So they could use an extra hundred men, right?"

"They could," Algar agreed. "Though, we could use those men too."

Bob shrugged. Algar observed him a moment. "Who is your lord?"

"Hemming."

Algar was surprised. "Hemming is with the Ottals."

"He might be, but his sergeants heard tell of this plan of your king's, and they told us, and we all agreed that we'd rather be with your king, seeing as how we don't agree with this war 'n all."

"You mean you aren't convinced by all the talk of saving souls?" Algar asked mildly.

"We've heard rumours that some Ottal started this war for revenge."

"Really? I hadn't heard as much."

"I had," Grunt noted. "You see, this Ottal attacked the clan that a prince of the Baveii's wife belongs to, only his men were all killed, and he got mad and started a war."

"I'm sorry, what?"

"There's this prince of the Baveii, see," Grunt started again slowly. "Ah, forget it. Just take my word for it that Bob here is right."

Algar grunted. "Figures." He turned to Bob. "How did you get those necklaces if you're with Hemming?"

"Lord Betsy had a few extra. Not enough for all of us mind, but we reckon we can send those without 'em back here where they'd be less like to need 'em."

"Please tell me there isn't actually a Lord Betsy," Grunt said to Algar.

Algar grinned. "His name is actually Betsworth."

"Oh."

"All right," the ranger Blue Ghost said, standing. "The sun is up. Let's get to work."

Algar stood, a little shakily.

"Not you," the Prince of the Pamisii said with a smile. "You and your men would get in the way. Just watch."

"I'd rather help."

"I know, but this is better done with fewer people."

Algar sighed, but did not argue the matter. He and his men stood aside and watched as all the rangers save the boy they called Blue Ghost vanished from sight, returning with armfuls of very carefully carried thick rectangles of dark clay. They lined up and one by one handed the slabs of clay to Blue Ghost, who laid them carefully over the stones of the cairn beginning at the top and working his way down in an anti-clockwise spiral.

With the application of the thick slabs of clay, the cairn looked more like a smooth, dark bubble in the otherwise pale, jagged landscape. The rangers dispersed and each returned with fistfuls of uprooted grasses of all kinds. Kneeling at the base of the cairn, they pushed the grasses into the clay. They stood, stepped back and bowed their heads in silence.

Algar and his men remained at a respectful distance and waited patiently until the rangers had finished their prayers and rejoined them once more.

"The grass will grow over and protect the clay," the young ranger who may or may not be Blue Ghost told Algar. "It is good that they died in the spring. The grass will spread quickly."

Algar smiled a little. "It is good they died in the spring?"

"Well yes," the ranger said with a smile. "If one must die at all, spring would be the time to do it."

Algar laughed, setting the ranger grinning.

"We will return to the woods now and await the other rangers who should arrive soon."

Algar nodded. "I will go to sleep now, and return to the army in the morning."

The ranger laughed. "Indeed. Well then, have a good sleep, Lion Spear. We will see each other again soon."

"Very soon," Algar agreed. He was not looking forward to the oncoming battle. It was some, albeit small, consolation that it meant there would be no protracted siege. "Take care, Blue Ghost."

"Not you too!"

Algar laughed and they shook hands. He watched the rangers leave before he turned to the ten men who waited patiently for him.

"Do what you want," he said to them. "I'm going to sleep."

The men grinned and nodded and then scurried away. Algar had no idea where they were going or why, and he didn't particularly care. He turned back to his blankets and lay down, falling asleep quickly.

* * * *

"Ready for training?" the elder Algar asked.

Algar groaned. "You cannot be serious! I haven't slept a quiet night in days!"

"You're at war, little cub," Algar the elder noted.

Algar groaned again.

"Come on, then," the Chief of the Lion Clan said, slapping Algar's thigh hard. "Time to work."

* * * *

Roger paced as the camp settled in for the night. It had been four days. Algar had not returned yet and Roger was concerned. The Yellow Robe noted it. "He was probably killed by the savages in the woods," he said to another lord, loud enough for Roger to hear.

The King of Misoua glared at the Yellow Robe. The lord he spoke to offered Roger a look that was at once apologetic and sympathetic. It only served to irritate the King further and he turned and resumed his pacing as his servants scurried to make him a shelter for the night.

"They haven't you know," a familiar voice said from a nearby rock.

"Go away bird," Roger growled.

"All right. But you should know that a yellow flag will be raised over the main gate when you are cleared to attack."

"Shhhh... woman! You're talking loudly and everyone can hear you!"

"No, they can't. They're hearing a particularly curious osprey whistle. You're the only one who can understand my words."

"And why is that?"

"Because you are the only one who I am talking to, you overgrown dolt."

"Even better, I look like a lunatic because I'm standing here talking to myself."

"Something like that. Now listen, the fortress defenders will cease operationing their engines when the Sierran host arrives. They will attack on the same signal as you. Once you're fully engaged, they will open the fortress and ride out to your aid. Is that clear?"

"I suppose."

"Good. The rest is up to you. Plan whatever you like, but be certain to attack as soon as you see the yellow flag."

"Yes, ma'am."

"Good. Now shoo me away."

Roger frowned but was so eager to get the talking bird out of his sight, he did as he was bid. The osprey shrieked and took to the air.

"I'm going insane," Roger muttered to himself.

No sooner had he done so, than eleven men rode at full tilt into the camp. It was Algar and the ten soldiers who had left to help him.

"About bloody time!" Roger roared, less pleased than irritated.

Algar grinned. "Sorry, Father."

"It's not funny."

"Of course not. I imagine you were worried."

Roger grunted and turned away as the irritation yielded to relief.

"Are you all right, Father?"

"No," Roger growled. "I was beginning to think I had lost another son."

Algar's smile vanished. He dismounted and grasped his father's shoulder as a squire led his horse away. "I'm sorry," he said gently.

Roger took a deep breath. "It's nothing," he said at last. "This is war. A father should expect to lose a few sons."

"And no one should expect him not to grieve."

"Later. We have things to discuss."

"Yes, we do."

Algar and his father retired to their campfire and were soon joined by their allies. Before long they were deep in discussion about their plans. In the midst of those who would very soon be their enemies, they very cleverly spoke in code and to the outside ear, it sounded as if they were simply having a crude conversation about loose women.

* * * *

"I always imagined myself an upright, moral person," Lord Kildurrow mused. He lay naked on his bed, Amwyl in his arms, her head against his chest. "Yet I am in bed with my king and friend's wife. I lost a son to treason. Now I follow him."

Amwyl smiled sadly. "I am no less to blame."

Lord Kildurrow grunted.

The tryst had been unexpected. Lord Kildurrow had not joined the royal family at breakfast that morning. He gave the excuse that he was not feeling well, but the truth of the matter was that he could not keep his eyes or his imagination away from Amwyl and he was afraid that his deepening feelings for her would be discovered. He was also afraid that he would not be able to restrain himself in her presence. It had been a long time since Lord Kildurrow was so moved by any woman.

The close confines of the fortress had ensured many painful encounters with Amwyl, encounters where Lord Kildurrow teetered on the edge of reason. They had been filled with awkward silences and hopeless longings.

Fate, it seemed, would have its way regardless. Amwyl had called upon him immediately after breakfast, concerned for his health. No sooner had she set down the tray of food she carried than Lord Kildurrow lost control. To Amwyl's credit, she had protested at first, but it was not long before she caved to Lord Kildurrow's persistent kisses.

Lord Kildurrow pulled Amwyl closer for a moment. He breathed deep the sweet scent of her and found his heart torn in two. He loved Amwyl, and he loved his king; the king he was at this very moment betraying.

"This can never happen again," he whispered.

The words hit Amwyl hard. Tears struck her eyes even as she nodded. "I know."

"Gods but this is cruel."

"I know."

Lord Kildurrow struggled against the sleep that hovered at the edges of his mind. He fought it as hard as he could, but all the nights of restless longing had finally found a release and his eyes closed in spite of himself.

Amwyl sighed and let her own eyes close, enjoying the warmth and strength of the man who slept beside her until she too fell to sleep.

Amwyl and Lord Kildurrow were woken early in the afternoon by three slow, very loud knocks on Lord Kildurrow's door and Bran's muffled voice. "Mother? Are you in there?"

Cursing loudly, Lord Kildurrow sprang from his bed, Amwyl close behind. Wrapping herself in a sheet, she hurriedly picked up her clothing and dashed into the wardrobe as the door creaked open. Lord Kildurrow himself barely had time to get his undershirt on when Bran came striding in.

Bran bowed to Lord Kildurrow and with an apologetic smile said, "I'm sorry to disturb you, my Lord. I'm looking for my mother. Is she here?"

"No," Lord Kildurrow managed to say. His breath was still ragged from panic. Bran raised his brows and his eyes shifted to the wardrobe, where a small triangle of white sheet stuck out the bottom of the door. Trying hard not to laugh, Bran walked over to the wardrobe, grabbed the door handle and pulled.

Amwyl shrieked and pulled the sheet closer to her as the doors swung open.

"Hello, Mother," Bran said with a broad smile.

"Bran," Amwyl managed to breathe. "I was... I was just cleaning:"

"In a bed sheet?"

Amwyl looked down at the sheet she was wrapped in and looked back up at her son's sparkling blue eyes.

"You'd better get dressed. Father wants everyone in the dining hall for lunch." Bran held out a hand for his mother, who took it and stepped from the wardrobe.

"How did you know I was here?" Amwyl asked quietly.

"Aunt Cat. I asked if she knew where you were and she blushed a delicate shade of crimson. You'll have to find a better liar to cover for you mother."

Amwyl felt like crying. "Bran...."

Bran put up his hand and Amwyl fell silent. "We've already talked, and my sentiments haven't changed."

"You won't tell your father, will you?"

"No. It's not my business. Now hurry. They're going to serve lunch soon." Bran turned and, nodding to Lord Kildurrow, strode from the bedchamber, taking care to close the door firmly behind him.

Lord Kildurrow walked to Amwyl and put his arm around her. "Your son is singularly understanding," he murmured.

Amwyl sobbed. "I am so ashamed."

Lord Kildurrow turned and pulled Amwyl into a tight embrace. "You and I both." They embraced for a moment longer before Amwyl pulled herself away.

"We'd best get dressed," she said.

Lord Kildurrow nodded and in awkward silence, they did just that.

They arrived at the lunch separately, Amwyl having returned to her chambers to brush her hair before presenting herself to her husband. Lord Kildurrow was the first to arrive.

"My Lord!" King Gofron bellowed with good cheer. "I have saved you a seat. Come, sit!"

His open warmth was like a dagger in Lord Kildurrow's chest. Lord Kildurrow tried to smile as he made his way to his friend's side. He sat slowly.

"You are unwell," Gofron noted, pouring Lord Kildurrow a goblet of wine. "You are horribly pale."

Lord Kildurrow sighed. "I suppose."

"Do you have a temperature?" Gofron asked. His genuine concern hurt Lord Kildurrow all the more.

"No, but I fear I am not myself."

"You haven't been for a while," Gofron noted. Lord Kildurrow wanted to hit himself. Had he been so obvious?

"Is it your son's death?" Gofron dropped his voice so his conversation with Lord Kildurrow was private, despite the many pairs of ears around them.

"No."

"Is it the thought of siege?"

Lord Kildurrow smiled at this. "No, your Majesty," he assured. "The Kildurrows are well used to sieges. Why do you think we have a fortress for our seat?"

Gofron shrugged. "What is bothering you then, Kildurrow? You should know by now you can speak to me about anything."

"Perhaps," Lord Kildurrow said quietly. "But not now."

"After lunch then. We shall play chess and talk."

Lord Kildurrow nodded. He had decided that King Gofron deserved to know the cause of Lord Kildurrow's present state of mind. How to present the matter delicately absorbed most of Lord Kildurrow's mind and he paid no attention to the conversations around him, or the food before him. He did not even notice Amwyl arrive, looking resplendent in a gown of purple crushed velvet.

Amwyl's sister, the widow Catrin, accompanied the third wife of the King of the Baveii. They chose to sit together with Bran who, being the youngest of the King's children, sat at the end of the royal tables.

"Good afternoon, Mother," Bran said with a smile. Amwyl's mouth twitched in return. It was her best attempt at a smile.

"You look lovely," Bran continued, pretending everything was in order.

"Thank you," Amwyl murmured.

"Aunt," Bran greeted.

"Bran," Cat replied. She threw her nephew a bright smile and Bran grinned in return.

Conversation in the dining hall was loud and informal. The Greyls were in good cheer, despite the impending siege. After a long spell of loud chatter, King Gofron of the Baveii stood and the hall fell silent.

"My friends," he began. "For the first time in memory, all the Greyl lords and their families are housed together under one roof. And, wonder of wonders, we all seem to get along."

"Aye," one lord called. "Just as soon as you give me back those cattle your grandfather stole."

King Gofron laughed. "My friend, if we win this war, you are welcome to come and try to take them." He paused and scanned the proud faces in the crowded room. "And that, my lords is the point. The Ottals and the Touans are now massing on the pasturelands immediately before this fortress. It cannot be more than a day or two now before the siege commences."

These words sobered the good cheer of the gathered lords and their families. Bran's mind immediately turned to the conversation he once had with the Lord of the Hunt. Otsana was coming to war.

He would next see his beautiful wife fighting viciously against their enemies, and she would be separated from him by a hostile army. Bran felt suddenly homesick for the tundra and yearned for his wife's arms.

Amwyl, noting Bran's sudden, uncharacteristic melancholy, reached out and took his hand. Bran was supremely grateful for it. He squeezed her hand gently.

"My friends, at this juncture, I wish to thank you all for everything you've done up until now. Thank you for possessing the foresight to see that it is not just for ourselves we fight, but for our children and their children and their right to live as they choose."

"Here, here!" the gathered lords cheered.

"And so I raise my goblet to each of you. May we all gather here again and celebrate victory!"

"Victory!"

Gofron drank deeply then sat down and the meal began.

Twenty-Seven

"This is all you came through with?" the representative of the Yellow City assigned to the Touans asked the representative of the Yellow City who rode with the Ottals when the two armies met.

"It was less the nomads than the terrain of the tundra," the latter said apologetically.

"And the wolves," one of the Tigils growled.

Algar overheard, as did Robert and the pair exchanged a knowing look before they dismounted and prepared for the evening's meeting. The two armies had met at long last before the gates of the Greyl fortress that abutted the tall Speckled Rock Mountain Range.

Both sides were disappointed with what they saw. The Ottals had lost nearly half their hot-blooded horses to the tundra and many of their men seemed mad as they shuffled into their ranks, twitching and whispering to themselves. Even still, they outnumbered the Touan fighters by a few hundred.

The Touans themselves had three quarters of their number left, having lost less than the Ottals. Both armies, however, were a great deal smaller than anticipated at the planning stages of the war.

"We still outnumber the defenders some five to one," the King of Jitoua said.

"Such numbers are only a boon in open combat. In sieges, we must be prepared to lose a great number of men. We may end up outnumbered by the defenders before the first day is done."

"Not if we're smart about it."

On and on the debates raged while the regular soldiers and the vassals of the nobles set up camp. Algar grew quite bored of it. He ceased to listen. His eyes began to wander as his mind did the same. In their wanderings he chanced across an osprey, sitting quietly in a nearby tree and preening. He couldn't help himself. He grinned. The bird ignored him and continued to clean her wings.

"Why are you grinning like an idiot," Roger whispered to his son.

"It's nothing," Algar whispered back. He turned his attention back to the meeting.

"Then it's decided," one of the Yellow Robes said. "We wait while we build the engines."

"It's the only thing you can do," Roger said grumpily. "There's no point in storming the walls without ladders."

"Thank you," the Yellow Robe noted in a tone that was nothing akin to gratitude.

"We didn't sit through a three hour long meeting to state the bloody obvious. Now I'm hungry and tired, and I'm going to eat some of that delicious food I smell cooking, and then I'm going to bed." Roger stood.

"You will remain in your seat until you have been dismissed," an Ottal said quietly, dangerously.

"King Roger of Misoua," the Yellow Robe said with a twisted smile. "We did not conduct formal introductions earlier. Let us now correct that mistake. This," he indicated the Ottal who had spoken. "Is the General of the Holy Army. That means he is your commander."

Algar saw his father's shoulders tense as Roger halted his rise from his seat. He reached out and placed a hand on the King's back to calm him. King Roger sat slowly down.

"My apologies," he said in a tight voice. "I am weary from travel and momentarily forgot myself."

"I understand your fatigue," Guild Master Mtsusa replied. "So there is no harm. Though, do be warned your Majesty, I have executed men for less."

Roger raised an eyebrow, but did not respond save to mutter "bastard" under his breath. Algar pressed his lips together and the pair of them remained silent until the meeting was at last concluded.

"I want to kill that bastard myself," Roger growled quietly to his son as they took their places around their hearth and were immediately served by their vassals. Roger had never been more grateful for soup in his life.

* * * *

Lord Kildurrow sat uneasily in the plush seat wedged too tightly against the chess table in King Gofron's study. He could not bring himself to look his friend in the eye.

"What is it, Kildurrow," Gofron said gently.

Lord Kildurrow swallowed past the lump in his throat. He forced himself to look up. "I am... I'm in love with your wife," he said. His voice was measured and calm, but his eyes were slightly wild and desolate. They watched as Gofron's shoulders tensed.

"Which one?" Gofron asked slowly.

"Amwyl."

Gofron sank back into his chair, the game of chess now quite forgotten. He cast his eyes to the ground and his face became stony and unreasonable. "Have you...?"

"Have I what? Slept with her?" Lord Kildurrow asked. "No." It was a lie, but one Lord Kildurrow did not mind uttering, for it was designed not to protect himself but to protect Amwyl. Gofron relaxed a little.

"So that is the reason you have been so tense of late."

Lord Kildurrow nodded, turning his eyes to the floor. "I did not think I could love again, after so long without. I did not want this, your Majesty."

Gofron sighed. He himself did not love Amwyl in the same manner, but his fighting instincts had been roused all the same. He wondered greatly at himself then and at the selfishness he did not know he possessed. "No. I imagine not." He observed Lord Kildurrow a moment. "You barely talk to each other," Gofron noted.

"I have been trying to avoid her of late. It is not easy in the confines of these walls, as a close advisor to her husband." Lord Kildurrow's mouth twitched into a bitter smile.

"Does she share your sentiment?" Gofron asked carefully.

Lord Kildurrow hesitated. "I don't know," he answered slowly.

Gofron scoffed. "That sounded too close to a 'yes' for my liking, Kildurrow."

Lord Kildurrow remained seated in silence. Gofron sighed and rubbed his forehead.

"I didn't even want to marry her," he said, frustrated at himself and at Kildurrow and at all women everywhere. "It was nothing more than a political arrangement. They all were. If my reputation did not matter, I would give you my blessing, Kildurrow."

Lord Kildurrow looked up in surprise.

"But what army would follow a cuckold?" Gofron continued. "What sort of a king is a man if he is cuckold?"

"I understand, your Majesty."

"Damn it Kildurrow, we are friends! You will use my name!"

Lord Kildurrow nodded, but did not speak. Gofron sighed.

"I know nothing. This conversation never happened."

Lord Kildurrow nodded in miserable silence once more.

"Good. You are dismissed. We can forget about this whole affair and move on."

Lord Kildurrow stood and looked sadly at his friend. "You and I both know that isn't going to happen," he said quietly. "Forgive me, my Lord, for bringing such trouble on your house." Lord Kildurrow bowed and left the study.

Gofron watched him leave and, once he was certain the door was shut and he was perfectly alone, he let his temper loose. He kicked over the chess table and overturned one of the chairs before he vanished into his bedchamber to brood.

* * * *

Bran felt the absence of his wife all afternoon. He spent much of the day wandering lost within the labyrinthine halls of the fortress as he daydreamed of her. So lost in his private world was he that he almost collided head on with Lord Kildurrow as the man stormed around a corner like an angry ouruq. They both pulled up short in surprise.

"Forgive me," Lord Kildurrow muttered before passing Bran and continuing on his way.

"Wait," Bran said. "Wait!" He jogged to the place where Lord Kildurrow halted. "Are you all right, my Lord?"

"Fine," Lord Kildurrow lied.

"Clearly," Bran noted with a raised brow. He observed Lord Kildurrow's pale, stony face. "You told him, didn't you?" Bran guessed.

Lord Kildurrow shook his head. "He knows only that I love her."

Bran smiled. "You love her?"

Lord Kildurrow's head snapped up. "I should fall upon my own sword for what I have done!" he snapped. "I am no different from my treacherous son!"

"Your son betrayed the entire Greyl people in unchecked ambition," Bran said gently. "You, my Lord, are in love. The difference is profound."

"How do you not hate me?"

Bran sighed. "Come with me. Let's have a drink and we'll exchange love stories."

He clapped Lord Kildurrow on the back and the pair of them walked to Bran's chambers. Once settled, and the wine brought before them, Bran leant back in his chair and propped his feet up on the footstool.

"I loved Otsana the moment I laid eyes on her," Bran said with a wistful smile. "I thought I was hallucinating when I saw her stumble from the woods in her heavy leather clothing, dragging a thick fur coat behind her. Gods," Bran breathed. "I'll never forget that sight."

Lord Kildurrow listened in silence.

"She doesn't love me though," Bran said. This caught Lord Kildurrow's attention. "The only reason she married me, I'm sure, was for political reasons."

"To get help against the Ottals," Lord Kildurrow noted.

Bran nodded. "She is in love with another. Do you want to know who?"

Lord Kildurrow did not answer.

"The Lord of the Hunt," Bran scoffed. "A god. How can any man compete against a god?" Bran sighed. "But I can't help myself. I love her, and gods be damned if I ever stop. I made a vow once. I swore that as soon as this war was over, I'd let her go. She'd be free of me, forever."

Lord Kildurrow drained his glass. "That is not a good love story."

"No," Bran said. "It's not. And that is the reason why I don't hate you. My mother loves you, I see it every time she looks at you. The best part is, you love her in return. What you two have, it's precious. Don't ever resent it. I'd give my soul to have Otsana love me in return."

"How can I not resent it? She is another man's wife, and that man is my friend!"

"She is another man's third wife. Father does not love her. Not the way you do."

"And still I can do nothing about it. I either yield to my selfish desires and commit treason, or I do not. How can I betray my friend, my king?"

"It would be different if Father loved her," Bran said quietly. "I'd hate you then. As it is, I cannot hate you. You've made my mother happier than I've seen her in a long time."

"Not anymore," Lord Kildurrow grunted. "I will not be a traitor."

Bran nodded. "I understand." There was a long silence.

"I wish it was different," Lord Kildurrow whispered. He did not know it, but he wept. Small trickles of tears made their slow way down his cheeks. Bran smiled at him and finished his wine. The two sat in comforting silence as the daylight faded away.

When dinner was called, only Bran answered. Lord Kildurrow retired to his chamber without food and went to bed. Dinner was a quiet family affair in Gofron's chambers. Gofron's three wives sat nearest him, while the children sprawled all over, talking to each other and laughing together.

Bran watched his father, noting that he often looked at Amwyl. There was no accusation in his eyes, rather the gazes swung between appraising and thoughtful. Sometimes Gofron looked unhappy, other times resolved and yet other times angry. Bran could well imagine the fury of emotions that raged inside his father. When he had learnt Otsana loved another, he had struck out in a temper.

It was not quite the same for his father, Bran knew. Gofron had resented being married. The King of the Baveii felt that marriage had prevented him from experiencing all manner of adventures. He had expressed his resentment about marriage to each of his wives many times before this.

The issue was not that Amwyl loved another, Bran was certain, but that his reputation as a king depended upon him keeping all his wives. No one would follow a man who could not even keep his own wives.

Dinner did not end in a hurry. If there was one thing Gofron revelled in, it was his children. He loved having them near to him and he took great delight in each of their varied skills. Bran sat with his sisters, finding them far more entertaining than any of his brothers. He had them laughing so hard with tales of the tundra that wine came out of one of his half-sister's noses. The laughter was slow to die down.

At length the royal family was dismissed.

"Bran," Gofron said. "Will you stay a moment? There's something I wish to discuss."

Bran nodded. "Of course," he said casually. He grinned at his half-sisters as they left, still giggling, and lounged happily on a chair. Gofron watched him for a while.

"It's about your mother."

Bran raised his brows. "Is it?"

"Háve you noticed anything... unusual about her lately?"

"Not really," Bran lied. "Why?"

Gofron sighed. "Lord Kildurrow, that's why."

Bran frowned and waited in silence.

"The servant who was sent to fetch you happened to note that you and Lord Kildurrow were drinking together."

Bran sighed. "He told me what happened."

"That he told me he was in love with your mother?"

"Yes."

"And that didn't disturb you at all?"

Bran shrugged, not speaking until compelled to by his father's stern gaze. "It doesn't upset me," Bran admitted. "In fact, I thought it was rather sweet."

Gofron slammed his cup on the table and stood abruptly.

"Father...."

"Sweet. You thought it was sweet?"

"Well, yes. Lord Kildurrow's wife died a number of years ago now. He, and everyone else, thought that he'd never find another woman worthy of the love he had for Isabelle. Apparently, everyone was wrong."

"She is *my* wife!"

"A wife you never wanted," Bran said patiently. Gofron stood up straight and glared at his son before suddenly collapsing back into his seat.

"I know," he moaned. He sighed. "I care for her, Bran," he said at last. "More deeply than I thought I did, but it still is not love, not the love that you have for Otsana."

Bran smiled a little sadly at this. "Be grateful for that," he said quietly. "The pain is tenfold when a love given is not returned."

Gofron looked at his son a moment before he nodded. "I need your advice, Bran. A cuckold king will not be king for long, but Kildurrow is like a brother to me now. I want him to be happy. I want Amwyl to be happy too. What should I do?"

Bran did not hide his surprise. His father rarely asked for advice. He sighed.

"I do not know, Father," he admitted. "All I know is that I want both mother and you to be happy."

"So I should turn my back and allow the affair?"

"Only if it makes you happy."

Gofron snorted in exasperation. "I should never have been king," he muttered darkly. "Damn my brother!"

"He died in a training accident," Bran said with a smile. "There's nothing that can be done about it now."

"I could annul the marriage," Gofron mused. "No, I can't. That would also annul the contract of peace, the whole reason for the marriage in the first place! Damn the gods for this mess!"

Bran sighed. "I don't know how to be more helpful."

"There's nothing I can do. There is no recourse for Amwyl and Kildurrow."

"Not yet, I suppose," Bran agreed.

Gofron raised his brows at him.

"I just mean that we do not know what the future holds for us. Perhaps a little time and patience will reveal a possible solution."

Gofron grunted again. "Perhaps." He did not sound hopeful. He watched his son a moment. "Why does none of this bother you?"

"To be perfectly honest, I don't know. Lord Kildurrow is a good man. He was threatening to fall on his own sword, tortured by what he called his treason against you. He is torn in half. I'm certain he never wanted this, and he certainly never wanted to jeopardise your friendship."

"No. I imagine not."

"And mother, well, she was as much resigned to your marriage as you are."

"I've never mistreated her."

"I was not implying you did," Bran said gently. "But just as you dream of being free, so does she. Even women dream."

Gofron shook his head. "I envy you Bran. You have seen more of the world than I ever shall. You've ridden the tundra. Do you know how much I used to dream about that as a boy? It always seemed so distant and its people so elusive. You married one."

"Who does not love me. She is like mother, resigned to her marriage because it cemented aid for her people and no other reason."

"Yet even so, she had brought you to the tundra. You are now one of them, and they have honoured you with that ridiculous turkey-cape."

Bran laughed and his father smiled.

"I promise that once this war is over, I'll take you through the tundra myself," Bran said. "I'll show you everything they have shown me, and we shall both attend the Great Gathering."

"I'd like that very much." Gofron sighed. "Thank you, Bran. I feel a little better now."

Bran nodded. "With your permission, I should like to retire to bed."

"A good idea. Go then, I'll not be long behind."

Offering a reassuring smile at his father, Bran stood and left the room.

Gofron shook his head, poured himself another goblet of wine and stared out the window at the campfires that littered the pastureland before the imposing walls of the fortress.

* * * *

The attack was sudden and unexpected. The Winter Wolf had only just turned her snout east in warning when the Ottals attacked. They were not members of the Ottalan army that the Sierran nomads had been chasing across the tundra. These men were fresh, if not experienced.

"Reinforcements!" Inna had barked as the first wave of Ottals stormed their disorganised camp. The fight was vicious and many Sierran warriors were slain before they could muster their defence.

The Winter Wolf and her pack were embroiled in a fierce battle with Ottalan horsemen. The Ottals had chosen an advantageous area to attack in. The land here was relatively flat. Their horses could run with ease.

When the din of battle ceased, Inna looked around him. The Sierrans, although victorious, had lost fully a third of their number and, Inna noted with a sinking feeling, the Winter Wolf was wounded.

"Otsana!" Ur shouted. He dismounted and ran to her side.

The Winter Wolf lay on her side, a cut across her cheek and two other slices on her back. Her thick fur had prevented a great deal of damage and the wounds, given time, would heal well. Still, she lay on the ground and whimpered. It did not take long for Ur to discover why.

Millen laid on the ground, a lance thrust into his chest. Dead eyes stared unseeing at the sky.

"Oh," Ur whispered when he saw. "Oh, Otsana! I'm so sorry. I know you were fond of him."

Bull was the next to arrive. "Is she all right?" he asked Ur.

"Her heart is hurt," Ur answered, pointing to Millen.

"Oh," Bull replied. "Otsana," he said gently. "I'm sorry."

The Winter Wolf snarled, startling even Ur, who jumped away. The horse-sized beast pulled herself to her feet and threw her head back, unleashing a howl so full of pain and rage that it froze the blood of all who heard it.

Bull straightened and turned to the Sierran warriors. "All who can still fight, now is the time to wear your war clothes. The rest must stay. Tend to the dead. Dead or alive, we will return to you."

The warriors immediately returned to their pavilions to dress.

It did not take them long, though they placed on all their fetishes and talismans. As they dressed, the Winter Wolf stalked around the camp, snarling and snapping. So fierce was her wrath that the other wolves cowered in fear, and the normally steady horses pranced nervously.

It took less than a half hour for the Sierran nomads and the Ayals to gather their horses and mount up, ready for battle. Bull looked them over critically. Many were still bleeding from wounds they had no time to tend.

"We fight," he said simply. It was all Bull need have said. The Winter Wolf's anger was infectious. The warriors rose in their saddles and roared. Bull turned his horse around and rode forward at a gallop.

* * * *

It had been a little less than a week. The siege engines had all been built and were ready to be put to work. For the first few days, the rangers in the woods had harried the soldiers cutting the trees at the edge of the forest. However, the size of the guard that had been sent to accompany them soon made any attacks unfeasible, so the rangers were forced to sit in frustration, unable to do anything.

Bran had spent his time watching the Ottals and Touans prepare for the siege. He remained in the lookout tower all day for days on end, dressed for the battle that might commence at any time. He chose to wear his feathered cloak with a crow's head helm.

Though he hated to admit it, there was a certain power that came from wearing it, no matter how ridiculous he thought he looked. The cloak was comforting, protective and, most importantly, connected him with the tundra and his wife.

"I miss you, Otsana," he whispered as he watched the Ottals begin to fall into their ranks. He straightened when he realised what he was seeing. He ran up the small flight of steps to the very peak of the tower to sound the bell. The attack would commence in just a few moments.

Bran was almost grateful for the battle, he mused as he pulled hard on the chord. The bell peeled in clear, deep tones. It would mean Otsana was closer to him now, as long as everything went according to plan. Not knowing where Otsana was at the moment was almost as terrible as the waiting for battle to start.

Bran released the chord on the fourth pull and immediately sprinted down the stairs and down and out of the tower. Before long he was standing by his father and Lord Kildurrow atop the inner gate of the stronghold.

"You look like a giant turkey," Gofron noted absently as he watched the enemy ranks form.

"Crow," Bran answered. "I look like a giant crow."

"If you insist."

Bran laughed. "Is everything prepared?"

"Yes. The talking bird-woman tells me that the kingdom of Misoua will attack the Ottals once they see the yellow flag. At the same time, the troops that have gathered in the forest and, with any luck, the Sierrans also will attack."

Bran nodded. He thought of Otsana and imagined seeing her again. He became so distracted by that thought, he did not notice the launch of the first of the missiles from the trebuchets. Only the earth-shattering thudding of boulder against stone wall woke him from his reverie. The siege had begun.

* * * *

The first day of the siege proved dull. It began as most do, with the Holy Army of the god of the Yellow City testing the fortress for any structural weaknesses. They watched carefully for cracks that appeared in the walls that might be large enough to send the wall crumbling with the next hit. The bombardment ceased once night fell, and the soldiers on the walls of the fortress retired to bed, replaced by fresh fighters.

"That was tedious," Bran noted as he removed his cloak in his chamber. Amwyl and her sister had gone there once the bombardment had commenced. Somehow she felt safer in her son's room. Perhaps it was the masculine nature of the space.

"Hello Mother, Aunt," Bran added as an after-thought.

Amwyl managed a small smile. Bran looked her over.

"Frightened?" he asked. Amwyl nodded.

"Don't be. The Ottals will break upon these walls."

"You sound so sure. How can you know?"

Bran shrugged. "I don't."

Amwyl laughed a little. "I need some tea. Would you like some, dear?"

"Yes please, that would be lovely."

"I'll make it," Cat said. She rose from her seat and stoked the fire, leaving momentarily to fetch a kettle and water. Amwyl tried to pay attention to her embroidery, but it was no use. With a frustrated sigh, she cast the embroidery away, missing the fire by mere inches.

"Mother!" Bran admonished gently. He went to the fire and picked it up. He looked down. The scene was beautiful – tall grasses in pale green and purple with grey-green rocks and patches of snow visible throughout.

"I'm trying to make it for your father," Amwyl said quietly. "I know how much he's yearned to ride the frozen north. I thought this might help ease that yearning a little."

"You care for him, don't you?"

"I do. He has been a good husband." Tears struck Amwyl's eyes. "And I a terrible wife," she whispered.

Bran went to her side and wrapped his strong arms around her slender shoulders. "That's not true." Bran's tone was so gentle that Amwyl burst into tears.

"I have!" she wailed. "I... I... want another... I've been unfaithful. I am a terrible wife."

"One cannot help their hearts," Bran said, remembering a conversation he once had with an Arrluk Clan Shamanka. The quote belonged to her, and Bran thought it useful under the circumstances.

"It doesn't matter," Amwyl said, collecting herself. The tightening of her voice gave a bitter tone to her words. "The man I love will have nothing to do with me now. It is settled."

"What happened?" Bran asked.

"He will not speak to me. He will not be in the same room with me, unless my husband accompanies me. He will not even look me in the eye. He never loved me, I fear."

"That's not true."

"It must be. Why else will he not face me?"

"Because he is hopelessly in love with you," Bran answered. "And he is torn between his love for you and his love for his king. I think he is just trying to avoid the temptation altogether. It is not that he doesn't love you but that he does that is responsible for his current behaviour."

Amwyl frowned at her son. "It is easier to hate him if I believe he does not love me, that he took from me what he wanted and is done with me."

Bran laughed. "I imagine it is."

"Damn it, Bran! I was ready to be resigned to my fate once again. Now I detest it even more!"

"Sorry."

Amwyl laughed through her tears. "No, I'm sorry. This is not your affair. I should not drag you into it."

Cat returned with the kettle and Amwyl hurriedly dried her eyes.

"Is everything all right?" Cat asked.

"Fine," Amwyl said.

"Mother is upset about the position she finds herself in."

"Bran!"

Cat laughed. "Your son knows you can't keep anything from me, and he just saved us both a lot of trouble. Thank you, Bran." Cat placed the kettle on the kettle hook over the fire and returned to her seat.

Bran shrugged. "My pleasure."

"What a charming boy."

Bran laughed and Amwyl took her embroidery from him. She sat down and began working again, Bran watched a moment before turning to his aunt.

"So, Aunt," he said casually. "Have none of the many lords gathered here for war caught your attention?"

Cat scoffed. "My first marriage was hell," she said darkly. "I'll never put myself through that again."

"I never said you had to *marry* him."

"Bran!" Amwyl admonished as her sister burst out laughing.

"You little imp!" Cat giggled.

Bran grinned. "I blame mother," he said lightly. "She raised me."

Amwyl found a new target for her embroidery and Cat laughed harder.

Twenty-Eight

"Well, however quickly it was built," Roger noted to the gathered war council. "It certainly is sturdy."

"That monstrosity will be brought crumbling down!" one of the Yellow Robes uttered with such vehemence that spittle sprayed the front of his robe. Algar coughed to keep from laughing aloud, earning him a hard elbow from his father.

"It's no use attacking the gate," Roger continued. "We should concentrate here." He indicated the section of wall that was the longest uninterrupted section on the hastily scribbled drawing of the fortress. Much of what was drawn had to be guessed. "It is unlikely that they've had the time to reinforce this section, and there are no turrets to ground it. This section ought to be the weakest."

"Know a great deal about sieges, do you, Touan?" the Guild Master asked him.

Roger shrugged. "My kingdom borders the Greyl kingdom of the Baveii. I've sat in my fair share of sieges. All of them minor, of course, but one siege is much like another when you get down to the bare bones of it all."

Mtsusa grunted. Roger moved carefully around him. He knew that the General of the Holy Army of the Yellow City had taken an immediate dislike to him and his son.

Roger was also aware that the General was a man of volatile temper, who would willingly kill one of his own, let alone a complete stranger, if they posed any sort of threat to his power. Roger remained mild and unassuming around the frightening Guild Master.

Algar, being young and arrogant, had to be checked by his father often. Though Algar hated the continual censorship, he very much appreciated his father's efforts to keep his foolishness in check. It kept him alive. The General certainly had the Yellow Robes' favour. They would not stop the Ottalan General from killing as many people as he pleased, should the General convince them that it was all for the cause.

Fanatics, Roger thought bitterly of the Ottals. *By the gods, I hate them.*

The meeting wore on into mealtime. All manner of possible strategies were put forward and discussed, but the General had his own ideas. Even still, he diplomatically listened to each lord's opinion when they cared to voice one before returning to his original ideas. They were sound plans, Roger had to admit. Though inexperienced, this Ottalan was no fool.

At length, and largely due to the ever-increasing volume of rumbling stomachs, the council disbanded for the night. The attack would continue on the morrow. For now, however, they would eat and rest.

Algar and Roger did not discuss their impending treason against the Touan Federation with their allies that night. Instead, they ate their bread and hearty soup and exchanged tales of the idiocy they perpetrated during the various stages of their lives. It made for some hearty laughs around the fire and did wonders in easing the tension the lords were feeling.

During one such round of laughter Algar happened to look back to the distant line of trees that marked the forest. He plainly saw Blue Ghost there, standing at the very edge of the woods, glowing faintly despite the night being as black as pitch. There was yet a more disturbing sight.

Through the trees flitted silver shadows. Algar watched with a pale face as the silver streaks left the woods and poured over the rocks like silken ghosts only to disappear in the cracks and crevices of the ragged terrain the Touans had left behind them.

"What is it, Algar?" Roger asked when Algar failed to laugh at one of his better jests.

"Wolves," Algar whispered. "Hundreds upon hundreds of wolves."

Robert turned to look at where Algar's gaze fell and saw only pale rock and the silent blackness of the forest line. He frowned. "I see nothing."

Algar shuddered and turned back to the fire. "We have angered the spirits here," he said to his father. "The Touans will face more than Greyl steel come the morrow."

"Shut-up Algar," one nobleman complained. "You're spooking us."

"Sorry," Algar said with a lopsided smile.

"That's nothing," another lord said with an evil grin. "You should hear the tales of the ghosts that inhabit our keep. There was this one time, when I was just a boy, I spied an old maid, skinny as a rail and dressed entirely in white. Only I could see straight through her, and her feet never touched the ground...."

The jokes about youth and foolishness were traded with a long barrage of ghost stories. So compelling were some of the tales, that all the men went to bed with prickled skin and had strange dreams.

* * * *

The dawn spread her fingers in a thin line of grey. The skies had clouded overnight. A bitterly cold wind howled in from the north. So strong were the northerly gales at times that they blew the boulders thrown by the trebuchets off their targets. Pavillions ripped free of their pegs and blew away.

Bran was glad for it. It would make it that much more difficult for the Touans. The men of the more southerly Greyl kingdoms were not pleased, but they too understood the tactical advantage such weather gave them, so they did not complain.

"Do you feel that?" King Gofron bellowed down at the army of the Holy Yellow City. "That is the Lady Tundra! She is angry with you. You shall feel her wrath!"

Bran couldn't help himself. He laughed.

"What?" Gofron asked his son innocently.

"You've never been the religious type," Bran noted, still smiling. "You sound as fanatical as they do."

Gofron grinned. "Should put them off a bit. Besides, I've seen things enough to make me believe."

Bran nodded. "As have I."

"You? The greatest sceptic known to mankind?"

"How else can you explain an elder woman of the Sierran tundra turning into a bird and flying away?"

Gofron nodded and grunted, but the sound was drowned by the thunderous crash of stone against stone as the invaders commenced the day's attack. Gofron, Bran and Lord Kildurrow watched closely as the boulders rained down on the wall.

"They're concentrating their attacks," Lord Kildurrow noted.

"Will it hold?" Bran asked his father.

"Unlikely," Gofron noted. "The men on the right will be stranded once the Ottals and Touans break through."

"There's nothing to be done for it now," Lord Kildurrow growled.

"They're not attacking." Bran was perplexed.

"They're waiting for the wall to come down. They weren't expecting a siege," Gofron noted. "They did not think to bring scaling ladders, and making the engines took all their timber and time."

"That's no way to win a siege," Lord Kildurrow noted sourly.

"Can they not see that we have another wall?" Bran asked.

"I believe they can."

"So…."

"So the only available recourse for them is to take the outer wall and move the engines closer, then work on the inner wall. Your Majesty…."

"It's Gofron, Kildurrow. Don't make me beat it into you."

Lord Kildurrow's mouth twitched slightly, but did not form into the smile that threatened. "I suggest we pull our forces back as soon as the wall is breeched. We'll lose less men that way."

"The plan was to engage them on the field once the Sierran's arrive," Bran said with a scowl.

"And it is a sound plan," Lord Kildurrow noted. "But I might add that we do not know if the Ottals have engaged the Sierrans and won."

"Don't even suggest it!" Bran growled.

"Stay calm, Bran," Gofron murmured. "Lord Kildurrow makes a good point. We're fighting blind at this point. Buddy!"

The messenger boy appeared from seemingly nowhere. He had never lost the awed sparkle in his eyes that had appeared the day the King of the Baveii made him the King's Personal Messenger.

"Your Majesty," he said with a deep bow.

"I need you to run a message to the King of the Pamisii. You know who he is, don't you?"

"Yes, your Majesty."

"Good. Tell him this exactly. 'Fighting blind, don't know about aid, pull back if breeched.'"

"Very good, your Majesty." Buddy bowed and vanished at a dead run.

"You aren't going to make him repeat the message?" Bran asked.

Gofron shrugged. "He's never made a mistake yet."

"Let's hope this isn't the day he does."

Gofron glowered at his son a moment before turning back to the siege. "You know," he noted sourly. "Until we get to the actual fighting, sieges are dead boring."

Lord Kildurrow burst out laughing and Bran grinned. No sooner had Lord Kildurrow laughed than a large boulder struck the wall and it cracked. The fissure was enormous and its creation shook the entire fortress.

"One more stone and that wall is down," Lord Kildurrow growled.

"Pull back!" Gofron roared as the massive Touan and Ottal alliance cheered. Keen as the Greyls were to battle, it seemed the Touan and Ottal alliance were more so.

"I don't like the sound of that," Gofron muttered as the cheers of the enemy reached his ears. Bran barely heard. He was scanning the northern horizon.

"Come on, Otsana," he whispered. "Where are you?"

Two more boulders pummelled into the wall, but neither of them close enough to the crack to do much else but shake the wall a little.

"Archers prepare," Gofron said.

"Archers!" Lord Kildurrow bellowed. The order spread down the inner walls as the gate opened to allow the retreating warriors into the inner circle in which the main stronghold stood.

One last boulder sent a large portion of the outer wall crumbling down. Roaring in rage and bloodlust, the Ottalan host and their Touan allies surged forward.

Though the Greyls rained arrows and stones upon them, it seemed that the invader's numbers did not dwindle. They rushed forward and, precisely as Lord Kildurrow had predicted, sought to take the outer wall first.

The King of the Pamissi had not yet finished retreating when the Ottals and Touans reached him. Knowing that the Greyls would have no choice but to shut the inner gate or risk yielding it to the invaders, the King drew his sword. Those who had remained with him did likewise.

"What the hell is he doing?" Gofron growled. He raised his voice to a bellow. "Get inside! Your Majesty, get inside!"

The King of the Pamisii heard, despite the roar of the oncoming enemy. He turned his head briefly and yelled in reply, "Shut the damned gate, you fool!"

Gofron stood in utter disbelief before he noticed that the Pamisii warriors who had wanted to retreat had done so. Most of the Pamisii who remained behind, defiant alongside their king, were the younger sons of the nobles. They stood proud, facing annihilation with drawn swords.

"Shut the gate," Gofron commanded.

"My Lord?" a guard asked.

"I said shut the damned gate!"

"You're leaving them out there?"

"His Majesty believes that the Sierrans will come in time, sire," a young Pamisii nobleman said as he arrived at the top of the inner gate.

"You are?"

"Strong Oak, your Majesty," the boy replied. "Bastard son of his Majesty, King of the Pamisii by a ranger."

"You seem proud of the title 'bastard,'" Lord Kildurrow noted without any malice.

"With such a man for a father, who could not be?"

"Well, Strong Oak, I hope to high hell your father is right."

Below the attackers had pulled up short and observed the small circle of Greyl warriors that now stood between them and the inner wall. They burst out laughing. The laughter was cruel.

Gofron watched in awe as the king of the Pamisii pulled himself upright.

"I am the king of these lands," he bellowed at the infantry of mockers in perfect Touan. "Who dares challenge my right to rule?"

"I do," a Yellow Robe said, stepping forward. It was an odd sight to observe a holy man, still dressed in the traditional yellow robes, but decorated in mismatched armour. "On behalf of the god of the Yellow City, whose divinity overcomes all."

This time it was the King of the Pamisii's turn to laugh cruelly. "Do you not feel the bitter winds of the tundra? They are not the dry, hot winds of the desert, my friend. The Winter Wolf is coming and your god has abandoned you."

"Our god never abandons his children."

"Even your god is terrified of the Winter Wolf, and of the men who fight now to defend her."

"Our god fears nothing!" the Yellow Robe shrieked.

The King of the Pamisii laughed loudly. His guard of lords grinned. They did not respond to the Yellow Robe, but began to beat their swords against their steel-plated breasts. The deep voices of the tall men as they took up the traditional Pamisii war chant soon joined the rhythmic clanging. Their voices were joined by those who had chosen to remain amongst the living and defend the keep with the other Greyl warriors. The whole fortress came alive, singing the ancient chant from its very stone.

The chant ended abruptly. The small circle of Pamisii warriors sank low into a fighter's crouch, awaiting the onslaught that was sure to come. Gofron smiled grimly as the invaders hesitated, looking at each other for reassurance. The King of the Pamisii wore the same grim smile.

In a combined and unusually undisciplined rush, the invaders surged forward en mass. It was precisely what the King of the Pamisii had hoped for. In such an undisciplined rush, he knew he and his men could last longer, prolong the fighting as much as possible, giving the Winter Wolf a little more time.

The Pamisii warriors proved incredibly proficient. They maintained their circle, never straying too far and always returning to their position should they be goaded from their formation. The result was a startling loss of life for the attackers, with not even one of the Pamisii defenders taken down.

At length the combined forces of the Ottals and the Touans were forced to retreat and regroup in order to find a better way of breaching the tightly formed circle that stood defiantly before them. No sooner had they retreated then Mtsusa, General of the Holy Army of the Yellow City, rode through the ranks.

The man observed the small circle of warriors impassively for a moment before dismounting and drawing his own sword. His presence seemed to fortify his confused and haggard infantry. They formed their ranks close to him. The entire battle had ground to a halt as both sides watched with bated breath.

"Do you know who I am?" the Guild Master asked the King of the Pamisii in a soft, gentle sort of voice. The Pamisii warriors remained crouched in silence.

"I am a god," he said gently. "Your god. The last words from your lips shall be a prayer to me, that I might have mercy on your tattered soul. You will be saluting my name, Greyl."

The King of the Pamisii's lips twisted into an odd smile, but he did not answer him.

"You know your precious Winter Wolf?"

The flash in the King's eyes was dark and dangerous.

"She is dead. I skinned her myself." He said it so gently it was almost loving.

The uncertainty that crossed the King's face was all the Guild Master needed. In a strike so rapid it could not be seen with the naked eye, he attacked, engaging the King of the Pamisii with a series of strikes that only instinct allowed him to survive. The combined Ottalan and Touan infantry attacked again and the two sides were once more embroiled in a vicious battle.

The defenders along the walls seemed to wake from their morbid reverie and began firing their arrows once more, taking careful aim in order to best help the Pamisii warriors who stood staunchly before the inner gate. It was not enough.

Disarmed and badly wounded, the King of the Pamisii was dragged forward by his ear and thrown onto the ground. The man rolled once, found a fallen sword and rolled onto his feet, facing the Guild Master once more, but now entirely without the support of his warriors.

"My Lord!" called one as he pulled his sword from a Touan soldier's gut.

The King of the Pamisii looked over briefly and shook his head. The circle was not to be broken under any circumstance. With a growl, the King of the Pamisii attacked.

* * * *

"Gods," Bran breathed as he watched. He looked over briefly at Strong Oak, who stood proudly, but nonetheless looked terrified as he watched his father and the General of the Holy Army of the Yellow City battle fiercely. Bran reached out and took the boy's shoulder. The bastard son of the King of the Pamisii, who loved his father dearly, did not notice.

* * * *

The strike to his wrist was unexpected. The King of the Pamisii grunted as he lost the use of his hand. His sword fell uselessly to the ground. His left knee and right thigh were sliced in close succession and he buckled, landing hard on his knees. He felt his helm being pulled off. A hard, calloused hand gripped his head by his short dark hair. His head was tilted back roughly.

None of it seemed real to the King. The once intense pain was now distant. He was calm, and though the din of battle raged all around him, he heard only the wind and the bright sounds of birdsong as all around him, ignorant to the follies of men, the land continued to live.

The thought made him smile even as his foe roughly shook him.

The sharply pointed tip of a sword touched his collarbone and was pressed just hard enough to break the skin. The King of the Pamisii winced, but it did nothing to quell the benevolent smile that painted his face.

"Say it!" he heard the General of the Holy Armies hiss. "Pray I spare you."

The King of the Pamisii turned his head to look once more on the northern horizon at that small rocky hill that divided Pamisii lands from the tundra.

That line he had crossed only once when he was very young. He had become lost in the vast expanse that was the tundra. A Shamanka of the White Fox Clan found him wandering through the tall grass.

How that old woman had laughed to see his beaming face. She had taken him in her strong arms and walked back to that very hill and placed him in his frantic mother's warm, very grateful embrace.

That woman had wanted nothing more from the exchange than to see a mother's relief. She bestowed upon him a small gift, a necklace made from the stuffed paw of a white fox. In turn, he had given her a child's love, a love that had never dimmed though he had grown and his hair had greyed.

As the King remembered this sacred exchange, he could see her, that wise old woman of the tundra, standing there on the crest of that hill.

His eyes filled with joyous tears when he saw her smiling face, shining as if it were made of the moon. He was once again that innocent babe.

Beside the Shamanka, a giant wolf crested the hill, her sharp green eyes catching his immediately. His heart rose in his chest and he smiled broadly.

"Otsana," he breathed. It was the last thing he said.

Angered that the Winter Wolf should be mentioned when it was he who had the King's life in his hands, the Guild Master and General of the Holy Armies plunged the sword down into the King's chest, sundering his heart. He gleaned satisfaction from hearing a lone wail of despair from atop the walls, but that satisfaction was short-lived.

A long, low howl filled the air, freezing the combatants where they stood. Several of the Ottals, their minds held by threads, screamed and fell to their knees, throwing their arms around their heads.

The Ottalan General turned slowly towards the sound. His heart stopped beating as he spied the Winter Wolf, standing alone on the crest of the hill that divided the tundra from the Greyl kingdom of the Pamisii. Her green eyes bore into his, even at that distance, and her snarl chilled him to the core.

The Winter Wolf threw back her head and howled again. This time, her call was answered. The entire hill was soon covered in Sierran warriors, some atop their enormous black horses, some on foot. All of them wore strange war fetishes and carried an array of weapons. They rose in their saddles and whooped and howled while their horses, reinvigorated by their riders, pranced and shifted.

Hundreds of wolves, some ninety of them tundra wolves, standing almost as tall as Otsana, joined the new army. They were accompanied by wolves of a more typical size and slightly larger Black Hounds by the score. Together, these wolves and hounds were an army unto themselves.

Astride his tall black horse was the figure of the stag-man that the Guild Master had met when he was still only a Tigil. The one who, it was claimed, was a god of very archaic origins. Beside him rode a boy with no eyes, yet the Guild Master felt sure that boy was looking at him, *into* him. Perhaps the greatest surprise General Mtsusa received was the appearance of the former Guild Master, dressed now as a Sierran nomad and riding a tundra horse.

The Guild Master was so taken aback by his predecessor's reappearance that he failed to notice the Braddard attached by a rope to the Ottal's saddle until the former Guild Master undid the knot and kicked the haggard-looking man forward. Gibbering incomprehensibly, the man tore down the hill, stumbling as he hurled himself unchecked towards his countrymen.

To the south, the Ottals and the Touans were faced with a similar sight. The one they called Blue Ghost stood on the tallest of boulders on the field of rocks immediately before the pastureland. He stood naked and unarmed. None could deny now that he did indeed glow.

Behind him stood another force of Greyls; an infantry numbering close to a hundred. They were surrounded by wolves of all hues, each of whom pointed their eager, snarling snouts towards the battle.

The Winter Wolf howled once more and, not waiting to see if her children followed, she loped hungrily into battle. It seemed the pouring of wolves and hounds over that small hill would never cease as they surged forward in one, snarling, snapping mass, the Sierrans in their midst whooping and calling savagely.

"Mount up!" the Guild Master screamed, running to his horse.

In an instant, the walls of the stronghold were forgotten as the Holy Army rode forward to clash with the attacking forces of the tundra.

* * * *

"Otsana?" Bran whispered as he spied the massive wolf on the crest of the hill. It seemed impossible that his wife could indeed be the enormous white wolf he saw before him, yet somehow he knew it was her. His heart would recognise his wife in whatever form she took.

"The flag!" an osprey screeched as it dove passed Bran's ear. It turned and circled and dived again, screeching urgently. "Raise the flag! Now!"

Bran was roused from his shock. Taking up the small brass horn he had strapped to his side, he issued three short blasts. Immediately a yellow flag rose over the tallest tower and waved frantically.

* * * *

Algar looked up when he heard the horn blasts issue from the wall. The waving of a bright yellow flag caught his eye.

"That's the signal!" he bellowed to his army. He pulled his charging horse up short and spun around, drawing his sword. His father and the loyal lords and their fighters did the same.

"For Misoua!" Algar screamed.

He kicked his horse. The charger reared with a piercing scream and bolted forward, eager now for battle, as if it sensed the importance of its role. Algar took down eight men before he was met with resistance.

"Traitor!" the Touan soldier shrieked at him, spitting fiercely.

Algar grinned. "I am loyal to my kingdom, are you?" he asked between clashes.

The Holy Army was in disarray. Half of them had been held back by the surprise attack by the army of Misoua. The other half was embroiled in a vicious battle with the wolves and the Sierrans. The number of dead was excessively high on both sides of the battle. The southerly edge of the front fared little better.

"Prepare to open the gate!" Gofron hollered as the shock of seeing his strange allies passed.

Lord Kildurrow, Bran and Strong Oak all unsheathed their weapons.

"No," the King of the Baveii barked. "You remain here with me."

"I will not be kept from this battle," Lord Kildurrow growled.

"The hell you won't. You're staying here."

"I am not."

"Nor am I," Bran said.

"You especially."

"That is my wife out there." Bran pointed.

"It's a wolf!"

Lord Kildurrow smirked, taking a moment for sarcasm. "I had heard as much."

Bran ignored him. "I am not staying!"

"Yes, you are," his father shot back.

"I will go now," Strong Oak said quietly, though his dark eyes burned fiercely. "I will avenge my father."

To this, Gofron could say nothing. The boy turned and joined the remaining Pamisii forces. Lord Kildurrow turned to follow and Gofron grabbed his arm.

"You will stay!"

"No, gods damn it!" Lord Kildurrow barked. His eyes blazed with a strange crazed need for battle. In an instant Gofron understood and he slowly released his grip.

"You will lead the Baveii," he said. "If anyone complains, take their heads."

Lord Kildurrow nodded and left. Bran glared at his father.

"Let me go."

"No Bran," Gofron said gently. "Not this time."

Tears blurred Bran's vision as he watched the armies of the Greyl Kingdoms pour through the open gate beneath him and into battle. Many Greyl warriors remained to defend the walls should the battle go sour. The outcome remained uncertain and the chaos made even the most educated guess mere conjecture. The Holy Army of the Yellow City had the advantage of numbers. Their hatred for the Sierrans and the Greyls had solidified into terrible resolve during the course of their trials.

Bran found that he cared little for the fate of even his own brothers, let alone countrymen. His eyes followed only the Winter Wolf and he prayed that she come through this battle.

Twenty-Nine

$\mathcal{A}$lgar found himself unhorsed and fighting for his life. Thrice he was thrown onto his back and thrice he had fought his way back up to his feet. He felt his sword slip as his opponent twisted awkwardly. The man's sword would have sliced his head in half had he not been taken to the ground by the sudden leap of a wolf. The dog clutched the man's neck and shook violently as the man tried to shriek through the gurgle of blood and a crushed throat. Algar's stomach twisted as the sounds of teeth grinding against spine reached his ears, and he had to pause to fight the bile bubbling up from his stomach. He was barely upright again when a tundra wolf crossed his path and bared its blood-soaked teeth at him.

The wolf growled low and prowled forward before its cold yellow eyes fell to the blue bead around his neck. Looking thoroughly disappointed, the wolf turned away and bounded down the field to find another throat to crush. Algar had no time to still his heart as an Ottalan soldier bore down upon him.

The man was taken clean off his horse, his head caught between the jaws of the Winter Wolf. Upon landing, the wolf shook him viciously, snapping the poor man's neck several times over. She released him and the body slumped to the ground, lifeless.

The Winter Wolf barely spared Algar a glance before leaping away to her next victim.

Algar was attacked immediately following. By his armour, the Prince of Misoua could tell his opponent was a Fortu swordsman. Legend of these hired swords had reached his ears and Algar's heart beat an irratic rhythm as he squared off against him. In three devastatingly quick blows, the Crown Prince of Misoua was stripped of all his weapons save his spear. A fourth strike cut a deep scar into his cheek, instinct saving him from losing his head altogether. Feeling anger replace fear, Algar yanked his spear from the make-shift holder he had strapped to his back.

The Ottalan grinned when he saw Algar's choice of weapon. "I'll be sure to carry your head upon that," he laughed. Algar's legs trembled with the effort of keeping him upright. The man before him was more than his match.

Lion Spear.

The words echoed formless and unheard down the battlefield until they reached Algar's ears. Algar chanced a glance around and saw, if only briefly, Algar Toua, Chief of the Lion Clan, standing on the crest of the hill that separated the tundra from the Greyl Kingdom of the Pamisii. The chief was watching Algar intensely and gave him a simple curt nod when their eyes met.

"Trust in the strength of the lion..." Algar whispered. He faced his opponent, now strangely calm.

"What was that, blonde ape?" the guildsman asked, mocking.

"My name is Algar Toua," Algar said, hearing a peculiar rumble in his voice. "Son of Roger, King of Misoua, and I am the Lion Spear."

"If you say so."

This time it was Algar who grinned. With a yell that sounded more like a roar, Algar sprang forward. It had been thousands of years since men had fought with weapons of stone. They had forgotten how to move. They had forgotten how to dance.

Algar remembered, taught for so many nights by his namesake. In two strokes, the Fortu guildsman fell to his knees, blood gushing from his neck, his eyes wide in shock and disbelief.

Algar raised his spear high. "I am the Lion Spear!" he bellowed.

The Misouan soldiers and commanders had heard. They saw Algar standing in the middle of the battlefield, his spear raised high. It was a call that sung in the hearts of all Misouan fighters. They answered it boldly, slaying their opponents and immediately joining Algar in the centre of the battle.

With a roar, Algar led them forward, his spear darting back and forth like a dancing snake as enemies fell by the score around him and his core group of men.

"Lion Spear!" they roared and chanted as they plunged into the thickest conflicts, rescuing their kin and countrymen.

* * * *

"Do you see that?" Bran breathed, pointing.

His attention was drawn from the vicious attacks of the Winter Wolf to the shadow that danced between the steadily growing number of Misouan warriors behind Algar.

It seemed to Bran to be in the form of a great cat, tawny and maned in blood. It's head looked where Algar looked and once it turned to Bran. Bran saw nothing of the face of that shadow, but its eyes bore into him nonetheless.

Gofron could not reply. He was struck dumb by the chaos that surrounded the stronghold. Battles were won or lost on strategies, but neither side could maintain theirs. The sudden appearance of the savage Winter Wolf had dissolved all plans and now each faction fought only to survive.

As groups were split and separated from each other, a commander was informally chosen, and each attempted to make their own ploys. What resulted was a haphazard back and forth between clusters of opponents without direction. The aim was simply to kill.

This gave Algar the advantage. He moved methodically from group to group, adding to his followers and eliminating their opponents. All this with an ancient spear tipped in stone.

"Gods," Gofron breathed.

Elsewhere, the battle raged fiercely. The wrath of the Winter Wolf seemed insatiable. With every kill, the Winter Wolf grew more and more savage, her snarls and snaps ringing in the ears of every warrior present. Yet such was the hate-filled resolve of the invaders that they refused to shrink before her. Indeed, their General drove his heels into his horse's flanks and charged.

Even as she leapt to take him off his horse, he dove from his saddle to meet her.

It was not the hands of a man that greeted the Winter Wolf, or the blade those hands held, but the sharply honed talons of an eagle as tall as a man with wings so large they blotted out the sun.

The battlefield fell silent; attackers and defenders alike watched on in astonishment as the great eagle rose with the yelping wolf in his great talons and, with cruel intent, threw her hard on the ground. She yelped just once as she hit the ground awkwardly. She struggled to rise to her feet.

Bloodied already, the wolf turned to face her opponent, who wheeled high overhead before plunging down with a shrill cry. Growling low, the Winter Wolf did not cower before the diving eagle, but rose to meet him, closing her jaws around a leg and pulling down hard. She shook with all her might, but the talons of the free leg clawing her throat forced her to let go. She collapsed as the eagle flapped away.

Again the eagle soared high, and again it dove down. The Winter Wolf rose again to meet him, but he swerved at the last and came down hard with razor sharp beak and talons on her flank. The Winter Wolf howled and spun, narrowly missing as the eagle wheeled away again.

* * * *

"Otsana!" Ur called in agony. He took up his reins and kicked his horse, but the Lord of the Hunt, who had sat quietly beside him, pulled the beast back.

"No," he said quietly.

"I have to do something!" Ur cried. "I have to help!"

"You must watch, Ur," the god said softly. "You must watch and remember. She needs you to remember."

Ur swallowed hard and watched with tearless grief as the eagle tore at the wolf.

* * * *

From atop the second gate, Bran's eyes clouded with tears as he too watched on, helpless to do anything. Otsana limped, her sight obscured by the blood that gushed from her head. It was easy to see that she was almost defeated. Her steps were shaky and unsteady. Twice she stumbled as she tried to turn and keep the eagle in her sight. A high-pitched whine escaped from deep in her throat; a whine thick with blood.

Bran's breath caught in his own throat as he saw the eagle dive once more, taking the wolf down to the ground. When the eagle caught the currents and rose, the Winter Wolf did not follow. She lay panting on the ground, struggling to find her footing and stand. The eagle dove once more.

"No!" Bran cried. Before his father could stop him, he jumped from the gate. Bran's body never hit the ground. He was carried high into the air on the wings of an enormous crow.

The eagle expected no attack from the air, and his call was triumphant as he extended his talons towards the Winter Wolf's throat. The crow crashed heavily into the eagle, sending it past its target and onto the ground with a roll. Both eagle and crow were men momentarily before they launched themselves at each other again, becoming birds once more moments before impact.

The eagle struggled to rise to the air, but the crow was as fast and fierce as he was clever. No sooner did the eagle leave the ground than did the crow bring him back down again. The squawking and screeching drove some men mad. They fell to their knees, clutching and clawing at their bleeding ears.

At last the eagle gained the upper hand. It struck the crow hard with its razor sharp beak again and again, while his weight kept his squawking victim firmly on the ground.

Sharp sight was ever the gift of the eagle. Humility was not. Believing itself to be victorious, the eagle spared neither thought nor glance at the Winter Wolf until it was too late. Mustering what strength she had left, the Winter Wolf rose and leapt at the eagle, catching the raptor by his neck. With a sharp crunch, the Winter Wolf closed her jaws and life fled the eagle. With a twist of her neck, Otsana tossed her opponent away. The body of the eagle landed and rolled, coming to a stop as the Guild Master once again, bloodied and dead, at the feet of his horse.

The Winter Wolf collapsed, once again a woman. The crow, upon seeing the Winter Wolf fall, struggled to his feet, becoming a man once more. He ran to Seraphimé's side and gently rolled her onto her back. He scooped her up into his arms and tenderly removed her shattered wolf's head helm.

"Otsana," he whispered, tears striking his eyes.

The woman stirred and her eyes fluttered open. Her vision was hazed and unfocused as she searched her swimming vision for the owner of the voice.

"Otsana, it's me. It's Bran."

At last her eyes found focus and looked into his. She smiled at him. "Bran," she whispered, reaching up to touch his bloodied cheek.

Bran nodded. He took her hand and brought it to his lips. He kissed it.

"I've missed you," Seraphimé said.

"I've missed you too."

Seraphimé smiled again. It was replaced by a frown moments later. "The battle?"

"It has not yet been decided."

"I cannot fight any longer."

"I know."

"My weapons... They are yours now. Take them."

"No, Otsana," Bran whispered, trying to keep his voice even through his tightening throat. "They were a god's gift to you. I am not worthy to carry them."

"You are worthy, Southern Crow," Seraphimé answered, smiling once more. "Because you are my husband, and I love you."

Bran's lungs ceased to function as his breath stuck in his throat, caught between a sob and a wail. He stared down at Seraphimé in surprise.

"I love you," she whispered again. "I am sorry I did not say it before. I love you, Bran."

Grief overcame Bran. He stared down through streaming tears as the light slowly faded from his wife's green eyes. When she released her last breath, he pulled her close and sobbed into her hair. He lifted his face to the heavens and wailed.

Friend and foe alike were moved to tears before the grief of the Southern Crow. Not one moved; no sword was raised, no battle cry was uttered. All combatants stood, watching Bran cradle his dead wife.

Gathering his strength, Bran gently laid Seraphimé's lifeless from onto the ground and unsheathed the long sword and short sword of black glass that she still had strapped to her.

He slowly rose to his feet, his feathered cloak and crow's head helm torn. They flapped in the gentle breeze that blew silently across the battlefield.

He stood there, his blue eyes now dark as pitch as his pupils widened to take in the entirety of the scene before him. He was trembling for the rage that flooded his veins like liquid flame.

Algar moved, taking only a few of his warriors with him. He moved behind Bran and placed a strong hand on Bran's feathered shoulder.

"The Lion is with you, Crow," he said gently.

An Ayal, still in his hound form loped to Bran's other side.

"The Hounds are with you, Crow," the black mutt growled.

Bull, too, moved forward and stood behind Bran. "The tundra is with you, Crow."

Bran took a slow step forward, and then another, and another until he was running at the front line of the Holy Army of the Yellow City. With a unified roar, Algar, Bull and the Ayal followed, their respective commands fast at their heels.

The elder of the Yellow Robes raised his weapons high. "Lord Susa!" he screeched.

The Holy Army of the Yellow City surged forward. The two armies clashed with a terrible tumult, the din of battle echoing from the uncaring stones of the newly built fortress.

Bran and Algar could not be stopped. They fought bitterly, one with spear, the other with glass sword. Though stone and glass met steel, they neither broke nor chipped.

When Bran reached the elder Yellow Robe who stood, urging his troops onward with barely comprehensible screaming, Bran snarled and sliced his head off. It tumbled to the ground, mid-screech, the mouth still moving even as it lost the connection to its voice.

Now devoid of their fanatical leadership, the Holy Army broke, turning to flee. Many could not. Trapped between the walls of the stronghold and the army of defenders they were slaughtered.

With a mighty roar, Bull called the victory and the warriors on the field and on the walls cheered, hollering their war-chants and dancing in sudden exultation.

Bran could find no joy in himself. He walked back to where Seraphimé lay, her wolf cloak torn and matted with blood and there fell to his knees and cast aside his weapons. Gathering her once again in his arms, he rocked back on his heels. He remained there, weeping bitterly until the sun sank low on the horizon and he had no tears left to shed.

"Bran?" It was Gofron. Bran's father had left the gates to join the battle as soon as Bran had leapt from them. He was timid now, afraid of his shape-shifting son. Bran did not turn his head at the sound of his father's voice but stared blankly ahead, seeing nothing.

"She is with him now," he whispered at length. "She is happy."

"Bran," Gofron said again. "Come inside now. Night is here. There is a lot to be done come morning. Come inside and rest."

Bran shook his head. "No. I will stay here. I will not leave her side until she is buried."

Gofron looked up at the faces of the other leaders who had gathered around Bran and Seraphimé. Lord Kildurrow was present. Crown Prince Algar was there, with his father. Ur had come and was standing between Inna and Bull, two men Gofron did not recognise. With them was an Ottalan dressed as a Sierran. The blind boy's face was twisted in agony and he trembled as violently as did Bran.

They seemed to have no objection to Bran remaining the night out in the open battlefield and so Gofron simply nodded.

"Then I shall stay also."

The gathered men exchanged looks. In silence they agreed that they too would remain with Bran. Behind them, the Crown Prince Algar and the new King of the Pamisii had taken charge. They directed the extraction of the wounded, while surgeons of all levels flowed from the fortress and tended to the worst on the field. Torches were brought out and no man was permitted to sleep until all that remained on the field were the Black Hounds, the wolves and the small group of men that surrounded Seraphimé's corpse.

Without a glance at the activity that buzzed behind him, Bran laid Seraphimé's body back on the ground and curled up beside her like a small child. On the other side, Ur did the same. The gathered men, one by one, found a space around Seraphimé and lay down for the evening.

The Black Hounds and the wolves gathered also, each finding a space and keeping the men who remained by Seraphimé warm as the temperature plummeted in the absence of the sun.

Thirty

"Hello, my Crow," Seraphimé said to Bran with a warm smile.

"I'm dreaming, aren't I?"

"I suppose, since we meet in your slumber."

"Then I do not want to wake."

"You must Bran. The tundra needs her king."

"I am nothing without you."

"I am the tundra, my love. I surround you, I fill you."

"But you will never again be in my arms."

Seraphimé smiled and held out her smooth, strong arms. No sign of battle marred her skin. Her dark green dress fluttered faintly in a breeze that was neither heard nor felt. Bran gratefully collapsed into her embrace.

"I love you," he whispered.

"And I love you."

Bran sobbed a moment. "Gods!" He took a deep breath. "Otsana," he said quietly. "The day I struck you, I went to the graveyard. I cut my arm and with the blood that fell to the ground, I promised that when this war was over, I would let you go."

"Yes," Seraphimé said with a small smile. "I know."

"Then to that I hold. I release you."

Seraphimé laughed. "I was given a choice," she said. "And I chose you, Bran."

Bran's sobbing started once more. "But you are dead and I am not."

"And though you will not be able to see me, I will be there, standing beside you. And every night when you sleep, I shall be there, sleeping beside you. For I am the tundra, and I choose my own kings."

Bran shook his head. "And the Lord of the Hunt?"

"Will not have me for as long as you live, my Crow."

"And when I die?"

"You will never truly die, Southern Crow, but sleep. In the summer you shall live, born in the spirit of every king of the tundra until the tundra has no more kings. And I shall be there, beside you, in the spirit of every queen. In the winter, you shall slumber."

"And you shall go to him."

Seraphimé shrugged. "If he remains on good terms with me."

Bran laughed suddenly. "It really is you!"

"Do not fret, Bran. There will never be a day I am not by your side," Seraphimé said with a smile.

Bran was caught by a flurry of emotions. He felt so much joy his chest might burst, yet it was darkened by jealousy and grief and a strong desire to never wake, for when he did he would find himself by Seraphimé's side, and she would be cold and dead.

"I hear the cock," Seraphimé said gently. "The sun will come soon. It is time to wake."

"No," Bran whispered. "Please. Let me sleep evermore, here, in your arms."

Seraphimé smiled and kissed Bran deeply. "Do not fear, my Crow," she answered, even as the air in the dream brightened and she faded away.

"No." Bran could not help the tears that flowed then. He knew what morning and wakefulness would bring.

"Do not fear," Seraphimé's disembodied voice floated in Bran's ear. "I am the tundra, ever around you. I love you, my Crow."

* * * *

"Bran? Bran?"

Gofron shook Bran gently as he slept on the grass beside Seraphimé's body. Bran's eyes fluttered open. He frowned up at his father.

The sun had begun to rise, spreading a warm glow over the battlefield and dispelling the frigid cold of the night. Gofron looked concerned.

"You were crying in your sleep," he said gently. Bran reached up and touched his cheeks, noting that they were wet with briny tears.

"I dreamt of her," he told his father quietly. "And did not want to wake."

Gofron nodded. Behind him, the battlefield had already become busy. Bodies were stripped and carried over to the far right to await the graves that were being dug there. Friend and foe alike were to be buried together at the new King of the Pamisii's command. All men, he had said, fought bravely and none should be punished. His own father had been buried in the night in a single cairn that had been built at the foot of the mountains within the stronghold's walls.

Noble families were given the option of taking their loved ones to be buried in their homeland and a few bodies were now being cleansed and anointed for the long journey back.

Like the Pamisii, the nomads of the Sierran tundra believed that their dead should be buried where they died, so that their spirits could protect the lands they fought for. For this reason, the Sierran warriors who were slain in this war were each buried at the very edge of Pamisii territory, that their spirits may guard both the tundra and the stronghold.

"Southern Crow," said a masculine voice that was a chorus of voices, both young and old. Bran turned his attention away from his father's concerned gaze and found himself looking at a man, entirely naked and glowing blue. "We are Blue Ghost. We have come to pay you our respect."

Bran frowned.

"The tundra has chosen her king," Blue Ghost explained.

"I am no king," Bran replied.

"You are married to the tundra," Blue Ghost said with a smile. Bran's frown did not move. "We must return to the woods. We and the sun are not friends. Before we do, however, take this." From around his own neck, Blue Ghost removed a leather thong on which was strung a single glass bead of dark blue. "Wear this ever more as a symbol of our gratitude for all you have done. All who see it will know you as friend."

"Thank you," Bran said as he bowed his head. Blue Ghost placed the necklace on Bran's neck and bowed before him. He turned and shimmered, vanishing into pale grey mist, drifting back across the field towards the forest.

"What now?" Bran asked his father.

"Otsana must be buried," Ur said quietly. "But not here."

"Then where?"

"In the Northeast there is an old quarry, used by our ancestors in the time before the Winter Wolf tore down their false caves. It is close to the river of ice upon which the others are camped. She will be buried there."

"Why there?" Inna asked.

Ur shrugged. "She told me that's where I should take her."

"You dreamt of her also?" Bran asked.

Ur nodded. "Very briefly."

Bran sighed and stood, the others following slowly. "We must help with the burials here."

"That will not be necessary," Strong Oak said. He stood behind the small gathering of men. How long he had been there no one could guess. That he braved the mass of hounds and wolves to come was something of a marvel. Many others would not have done the same.

"I am come at my half-brother's request. He wished me to pass along his regret at the cost of our victory, and also his sadness that he will not be able to attend the Winter Wolf's burial. He requested that I attend in his stead, so that the gratitude of the Pamisii will be known."

"And the burials here?"

"We have more than enough men to take care of it," Strong Oak said with a shrug. "A stretcher will be brought for the Winter Wolf and wagons for the wounded amongst the Sierrans. Is there anything else that you might require?"

Bran shook his head. "No."

"Very good. It should take no more than a day to organise, thus we may leave on the morrow."

Bran nodded. "Thank you."

"It was the very least I could do. Come now, we must eat."

Strong Oak's skill in organising was impeccable, and the respect the men of the Pamisii afforded him struck Bran as odd, since bastards were so poorly looked upon in the eastern reaches of the Greyl Kingdoms. Nevertheless, Bran could easily see that such respect was well earned. The young man had proved a proficient fighter, equally as humble as he was skilled. He spoke little and plainly, but what he had to say was worth the hearing.

Bran found he very much enjoyed his company. As with the Crown Prince of Misoua, who was also called Lion Spear. There was something frighteningly hypnotic about the quiet strength Algar possessed, the unadulterated self-assuredness, that men found themselves drawn to him without thought.

Bran found a great deal of comfort in each of them, their strength supporting him in a time where he felt his own had been stripped away. The small group of men, which included Lord Kildurrow, Guild, Inna, Bull, Ur, Algar, Strong Oak, and Bran and his father ate in silence, each lost to their own thoughts.

Eventually, Gofron turned to Lord Kildurrow. "I will be accompanying my son on the journey to his wife's burial place. Please remain behind and help my eldest in any way you can."

Lord Kildurrow looked Gofron over. "I would much prefer to remain at your side," he said quietly. Though it seemed a normal statement to say to one's friend, Gofron heard and understood the underlying fear that laced Lord Kildurrow's words.

"I know," Gofron replied. "It's all right, Kildurrow. All of it."

Lord Kildurrow looked at Gofron in open surprise and the King grinned. "We'll talk more of it on my return."

Lord Kildurrow shut his open mouth and nodded, frowning. The party returned to silence.

Strong Oak's prediction proved correct. The nomads of the Sierran tundra were ready to return home at dawn the following morning. Upon mounting, Bran noticed that all the Black Hounds, save three, had vanished.

"The Ayals are gone," Ur said, as if he were simply voicing Bran's thoughts. "They left in the night and returned to Aqyn. The danger has passed. Their task here is done."

"And those three?"

"They are his hunting hounds, not Ayals."

"I see."

Ur put up his hand and kicked his horse. With Guild trailing half a horse behind, Ur led the party of Sierran warriors from the battlefield. Behind them the Pamisii warriors had stopped working. They saluted their departing allies

Remaining behind also was a large number of southern wolves, who watched the group leave and then, snarling at each other, separated into their packs and fled the battlefield, returning to their traditional hunting grounds.

In less than two day's walk, the group met up again with the wounded they had left behind. A few had left the world of the living and were buried. The rest silently joined their companions, noting in sadness Seraphimé's body on a stretcher that was strapped to the broad backs of two tundra wolves.

Bran refused to remove his ruined feathered crow cloak and walked in distracted silence next to the wolves that stood as tall as his shoulder. His father rode a tundra horse a few paces behind, keeping one wary eye on his son.

When the party stopped for the day, the stretcher bearing Seraphimé would be lifted off the wolves and Bran would lie down beside the stretcher. The wolves curled around him for warmth.

Once he was asleep, the wolves would let no one near Bran to disturb him. The beasts barely had to curl their lips for the offender to be sent running in the other direction.

All members of the party noticed how, every so often, small packs of wolves would peel away from the group and head north or south, back to wherever it was they came from before the Winter Wolf called all her children to battle. It was much the same for the human members of the group.

As each clan arrived at the borders of their traditional territories, the wounded and a few able warriors would take their leave of the group and head to their summer camps to await the arrival of the rest of their clan, when so ever they returned from their camp atop the river of ice in the far north.

Slowly their numbers dwindled until only Strong Oak, Bull, Guild, Inna and Ur, as well as Bran and his father were left. The six of them walked easily amongst the tundra wolves, none of whom returned to their secret northern homes. The wolves numbered now only ten of the hundred or so that had come at the Winter Wolf's call.

It made Bran sad, and he spent a great deal of time with the wolves, speaking to them and comforting them. He felt that they too mourned the loss of Otsana. It seemed that the wolves had accepted him as one of their own.

They travelled many months. In the south, summer had bloomed with all its usual glory, but the tundra remained frozen, despite the warm sun. Several times, though it was high summer, it snowed.

"It is good," Ur remarked during one down-pouring of think white snow. "She will remain whole now."

All looked over at the wolves to which Seraphimé's body had been tied. Bran walked steadily beside her, one hand resting gently on one of the wolves' great neck.

"Will he be all right?" Gofron asked Ur.

Ur nodded. "I believe so. The Southern Crow has a strong heart. The tundra did well in her choice."

Gofron sighed and turned to face forward again.

It was several more weeks before the Quiranese Mountains came into view. Immediately to the left of that great, spiny range glistened the blue white river of ice that was the southern-most example of its kind. It had come far down into the south over the winter and did not retreat this summer.

"They are waiting," Ur said sadly. He picked up the pace a little. The horses and wolves broke into a trot.

The party travelled for three more weeks before they reached the quarry. It was halfway up a slope that stood on the rim of a circular cavity that had been dug free of the mountain. A large post and lintel gate that had collapsed many years before marked the entrance.

Bran gasped when he saw the quarry itself. A large square pit of carved white stone continued into the belly of the mountain in levels, with each level becoming successively smaller. The bottom two levels had filled with water so blue as to be the colour of sapphire. At the edge of the pit, in the shadow of the mountain, waited a small group of Shaman and Shamanka, along with Gabija.

Gabija sobbed audibly when the wolves that carried her sister's corpse entered the quarry. Not heeding the predators' massive size and equally massive teeth, she rushed forward, throwing herself against one of the wolves and reaching up to grasp Seraphimé's cold hand. The wolf whined in response and lay down on its belly. Gabijia threw herself across her sister's lifeless form.

Bran let her weep a moment before gently prying her away.

"Oh Bran!" she wept as she collapsed in his arms. Bran said nothing, but pulled Gabija into a tight embrace. She remained there and wept until exhaustion took her and she was gathered by the Shaman of the Osprey Clan.

"Come love," the Shaman said gently. "Come. We must let her rest now. Let go."

Gabija stood bravely and walked back with the Shaman to the group of waiting Shaman and Shamanka as Bran, Bull, Inna and Guild removed the harness and stretcher from the backs of the wolves.

They were gently shooed aside by the Shamanka and they retreated to the far corner of the quarry. Bran and his company withdrew to the pit to talk and find consolation as the holy women prepared Seraphimé for burial.

Gabji went to them also. She took Bran's hand as he held it out to welcome her. They embraced once more.

"I am so sorry, Bran," she whispered.

Bran nodded. He turned and saw his father staring. "Come," he said to Gabijia. They walked together to Gofron and the king of the Baveii bowed low. Gabija did not.

"Gabija, this is King Gofron of the Baveii, my father. Father, this is Otsana's sister, Chieftain Gabija of the Osprey Clan."

Gofron could not speak, so Gabija did so for him. "I am honoured," she said simply.

"No," Gofron croaked, roused from his stupor by her sweet voice. "It is I who is honoured." There was an awkward pause. "I am so sorry for your loss," he added at last.

Despite himself, Bran managed a smile. He had never before seen his father trip over himself.

The others had noticed it too, and were trying very hard to conceal smiles and play ignorant. In Algar's case, it was not very successful at all. His grin could have put a jester to shame.

The group remained and talked awhile in low tones. Gabija had asked only once about the battle. For a response she was simply told that very few of the invaders had escaped. The rest were slaughtered and buried at the stronghold.

"I should like to go one day and visit the graves there to pay my respects to those warriors who died defending us."

"It would be my pleasure to take you," Gofron offered, realising too soon that he was being much to forward. A woman travelling alone with a man she barely knew? It was a ridiculous thought.

Gabija simply smiled gratefully. "I should like that very much."

"You would?" Gofron winced at the squeak that escaped his throat as he spoke. He silently cursed himself and looked away at the distant glacier to hide his sudden discomfort.

"I would," Gabija confirmed. Her gentle smile and soft voice immediately put Gofron at ease and he smiled at her. His gaze did not leave her face.

"We are ready," a Shamanka said, breaking the long gaze. The group turned.

Seraphimé was laid on the stretcher. Her armour had been removed and laid at her feet. The Shamanka had dressed her in a simple, sleeveless white gown that tied at the shoulders. Her pale, tattooed arms rested easily on her stomach and her hands held a bouquet of wildflowers and smoking sweet grass. Her thick auburn waves fanned loosely about her neck.

Across the top of her head she wore a band of plated sweet grass dotted occasionally with wild flowers of white and pale blue. All of her weapons were strapped to her person, with the exception of the long sword which ran the length of her body by her right side.

Bran's eyes misted at the sight of his wife once more. She appeared as if asleep, and his heart ached knowing that she would never again wake. He heard Gabija gasp and felt her grab his arm for support. He was not certain he could give it; he verged on collapse himself.

The stretcher had been removed from the harness and to each of the four posts was tied a very long length of rope. The Shamanka pointed at Bull, Inna, Guild and Bran and indicated for them to follow. She handed Guild and Inna an end of one length of rope each and pointed at each of the far corners of the pit. They understood and, dragging the ropes behind them, they took their positions at the corners. To Bull and Bran she did the same, indicating that they should stand at the nearest corners of the pit.

Bran understood. They would lower Seraphimé's body into the water at the bottom of the pit. The thought tightened Bran's chest. That water was cold, rarely seeing sun but for the middle of the summer's day. Nevertheless, he took up his rope end and stood where he must.

The gathered mourners lined each edge of the pit and the Shaman and Shamanka handed out lit sweet grass until each mourner had one in their hands. One at a time, they began to sing, blending their voices in a beautiful dirge that threatened to break Bran once more.

Slowly Inna and Guild pulled, their efforts guided by the tension kept by Bran and Bull. Once the stretcher hovered in the centre of the hole, all four men began to let the rope slide slowly through their grips and Seraphimé was lowered down into the quarry pit.

Bran found that he was weeping again as Seraphimé disappeared from view. He knew that she had not hit the water yet by the thick trail of smoke that rose steadily from the centre of the pit. All four men continued to lower until the rope ceased sliding. She had touched the bottom.

"Let the rope go," the Shamanka told the men gently. All did except for Bran, who clutched his last remaining connection to his wife with trembling hands.

"Little Crow," the Shamanka said, placing her hand on his arm. "You must let her go."

Bran tried, but his hands would not ease their grip. He fought with himself as tears streamed down his face. Seeing this, Gofron abandoned his place at the edge of the pit and went to Bran, wrapping his strong arms around his son's shoulders.

"Son," he said gently. "It's time to let go."

Bran's hands relinquished their prize and Bran fell to his knees, clinging to his father and gulping back air as he fought the sobs that threatened.

"There now," Gofron said, pulling Bran close when the end of the rope slithered across the edge and away from sight. "It's done now. It's over. There now."

Bran remained in his father's embrace for the rest of the ceremony. He watched dully as each of the Shaman and Shamanka came forward and uttered a blessing, throwing flower petals down into the pit as they did so. The others continued to sing quietly as each spoke their benediction.

It came time for the mourners to do the same. Bran was the last. He stood for a moment, holding what was left of his smoking sweet grass. He thought for a moment of dedicating his body to the water, but knew that it would not be right. He was lost for words. There was no blessing he could ever utter that had not been said before.

Bran drew a deep breath, inhaling the sweet scent of the smouldering grass and said, "I love you." He released the sweet grass and watched thoughtlessly as it fell into the water with barely a sound.

"It is done," the Shamanka said.

* * * *

"Well," the osprey said to the man in the stag-skull helm who sat on the rocks high in the Quiranese Mountains, unnoticed by the mourners below, as he observed the funeral. "I suppose this means my use on this plane has been spent and I must return below." The bird had perched on the man's broad shoulders, her sharp talons barely noticeable beneath the thick hide cloak.

"I suppose so."

"Will you miss me?" she asked cheekily.

The man scoffed, the movement dislodging the osprey who twittered in annoyance.

Then she sighed. "I shall miss you, even if you are an idiot."

"Get out of here, you old harpy."

"I love you, too."

The man reached around to grab the offending bird, but she jumped backwards and took to the air. He watched her leave before turning his attention back to the funeral. He sighed.

"It is done."

Epilogue

*B*ull returned alone to his clan whilst Ur and Bran remained in the Quiranese Mountains for the rest of the year. At Gabija's invitation and Bran's insistence, Gofron had elected to journey with Gabija and her people to the traditional summer hunting grounds of the Osprey Clan.

Inna and Guild, now firm friends, journeyed together to the territory of the Ice Bear Clan and there Inna applied the traditional tattoos that marked the Ottalan as a warrior of his clan. Inna took great care to teach the southern desert man about the ways of the Ice Bear Clan; how to build houses from blocks of cut ice and packed snow, when and where to hunt, what to hunt when and why, and even his famous soup recipe.

Though they did not share blood, Guild and Inna were brothers. They were both later married to Gabija's half-sisters and fathered many children. In just a few short centuries, the Ice Bear Clan revived, becoming even stronger than they were before the first of the Ottalan raids.

In the south, that very summer, upon the return of Algar to Misoua, King Roger formally announced Misoua's detachment from the Touan Federation.

The maps in every scholar's household in that kingdom were immediately changed and the new marking above their kingdom read, 'The Independent Kingdom of Misoua.'

The Touan Federation did not have the manpower to contest the declaration until three years after. When they tried, they found not only the army of the Kingom of Misoua, but the entire fighting force of the Greyls awaiting them on the field. Still wounded from the failed Holy War, the army of the Touan Federation turned around and marched home. No battle was fought then or since. Misoua remains an independent kingdom.

King Roger retained the religion of the Yellow City as the official religion of Misoua until his death. Upon Algar's ascension to the throne, he declared Misoua a kingdom of all faiths and revoked the creed that made other religions illegal in Misoua. No sooner had he made that declaration than the shrine of the Queen of Dreams, long abandoned at the edge of the kingdom, came to life once more. It quickly became one of the strongest cults to take root in Misoua.

Algar's rule was a prosperous one. His long years of study and the war he had fought created of him a firm ruler, but fair and just. He quickly became one of the most beloved kings of that age. It is said he carried a stone-tipped spear when he presided over court. That spear remains in Algar's bloodline to this day, though they are kings no more.

The desert dwellers suffered greatly after their defeat. Famine struck the land and several slave revolts took place. The riots resulted in a hundred long years of bloodshed and starvation as slave after slave refused to work. They were reduced to poverty until, at length, a charismatic young Yellow Robe was elected Elder of the Holy Council. His methods were brutal, but they swiftly restored order in the Ottalan Desert.

That elder was primarily responsible for the disbandment of the Fortu Guild and the establishment of a professional army controlled by the Holy Council of the Yellow City.

Their mandate was defensive, as the Holy Council was concerned that the nomads of the Sierran tundra would seek retribution, or land, or both. It never did happen. However that army remains one of the best in the known world.

In the summer following Seraphimé's burial, a Great Gathering was held. There, by unanimous vote, Bran was pronounced High King of the tundra. It became his role to convene successive Great Gatherings, wed couples and bless their union, as well as resolve issues between clans that could not be resolved by any other means.

One of the marriages he blessed was that of his own father to the Chieftain of the Osprey Clan. King Gofron had, on advice of the ranger Strong Oak, abandoned his duties as King of the Baveii and remained for the rest of his days in the tundra by Gabija's side.

Word was sent to the Baveii that King Gofron was killed in a hunting accident in the tundra, thereby releasing all his wives without destroying the marriage contracts that he had undertaken.

This little deception freed Amwyl and Lord Kildurrow. Three years after hearing the news, Amwyl and Lord Kildurrow married. According to the Kildurrow family, King Gofron sent a note from the tundra congratulating them and wishing them well in their new life together.

As the Kildurrow family has refused access to their records, this has been impossible to verify.

King Gofron's eldest son succeeded his father and, aided by his mother, became a fine ruler.

The Baveii received unexpected surplus in crops and became very wealthy and powerful until its decline in the next epoch when it was taken over by a distant relative of King Gofron's second wife.

Sightless Ur returned to the burial place of the Winter Wolf and set to work establishing a sanctuary there. He was the sole power behind the Cult of the Winter Wolf. It attracted all manner of pilgrims and grew into the largest single cult of the Sierran tundra. It remains thus to this day, and has spread even beyond the tundra with shrines appearing as far south as Bulga. Ur died quite young, struck by a mysterious illness. He was laid to rest in what is now the Quiranese Crypts carved into the mountains at the shrine of the Winter Wolf, where all the grey robed priests are now buried.

High King Bran himself lived to be quite old. At his request, he was buried beneath the plaza at the centre of the Great Gathering location. All the leaders who had survived the Ottal-Touan invasion attended his funeral.

It is said that one thousand crows carried his soul to the Otherworld and to this day, the High King of the tundra is associated with these birds. There is a story the Shaman and Shamanka of the tundra tell when a wolf and a crow are seen together in the long winter months.

They will note, with a sly wink, that the King and Queen of the Dead have had a row, and she has escaped Aqyn to be with her consort. Since wolves and crows are often found in one another's company, I can only imagine that the Lord of the Hunt and his wife fight frequently.

Despite his longevity, Bran never remarried.

> \-   ***After the War (translation).*** **Author Unknown. Bulgan Royal Library, r. W s.KI p.XI-XXI.**

Glossary of Terms

Aqyn: Home to the spirits of the deceased, Aqyn is a series of islands, rather than a single landmass. Ruled over by the King of the Dead and guarded by his three Black Hounds, each island is said to have peculiar properties specific to that island. The spirits of the dead inhabit only one of these islands. This island appears no different from the Sierran Tundra. *See also: Black Hounds, Lord of the Hunt.*

Ayal: Servants of the Lord of the Hunt, ayals are stag-helmed warriors returned from the dead and assigned to a clan. There may be only one ayal per clan at any given time, though it does not follow that all clans will have an ayal. They are said to appear when times of strife approach. *See also: Lord of the Hunt; Sierrans.*

Black Hounds: The famous hunting dogs of the Lord of the Hunt, there are three Black Hounds – Cabal, Guira and Valla. They are said to guard the gates of the Otherworld when not accompanying their master on a hunt. *See also: Lord of the Hunt.*

Braddard: In the hierarchy of the Fortu Guild, the Braddard stands second only to the Guild Master. There are only five Braddards in the Guild. They are given the same status as Lords in Ottalan society. *See also: Fortu Guild, The; Ottalan Empire; Ottals.*

Bride of Fire: Goddess of fire, healing, and artistic inspiration for the Sierrans and the Greyls. Her shrine is located at the same site as the summer solstice festival called The Great Gathering, where a perpetual fire dedicated to her is tended by virgins – one from each clan of the Sierran Tundra. Unlike her masculine counterpart, the Lord of the Hunt, she is referred to by only one name. *See also: Great Gathering, The; Greyls; Sierrans.*

Cabal: The Lord of the Hunt's favourite hound. *See also: Black Hounds.*

First Hunter, The: *See Lord of the Hunt.*

Fortu Guild, The: A guild of Ottalan hired swords. They are hired as assassins and soldiers, though more often are used as guardsmen for trade goods en route. The structure of the guild is feudal, with the Guild Master presiding over the entire Guild. Next in command is the Braddard. There are only five Braddards in the Guild at any one time. They command the Tigils, who in turn recruit and command their own regiment of hired swords. *See also: Braddard; Tigil.*

God of Death: *See: Lord of the Hunt.*

Great Gathering, The: Occurring once every three years during the summer solstice, this is the largest festival of the Sierran Clans. It is so famous that it is known to the Greyl kingdoms and the Touan Federation. The festival begins with the ceremonial relaying of important events to the clans. A spokesman from each clan, usually a chieftain, joins in a circle and speaks only when a lit sweet-grass stick is handed to him or her. This is followed by three weeks of feasts, trade, contests of skill and matrimonial negotiations. *See also: Greyls; Sierrans; Touan Federation.*

Great Stag, The: Taking the form of a breed of deer made extinct by excessive hunting (giant deer), the great stag is said to be the Lord of the Hunt's preferred corporeal form when walking in the land of the living. *See also: Lord of the Hunt.*

Greyls: The general cultural name given to the peoples of the kingdoms of the southwest. Descended from a singular tribe, the Greyls live in autonomous kingdoms and are as prone to raiding one another as much as anyone outside of Greyl territory. The Greyls hold to the archaic gods of their past, sharing two of them with the Sierrans. *See also: Bride of Fire; Lord of the Hunt; Sierrans.*

Guira: A Black Hound; one of the three hunting dogs of the Lord of the Hunt. *See also: Black Hounds.*

High One: The name the Sierrans use when speaking to their Shaman or Shamanka. *See also: Sierrans; Wise One.*

Holy City, The: *See Yellow City, The.*

Ice-Dweller: Though strictly the name of the people who lived in the tundra before the Sierrans, it is used most often as a derogatory term to describe the Sierran nomads. *See also: Old Ones.*

Keeper of the Otherworld: *See Lord of the Hunt.*

King of the Dead: *See Lord of the Hunt.*

Lord of the Hunt: The masculine counterpart of the Bride of Fire, the Lord of the Hunt has many functions. He is responsible for the care of the wilds, and the wild animals, on which the Sierrans and Greyls both rely for food. He is also the spirit that aids or hinders a hunter, and sometimes punishes a hunter should they hunt needlessly or carelessly. He is also considered King of Aqyn, the Otherworld, and rules over the spirits of the dead who dwell there.

He keeps for company three Black Hounds, Cabal, his favourite, Guira and Valla. It is believed that he takes the form of the now-extinct giant deer most often, though some sightings of him in his more human form have been reported. It is considered rare that he would walk the land of the living, and any sighting of him is considered an ill omen.

Unlike his female counterpart, Bride of Fire, the Lord of the Hunt goes by various names including, but not limited to, God of Death, Master of the Wild, The First Hunter and Keeper (and sometimes King) of the Otherworld. Use of any one of his alternate names seems to be indiscriminate. *See also: Black Hounds; Bride of Fire.*

Master of the Wild: *See Lord of the Hunt.*

Old Ones: The term by which the Sierrans most often refer to the people who came before them. According to Sierran tradition, it was the Old Ones who first taught the Sierran ancestors to live on the tundra. *See also: Ice-Dweller.*

Ottalan Empire: Named for the first man to unify the slaves of the eastern desert, Susa Ottal. The Empire now spans the entire desert, unifying all the peoples therein under one religious rule. *See also: Yellow City, The.*

Ottals: The name of the people of the Ottalan Empire. They live exclusively in the desert of the east. *See also: Ottalan Empire.*

Queen of Dreams: More colloquially known as the Lady of Light, the Queen of Dreams lives in freshwater and is responsible for healing, as well as pleasant dreams; unless the dreamer has been wicked. Then she is tasked with punishing them in their sleep. She is rarely seen, though some claim to have seen her striding over a body of fresh water wearing a crown of candles on a cold winter's night.

Roib: A medicinal desert shrub the flowers of which are chewed before battle. It is said to numb the fear response and increase aggression. It can be addictive and prolonged use can result in severe mental disorders (psychosis, paranoid delusions, etc.).

Sierrans: Also Sierran nomads. The general cultural name used to describe all peoples who live in the Sierran Tundra. Unlike the people of the other regions, it was the name of the land that was bestowed upon the people, and not the other way around. The society itself is divided into large family groups, or clans, each ranging within a defined territory. Each clan lives independently of the others save for once every three years, when all clans attend the summer solstice celebration known as The Great Gathering. *See also: Great Gathering, The.*

Suma: The title afforded to merchants of the Ottalan Empire, specifically those who deal in the slave trade. *See also: Ottalan Empire.*

Tigil: The Tigil is an officer of the Fortu Guild. Answering directly to a Braddard, the Tigil is responsible for recruiting, training and commanding their own regiment of hired swords. The number of Tigils in the Guild varies in accordance with a man's ability to recruit. There are generally around thirty Tigils at any given time. Tigils do not get to choose which Braddard commands them. *See also: Fortu Guild, The, Braddard, Ottalan Empire, Ottals.*

Touan: The name given to any citizen of, or anything to do with any kingdom within the Touan Federation. *See also: Touan Federation.*

Touan Federation: Though strictly sharing ancestry with the Greyls, the Touan Federation is a conglomerate of formerly independent kingdoms that were converted to the religion of the Ottalan Empire. Though given some independence from Ottalan rule, all kingdoms of the Federation answer to the Yellow City, share currency with the Ottalan Empire and are expressly forbidden to make war upon one another. *See also: Greyls, Ottalan Empire, Ottals, Yellow City, The.*

Valla: One of the three Black Hounds of the Lord of the Hunt. *See also: Black Hounds, Lord of the Hunt.*

Wetouan Council: A branch of religious officials assigned by the Yellow City to rule over the Touan Federation. They hear matters concerning the Federation that are not deemed important enough for direct intervention from the Yellow City. *See also: Yellow City, The.*

Wise One: The Greyl equivalent of the Sierran "High One." *See also: Bride of Fire, High One, Lord of the Hunt.*

Yellow City, The: The name of the Holy City of the Ottalan Empire, and the heart of the Empire itself. From the Yellow City come all laws and edicts, as well as commands to battle. History states that the Yellow City was destroyed by Susa Ottal in his bid to escape slavery and avenge his family. It later became the seat of his rule. *See also: Ottalan Empire.*

About the Author

Born in 1983 in Quito, Ecuador, S.M. Carrière has lived in five countries around the world including Ecuador, Gabon and The Philippines. The family moved to Australia from The Philippines shortly after the commencement of hostilities there in 1989.

After graduating High School, S.M. Carrière worked full time as an Office Junior at a law firm in Brisbane, Queensland before moving to Canada in 2001. In 2002 she began her academic career in Criminology, but switched to Directed Interdisciplinary Studies (focusing on Celtic Studies) after her first year. She graduated with honours, earning a B.A. Hon from Carleton University in 2007.

It wasn't until well after graduation that writing found her. She hasn't looked back since.

S.M. Carrière now resides in Canada with her two cats and a growing collection of books.

www.smcarriere.com